**This whole expedition had been one case of bad luck after another, and now this. What else could go wrong?**

That night, after the group retired to their sleeping bags, Harry lay awake, sleep not forthcoming. He tossed and turned, long after the others were breathing regularly. His mind was a jumble of thoughts of his mother, the monk, Yetis, and Dixie. And Jing. He had hurt her feelings, he knew. For the rest of the evening, she sat silent, sipping her tea, looking at the stars. The fact that his research had been interrupted by this Yeti business unnerved Harry. It was a distraction to the main purpose of the expedition and his career.

He wanted dearly to leave this place with enough artifacts to eventually provide material for an earth-shattering scientific paper, one that would redeem his reputation in the professor's eyes. Was that such a horrible, selfish goal? He was tiring of field work and hoped the Mongolian dig would be the last he would be required to endure. Someday, Professor Kesler would retire and Harry hoped to fill his shoes.

A monumental discovery would cement his place as *heir apparent*. And maybe repair their damaged relationship.

But now, what else would slow his progress, and threaten to derail the research?

Harry had a distressing premonition that something dreadful was about to happen.

And when the sun rose in the morning, it had.

Dixie was missing.

Deep within the remote Altai Mountains of Mongolia there exists a heinous mystery, one the locals have attempted to keep secret for generations. Now, Harry Olson, an American paleoanthropologist, is in the area excavating for early human fossils. What his team discovers threatens to turn modern scientific knowledge on its head and disrupt the peaceful harmony of the largely superstitious country. It is a discovery so appalling, so sinister, that the lives of the expedition members are at risk from a determined fossil pirate who learns of their discovery and vows to make it his own. Harry and his research team fight to outwit the man who is out kill them and steal their find, but first they must escape the terrible evil they have uncovered...

# KUDOS for *Yeti*

In *Yeti* by Richard Edde, Harry Olson is a disgraced and troubled scientist on an archaeological dig in Mongolia, looking for signs of ancient humans. They uncover bones and teeth (in the wreckage of a Soviet airplane from the late 1960s, of all things), a discovery that starts them on a journey of terror, danger, and death, taking us along with them through the beautiful and rugged country of mountains, steppes, and monasteries, where they inadvertently discover a horror more terrifying and deadly than the wealthy pirate who wants to kill them and steal their find. The book is incredibly interesting, and I learned a lot about both Mongolia and archaeology. With a strong plot, lots of action, and plenty of heart-stopping suspense, it's a hard book to put down once you pick it up. ~ *Taylor Jones, Reviewer*

*Yeti* by Richard Edde is a fascinating tale, set in the mountains and steppes of Mongolia. Our protagonist, Harry Olson, is in Mongolia digging for ancient human remains. Wanting to recoup both his self-respect and his mentor's forgiveness after making a disastrous and unethical mistake, Harry is desperately hoping for an important find to cement his reputation. When they discover the remains of a plane crash, he is naturally disappointed—until they find ancient bones and teeth among the wreckage. Little does Harry realize the effect those bones will have on his life, on the lives of his associates and friends, or on science itself. Their quest for the truth takes Harry, his assistant Dixie, and their foreman Li on a hazardous journey into the remote backcountry of Mongolia, where they stumble upon horrors they could never have imagined. *Yeti* is well written, with a solid plot, a number of smaller subplots, plenty of fast-paced action, and enough edge-of-your-seat tension to keep you turning pages well into the night. ~ *Regan Murphy, Reviewer*

# Yeti

**Richard Edde**

*A Black Opal Books Publication*

GENRE: PARANORMAL THRILLER/ROMANTIC ELEMENTS

YETI
Copyright © 2015 by Richard Edde
Cover Design by Jackson Cover Designs
All cover art copyright © 2015
All Rights Reserved
Print ISBN: 978-1-626943-77-3

First Publication: DECEMBER 2015

Published by Black Opal Books **http://www.blackopalbooks.com**

# DEDICATION

*To*
*Karin, Greg, Chad, & Danielle*

I saw it today.
I know now the tales my father
told around our hearth were true.
Early in the morning the mist was heavy,
but it was unmistakable.
Barely identifiable, but nonetheless real,
it moved with lumbering precision
then disappeared into the mist and fog.

~ *Quang Tre, Mongolian Altai, 1929*

# Prologue

*Mongolia 1964*:

The dark Lisunov Li-2 sat perched like a giant insect on the short runway amidst the driving snow and freezing rain. Its somber hulk housed two Shvetsov-Ash engines and the aircraft was alone on the isolated field. Earlier, the day's gray light had faded into a grim darkness leaving the men in the small Flight Operations Office shivering in their Soviet great coats. An antique oil lamp filled the single room with a soft, yellow glow. The plane's pilot, bent over the counter, studying an aeronautical chart while his copilot, at the end of the counter, spoke softly into a telephone.

It had taken some doing to find this small landing strip in the middle of the Mongolian steppe, far from any known civilization. There were no radio beacons by which to navigate, and it was only by luck that the pilots had spotted the field at the last moment. Now, a winter storm ravaged the steppe, making their upcoming flight a perilous one. The maintenance crew sprayed the Lisunov's wings with de-icing foam in preparation for take-off as soon as the men inside the small shack completed their work.

Engaged in their duties, the pilots did not see the headlights of the Soviet vehicle approach the office. The copilot hung up the phone, stood next to his superior, and pointed at the chart. The office door opened, ushering in a blast of frigid air, and the pilots turned as two men in similar uniforms tramped into the office and shook the snow off their coats. After exchanging salutes, they addressed the pilots with heavy Russian accents.

"Your cargo is in the jeep, Major. Are you about ready?"

"Just about, Sergeant. A few last minute details."

"What's this all about, sir?" the other enlisted man said.

The pilot shook his head. "Sorry, state secret."

"What is in the box?" the sergeant said.

"That I can answer. I have no earthly idea."

The two enlisted men turned and tramped toward the door.

"We'll get it loaded for you, Major, so you can be on your way."

The copilot followed the men out of the office into the blizzard and led them to the large, solitary aircraft.

Inside the Li-2 the pilot made his way to the cockpit while the three men secured the wooden box, which was the size of a footlocker, in the cargo bay. Once they had the box strapped down, the enlisted men waved and crawled out of the plane. The copilot closed and latched the door then settled into his seat next to the major. He retrieved the checklist and began reciting.

The pair quickly ran through the *Before Start* list, which included the batteries, magnetos, lights, throttles, trims, and instruments.

"Did you unplug the oil heaters?" the major said.

"Yes, sir, just before our preflight."

"Good. This weather is going to be a bitch. Icing is going to be a constant worry. Ever flown is weather like this?"

"Never this bad at night. I was copilot on a flight over the Urals in a snowstorm a few years ago. That was more than enough excitement."

"Well," the major said, pulling on his leather aviator cap, "you are liable to age a few years tonight."

The copilot smiled briefly and, without looking at the major, said, "I feel comfortable with you at the controls, sir."

"Let's continue then and get this baby airborne."

The copilot ran his finger down the checklist. "Right engine, start," he said.

"Check," returned the major.

"Battery master."

"On."

"Right boost pump."

"On."

"Right starter."

"Engaged."

"Right propeller."

"Blades correct."

"Right engine mixture."

"Auto rich."

"Right engine magnetos."

"Both."

"Right throttle."

"Advance slightly."

"Right engine primer."

"On."

"Right engine starter."

"Off."

The pair ran through the same checklist for the left engine. The snowfall had lessened but the wind continued to beat against the plane's fuselage. It creaked and groaned. When the pilot actuated the primer switch, the right engine propeller started turning slowly, then, with a loud explosion, the engine started and its RPMs began increasing. When the left engine was similarly started, the aircraft rocked heavily on the runway.

Both men studied the instrument panel while the major pushed the throttle forward until the RPMs reached 1700. Satisfied with the run-up, the pilot eased off the brake and the Lisunov slowly rambled to the end of the runway. When the plane was positioned for takeoff, both men stared into the dark night ahead. Large snowflakes beat against the windshield and not a star was seen in the densely overcast sky.

Airborne, the aircraft, buffeted by the wind, banked in a long turn to the northeast and locked into a great circular route toward Moscow. The slow climb through the clouds was bumpy, but soon the plane punched through the storm and into clear stable air. The major and his lieutenant copilot settled into their seats and began checking their flight plan.

"Where is our refueling stop, Major?" the lieutenant said.

"Camp Zulu on the West Siberian Plain," answered the pilot as he feathered the Lisunov's powerful motors. "You can find it on the chart. It's halfway to Moscow."

"Aren't you curious as to what we are ferrying to the Kremlin, sir?"

"Lieutenant, I have learned over the years to keep my thoughts to myself. I once flew for the Air Defense Force and our mission was to shoot down US planes if they entered our airspace. Quite an elite group of men. But I questioned an order back in '61 and now look at me—flying a taxi service for the KGB and during a blizzard, no less. Our KGB friends don't take kindly to questions. No, take my advice—keep your mouth shut and follow orders."

"I hope one day to fly for the Air Defense Force but my wife does not like my flying. She says it is too dangerous."

"My friend, on nights like tonight, she is right."

"But I still cannot help but wonder what is so important that we must fly in this weather. That it could not wait a couple of days."

"I'm sure it has something to do with national defense."

"Must be damn important," said the copilot.

The plane droned on through the night and, after a snack of coffee and sandwiches, the lieutenant spelled his superior at the controls.

Then the drone of the engines changed.

Not a large change but to the experienced ears of the pilot it was enough to cause him to notice. He scanned the instrument panel.

"RPMs on both engines are down," he said. "Take a look out your window."

Both men glanced at their motors, which seemed to be functioning perfectly in the winter air.

"Wing looks okay as well," said the copilot.

"I'm switching on carb heat," the major said. He flipped a switch on the panel and continued to watch the tachometers.

"RPMs still dropping a little, sir," the copilot said.

The pilot pushed the throttle forward, but there was no response in the RPMs. A glance at the altimeter revealed they had dropped five hundred feet.

"We may have some carburetor icing," he said. "Need to get lower."

"But sir," the copilot said, voice quivering, "the Altai are just ahead. We have to get over them."

"I don't think we can make it, Lieutenant. If we keep icing up, this plane won't fly at all. I think we should turn around."

By this time, the engines were definitely turning at much lower RPMs and the Lisunov was losing altitude at a rapid rate. The pilot began a slow bank to the southwest. Suddenly the stall warning alarm began beeping. He pushed the nose down for more airspeed. Added more throttle.

But there was no additional power.

The wings shuddered violently as the airfoil was interrupted and the plane quit flying.

"I'm flipping on the landing lights," said the pilot over the engine noise. Maybe we can find a place to glide this thing down."

Passing through the cloudbank created a zero visibility situation. The major shot a glance at the instruments. They were in a sharp bank and nose-down attitude.

"Pull up!" shouted the copilot.

The pilot fought the yoke in a vain attempt to right the aircraft and get it flying again.

It was no use.

The physics of carburetor ice, combined with the dynamics of drag and lift, produced a tragedy that frigid winter night. The Lisunov Li-2 never made it out of Mongolia. When the plane crashed somewhere in the Altai Mountains, its secret cargo was buried with it.

The Kremlin wisely never attempted to locate it.

# Chapter 1

E ven the crisp mountain air could not temper the blood boiling in Harry Olson's veins. His patience dissipated, Harry let his ire spew forth like mad hornets. Standing before him was Li Chao and Harry pointed a dirty finger at a map overlaid with dark lines forming squares, each identified by a number.

"How many times, Li, do I have to repeat myself? You have to do the digging systematically and not skip over a section. You know that."

Harry, affectionately known as Harry O—after the 1970s television program of the same name—to most members of the expedition, was finding it difficult to keep his temper in check.

Li Chao was the expedition's guide and foreman of the Mongolian workers who were spread out over the lower side of the mountain. Short in stature by Mongolian standards, he had large dark eyes and hair that hung straight over his ears. He shifted his weight and stared at the map as Harry continue his tirade.

"Understand, Li?" Harry waited for the man's nod before finishing. "So please, let's try to do better. I need your help in this. All right, let's get back to work."

Dismissed, Li turned and strolled back to the group of workers bent over their tools. Harry folded the map and made his way to the expedition's command tent, dug a bottle of wa-

ter out of a box, and collapsed into a canvas chair. His breathing slowly returned to normal, the air hunger brought on by the
elevation and his momentary outburst at Li Chao.

Harry's tall frame didn't fit the small chair. Rubbing his
temples, he tried to ease the pounding in his head, a head covered with dirty-blonde hair that receded at the temples. Since
he had arrived at the expedition site, its high elevation had in-
terfered with his normal sleep, leaving him with a constant
headache. Soon, he hoped, he would acclimate to Mongolia's
steppes. It had taken several weeks to get the compound organized and, as site foreman, Li had excellent credentials, but
Harry couldn't tolerate shortcuts as had just occurred. It would
place the whole expedition's discoveries, if any were found, at
risk. He set the water on a large table in the tent's center as
Dixie Zinn, his graduate assistant, entered.

"What was that all about," she said, brushing a lock of
brown hair from her face.

"I was just telling Li, once again, how important it is to follow the map section by section and not skip over one. It puts
the entire dig at risk if he allows that kind of mistake to happen. He should know better, Dixie." Harry took the map out of
his pocket and spread it out on the table.

"I think he knows. Between overseeing the workers and
keeping us all provisioned, he's got too much on his plate,
that's all. I wouldn't be too hard on him. Li does a good job."
Dixie leaned over the map and squinted. "Which sector did he
overlook?"

"Right here," Harry said, pointing. "G2. I sent him back out
to get a few people over there now."

"You're not thinking it was a mistake bringing him on the
expedition? He had good references and he supposedly knows
this area well. He guided us here without any difficulties. Remember?"

"Of course. He has worked several digs in this general area
of Mongolia where the teams were searching for hominid fossils, as we are. He seems familiar with the routine. Besides, he
speaks English, which helps, since most of the workers only
know Mongolian or some Russian."

"More people speak English in the capital, but you're right—out here, not many. Like I said, however, I think he does a good job. It would be hard to replace him if he quit." Dixie looked out the tent's door at the Altai Mountains with their snow-capped peaks in the distant haze. "Would you be offended if I offered a suggestion, Doctor Olson?"

"Not at all, Dixie. I value your input. Go ahead."

"Well," she started, averting her eyes, "you might consider giving some of Li's chores and responsibilities to someone else. Let him concentrate on the digging and the workers. Someone else can worry about the kitchen and the commissary. I think if you would do that, you'd find Li a much better foreman."

Harry looked at Dixie and smiled. "How can someone as young as you be so wise?" he said. "I don't know why I didn't think of it."

"You've got a lot to be concerned with, that's all."

"I'll tell Li of the change today. And thanks. This is a big undertaking, this project." A figure appeared in the doorway of the command tent. Harry waved. "Ah, Sube. Dixie, this is my friend from the Mongolian Academy of Sciences."

Dixie nodded to the man who was dressed in jeans and a denim shirt.

Harry picked up the coffee pot, beckoning the man inside. "Care for some coffee, Sube? We were just discussing the day's work."

"No thanks, Harry. How is the work progressing? Does it look good?"

"Yes, very. We know this region of Mongolia is promising for hominids," Harry reminded him. "When the team of researchers from Germany, France, and the United States found that skull in the Republic of Georgia that dated 1.7 million years ago, it seemed to prove your hypothesis—that our early ancestors left Africa on their way to Asia. That skull showed clear signs of African ancestry and is probably *Australopithecus*. If early hominids crossed the Asian land bridge on their way to North America, it stands to reason that there should be hominid fossils here in Mongolia." He paused to take a gulp of water.

Dixie smiled at Sube. "And in addition, our colleague Ross and his team found some rudimentary stone tools in the Gobi Desert last year. Remember, Harry?"

"Of course. Their paper in *Anthropology* made all the news outlets. Isotope analysis of the basalt places the age of the site at about 1.77 million years old, but the paleomagnetic signature of the sediment burrows themselves encompasses a period from 1.77 million to a little over a million years ago. So it is still far from conclusive."

"Interesting," Sube mused. "Do you hope for similar finds here in the Altai Mountains?"

"One never knows," Harry confessed. "Those same researchers found and recorded nearly four dozen of the stone artifacts and rodent fossils known to have lived more than a million and a half years ago which were found with the tools confirming the age. So it's a very good possibility."

Harry found another two bottles of water and offered one to Sube and one to Dixie. Then he got a bottle for himself. After taking a couple of big gulps, he continued. "Of course, these theories beg the question as to why the hominids left Africa. Most plausible would be they left to find food as the African savannas began to shrink in size."

Sube gazed at Harry and rubbed his chin for a moment. "I have heard that theory. But have you any plausible reasons for being in the Altai other than the Gobi Desert find?"

Harry nodded. "Yes, there are rumors that Yves Montague has uncovered a frontal bone and possibly more from just over the border in Russia, but it is unconfirmed at present. From what I have heard, it supposedly came from a pit dug for gold mining. Then, a small fossil finger bone was found at the Denisova Cave in these Altai Mountains in southern Siberia. Nothing about the bone seemed unusual, and it was assumed to belong to one of the Neanderthals living there in that time period, between 30,000 and 48,000 years ago. When the mitochondrial DNA of the bone was sequenced, however, it belonged neither to a Neanderthal nor to a modern human. This could, quite conceivably, be a landmark discovery, changing the way we view Asian hominid history. The finger bone was nicknamed the X-Woman, X for *unknown* and *woman* because mitochondrial DNA is maternally inherited but, in fact, it didn't necessarily belong to a female. As you know, males have mitochondrial DNA too—they just don't pass it on to their children."

"I see," Sube said. "So the Altai could be a potential source for early human remains?"

"Absolutely," Harry assured him. "And your government has been kind enough to grant us the necessary permits. We are very grateful."

"My field is geology," Sube replied, "so I am in the dark when it comes to DNA. It seems quite complicated."

"Yes, it is," Dixie said. "But it is an invaluable tool. With an upper molar tooth found at Denisova, which also had the mitochondrial DNA sequenced, that mitochondrial DNA sequence was very similar to that of the finger bone, indicating that both individuals probably belonged to the same population."

"It gets involved and complicated in a hurry," Harry said, taking a gulp of water. "Where Neanderthals differ from modern humans by an average of 202 positions in the mitochondrial DNA genome, the Denisovan individual differs from modern humans by an average of 385 positions. This implies that the most recent common mitochondrial DNA ancestor of the Denisovan, Neanderthals and modern humans lived an estimated 1,000,000 years ago. This made them about twice as old as the most recent common mitochondrial DNA ancestor of Neanderthals and humans. There is speculation that the Denisovan might belong to a previously unknown species, but it is also possible that it belongs to a relic *Homo erectus*, or to a Neanderthal that had retained an archaic mitochondrial DNA sequence, or even to a modern human."

Sube shook his head. "An unknown species? I thought—"

Harry Chuckled. "Archeologists are constantly finding new hominids that take years to sort out. So, the theory goes, the Denisovans then headed east. Some 50,000 years ago, they interbred with humans expanding from Africa along the coast of South Asia, bequeathing some of their DNA to them. Researchers have looked for evidence of interbreeding comparing the Denisovan genome to the complete genomes of five people, from South Africa, Nigeria, China, France and Papua New Guinea and much to the scientist's astonishment, a sizable chunk of the Denisova genome resembles part of the New Guinea DNA."

Sube rubbed his eyes as if pushing away fatigue. "And from New Guinea?"

Dixie patted his shoulder. "And they may have come out of the Caucasus and Pamir Mountains of central Asia, before crossing into the Altai Mountains here in southern Mongolia."

Harry smiled at Dixie, glad she had finally decided to come on the expedition. She was energetic and good-looking. Her left cheek sported a small dark beauty mark that turned darker when she became excited. When he had approached her with the idea, she was skeptical, not sure she wanted to spend time alone with an unmarried professor in a distant land.

She told him that, when she had called her parents for their opinion, they quizzed her repeatedly about his background, who his parents were, and if he had ever made a pass at her. She answered all their questions, but they still were not sure if it was a good idea.

But he convinced her that, as her major professor in charge of her doctoral thesis, he was not the least bit interested in her as a woman and only desired a competent colleague. He had no time for such doings right now. However, he had asked her to call him by his first name.

She had proven him right, for she was as energetic as she was competent, always willing to listen while he bounced ideas and new theories around. As she sat across from him now, he realized she was as beautiful as she was intelligent. She smiled at him now then turned back to Sube. "We think *Australopithecus* became extinct somewhere around two million years ago so if Ross's skull is indeed an *Australopithecus* it would cast an entirely different light on our current theories of hominid development. To find such an early fossil here in Mongolian Asia would not only be earth-shattering news for the scientific community it would cause most of us to rethink how we as *Homo sapiens* came to be."

"This has been most interesting. Thank you, Harry, and you too, Dixie." Sube stood shook both their hands. "I can now report to my government that there is much hope for a successful excavation."

As Sube left, Harry noticed that Dixie was gazing at the mountains. He exhaled a long, slow breath. "Beautiful up here, isn't it?"

She smiled and brushed a lock of hair from her face. "It is, indeed, Harry. I don't think I've ever seen anything quite as enchanting. Even our rustic living conditions haven't dampened my enthusiasm."

Harry stood and stretched. "Well, I need a short nap before dinner. Still haven't completely acclimated to the altitude yet. I will see you when the dinner bell rings."

With that, he walked out of the command tent and headed to the rear of the expedition compound and his personal tent. He zipped the mosquito netting shut, reclined on his cot, and closed his eyes. His thoughts drifted to Dixie. He was glad she was along for the ride. He made a mental note to apologize to Li for accosting him earlier. Li was a team member Harry couldn't afford to lose.

છળળ

When Harry awoke, the sun was setting behind the peaks casting long purple shadows over the Altai Basin. He could hear music emanating from the mess tent, indicating that dinner was almost ready and everyone was congregating, socializing, and discussing the events of the day. The quiet hum of the camp generator pulsed in the background as Harry made his way to dinner.

Soft yellow lights burned inside the large tent that served as both kitchen and dining hall. Entering, he found Dixie sitting at a long table, chatting with Li Chao, and sipping a soft drink. The young man frowned at Harry's approach.

"Li, I owe you an apology," Harry said, sitting next to Dixie. "I was frustrated earlier today and I'm afraid I took it out on you. Unfairly. I'm sorry."

Li looked up from his folded hands and smiled. "Li accepts apology, Harry. All forgiven. When I was studying at Brandeis, I heard of this new professor at California Pacific University and his theories. I have wanted to work with you for quite a while and I am thankful for this opportunity. I understand and there is no reason to apologize."

Harry extended his open hand. "Nevertheless Li, I am sorry. I'm glad you're with us. And I want you to appoint someone else to oversee the kitchen and commissary duties. It will free you up to devote your time to the dig and we can spend more time together going over everything."

Dixie tossed her head back and laughed. "Good, that's settled. Now, let's eat. I'm starved."

Over dinner of stewed chicken and boiled potatoes, Li continued a discussion he had started the previous evening. "This past week here in the Altai steppe has been like coming home for me. I remember this place from my teenage years. The major factors that make the Altai Mountains a recreational domain of great value for Mongols are the amazing natural diversity, along with a small population of people who are historically nomadic and who have a very natural way of life. Finally, remoteness from any industries. The people here live only for tourism and agriculture. All this has ensured that the Altai region stayed untouched by industrial development and remains a very special place.

"During the Soviet times, Altai was a mecca for adventure tourism, especially rafting. Altai Mountains have a lot of rivers, Katun, Biya, and Chuya, being the longest of them. There are also dozens of smaller mountain rivers that are fed by Altai's glaciers. Along all these rivers, there are a lot of places for recreation and fishing. As you have seen, you can easily put a tent anywhere you want."

Dixie nodded. "The vast expanse and remoteness of this area astounds me. Trekking to this site I didn't see any other people except our group and we traveled for days."

Harry held up a hand in protest. "Oh, please, don't remind

me of that pack trip. My backside is still aching from being on that horse for days. And those camels. Whew."

"Camels and horses have been a way of life of my nomadic ancestors for generations. My grandfather used to tell stories of packing his family and possessions onto three camels and trekking for a week, searching for new grazing for his small herd of yaks. Fortunately, my father moved to the city so my sister and I grew up in a more conventional environment. But my close friend Bao, who tends our animals, grew up in this basin. The modern population is a mixture of indigenous Altai and Russian settlers, some of the latter still leading the life of Old Believers in their villages, with strict rules and very much isolated from civilization. There are a few remote villages in the Altai where you can see wool being spun on a hand loom and hear traditional Altai throat singing."

"You grew up in a city?" Harry said, pushing his plate of chicken bones away.

"Yes, in the town of Kosh-Ut on the Katun River. Seems a long time ago."

"Your parents still living, Li?" asked Dixie.

"No, they died several years ago. My sister moved to Beijing and is a nurse there. How about you, Dixie? You ever going to get your doctorate?"

Dixie shot a glance at Harry, who took his plate and excused himself from the table.

"If Harry—er—Dr. Olson ever approves the final draft of my dissertation, I could defend it this fall. I think he's dragging his feet."

"Doesn't want you to leave, eh? I don't blame him. You have been a tremendous help to him already on this expedition."

"I don't see how. We haven't found anything of note yet. He just has me busy keeping a journal and making sure the sectors are dug properly. It's getting pretty boring, actually."

"I guess you have to put in your time, as they say. I do hope we can find something of value before the weather closes us down for the year."

"Me too," Dixie said with a long sigh.

The pair left the mess tent as the cool evening dusk was settling over the camp.

# Chapter 2

Harry had grown up in a poor neighborhood in the south side of Chicago. From an early age, he was frequently in trouble at home and at school. Being a quiet, introverted child—some called him shy—led to numerous fights with other children who confused his quiet ways with pretentiousness. At Phillips Academy High School, he grew tall and lanky with sandy blond hair. Steel-blue eyes held a natural curiosity of the world around him and for all forms of life. He kept a butterfly collection until he went off to college. His father, an obese man with a bulbous ruddy nose, was an alcoholic and abusive to his mother, a fact that caused Harry to lie awake at night, plotting the man's demise. Once, he thought he had devised the perfect crime to rid the family of the man but was too scared to implement it.

His father rarely worked, spent most of the family money on cheap beer, and sat drunk at night in his shorts, watching late-night movies. Many an evening Harry locked himself in his bedroom while he listened to his father scream and berate his mother until she ran, crying, to a neighbor's house. To escape the cruelty, on Saturdays he would ride the bus to Lake Shore Drive and Lake Michigan and watch the planes take off and land at Meigs Field. Sitting on the rocks overlooking the lake, Harry plotted his escape from the insanity. But as he grew older, he realized there would be none—he was stuck. He became depressed and his marks in school suffered as a result.

Harry's brother, Max, was two years older. Max was his father's favorite and, when the man was sober, he took the boy with him everywhere. His brother was fastidious, fearful, but due to his father's loyalty, developed a sense of entitlement at an early age. As the years went by, Harry and Max drifted apart, only seeing each other or talking to each other at family holiday dinners.

While at Phillips Academy, Harry made the basketball team and, by his senior year, had won all-city honors, his only note to fame. Not having many friends, he kept to himself, wondering what life had in store for his future. His father was noticeably absent at his graduation, a fact that troubled him not in the least. Mother was there, all decked out in her best ten-year-old dress. He was awarded a basketball scholarship to Perdue, where he majored in history. College was good to Harry, for it afforded him time away from his father. The day he left for Indiana, the old man grabbed him by the arm, predicted he would never make good, and told him to never return home. He didn't want him around anymore.

Harry kept his mother informed of his progress by frequent letters he wrote and she, in turn, encouraged his every step in letters of her own.

One semester during a course in anthropology, he attended a seminar on human evolution given by the distinguished professor at California Pacific University, Dr. Julius Kesler. The seminar changed Harry's life. From that week onward, he only desired to study the human race and its development. After graduation from Perdue, he gained admittance to Dr. Kesler's graduate program in anthropology and wrote his doctoral thesis on hominid evolution and their fossils. Following Harry's doctorate, Dr. Kesler begged him to stay at California Pacific on the faculty. He accepted and began teaching a course in African hominids.

Those first years on the faculty were spent in the lonely pursuit of an academic career, writing, and teaching. But he could not escape the vague notion that he was not good enough, not smart enough, to warrant Dr. Kesler's confidence in him. It was made all the worse by the knowledge that, after two years of being the professor's pride and joy, he had let the man down in a way that almost destroyed his career. Now, when Kesler looked at him, Harry saw the hurt in the man's eyes. He had become a father to Harry and now, with no self-respect left, Harry thought about leaving the university.

Then Kesler asked Harry to lead the expedition to the Altai Mountains in Mongolia to search for hominid fossils. Harry jumped at the chance. The professor, as his students and colleagues called him, gathered the necessary funds to finance such an outing and seemed pleased that Harry was heading it. It had taken six months for Harry to coordinate all the details, including finding Li Chao to guide the expedition. Purchasing and packing the scientific equipment involved countless hours of checking and rechecking. When Dixie signed on, things went smoother. She had a knack for details. The professor knew Li Chao from a meeting he attended and Harry convinced Li to take on the job as guide and foremen of the local workers they would use for the backbreaking labor.

The Altai research was Harry's big break and his chance at national notoriety in academic circles. With a monumental discovery to his credit, he could write his own ticket—a full professorship, a departmental chairmanship, a huge research grant. His career would be set. He would be able to settle back and enjoy life, maybe have a family. He had worked long and difficult hours to get where he was and, if the Mongolian research project was productive, he might even succeed Professor Kesler. It would be a dream come true.

The expedition flew on a chartered jet to Beijing and, there, boarded the Trans-Mongolian Railway to Kastum. From Kastum, it was another three-day journey by camel and horse to the expedition site Professor Kesler had chosen.

*ᑭᑐᑭ*

Breakfast over, Harry sat in the command tent and studied the map's layout of the diggings over a cup of coffee. The digging site was represented on the map by a grid, made up of lines that conformed to one-meter-by-one-meter squares on the ground. The site had been surveyed using GPS, and the grid, constructed with stakes and twine, had taken the better part of a week to set up. The resulting grid had been transferred to the map and the expedition computer. One worker was assigned a square on the grid, shown how to dig into the earth, sift its contents, then make appropriate notations in a log. Twice each day, the log's entries were typed into the computer and, in so doing, an accurate inventory of all unearthed items was made as they were found. Satisfied that the morning's work was going as scheduled, he settled back in his chair and waited for Dixie. They usually had their morning conference shortly after she made her rounds of the work site. He looked up as she sank into a chair next to him.

"Good morning, Harry," she said. She wore jeans and a denim shirt, along with brown hiking boots. He noticed her hair needed combing and, with her shirt tucked into her jeans, it enhanced her buxom figure.

"Yes, it is," he said. "How goes the camp?"

"Everyone is settled in for now. Li is down at section H9, called down there about something."

"A problem?"

"I dunno. We should know soon enough. Here comes a runner." Dixie pointed out the door of the command tent to a short Mongolian boy making his way toward them. He wore cutoff shorts, a white tee shirt, and sandals. The boy came to a stop, out of breath, at the tent's entrance and waited.

"Yes?" Harry said, approaching the boy.

"Dr. Harry, come quick. Now. Li needs." The boy took Harry's arm and pulled him toward the diggings.

Harry ran behind the boy, squinting past him, trying to make out the commotion at section H9. Dixie followed.

At the site, they found Li bent over in a square hole and talking rapidly in an unknown dialect to a worker. Li crawled out of the hole when he noticed Harry standing above him.

Harry wiped the perspiration from his forehead with a large bandana. "What have you got, Li?"

"Jump down there and take a look," Li said. "Yen Po uncovered it just now. I thought you ought to have a look before we removed it."

Harry scrambled into the pit. "Something interesting, I hope."

He noticed a piece of cloth nestled in the loamy soil at the bottom of the hole. As he scraped dirt away, an olive green object came into view. Meticulously, he worked with a trowel, exposing more of it until it was in full view. It was some sort of canvas and leather cap.

"Get a camera down here," Harry called to Li. "And a plastic container, as well."

More digging with the trowel revealed the cap's entirety. When the camera arrived, Harry took several dozen photographs then carefully placed the cap in the container.

"Dixie, take this up to the command tent and wait for me. I'll be along in a few minutes."

Dixie climbed out of the hole and made her way to the command tent with the container.

Harry turned to Li whose face bore a deep frown. "Li, I want you to move the workers to the sectors immediately adjacent to H9. That would be H8, H10, G8, G9, and G10, along with I8, I9, and I10. Have them carefully sift through all layers. Maybe there's more down there to find. I'll be in the command tent if you need me."

Li nodded and began moving workers to the respective sections as Harry moved to join Dixie. He found her examining the cap with a magnifying glass, gently brushing dirt from its surface with a brush.

"Christ, Harry, look at this." Dixie moved out of the way and handed the magnifying glass to her boss. "Can you believe it?"

Harry bent over the container, studied the cap for a while, and then let out a low whistle. He stared at a pilot's cap, drab olive green in color, with padded earflaps. On the front of the cap was an insignia. A red star with a yellow hammer and sickle in its center.

"What do you make of it," she said.

"I'll be a monkey's uncle," he said. "It's a Russian cap. The insignia belongs to the old Soviet Union before its breakup in 1991. I wonder what it's doing here in these mountains." Harry put the magnifying glass on the table and eased his tall frame into a chair.

Dixie slumped into a chair next to him, shaking her head. "How do you know it's from the old Soviet Union?"

"I took a Russian history course in college. And I remember seeing old Gorbachev wearing a hat with that insignia on it."

"Well, Russia is right over there, beyond those peaks, so it could have made its way here with tourists or other travelers. Or the military. Could just be someone's memento that got lost. It is interesting though."

"Military? I don't think the Russian army or air force would be conducting maneuvers in Mongolia."

Harry opened a soft drink, passed it to Dixie, then retrieved one for himself. Back in his chair, he sat in silence for a few minutes, allowing the discovery to sink into his brain. It was an odd discovery, no doubt about it. What he had learned about Mongolia in preparation for the expedition was that the country came under Soviet influence, resulting in the proclamation of the Mongolian People's Republic as a Soviet satellite state in 1924. It was only after the breakdown of communist regimes in Europe in late 1989, when Mongolia saw its own Democratic Revolution in early 1990. It led to a multiparty system, a new constitution in 1992, and transition to a market economy. He rubbed his temples, attempting to relieve the built-up pressure there.

A Soviet Union military cap in Mongolia. Harry couldn't fathom the significance of the find, if indeed, there was a significance. It could have found its way here on the head of a Mongolian yak or sheep herder, bought at some bazaar in any village out here on the steppe. Or maybe the Russians were in Mongolia at some point in the past. He made a note to ask Li what he knew.

"Well, I asked Li to make sure the adjacent sectors are dug up and sifted, just in case there's something else interesting," he said. "Certainly not what we came to find, however. I came all this way to hopefully find some hominid fossils not twentieth-century trash."

಼ಎಎ

Dixie sat in her tent, entering the morning's activities and the finding of the Russian cap into the expedition journal. Finished, she allowed her mind to wander and consider Harry. His personality was certainly different from hers. Harry was quietly sensitive but at times, forceful. She was outgoing, talkative, energetic. He was a private person, at times socially uncomfortable. She wanted to be the life of the party, was considerate of others, and group oriented. Harry was focused on his research while she hoped for a family in the future. It was no secret to any of his students that his academic career was Harry's primary interest. No, even though she was drawn to him, they were too dissimilar in temperament and personalities to ever hit it off. They got along well at the university and on the expedition because she played the submissive role around him. Even though she called him *Harry,* he was still her professor and team leader and she was focused on obtaining her doctorate.

She was raised as the privileged daughter of a Wall Street banker and lived on Long Island in a big house with two servants. She attended Smith College on her father's money. During her freshman year, while pledging a sorority, she became a pot-smoking liberal. The marijuana led to stronger drugs, supplied by several sorority sisters, and the small group used to snort cocaine in each other's rooms. Some of her sorority sisters were lesbians but that did not interest her. She lost interest in college, lost a lot of weight, and argued with her parents all the time. After she flunked her courses that spring, her father was at the end of his rope and, at the suggestion of their family physician, had her tested for drugs and that ended her semester-long party.

Reluctantly, she agreed to go to the Betty Ford Clinic for rehab. However, she didn't excel in the program until tragedy struck. Her younger brother, Bill, was killed in an automobile accident. The shock devastated her. She had held Bill on a pedestal. He was a special brother. He knew of her struggles with drugs but was never judgmental, although he had tried to get her to stop. He was handsome, funny, and she loved him more than she loved herself. At his funeral, she broke down and sobbed for a week, never venturing out of the house. But, in the end, she vowed to begin again in earnest. Returning to Smith on probation, she attacked her studies with renewed zeal.

The first semester back she struggled with her studies, having to relearn how to learn. Then she made the Dean's Honor Roll the remainder of her time in college and, upon graduation, moved to San Francisco to get away from family and the sad memories. She enrolled in the graduate school at California Pacific University. Interested in biology, she elected to study human evolution and anthropology. When she took a course taught by Dr. Olson, she immersed herself in it and flourished under his tutelage. She became Dr. Olson's understudy and, although she thought him rude and callous, she later found him to be highly intelligent and very shy. For four years, she worked hard trying to write a doctoral thesis that he would be proud of. Now on the threshold of finishing and defending it before the doctoral committee, she felt the butterflies forming in the pit of her stomach. She no longer possessed the confidence she had at the beginning of her graduate studies. That uneasy feeling sometimes gnawed at her insides, turning her stomach into a churning knot. To complicate matters, she'd noticed a change in Dr. Olson. He didn't look her directly in the eye like he used to, he spoke in soft tones, and he seemed awkward in her presence. Something in his life had dramatically changed him.

Later in the afternoon, as she and Harry sat in the command tent, planning the next day's activities with Li, she heard a commotion at the dig. Workers were shouting and waving their arms in obvious excitement. Something else had been found.

Dixie joined Harry and Li in sprinting to the dig site.

# Chapter 3

Harry was the first to arrive at the diggings. His lungs burned from the exertion. The workers were crowded around the large hole, all talking with animated gestures in a dialect he did not understand.

Amidst the confusion, Li arrived, took control of the situation, and calmed the crowd. He pointed into the hole. "Look," he said to Harry as Dixie arrived.

She peered into the giant crater as she held Li's arm for balance.

"What the hell is it?" Harry said. He jumped into the hole and pushed a worker out of his way.

"What does it look like?" Li asked. "They came across a propeller first, kept digging, eventually uncovering the whole thing. It's an airplane motor, Harry. A damned airplane motor."

"From a plane crash? Maybe that's where the pilot's cap came from."

Harry crawled out of the crater, heart pounding. He was still breathing hard from the run. *Damn*, he thought, *no bones or anything of scientific value. Just a damned airplane motor.*

"Li, I want that thing pulled up here where we can get a good look at it."

With the order, Li shouted instructions to the workers who went back into the compound and retrieved a block and tackle. Fixing it to the motor, they began to lift the large beast from its resting place. For the first ten minutes, the thing didn't budge then, with a group of workers using pry bars, the motor popped loose. After thirty minutes of hard labor, they were able to hoist the motor from the hole and set it on the ground next to Harry, Li, and Dixie.

It was a large, rusted affair. The engine cowling had been ripped apart exposing a myriad of multicolored wires and hoses. Harry noticed engraved on the motor block a series of letters and numbers partially covered with dirt. Dixie rubbed a finger over the lettering brushing the dirt away.

Й г щ ъ о р
75-3019

"Russian," Li said. "Belonged to a Russian plane, obviously." He sat on the ground, watching Harry examine the rest of the motor. "I wonder what kind of plane it was? It must have crashed up here some time ago. The pilot's cap you said was Soviet, before 1991—"

"It's a big motor," Dixie interrupted.

"—probably from a multi-engine aircraft," Li continued.

The cacophony produced by the workers had dwindled to a quiet buzz around them. Several of the men ventured close and touched the wrecked motor as if they found it enchanted. They murmured among themselves, seemingly transfixed by the sight.

"If that is true, then there is another engine around here as well as the rest of the plane. The fuselage shouldn't be far, I would think," Harry said, still inspecting the wreckage. "Well, we do have a mystery, don't we? The question is do we continue to search for this plane? We came here to look for human ancestors not investigate a plane crash that happened years ago."

"I suggest we discuss it over lunch and give these workers a break. They have been doing some heavy work this morning." Dixie smiled and pointed to the mess tent. "My stomach's growling."

"Good idea," Harry said. "Li, dismiss the workers for lunch and join us in fifteen minutes. Come on, Dixie."

*೭ൟ೨*

Lunch was a hurried affair of cold cuts and fruit, washed down with bottled water. Harry, Dixie, and Li sat around a long table alone, the lunch crowd having returned to their afternoon duties. A map of the site was spread out on the table in front of them. Harry eased back in his chair and let out a long, slow sigh. "Well, what do you both think?" he said, addressing no one in particular. Then, turning to Dixie, he asked, "Dixie? What's your opinion? What should be our next move?"

Dixie smiled softly, showing bright, white teeth. "Since you asked, Harry, this cap and motor business is just a distraction from the main reason we're here. We came on a research expedition, thinking there might be hominid fossils in this region of Mongolia. Soon, the colder weather will force us to shut down for the year and return home. We lose precious time if we divert our attention from our main purpose." She smiled again and ran a hand through her hair.

Harry nodded. "Li, what's your opinion?"

Before Li could answer, the satellite phone laying on the table started ringing. Harry picked it up.

"The professor," he said, glancing at the Caller ID. He hit the TALK button. "Yes, Professor? How are you? Close to midnight in San Francisco, isn't it, sir?…Yes, sir…They're sitting right here…Just a minute while I put you on speaker." Harry pushed a speaker's phone jack into the satellite phone and continued. "There, Professor, we can all talk now."

Dr. Julius Kesler's voice boomed over the speaker. "Yes, it's closer to one in the morning here. I waited up past my bedtime to be able to talk to you all. Harry, you and Dixie haven't killed each other yet?" Kesler's husky laugh caused Dixie to shake her head.

"Professor," she said, "he beats me every day. Make him stop, please."

"Professor," Harry interjected, "if I don't beat her, she sleeps all day."

The three at the table laughed and Dixie punched Harry on the arm.

"Now down to business," Kesler said. "How's the project coming along? I want an update. You've been there a week now. Finding anything of interest?"

Dixie and Li looked at Harry, as if wondering what he would say to the Professor.

"We found something, all right, sir. A wrecked motor from an old Soviet plane that crashed up here some time ago. The three of us have been discussing our next moves."

"You mean an airplane engine? How'd you come across something like that?" Kesler's voice sounded irritable over the periodic static on the phone.

"Just this morning the workers uncovered it in section H9. Along with a Russian pilot cap."

"Sounds interesting, Harry. But leave it for another time. The fall weather is approaching, and the snow will start falling in a few months. We will have to close down then. I want as much digging done as possible by the first snowflakes. So forget the plane. I'll call next week for another progress report."

"We understand, Professor," Dixie said. She patted Harry on the shoulder.

"No problem," Harry added. "We'll keep plodding along."

There was a pause before Kesler spoke again. "Harry, I got a call this morning from a doctor in Chicago. Your mother—"

"What's wrong, Professor? She ill?"

"Nothing serious at the present. The doctor was looking for you and when I told him you were out of the country, well, he confided in me. I hope you don't mind."

"Not at all. What's her problem?"

Dixie and Li rose and waved as they filed out of the mess tent, leaving Harry alone with Dr. Kesler, who continued. "The doc said she has a touch of congestive heart failure. Apparently, your brother is flying in from New York."

"Good. Max will check on everything. Did the doctor mention my father? Is he there at the house?"

"Didn't mention your dad, Harry. I will call later and give your brother your sat phone number so maybe he can call you when he gets in."

"Yes, please. And thanks. The woman is close to seventy-five and her health has been slowly going downhill for the past couple of years. Keep me posted if anything changes."

After hanging up, Harry sat for an hour then walked down to check on the digging.

ຂໆຊໆໆ

Li sat in his tent, its door open, allowing the cool evening breeze that blew down off the Altai peaks and across the grassy steppe to fill its interior. He was waiting for Dixie and Harry, a meeting Harry called because he wanted to discuss the aircraft motor. Dr. Kesler had sounded tired during their conversation, somewhat curt. Maybe it was only because it was the middle of the night in California. Li hoped so. He remembered Kesler as a man of graying dignity, a scientist who had made significant contributions to the field of human evolution. If they found anything worthwhile, it would look good on Li's resume, maybe even convince the professor to offer Li a position at the university.

He and Harry had hit it off from the start, a few minor bumps in the road along the way notwithstanding. The expedition leader had a good command of what he wanted out of everyone under him, issued precise directives, and was generally well-liked by the entire crew. The Americans paid a higher wage than anywhere he could find in Mongolia and he considered himself fortunate to be working here and alongside such amicable people. And being employed by a scientific research team afforded him a certain distinction in his hometown. He was about to doze off when heard someone outside his tent.

"Knock, knock," Dixie said.

"Come in, of course," Li said, waving Dixie and Harry in.

He got up, lit a small propane lantern, and returned to his chair. Harry and his assistant sat on his cot. The soft, yellow light from the lantern filled the tent with a warm glow. Dixie had worn a fleece pullover and Harry was wearing his field jacket.

"Okay, all," Harry began, "let's continue about this damned motor. I want to hear from each of you. Li, you first. What would a Russian plane be doing in Mongolia? It's your country, what have you heard? Any history here?"

"In the beginning stages of World War Two, the Mongolian People's Army was involved in the Battle of Khalkhin Gol, when Japanese forces, together with the puppet state of Manchukuo, attempted to invade Mongolia from the Khalkha River. Soviet forces under the command of Georgy Zhukov, together with Mongolian forces, defeated the Japanese Sixth Army and effectively ended the Soviet-Japanese Border Wars.

"The battle experience gained by Zhukov was put to good use in December 1941 at the Battle of Moscow. Zhukov was able to use this experience to launch the first successful Soviet counter-offensive against the German invasion of 1941. Many units of the Siberian Army were part of this attack. A year after flinging the Germans back from Moscow, Zhukov planned and executed the Red Army's offensive at the Battle of Stalingrad. He used a technique very similar to Khalkhin Gol, in which the Soviet forces held the enemy fixed in the center, built up a massive force in the area, undetected, and launched a pincer attack on the wings to trap the enemy army."

"I see," Harry said. "Go on."

"The Pei-ta-shan Incident was a border conflict between the Republic of China and the Mongolian People's Republic after the end of World War Two. The Mongolian People's Republic became involved in a border dispute with the Republic of China, as the Chinese Muslim Hui cavalry regiment was sent by the Chinese government to attack Mongol and Soviet positions. This area was eventually lost but the Soviet bombers aided the Mongolian Army.

"So you see, there has always been a close relationship between Mongolia and the Russians. At least until 1990, when Mongolia underwent a democratic revolution, ending the communist one-party state that had existed since the early 1920s. It was a democratic revolution, which started with demonstrations and hunger strikes, to overthrow the Mongolian People's Republic and eventually moved toward the democratic present day Mongolia and the writing of the new constitution. Mostly younger people, demonstrating in Ulaanbaatar, spearheaded the revolution. It ended with the authoritarian government resigning without bloodshed." Li took a deep breath and smiled.

"Very impressive summary," said Harry.

"So it's reasonable, and not at all alarming, that we find a Soviet airplane crashed in the Mongolian mountains. Is that what you're saying, Li?" Dixie said.

"That's correct. In fact, since Mongolia was so strongly linked to the Soviet Union in every way—from the military to civil services to governmental infrastructure—the fall of the USSR left Mongolia almost completely cut off from the rest of the world. Russian personnel, assigned to Mongolia for a tour of duty, staffed many military and some governmental professional specialty positions, such as medicine and engineering. When the Soviet Union became engulfed in political turmoil, most of these professionals either returned to their home republics of their own will or were reassigned by the Soviet military. This mass exodus of trained people left Mongolia extremely deficient of medical, dental, veterinary, legal, aviation, engineering, and scientific professionals. Most Mongolians with a college education had elected to go into governmental administrative professions, as these were the most promising for advancement in the Communist system. In fact, only about thirty per cent of all physicians in Mongolia were Mongolian citizens.

"The usual Russian domination," Li continued with a nod. "Though Mongolia was a communist state, democratic uprisings had been sweeping through the nation, beginning that summer. The Soviets desired to put these uprisings down. Also, the Soviets greatly desired the oil and mineral rich lands on which Mongolia rests. As the Soviet Union grew, more materials were needed to feed its growth, and Mongolia could provide that.

"The Soviets crossed the Mongolian border at 4:00 a.m. on 7 October 1967, as T-55 tanks and fifty thousand Soviet troops marched across the border, virtually unopposed. There was sparse fire from scattered Mongolian troops stationed in the area, but the Soviets only suffered one casualty during the initial border crossing. The Soviets made their way southwesterly along the Orkhon River, unopposed as they advanced toward the forty-five thousand Mongolian troops stationed just outside Orkhon.

"Surrounded, the Mongolians held out for two days, but heavy casualties eventually forced the Mongolian forces at Orkhon to surrender. The Soviets suffered only thirty-four deaths and ninety-five wounded during the battle, while inflicting over twenty thousand casualties upon the Mongolians. A few thousand Mongolian troops escaped the encirclement, but the remaining twenty-thousand-plus troops surrendered to the Soviets on twelve October."

"What happened then?" Dixie asked, seemingly mesmerized by Li's story.

"Well, NATO strongly condemned the invasion, but no repercussions were introduced. While NATO did not wish to see the Soviets invading nations such as Mongolia, they also were not interested in starting World War Three. Thus, a policy of appeasement was followed as the Soviets got nothing more than a slap on the wrist."

"Things are sure different now," Dixie said. "Ulaanbaatar looks like LA."

"Funny you mention that," Li said. "The city's Sukhbaatar Square—where a bronze statue of Lenin once stood—is now home to a luxury mall featuring outlets for Louis Vuitton, Armani, and lots of others. Our nation has gotten rich quick—well, at least its elite have—because of the vast mineral wealth buried in its ground, comprising deposits of eighty different minerals, from coal and copper to gold and uranium. Mongolia's extensive mineral deposits and attendant growth in mining-sector activities have transformed its economy, which traditionally has been dependent on herding and agriculture. In addition, molybdenum, fluorspar, tin, and tungsten deposits have attracted foreign direct investment. Not to mention oil."

Harry stood and stretched. He stood in the tent's doorway and watched a meteor blaze its way across the black, velvet sky. "I appreciate the history lesson, Li, but I, for one, have heard enough. I think we need to rededicate ourselves to our original mission, the reason we're here—hominids. Tomorrow we put this Russian plane business behind us. I'll see you both at breakfast."

With that, Harry disappeared into the inky darkness, leaving Dixie and Li alone. Dixie stared at the empty doorway.

Li shrugged. "Do not worry, Dixie," he said. "Harry is right. We came here for hominids."

# Chapter 4

The satellite phone rang continuously until Harry ran into the command tent and picked it up.

It was his brother, Maxwell. "Harry," he said. "I finally caught up with you."

"Good to hear from you, Max. It's been a few years. You at the folks' house?"

"Yes, I'm staying here a few days. At least until I know Mom's going to be okay. I hadn't realized it had been quite that long since we last saw or talked with each other. Really, a couple of years?"

"Three years this Christmas," Harry said. "Pop was even sober that time."

"Harry, please don't start in on him. I know you two didn't really get along very well, but save it for another time."

"You're right, Max. Of course. You said something about Mom. Is she all right?"

"She went to see her doctor last week because she was having difficulty breathing and her legs were swelling. After getting an X-ray of her lungs, he told her she had congestive heart failure and prescribed some medicine. So far it hasn't helped all that much. She spends most of her time in her chair, reading. Dad does most of the cooking and cleaning now."

Harry blinked in disbelief. "No. You're kidding. He always said that stuff was Mom's work. When does Mom see the doctor again?"

"Not until next week. I have an important meeting later this week so I'll have to fly back to New York in two days. You're stuck in Mongolia for a while, then?"

"Until the end of summer or unless you think I need to come home now."

"No, you stay put. Dad is bitching a lot but, for now, he has calmed down quite a bit from when you were around."

"The sonofabitch used to scream at her. I'll never forget that," Harry said, his stomach twisting into a knot at the memory.

"Now, Harry. Calm down. We don't need to rehash the past. I just wanted to fill you in on Mom's condition. How's the research going?"

Harry smiled at his brother's question. In all the years of their life his brother, Max, had never voiced any interest in his career. Max was all about himself, Wall Street, and the size of his bank account. Living in a big house out on Long Island, his brother usually felt the world revolved around him and he never called Harry. At family gatherings, he bored Harry with long tales of money made and deals accomplished. Harry thought Max was a jerk.

"Going pretty well, Max. Thanks for asking. Haven't made any earth-shattering discoveries but such is the nature of academic research."

"Okay, brother, I'll sign off. If there's any change in Mom's condition, I'll let you know. Bye for now."

Harry switched off the phone and relaxed in his chair. He replayed the conversation with Max over again. His brother, although meticulous and organized to a fault, was intolerant of differences, fearful of doing the wrong thing, and disliked change. He was their father's favored son and for that, he'd earned Harry's jealousy and resentment. Early on, Max realized that he could do no wrong in the old man's eyes and used it to his advantage. Being the favored son inflated Max's ego to supercilious heights and any mistake he made became Harry's fault. The bile that road in Harry's throat burned and the fire spread to his brain as he remembered the past. His abusive father, drunk most of the time. His arrogant, condescending brother.

Once in high school when Harry was playing in a basketball game with a crosstown rival, his father showed up drunk and disorderly, yelling obscenities at everyone present. Harry hid out in the locker room until the school principal called the police and his father was taken downtown to sleep it off. But his friends never forgot the day Harry's father turned up at the game. It was an embarrassment that he never forgot. And Max never forgave Harry.

When he left for college, he and Max went their separate ways and rarely communicated, except once or twice a year, at a holiday, when the two brothers gathered at the family home. There, under their mother's watchful and encouraging eye, they talked as brothers with each other. Otherwise, they simply didn't have anything in common.

As Harry got up to leave the command tent, another commotion was being raised from the direction of the diggings. He donned his cap and went to investigate.

෴

A much larger hole than previous one had been excavated and Harry pushed his way to its edge. A long rectangular pit greeted him, glints of green flashing in the bright sunlight. In its depth lay the broken, rusted, fuselage of an airplane. The moss-and-dirt-covered metal body was missing its wings and tail and had several large cracks where the plane had come apart on impact. Workers milled around the crater, speaking with garbled excitement, pointing and nodding. Harry climbed into the hole and worked his way over to the metal beast. It looked like a giant insect pupa at rest. The soft earth sank around his boots, causing him to stumble.

Harry worked his way over large rocks of limestone and piles of dark earth. At the wreckage, he was greeted by the musty smell of damp earth, mold, and decaying matter. Although most of the plane's markings were worn beyond recognition, its olive green exterior contrasted sharply with the surrounding soil.

Muddling along the body of the aircraft, he found a door

located toward what could have been the rear of the plane. The odor that emanated from the excavated skeleton tickled his nostrils, which caused his eyes to water. Harry wrapped a large hand around the handle and pulled. Nothing. He pulled harder and the handle popped off in his hand.

"Li," he called. "I'm going to need a crowbar and a flashlight."

No sooner had he turned back to the rusted door than Li was beside him with the requested items. Harry took the crowbar, fitted it into the narrow space around the door, and began to pry it open. With a loud screech, the door budged a fraction of an inch. He shoved the crowbar in farther and pulled again. The door creaked as it opened slightly more with his effort. After several minutes of work, the door was open enough for Harry and Li to grasp its edge and, together, they yanked it open.

Slowly, with each labored pull, the door gave way, allowing enough room for entry. A rush of stale fetid air, prompting Li to pull his bandana over his nose, greeted the men. In the dark interior of the cabin, Harry switched on the flashlight and began making his way forward. The beam of light danced eerily off the aircraft's walls as Harry and Li stumbled over a myriad of wires and rotting boxes strewn throughout the wrecked fuselage. Working their way through the dim light, the pair managed to get to the cockpit and peered into it. Amid cobwebs, spiders, and numerous cockroaches, two desiccated skeletons were strapped into the pilot and copilot seats, their heads cocked at an acute angle. A large insect, unknown to Harry, scampered out of the eye socket of the pilot's skull.

"Christ," exclaimed Li. "They have been sitting here all these years, just like that."

"I wonder why no one ever located them or the plane," said Harry. "Surely it was reported missing and a search party sent out." He began searching through the ragged, decaying pockets of the mummified corpses' flight jackets.

"It gets pretty bad here during winter. Place is mostly inaccessible."

"No identification on them," Harry said, moving his search

to the remainder of the cockpit. "That's odd. Why wouldn't they have some sort of identification?"

Li turned and started back into the fuselage. "I'm going to look around in the back. There might be something of interest."

"I'll follow," said Harry.

The two returned to the main cargo area and began rummaging through the wreckage. They talked as they worked.

"Know what kind of plane this is?" Harry said.

"A Lisunov Li-2. Basically, it's a DC-3. The Soviets bought a license from Douglas Aircraft sometime during World War Two. The aircraft were used for transport, partisan supply, bombing, and as ambulance aircraft. Some, I think, were even equipped with machine guns."

"How come you know so much?"

"Well, there was a time I wanted to be a pilot. I read everything I could get my hands on about airplanes."

"It puzzles me that neither of the pilots had identification, Li. Any ideas why that might be?"

"Maybe they were on a secret flight of some sort. The Soviets were famous for that, you know."

Toward the rear of the main cabin, Harry moved a brittle wooden crate to an empty space on the floor. Dirt and dust powdered the stagnant air.

"Shine that light over here, Li. Let's see what this is."

Li complied and the two men peered at a box the size of a footlocker. There were no markings on it. It was covered with dirt and dust. Harry pried open the crate with the aid of the crowbar while Li held the flashlight. Dust filled the cabin and the dank smell made breathing difficult. The two gazed into the box and took a deep breath.

"Bones," Li said.

"Let's have a closer look." Harry fumbled around in the crate and produced several long, heavy bones, which he handed to Li. Reaching back into the box, he retrieved a smaller, black metal box with the Soviet hammer and sickle stamped on its cover.

When opened, the small box contained numerous teeth. To

Harry they looked human but they were much larger than any teeth he had ever seen.

Li stared over his shoulder. "Teeth?" he asked Harry as the expedition leader handled a few of the items.

"Looks like it. More human than anything but unlike anything I've come across. Let's move this crate up to the command tent so we can get a closer look. I need to get Dixie down here to shoot a series of pictures for photogrammetric mapping and modeling. Get some men here now while I share the news with Dixie."

സ്ഥ

High atop a glass skyscraper overlooking Lower Manhattan and the East River, Rutherford Eastwood reclined in a tufted leather chair, while leisurely enjoying a ten-dollar cigar. From his towering perch, he had a grand view of the Brooklyn Bridge leading into Brooklyn Heights and the Brooklyn Navy Yard, now used commercially by two hundred businesses. He was finished scanning the stock reports in the *Wall Street Journal* and the paper lay on his ornate desk amidst numerous photographs of himself and others in various poses. At sixty, his graying hair belied the person in many of the pictures, for now glasses sat upon a ruddy nose. After a few puffs, he absentmindedly flicked a large ash off his Italian silk suit. This was the part of the day he enjoyed the most—watching the sun fade over the river after his secretary and assistant had left. He reached into the lower desk drawer, retrieved his favorite single-malt scotch, and poured himself a drink.

BioGen International was his brainchild, formed out of nothing but an interesting idea. Rutherford put legs on the company through diligent hard work and now reaped the rewards of heading an organization with a worldwide reputation. It was the result of equal parts of Herculean effort and luck.

BioGen had long arms, reaching into each of the world's seven continents. On its board of directors sat some of the nation's shakers and movers, men and women who saw the value in Eastwood's global vision. His mission was to scour the earth searching and uncovering the world's rare and exotic relics. Primarily interested in human and animal fossils, Eastwood also dabbled in other treasures, including rare art, gems, and documents. He collected things such as Australian banknotes of the King George V period, which were hard to find in good condition and commanded high prices. He once found an exceptional Maya Bowl—an extremely rare, 1,400-year-old vessel that told the story of a young prince and his bloodletting sacrifice—and pottery figurines from around 738 BC found during excavations at the archaeological site of Tel Motza on the western outskirts of Jerusalem. BioGen financed excursions all over the world, in search of these ancient specimens, then charged enormous fees to private collectors and museums. Over the years, this activity had made Eastwood an extremely wealthy man. As CEO of BioGen, he had exclusive use of its Hawker 800 corporate jet that cruised at over five hundred miles an hour and could take him anywhere in the world on a moment's notice. He owned a home in St. Moritz and another in Tobago. His chauffeur drove him around in a Bentley Mulsanne. Life had been good to Eastwood.

BioGen International had just concluded negotiations with the National Museum of Saudi Arabia for a complete fossilized skeleton of *Lycaenops,* a mammal-like reptile with a large wolf-like skull and big canine teeth. The creature lived around 250 million years ago in South Africa before becoming extinct. The Saudis were willing to pay sixty-eight million dollars for the skeleton, more than enough to pay the bills and finance BioGen's next venture. No one outside the company knew how he had managed to obtain the artifact.

Of course, this wealth had not come easily or without human cost. Some of the countries they had scoured had been hostile to Americans. Either the governments were not particularly interested in a group of foreigners removing their national treasures, or his men had been caught in the middle of hostile tribal factions. On more than one occasion his team had had to shoot their way out of trouble, a fact that left a few corpses in their wake. Sometimes, violence was unable to solve logistical problems, and those instances called for lots of accessible cash. The road to success had been difficult, and it necessitated a cadre of security and bodyguards watching over him night and day. Eastwood had made many enemies.

As he gazed out over the East River Eastwood mentally debated his company's future options. There was the possibility of looking for a Siberian mammoth fossil but there weren't many clues as to where to search. Possibly hunt for human remains in Indochina. Both ventures sounded somewhat promising, although nothing was a sure bet in the relic business.

He leaned back in his chair and savored the remaining puffs of the cigar.

 espeso

It was late afternoon in the Altai Basin, and dark clouds were pushing their way over the snow-capped peaks, obscuring any view of them. A front from Russian Siberia had moved past the region, leaving in its wake a north wind that blew lightly over the steppe, rippling the grasses like waves on the ocean. Harry and Dixie were in the command tent, waiting for the evening meal. The basin was quiet, the workers having quit for the day. Dixie typed on a laptop while Harry strummed his fingers on the table. The longer he strummed, the more exasperated she became.

Finally, she closed the laptop. "Okay, Harry, what's eating you?"

"Nothing, really. I was just thinking about the bones we found earlier today. They are just too large to be *Australopithecus* or even *Ardipithecus*. Of course, they could belong to a human antecedent hominid."

Dixie was puzzled. "You mean like the Miocene primates? The apes and gorillas? I know that, during the Miocene Period, these hominoids reached their greatest abundance and diversity. But I thought the crashed plane didn't interest you at all. Those bones stimulated an interest, did they?"

"Yeah, they have. The Miocene primates lived around twelve to fourteen million years ago. But they aren't considered human by any stretch of the imagination. They aren't hominids. That's why we call them hominoids, like hominids but earlier."

"I thought most every scientist believes that human origins lie somewhere within this group. Am I right, Harry?"

"Possibly. But it's a very confusing field now. The genetic difference between modern humans and chimpanzees is only a little greater than one percent, the difference with gorillas is more than that. No matter how the calculation is done, the big point still holds—humans and chimpanzees are more closely related to one another than either one is to gorillas or any other primate. From the perspective of this powerful test of biological kinship, humans are not only related to the great apes—we are one. The DNA evidence leaves us with one of the greatest surprises in biology—the wall between human, on the one hand, and ape or animal, on the other, has been breached. The human evolutionary tree is embedded within the great apes.

"Some of the tools found around the Caspian Sea have been associated with Neanderthal fossils, the Mousterian tools. As you know, they are tools with long tapered points. The Caspian Sea fossils could represent a stop of the hominid's journey on their way to Mongolia and the land bridge. That would be relatively recent, around three hundred thousand years ago."

Dixie frowned. "Our initial assessment is the bones in the plane don't match any previously identified hominid, do they?"

She opened her laptop and recalled the file with photographs of the bones and teeth. Together, they reviewed the pictures in silence before Harry continued.

"No. See? The teeth are too large and too thickly enameled. The bones are obviously from a lower limb but the articular surfaces are too extensive to be hominid. Frankly, I've never seen anything like them before."

They continued to look through the pictures Dixie had taken of the bones and teeth. The computer screen blinked as she scrolled through them.

"How old do you think they are?" she asked.

"I dunno, but my feeling is that they are pretty old. However, maybe more recent than the early hominid we know, possibly the age of the Neanderthals, but that would be just a wild guess. I think later this evening we need to shoot the pictures to Professor Kesler. Can you connect the satellite antenna to the laptop? We haven't tried a satellite transmission yet and now is as good a time as any."

"Okay, Harry. Can do after dinner."

"Did you manage to get pictures of the crash site, earlier?"

"Did that as well. But I don't understand the photogramme- try process yet," Dixie said, frowning.

"Not all that complicated," Harry said. "Photogrammetry is the science of making measurements from photographs. The output of photogrammetry is typically a map, drawing, meas- urement, or a 3D model of some real-world object. With these georectified images, we can produce photographic plans of sites and their stratigraphy, take accurate measurements direct- ly from the photo, and import photographic data into other computerized technologies for mapping and visualizing ar- chaeological features. We can rotate the image, zoom into a specific location, and measure distances between objects. We take the pictures, the computer software does all the heavy lift- ing."

Dixie smiled. "It's all over my head. Maybe one day I'll understand how it works. The computerized models are sure neat to play with. It will be interesting to see a 3D model of the crash site."

Harry rose, and his assistant followed suit.

"I think dinner's about ready," he said.

# Chapter 5

Dixie pointed the satellite dish into the southwestern sky, locked onto the Russian Express AM1X satellite, and punched up the VSAT Private Network. When the site appeared on the screen, she typed in Professor Kesler's university number, followed by her PIN number, and waited with Harry for the connection to link up. She adjusted the camera atop the laptop and primped her hair. The screen blinked and the professor's bearded face appeared on the screen.

"Good evening, Professor," Harry said. "I guess it's morning there. Good morning."

"Good morning, Harry and Dixie." The professor's voice boomed over the computer's small speakers. "My, you look wonderful, Dixie, I must say, for someone digging around on the edge of the earth."

"How nice, Professor," Dixie replied and moved her face in front of the laptop. She waved. "You certainly know how to make a girl feel special. Too bad you can't teach Harry some of those manners."

"I'm sorry, Dixie. Should I replace him with someone more suitable?" The professor's face lit up with a broad smile and he laughed heartily.

"If so, I'll let you know."

"Enough of this idle chatter," Harry interjected as he pushed Dixie away from the computer's camera. "I called for a very important reason. We have found something interesting.

At least interesting enough to discuss it with it you, Professor."

"Yes, yes." Kesler's voice was at a higher pitch, betraying his sudden interest.

"Tell him, Harry. Don't keep him waiting," Dixie said.

"Professor," Harry began, his voice modulating at an even tone, "we uncovered some teeth and a few bones in Section H9. However, they weren't in the ground like you might think. These artifacts were found in the wreckage of a crashed Soviet plane. We found a pilot's cap and confirmed it's from before the Soviet breakup, but the exact date is unknown. It's hard to say what these bones and teeth are right now. They could be from a hominid precursor, like *Proconsul*, but again, I can't be sure. They might belong to some hominid that we have never seen before, something unknown to date. We've gotten a few pictures of the items and Dixie can call them up. Right, Dixie?"

Harry waited while Dixie recalled the file with the photographs of the items in question and the images appeared on the screen. The group continued to talk while examining the photos.

"You can see, Professor, the teeth are quite strange for a hominid but even stranger for anything earlier. Too much enamel for a hominid and not sharp enough for any earlier primates. The bones are seemingly an upper thigh and lower leg bone, a femur and tibia. However, the distribution of the desiccated cartilage on the femoral head shows this species had a preponderance of joint surface on the anterior surface of the femoral head. When we placed these two bones together they resulted in a carrying angle greater than that found in apes and other hominoid primates."

"Yes, the angle created by the femur and tibia. In other words, the weight-bearing axis." Kesler seemed to be thinking out loud. "In hominids and humans, walking generates a torque that pulls the trunk toward the body's center so, as a counter, the buttock muscles contract, pulling the pelvis in the opposite direction. It results in a carrying angle, or the angle the femur makes with the tibia—we call it the valgus angle—greater in humans, placing the legs directly under the body.

The chimpanzee, for example, which is a quadruped, has a femur that comes straight out of the hip socket. Hence, the cartilage differences between the species."

"Hominid bipedalism?" Dixie asked.

"Yes," Kesler confirmed. "Anatomical evidence for bipedalism includes modifications of the hip joint and limb muscles that balance the thigh in an upright stance and keep the trunk erect. For example, the ilium supports enlarged gluteal muscles that are important for standing and running. Specialized knee and ankle joints place the foot underneath the hip joint. These features provide the ability to balance the body on one foot during upright standing and locomotion. The relatively straight leg minimizes the amount of active muscle needed to balance the body, acting much like a stiff column. The forelimb of bipeds also lost some specializations for climbing, but gained manipulatory capabilities—"

Dixie interrupted. "Yes, I know, Professor, I learned that last year in my advanced paleontology course. Harry is saying that the leg bones seem to be from some sort of hominid and not lower primates. And the teeth, well, we don't know."

"I must admit, after studying these photographs, I'm unable to shed any light on your confusion," Kesler told them. "I don't remember ever seeing teeth such as these. Hominid dentition is a confusing area of study at present. There are two basic directions in the evolution of hominid teeth and jaw anatomy. The first is for larger back teeth and is associated with *Australopithecus* who specialized their diet toward vegetation. Coupled with the large molars, massive muscular structures to aid chewing developed in these early hominids. These hominids shared the ability for bipedal walking. The reasons for the development of bipedalism in these early hominids would have been the same as for later hominids. They shared the freedom of the hands from locomotion, as well as the ability of the trunk to be controlled on the hind limbs during bipedal postures. Therefore, their hands could be used in many other activities besides walking.

"The other direction in the evolution of the dentition of hominids was for smaller teeth and a parabolic shape to the palate. The trend for smaller teeth was one that began with early *Homo* and continued through to modern *Homo sapiens*. The decrease in the size of the teeth is thought to be related to a diet that included a wide variety of foods where there was less emphasis on plant foods that required heavy chewing."

"Right," Harry said. "But that still doesn't give me any answers."

"Have you dated them yet?" Kesler asked. "Did the mass spec make it there in one piece?"

"It did." Dixie smiled as Kesler's face reappeared on the computer screen. "We haven't unpacked it yet or checked it out but it seems to have survived unscathed."

Harry was getting impatient, he was ready for bed and wasn't used to late night scientific discussions. "We'll get the beast calibrated tomorrow and do the analysis. One of the bones and two of the teeth have a shell of rock around them so we will shoot you the potassium-argon data and you can do the math to determine the age of these specimens."

"If I had the actual specimens, we could perform AAR on the bones themselves and compare the dates from both methods," Kesler said.

"Amino acid racemization?" Dixie asked, wanting to be sure she understood.

"Yes. If we can extract the amino acids found in the organic bone, we can calculate and compare the racemization rate for aspartic acid and isoleucine and get a date with which to compare the date we get with the argon method on rock."

Dixie frowned. "But that destroys part of the specimen, doesn't it?"

"Only a small amount," Harry said. "We're lucky to have a layer of rock around part of a bone and a few teeth. That fact makes the dating of a specimen much easier. Radiometric methods are more accurate."

"The circumstances surrounding the find are certainly intriguing, if not downright puzzling. It seems to be a mystery, for sure. If you just had a skull it would answer a lot of questions." Kesler didn't seem to want the conversation to end.

Harry sighed. "Yeah, but we don't. And you are right—the

fact that these specimens were found on an airplane insures that there is no telling where they came from. May not even be in Mongolia."

∽∾∾

The sun was just casting its first golden rays down the Altai Basin when Dixie entered the small tent dedicated to laboratory procedures and analysis. The kitchen crew was already up and had the coffee ready when she'd strolled through the mess tent, so she brought a cup with her. She took a sip of the hot liquid and opened the crate that housed the Duke 860, the miniaturized mass spectrometer they would use for dating the specimens. The whole instrument was the size of a small suitcase.

Like most mass spectrometers, the Duke worked in combination with a gas chromatograph where, after preparation, samples were placed in a combustion tube and heated to 800 degrees Celsius. The resultant vapor then passed through the gas chromatograph and subsequently analyzed by isotope ratio mass spectrometry. The resultant data was displayed on their computer screens using GRAMS/IT software. The mass spec data would then be beamed to Kesler who would calculate the dates of the specimens. Dixie never was able to understand the science behind the machine, she just knew that it worked.

Preparation of the specimens was the most complex and labor intensive of the procedures and required the utmost precision. Dixie took one of the teeth and dropped it into a beaker of mild acid to clean it of grime and organic matter. When it was clean and dry, she placed it into a ceramic mortar, chipped off a fleck of rock, and ground it to a fine powder with a pestle. Then the powder was passed through a Pyrex filter, using mild hydrochloric acid as the carrier. The residue was then freeze dried in a Guidon FP-5 freeze drier. After thirty minutes of preparation, the small residual sample was then ready for the mass spectrometer. Dixie placed the sample in a Vycor glass mass spec tube and laid it aside as Harry sauntered into the lab tent.

"Good morning," he said, placing his coffee cup on the table. "Started early, eh?"

"Thought I would start processing the specimens before you got here. Rock from one tooth is all ready for the mass spec. It's laying there on the table." Dixie pointed to the glass tubing next to the Guidon unit.

"Great. Let me down this coffee, then I'll help you."

"Sleep well?" she asked.

He nodded, coffee cup at his lips.

Dixie smiled at him. "If you want to run the tooth material, I'll prepare one of the leg bones. I know how you hate the tedious lab work, and I don't mind."

"Okay," Harry said. "The sooner we can get the professor the raw data, the sooner he can come up with some dates."

She picked one of the bones and began cleaning it while humming a tune.

"You sound pretty chipper this morning," Harry said. "Must have had an erotic dream or something."

"Stop it, mister," Dixie said, scowling at him.

They both laughed and continued working. Dixie continued to hum her tune.

Harry took the Vycor glass tube and fastened it into the mass spectrometer's inlet portal where it was vaporized by an electrical current. The resultant vapor, made up of various ions, was then pumped into the analyzing chamber where they were analyzed and quantified. The results were plotted on a curve for visual reference and the graph popped up on the computer screen. The conversion of this raw data into a usable age for the specimen was a complicated mathematical affair, best left to the larger computers back at Cal Pacific.

Harry pushed the start button and waited, while downing the rest of his coffee. He observed Dixie as she labored over the leg bone. She looked especially appealing this morning, with her freshly shampooed hair pulled into a bun. And she had applied a hint of makeup, something unnecessary on an archeological dig. He marveled at her delicate fingers as they ground bone fragments with the mortar and pestle. But the delicateness belied a strength that was characteristic of Dixie. In spite of her privileged upbringing, she was eager to do the heavy work of an expedition.

Today, knowledge of fossil ages came primarily from radiometric dating, also known as radioactive dating. Radiometric dating relied on the properties of isotopes—chemical elements, like carbon or uranium—which were identical, except for one key feature—the number of neutrons in their nucleus.

Usually, atoms had an equal number of protons and neutrons. If there were too many or too few neutrons, the atom was unstable, and it shed particles until its nucleus reached a stable state. The nucleus was like a pyramid of building blocks. If you tried to add extra blocks to the sides of a pyramid, they may stay put for a while, but they'd eventually fall away. The same was true if you took a block away from one of the pyramid's sides, making the rest unstable. Eventually, some of the blocks would fall away, leaving a smaller, more stable structure.

The result was like a radioactive clock that ticked away, as unstable isotopes decayed into stable ones. You couldn't predict when a specific unstable atom, or parent, would decay into a stable atom, or daughter. But you could predict how long it would take a large group of atoms to decay. The element's half-life was the amount of time it took for half the parent atoms in a sample to become daughters.

To read the time on this radioactive clock, scientists used a device called a mass spectrometer to measure the number of parent and daughter atoms. The ratio of parents to daughters could tell the researcher how old the specimen was. The more parent isotopes there were—and the fewer daughter isotopes—the younger the sample.

The mass spectrometer hummed and, with a *beep*, churned out a graph that displayed numerous peaks and valleys. Harry jotted the numbers in a notebook, saved the graph into a computer file, and refilled his coffee mug. When Dixie had the second specimen ready for the mass spec, he fitted the tube on the inlet and repeated the process. It was late morning when they had collected and recorded the last of the data. Dixie cleaned up while Harry walked back to the command tent. A brilliant sun was high in an azure-blue cloudless sky.

Along the way, Li joined him. "Finished with the specimens?" he asked as the two continued to walk.

"Got the data right here, as well as saved in the computer," Harry said, patting his notebook. "I'm going to send the graph and numbers to the Professor right away. It's late back home but I know he's waiting eagerly to hear from me."

"Where do we go from here, Harry? I gave the workers the morning off as you wished, but they're going to want to know. What do I tell them?"

In the command tent, Harry sat at the computer and turned it on. "Well, for starters, it's business as usual. Get them back to working, according to our original schedule. Then we'll see."

Li sat opposite him and shook his head. "What do you really think about these specimens, boss? Think they could turn out to be something big?"

"The mystery is intriguing, Li. Why would a Soviet military plane be carrying old bones and teeth? And to where? From where? Just how old is the plane? The questions are endless, but I'm not sure any of the answers are pertinent to us being here. After I've talked with the professor, I'll have a better idea of where we're going."

におの

Rutherford Eastwood sat behind his massive desk with a copy of the *New York Times* in front of him. Across the desk, ensconced in a burgundy leather chair, was Ben Doyle, his chief of security operations. Doyle was a large-framed, muscular man in his mid-forties who had a scarred and pockmarked face from an IED while serving in the Iraq War. After recovering from the injury, he had been transferred to the army military police corps which reported directly to the provost marshal general. Doyle had quit the service with the rank of captain after a disagreement with a superior officer nearly got him court martialed. Doyle was vacationing in the Bahamas for the past few weeks, recovering from Eastwood's latest venture in

Saudi Arabia, and had not sounded happy when Eastwood had summoned him to New York. But Doyle was all smiles as the two men chatted amicably about his fishing excursions in the clear waters around Eleuthera.

At a break in Doyle's story, Eastwood picked up the *Times* and smiled. "Look at this article, Ben." He passed the paper to Doyle. "I've circled it." He lit a cigar and sat back in his chair while Doyle read the newspaper article.

A few minutes later, Doyle handed the paper back, nodded, and waited for Eastwood to continue.

"This looks interesting, Ben. These guys in Mongolia may have stumbled onto something."

"This Dr. Kesler, he's leading the expedition?"

"No. He is a well-known anthropologist at California Pacific University in San Francisco. Heads the department there. His colleague is in Mongolia, leading the expedition."

"They're looking for human fossils?" Doyle asked.

"Hominids, Ben. Hominids. Human ancestors. They may have stumbled onto something interesting and possibly lucrative for BioGen."

Doyle shifted in his chair. "What's on your mind, sir?"

"Whatever it is could be worth a lot of money. Human fossils always make the news, Ben. Something that changes the way science looks at mankind would be worth a fortune. Especially if it were a human skeleton."

"I never understood why fossilized bones are such a big deal to these scientists," Doyle said. "I just don't get it."

"You don't have to get it," Eastwood retorted, flicking the cigar's ash in a crystal ashtray. "You just have to trust my judgement."

"You're thinking of appropriating their discovery?"

"Great choice of words, Ben. We'll let them process whatever it is, then move in and take it off their hands. That will be your responsibility. I want you to start getting your team ready to fly over there and begin surveillance. If they unearth what looks like an important relic, you are to notify me." Eastwood's intercom buzzed. He laid the cigar in the ashtray.

"There's a Mr. Sawyers on the line, sir," a soft, female

voice crackled. "He said he was an assistant with the White House."

"The White House?" Eastwood said, eyebrows raised. "What in the world?" He put the phone on speaker. "This is Eastwood."

Doyle excused himself and left the office.

"Mr. Eastwood, this is Garrett Sawyers. I'm an administrative assistant to the president. How are you?"

"I'm fine. How can I help you?"

"I'm calling, Mr. Eastwood, to inform you of the formation of a presidential charity commission. He has formed this commission to investigate compliance by charitable organizations with government regulations and make recommendations on how to improve oversight. He has chosen you to head this commission if you would be willing."

Astonished Eastwood sat silent, momentarily speechless.

"Mr. Eastwood," Sawyers asked, "did you hear me?"

"I'm flattered, Mr. Sawyer, but how did the president arrive at my name, if I may ask?"

"Well, the fact that BioGen International is a *Fortune 500* company didn't hurt. The fact that you built the company yourself without much outside help was the clincher."

"Like I said, I'm flattered but I really don't know." Eastwood puffed again on the cigar. Acrid smoke swirled above him.

"I perfectly understand, sir. The president would like to meet with you personally and describe his ideas more fully. Would that be acceptable?"

"The President wants to meet with me?" Eastwood's voice betrayed his excitement, though he tried to hide it. "Of course. I can find the time to come to DC. When would you suggest?"

"How about next week sometime? I can have my secretary call when the president's schedule is put together."

"That will be fine, Mr. Sawyer. I look forward to meeting him." Eastwood leaned back and smiled. A gray haze hung over the East River, making Brooklyn barely visible. *A meeting with the President of the United States. How far I have come, indeed.*

∾∾∾

Harry was on a satellite video conference call with Professor Kesler. Dixie and Li sat around the table, staring at the laptop's monitor. It had taken several attempts before a clear and audible transmission signal had been found. They worked with impatience, trying to get Kesler's wrinkled face to appear on the screen.

"Harry, about the age of the specimens. Are you ready for this? Approximately one hundred thousand years old. And I have examined the photos over and over meticulously, and they definitely are not Homo. Not modern human."

"Wow," Dixie said, surprise showing on her face.

"And they are nothing like the Neanderthals, either. That is way too late to be a hominid predecessor. At that age, I don't know what else they could be, other than a Homo species or a Neanderthal, but the specimens don't fit into either category. I haven't done a mitochondrial DNA analysis so they could turn out to be something along the lines of the Denisova fossils. At our current knowledge, there isn't anything else living in that time frame. Then, too, they could belong to a species entirely new and different, heretofore unknown. Of course, I need to wait on a final opinion until I examine the actual specimens.

"I don't know if you are aware, but K40 decays to non-radioactive Ar40. Argon is a gas and escapes into the atmosphere as soon as it forms, unless it's trapped in solid rock. With igneous rock formed from magma, argon escapes from the magma. Therefore, any Ar40 trapped in such rocks has accumulated since the rock solidified. By careful measurement of the amounts of K40 and Ar40 in igneous rock, it is possible to determine how long it has been since that rock formed."

"Professor, this is Li. Those specimens were found on the airplane so they, in all likelihood, are not even from around here. We don't really know why they were on the aircraft, where they came from, or where they were going. Who knows how long the plane has been here? The cap found near it is from before the dissolution of the old Soviet Union so the plane has been here at least fifteen years. Skeletons of the pilot and copilot are still strapped in their seats."

"Well, that does pose a problem, doesn't it?" Kesler said, his smile twisting into a grimace. "If that's the case, then I suppose you need to keep digging and see what else turns up. Not being able to determine the exact origin of these specimens makes them almost useless at this juncture."

"We are eventually going to have to inform the Mongolian authorities," Harry said.

"I don't know if that's such a good idea, Harry," Kesler argued.

"Why?" Dixie interjected. "They're going to have to know eventually."

"And have a bunch of uninformed lay people tramping all over the site, contaminating it?" Kesler said, his tone noticeably irritated.

"I think we can hold off on that for a little while longer, Professor," Harry said.

# Chapter 6

Dr. Kesler turned out the light in his office and walked out of the Physical Sciences Building to the parking lot. After leaving the university campus, he started the drive down the peninsula to his home in San Mateo. The stars hung like silver jewels in a black-velvet sky. Over the quiescent waters off to his left, an orange moon rose above the bay, the moonlight filtering across the water in shimmering waves of light. Once he passed the San Francisco International Airport, the highway hugged the coastline, coursing south then southeast. US 101 was the most historic highway in California. It followed the route the Spanish explorer Juan Gaspar de Portola followed in 1769, which later became El Camino Real, the King's Highway. This historic road connected the twenty-one California missions and served as the main north/south road in California until the 1920s. The missions were constructed about thirty miles apart, which was one day's journey by horseback, and the local padres lined the road with mustard seeds to mark the trail with bright yellow flowers.

Passing Candlestick Park, Kesler noticed a large two-masted sailboat moored in the bay with its lights reflecting in the water.

The events of the evening had left him confused but curious. He had rechecked his calculations on the computer numerous times but the results were the same. The bones were one hundred thousand years old, no doubt about it. Unless Harry and Dixie had made some mistake and Kesler doubted that possibility—for they were top-notch scientists. He switched on a Mozart symphony that was in the CD player and tried to concentrate on the music.

Kesler was Lithuanian by birth. He had escaped Europe, during the Nazi occupation of 1941, when a hundred thousand of his countrymen were murdered. Following the German Army, as it swept through the country, were the Nazi killing squads who began organizing the systematic murder of Jews. His parents took him to live with a non-Jewish family and they cared for him until the end of the war.

His mother and father were sent to Sobibor Concentration Camp and died there. His adopted family traveled to the States and Kesler finished high school in Baltimore. Educated at Penn and Harvard University, Julius Kesler had forged a career in anthropology and paleontology and become one of the country's leading researchers in the field. He once fell in love with a beautiful graduate student while at Harvard and, for a year, they'd lived a bohemian life together, partying, studying, listening to music, going to the opera. But one day she up and left him for a well-to-do professor of humanities and they got married. Kesler wasn't even invited to the wedding. The experience left him soured on the opposite sex. Although he could still appreciate their wit and beauty, he wasn't about to enter into another love affair. He wasn't much for entertaining or working the social set and spent his spare time on his hobbies of photography and coin collecting.

He had come to California Pacific University from Harvard at the request of his former dean, who was now the school's president. Prior to Harry joining his research team, Kesler had gained national prominence with the discovery of a new hominid species, *Ardipithecus Sensus*, with an almost complete skeleton located in Ethiopia. It had caused an international sensation, modifying the way scientists looked at human evolution. Those days were long past, and Kesler ached for a new, earth-shaking discovery.

Kesler pulled his SUV into the drive of his San Mateo home and killed the motor. Headlights from a large vehicle shone through the rear window, blinding him. He removed the key from the ignition but, before he could open the door, two dark figures opened it and yanked him out. He fought to get a look at their obscured faces but they were muscular and forced his arms behind him.

"What the hell," he yelled, pain shooting into his shoulders.

"Shut up and you won't get hurt," said one of the dark figures.

The two figures manhandled Kesler and shoved him into the rear seat of a dark Suburban. One of the figures piled in beside him, a bandana in his hand.

"Tie this over your eyes, sit still, and don't say a word. Move and you'll get a bullet in your brain."

Kesler did as commanded. The car's interior smelled of new leather, while the man next to him reeked of stale cigarettes and alcohol.

He felt the other man jump behind the wheel. The SUV lurched out of Kesler's driveway and sped away, lurching first in one direction, then another. He heard several car horns blast as they careened around a corner, hit a bump, slowed for a second, then accelerate again. His impression, by the turns the truck made, was that they were traveling north, back toward San Francisco.

His abductors did not say a word and Kesler decided to remain silent. He was dazed by the suddenness of the event and confused as to how he should act. Should he put up a struggle? Fight for his life? Not knowing what would happen next caused his hands to sweat and a pain to well up deep in his chest.

Was he having a heart attack? He couldn't die here, not before prying the secrets out of the Mongolian earth. His abductors hadn't hurt him yet and maybe they wouldn't. The man next to him lit a cigarette and blew smoke into Kesler's face, stifling, and choking him. The Suburban's tires squealed as they hit a long curve. Kesler struggled to breathe and said a silent prayer—*Blessed are You, LORD our God, King of the Universe, Who bestows good things upon the unworthy, and has bestowed upon me every goodness.*

Then he waited.

 birth

Harry dialed his brother's number in New York. Max picked up on the first ring.

"Max, it's Harry. What's the latest on Mom? How is she doing?"

Harry had debated on whether to call Max. During their last conversation his brother sounded curt and abrasive, leaving Harry to wonder if he could confide his concerns to Max. Harry doubted the man truly cared if he was kept informed with updates, probably only going through the motions. But what did he, Harry, care?

"I'm glad you called, Harry. Mom has taken a little turn for the worse. She—"

"What do you mean, worse, Max?" Harry said, irritation showing in his voice. "Or little? How come you haven't called?"

"Calm down, Harry. I was planning on calling but I've been working all week. Mom started getting more short of breath, so she went back to the doctor and he changed her medicine. Let's hope she improves in a few days."

"If she doesn't, then what?" Harry tried not to let his aggravation overcome the calm he relayed over the phone.

"I suppose she'll have to go to the hospital. Her spirits are good and Dad is helping the best he can."

"The asshole doesn't care about her, he never did. Or have you forgotten, Max?"

"Harry, don't start with that, all right? For Christ's sake, just keep it to yourself."

Max sounded annoyed and Harry chafed at his brother's tone.

"Max, listen to me. Don't find a reason to delay calling if Mom takes another turn for the worse."

"You know, if you were here, instead of on the far side of the world, things would be better."

Harry was losing his temper. His heart pounded and a lump formed in his throat. It was there, again—the reason he and Max never hit it off as brothers—his irritating, condescending, arrogant attitude. They were like oil and water, seeing the world through completely different sets of eyes.

"Dammit, Max, it's my career. It's what I do. I didn't choose to be here. Listen, just call if you have news. Now I have to get back to work."

♥⏎♥⏎

The grandfather clock in the West Wing's Roosevelt Room ticked closer to Eastwood's appointed meeting time with the President of the United States. He sat at the end of a long ma-hogany table, surrounded by red leather chairs. He couldn't believe he was actually here in the White House, about to meet the leader of the free world. His flight to Washington/Dulles had landed less than an hour earlier and a limousine had met his Hawker near the cargo ramp at the end of Runway 19. A short time later, they drove through the Northwest Appoint-ment Gate and entered the West Wing.

The door next to a fireplace at the end of the room opened and in walked a cadre of men in suits, followed the president. Eastwood stood.

"Good morning, Mr. Eastwood," the president said, extend-ing his hand. "Thank you for coming."

"Thank you, Mr. President. I am honored to be here."

"Well, let's get down to business, shall we." The president signaled Eastwood to be seated and took a chair next to him. "Would you care for anything? Coffee? Water?"

"No thank you, Mr. President," Eastwood said. The rest of the suited men took seats around the table. "How can I be of service, Mr. President?"

"Mr. Sawyers, I believe, has briefed you on my Charity Compliance Commission and that I hope to persuade you to lead it. It would entail a number of public hearings with you as the chair and the writing of a report, summarizing any recom-mendations the commissions feels appropriate."

Eastwood listened as the president outlined the details of his commission and his vision of its mission. Flags hung on poles and framed an idyllic Hudson Valley painting on one wall, while a painting of Theodore Roosevelt as a Rough Rider hung over the fireplace. Eastwood noticed that there were no windows.

"My vision is a commission comprised of twelve folks from the private sector of varied backgrounds and areas of expertise. Their mission would be to determine to what extent current charities abide by the tax code and whether more reform is needed. For example, could we maximize the efficiency and effectiveness of any incentives for charitable giving? Should we consider whether the availability of tax incentives for charitable giving be broadened to include more taxpayers? Do we need to closely examine the relationship between political activity and tax-exempt status?"

The president paused for a moment then continued with his outline. Thirty minutes later, he was finished. "That's about it, Mr. Eastwood. I can answer any questions you might have."

Eastwood thought for a moment then shook his head. "No, Mr. President, you covered everything."

The President stood. Eastwood followed suit. After shaking hands, Garrett Sawyers escorted him to a small office down the hall from the Roosevelt room.

"So, can we count you as being on board, sir? The president is certainly impressed with your qualifications." Sawyers indicated a chair and the men sat facing each other.

"I believe so," Eastwood said. "It would be an honor to serve the president and my country."

An hour later, he was seated in his Hawker 800, heading back to New York.

ↄↄↄ

Kesler opened his eyes. It was dark but he could just make out that the small room was bare, except for the hard chair in which he sat. His hands and legs were not bound so he stood and stretched, feeling the blood return to them. There were no windows. The single door was closed, a soft beam of light glowing beneath it. Voices, talking in hushed tones, emanated from the next room. Kesler's lips were parched, his mouth felt like cotton, his bruised and battered body ached. He searched the room for clues to his location but recognized nothing. An overwhelming musty smell greeted him and caused his stomach to convulse. The drive in the Suburban had lasted about an hour so he figured he must be close to San Francisco. On the drive, he had heard jets taking off so he was either near the San Francisco airport or possibly near San Jose. Most likely San Francisco, he surmised. He had been pushed up a few steps, shoved into the chair, and commanded to remain still. Hours passed as he waited.

Kesler struggled to wrap his mind around the *why* of his predicament and came up empty. He was no physicist working on government secrets, no politician trying to save the world. He was a simple anthropologist, teaching at a small university. He was not wealthy so ransom could not be much. His thoughts drifted back to Lithuania when he was accidentally locked in the family cellar. It had been dark and creepy with large rats scampering over his feet, bumping into him. His cries for Mother stayed with him into adulthood and now, in the dark room, old terrors began to surface. His pulse raced, droplets of sweat formed on his upper lip, his breathing quickened. He fought to keep a grip on the panic that was percolating deep inside his mind.

He focused on his breathing and methodically slowed its rhythm, blowing out each deep inhalation gradually before sucking in more air. As his pulse began to slow, he looked about the room a second time, again noticing the light under the doorway. The room was not decorated—no wall hangings and no graffiti. The voices he thought he had heard earlier were now silent. He was alone.

He returned to the chair and collapsed in it.

The door opened, flooding the small room with a yellow light. A husky man dressed in black fatigues entered and grabbed him by the arm.

"This way, Doctor," the man said, his voice a deep baritone pitch. The man pulled Kesler into the brightly lit room. "Sit there," he said, pointing to a chair.

Kesler sat, squinting.

A large, bulky man, his nose and chin in the air, entered through a side door and stood over him. "Hello, Dr. Kesler, My name is Doyle. I trust you have been treated with respect."

Kesler looked about the room and noticed two other men dressed in black fatigues. They were big and burly with hairy arms. One had a nose that was bent to one side.

"In addition to kidnapping, what other crimes are you going to inflict on me?" Kesler said through a dry mouth.

"None, I assure you, Doctor. My employer believes you can be of great assistance to his enterprise. My job is to convince you of the logic in cooperation. If you answer a few simple questions you will be returned to your home unharmed. If you don't, well..." His voice trailed off without finishing the threat.

"What are you talking about? I'm just a college professor."

"It is in regard to the expedition in Mongolia. Your interview appeared in the *Times*. Remember?"

Kesler nodded. He had been so excited about the possibilities of Harry's discovery that he had called the science editor at the *New York Times*—the man was a friend of his—and explained the discovery and its implications. A bit premature, yes, but it might help in garnering more funding for the project. And he had yet to inform Harry.

"My boss is very desirous of learning the exact location of the expedition. Exactly where they are digging. Give me that information, Doctor, and you will be home in a matter of hours."

"I don't know their exact location. We have talked only a couple of times by phone."

"Come, come, Doctor. You can do better than that. Otherwise, my burly friend here will have to extract the information from you. Trust me, you will tell him everything when he's finished."

Kesler shot a glance at the big man whose smile revealed a missing front tooth.

"I told you, I don't know the exact location of the team. Only in general terms. What are you going to do? What do you want?"

"Doctor." The way the man said the word *Doctor* made Kesler's stomach churn into a knot. "Just answer my question. I'm losing patience. Where the hell are they?"

As the big, burly man moved closer, Kesler slumped in his chair and gave him the information he wanted.

☙☙☙

Harry lay on his cot, waiting for dinner to be served in the mess tent. Low clouds had formed in the dull gray sky over the Altai Basin, threatening storms. A cool wind swept down off the peaks and over the steppe, causing the grasses to undulate in an ethereal way. As the interior of his tent darkened with the fading light, his thoughts rested on his mother and he wondered if her condition had improved. Being halfway around the world made it nearly impossible to keep abreast of her situation. His brother's bad attitude did not help either. She was older and plumper now but her laugh was still infectious. During all those years of growing up in Chicago his mother was his most ardent supporter, in spite of his own personal doubts regarding his talents. She managed to give her sons equal attention, much to Max's displeasure. Harry quickly learned that his father favored Max who he took everywhere but, rarely, if ever, paid Harry any attention. His mother came to his college graduation while his father stayed at home, inebriated on the sofa. His mother read his dissertation and praised his work, although she didn't understand a single word of it. She also saw him receive his doctorate hood and bought him a fine celebration dinner.

She lived simply, not having much in the way of worldly luxuries, but he never heard her complain. He sent her what little money he could save on a lowly professor's salary. He didn't know if Max helped or not. His father could not, or would not, hold down a job for any length of time so his mother worked at a hotel as a maid in order to support the family. Whether his mother loved the bastard, Harry never knew, never inquired. He didn't want to know. She managed to make a life for Max and him, feed and clothe them, fussed over them when they became ill. His mother deserved better than she had received in life.

It was Max who Harry never understood. The source of Max's arrogance and his airs of entitlement still mystified Harry, for his brother wasn't a very happy person. Divorced twice, he had been taken to the cleaners by his second wife until she died in a fiery automobile accident. Harry always harbored a deep suspicion that Max might have had something to do with it. His large alimony payments ceased after her death when the brakes on her car failed, she crashed into a bridge abutment, and the car caught fire. Pinned behind the wheel, she didn't make it out of the resulting inferno. Max had paid for an elaborate funeral. Neither of his marriages produced any children and, as far as Harry knew, there was no current love in his brother's life. Once, when they had been drinking together after Peggy's death, Max talked of depression and an unwillingness to continue living. But through counseling, he had managed to pull himself out of the depths of despair. Five years of dedicated work had allowed Max to get back on his feet financially and now he was raking it in. Harry had to admire his brother's tenacity and his single-minded purpose, but it was all about making money. Max had no other interest that Harry was aware of. Maybe that was the source of Max's condescending personality, his unending ability to make Harry feel subordinate, as if he were a small boy again.

So now, here they were the small dysfunctional family. Harry had only his career and Mother. Once she was gone, his family would cease to exist. No, he thought, it didn't really exist now. The only relationship that mattered to him was with Mom. His true family was his research family, his colleagues. Without them, he had no life, no future, no hope. But that too, had changed after what he'd done, and now he was struggling to regain his self-respect.

# Chapter 7

Doyle sat in a high-backed leather chair across Eastwood's massive desk while his boss toyed with an unlit cigar. Brilliant sunlight shone through the large window behind BioGen's president, backlighting him with an ethereal glow. The express ride up the elevator to Eastwood's penthouse office had left Doyle somewhat lightheaded and nauseous, which continued under his boss's scrutinizing gaze. He opened a canvas messenger bag, retrieved a sheaf of papers, and handed them to Eastwood.

Eastwood thumbed through his report on the Kesler kidnapping and interrogation. Impatient, Doyle fidgeted in his chair and tugged at his tie.

He was an action-oriented individual, prone to making quick decisions without thinking through all available options. It was this personality flaw, he realized, that had gotten him into trouble with his commanding officer while with the MPs. There had been a cocaine smuggling ring on post, and Doyle was assigned to find out who was dealing the drugs and how they were getting by security and onto the post. When his investigation began to implicate the post commander's chief of staff, things got dicey. The major was the colonel's darling and the commander did not want to hear bad news. The fact that the commander was having sex with the major's wife further complicated matters. Doyle knew the woman to be one that got around and had a reputation, but when she became the commander's mistress, it sent Doyle's investigation into a tailspin.

The colonel listened to Doyle's findings then promptly threw him out of his office. When Doyle threatened to go to the Provost Marshal with his findings, he suddenly found himself facing a court martial for dereliction of duty and failure to obey a superior officer. The charges were bogus, of course, but Doyle didn't have the stomach for a protracted military trial with the attendant publicity. He resigned and received his pension.

After leaving the service, he worked for several private security firms and was a deputy sheriff, until he noticed Eastwood's ad in a law-enforcement magazine for a chief of security. At his interview, the two men hit it off and Doyle had the job before the session was over. It was difficult, complex work, requiring long hours and numerous flights in the Hawker, for BioGen had its tentacles all over the world. But he found the work challenging and stimulating, leaving little time for romance. When he needed sex, he paid for it. His boss was an odd duck but he had big ideas. And Doyle was making more money than he ever dreamed possible.

Eastwood placed the report on his desk and lit his cigar. "Well done, Ben," he said through a haze of smoke after lighting the cigar. "What's the fallout going to be? Do you think he will go to the police?"

"What if he does? He can't identify anyone or how he got to the warehouse. We left no traces, I assure you, Mr. Eastwood." Doyle toyed with an ear as he spoke.

"I'm sure of that, Ben. From what this Kesler told you, the expedition is in the Altai Mountains of Mongolia. These bones they have uncovered—they may have stumbled onto something that merits our further scrutiny."

Eastwood leaned back in his chair and gazed out over the East River. Its water was a dark black and tiny whitecaps were visible. Doyle was uncomfortable in the long silence that followed. BioGen's leader was an unpredictable man with a hyper functioning ego and, while Doyle was used to the long periods of silence—when the man appeared to be weighing options—they still, nonetheless, made him uneasy.

Finally, Eastwood leaned forward with his elbows on the

desk. "Ben, I want you to take a few of your best men and get over there. You can take the Hawker. Find the expedition but keep your distance. I want to know what they're doing, their every move, so keep me informed. But don't do anything until you get orders from me."

"Yes, sir. Want to use encrypted email using the satellite connection? We have our own encryption method so it should be private and hacker-proof."

"That's fine. Or you can call, using the scrambler software. How soon can you get underway?"

Doyle relaxed. The silence was over. And finally he had a mission. It had been a while since the Saudi deal. "Two days, sir. I'll need to decide on who is going and brief them. Weapons?"

"Of course. A full arsenal. Always be prepared, Ben. You know that."

"Most certainly. Isn't Mongolia on the other side of the world?" Doyle asked.

"Yeah, and I don't know much about the country myself. Sticks mostly to itself, I believe."

Eastwood stood. Doyle followed suit, realizing the meeting was about over.

"Touch base with me before you take off. I want to know your flight plan. Probably through Beijing, I would imagine."

Doyle shook Eastwood's outstretched hand and left the office. He was glad for a new mission. He had never been to Mongolia before.

✍✍✍

It was late night at the expedition site. The compound was quiet as the worker's had long since gone to their tents. Professor Kesler was on the satellite phone with Harry. The connection wasn't perfect and the static made the conversation erratic, but his voice sounded nervous, a little frightened to Harry. A kerosene lantern's low light cast a warm glow about the command tent.

"You won't believe what happened to me, Harry? Two

thugs grabbed me, pushed me into an SUV, drove me some-where, and asked me all kinds of questions about the expedition. You know, where you all were, what you were doing, that sort of thing."

"Christ, Professor. Did you go to the police?" Harry raised his voice, on the verge of yelling into the phone's receiver.

"No. What could they do? I didn't even know what these assholes looked like. All the police would do is take a report. Why bother? I tried to keep from telling the thugs anything but—but I was afraid they were going to hurt me bad."

"*Why?*" Harry was still screaming into the phone. His professor kidnapped? How could it have happened? Why did it happen?

Kesler's voice dropped in pitch and his tone softened. "Well, it may have had something to do with the interview I gave that *New York Times* fella."

Harry calmed his voice and swallowed the bile that had crept into his throat. "What *New York Times* fellow? Professor, what exactly did you do?"

"Oh, I called a reporter friend of mine and gave him some information on our human ancestors. I mentioned the expedition and the specimens you found and what they might mean and—"

"*What?*" Harry screamed into the phone again. "Professor, please. You know better than to do that. This field is competitive enough without you broadcasting our secrets to the world before we know anything and have them published. You know it's way too premature for something like this."

He could not believe the professor's complete lack of judgement in this matter. *He knows better than to do something like this.* Harry tried to calm himself—this was his professor, his boss, after all.

"I know, I know. And I feel bad about it, too. Maybe I'm getting too old, Harry. Maybe I'll just retire and you can have my position at the university."

"Forget that, Professor. Exactly what did you tell them?" Irritation replaced the screaming as Harry probed for answers.

"I'm afraid I told them you had found some very interesting

specimens of a hominid skeleton in the Altai Mountains. That you were continuing the search for more remains."

"Anything else?"

"That these specimens could revolutionize our thinking about hominid development. Like the ones from the Denisova cave."

"You didn't? Really? We don't know anything about this discovery as yet. This is not like you at all." Harry bit his lip hard enough to bring blood. It tasted of metal.

Dixie and Li walked into the command tent. Dixie mouthed "What's up?" to Harry as the two seated themselves on opposite sides of the table.

"Well, Professor, what's done is done," Harry continued. "We will increase our security here and keep our guard up. And, sir, please try and avoid doing something like this again, okay?"

"I promise, Harry."

Harry signed off and turned to Dixie, who had made coffee and handed him a mug of the steaming brew. It stung the small cut on his lip.

"What was that all about?" she said.

Li had a frown on his face.

"The Professor blabbed all about what we've found and our location to a reporter he knows. No telling who has read the article in the paper. Not only that, but someone kidnapped him and got him to spill the beans about our research here. Who they were or why they wanted the information, he didn't know, but we can surmise that it was for no good. After they got the information they were after, they let him go unharmed."

"Kidnapped? Do the police know about it?" Dixie asked, her voice shaking. "He wasn't hurt?"

"Roughed up some but, otherwise, he's fine. And no, he didn't call the police. He couldn't describe any of them. I've already asked him *why* but he doesn't know. Said he's getting old. Maybe he's right. He's certainly repentant."

Li stopped strumming his fingers on the table. "So," he said, "what does it mean for us? I heard you mention more security."

"We'll need to beef up nighttime security." Dixie's voice was back to its normal tone.

"I think, during the day, there are enough people up and about that we should be fine," Harry agreed. "Li, you arrange for a couple more night sentries, okay? Other than that there's not much more we can do."

"What did the Professor tell this reporter?" Dixie said.

"Basically, that we may have found a new hominid species. Or the first Neanderthal remains in Mongolia."

"But that hasn't been determined yet," she said, standing and pacing the command tent. "Why would he have said that?"

"I dunno," Harry said. "He's getting older. He's overly excited because he thinks modern humans and Neanderthals coexisted at the same time and even interbred."

"What's the evidence, Harry?" Li said. "I'm not that familiar with current thinking."

"It's complicated, Li, but I'll try to explain without being overly simplistic. Since the discovery of the first Neanderthal relics in the mid-1800s, scientists have argued the relationship between Neanderthals and humans. The Neanderthals were not as tall as humans, had shorter limbs with thicker bones, a pronounced brow with a receding chin, and a different larynx. The big question is, were the Neanderthals a human variant or a distinct species?"

"Yes," Li said. "I have heard this question discussed at the university."

"Well, at one time in the past there was a common ancestor, which, over time, genetically diverged. This happened around 250,000 years ago. We know this from mitochondrial DNA analysis. They inhabited a vast area from Europe to Asia until around 25,000 years ago. In the middle 1800s, a discovery was made in Germany that finally sparked the recognition that these were, in fact, not just strange looking modern people. This was the discovery of a skull and a number of other bones from a limestone cave deposit in the small Neander River Valley. Thinking that they were from a bear, the quarrymen gave them to a local schoolteacher and amateur naturalist. He recognized them as being somewhat different from those of modern Europeans. When several leading paleontologists and medical pathologists in Germany became aware of the fossils, a disagreement arose as to who the newly discovered man was. There were many theories—that he had been an old Roman, a Dutchman, and even an Asian soldier in the service of the Russian czar during the Napoleonic wars. A completely different species was inconceivable back then."

"But it's the mitochondrial DNA that's helping answer questions now?" Li said. He found a bottle of water and took a large gulp.

Harry smiled and continued. "In addition, now we know that Neanderthals and modern humans are genetically similar to chimpanzees, indicating a common ancestor. Neanderthals and modern humans have forty-six pairs of chromosomes, and chimps have forty-eight. Why the discrepancy? Well, chimpanzee chromosome 2 has been fused in humans, resulting in the lesser number. We know this by comparing the way the genes on the chimp's 2A and 2B chromosomes line up on Neanderthal and human chromosome 2."

"The Neanderthals were physically diverse but, in general, they were larger boned and more heavily muscled than most modern humans," Dixie added.

"Yes, this was particularly true of the European Neanderthals," Harry continued. "Some of the Southwest Asian Neanderthals were less robust in appearance and somewhat more like modern humans. They probably stood as erect as we do and were fully bipedal. They were not only strong but also apparently quite flexible. The thickness and high density of their leg bones suggest that they did a great deal of walking and running. Their lower arm and leg bones were short, compared to modern humans. These traits were likely adaptations to an aggressive hunting and gathering way of life, as well as to the cold climates in which most Neanderthals lived. The fact that adult Neanderthal skeletons frequently have multiple healed bone fractures suggests that these people lived rough lives."

"And the DNA evidence suggests what?" Dixie said.

"It gets a little complicated here." Harry took a sip of coffee, made a face, and then continued. "DNA exists either in a cell's nucleus or in its mitochondria, the small intracellular organelle responsible for energy production. Evidence from studies of nuclear and mitochondrial DNA extracted from Neanderthal fossils and humans points to the types of interbreeding that occurred between the two species. When Schwartz and his colleagues first collected, then successfully analyzed, mitochondrial DNA from a Neanderthal fossil, it was groundbreaking. Mitochondrial DNA is more abundant than nuclear DNA and is only transmitted from the mother, which means that changes from generation to generation result from mutation alone and not a recombination of the mother and father's DNA."

Harry noticed a frown on Li's face and smiled. "Like I said, it's a little complicated. The researchers at Penn State have sequenced eighty percent of the Neanderthal genome. So when the professor gets our specimens, he might be able to say if they are Neanderthal or not. The big question is to what extent did Neanderthals and modern humans, meaning *Homo sapiens*, interact? By way of trade, cultural exchange, and interbreeding. What happened to the Neanderthal? Were they pushed aside by a smarter, larger-brained human population or were they absorbed by them? Or simply killed off in a mass genocide? We just don't have the answers at present."

Dixie shrugged. "The fact that certain Europeans have a small percentage of Neanderthal DNA in their genome certainly suggests interbreeding at least on a small scale."

Harry nodded. "None of these Neanderthals are left. All we have is a small collection of bones, tools, and a few pieces of art. Ten thousand years after their meeting with *Homo sapiens* all the Neanderthal groups were extinct."

"It does make one wonder what happened to them," Dixie said. "Makes for fascinating theories."

"Billions of people carry sizable chunks of DNA from Neanderthals and other archaic human relatives. There may be other, undiscovered humanlike beings lurking in our genomes. At the Max Planck Institute for Evolutionary Anthropology, the researchers had ground up a peppercorn-size chip of bone from a Neanderthal humerus. They doused it in chemicals that drew away all the molecules except any DNA it might hold. It did hold a lot of DNA, and most of that genetic material belonged to the bacteria that had inhabited its pores. After setting aside the microbial DNA, the Max Planck researchers were left with 379 base pairs of mitochondrial Neanderthal DNA. They compared the Neanderthal DNA to the same stretch of DNA from human mitochondria, as well as to equivalent chimpanzee DNA. The Neanderthal DNA was more similar to human than to the chimps."

"The bottom line is, then," Li said, "that there are humans carrying Neanderthal genes."

Harry took a bottle of water from the small ice chest. "Correct. And maybe other more archaic genes. We just don't know. What we have stumbled on to in this plane crash, may turn out to be extremely important. The age of the bones and teeth fit into the Neanderthal timeline. If so, it helps to confirm my hypothesis of early hominids in Mongolia. If not, I don't know who or what the hell those fossils are."

# Chapter 8

From his small cubicle, office in the West Wing, Garrett Sawyers placed a call to his friend, Jacob Middleton, at the FBI. Around him, all the president's men scurried about, running errands, making phone calls, working politicians. Sawyers waited until Middleton was off another call then proceeded to ask a favor.

"Jacob, how is everything at the Bureau? How're Janet and the kids?"

"We're fine, Garrett. The kids are at summer camp and Janet is doing her internship at MSNBC. What's shaking at the White House?"

Sawyer placed the phone call on speaker and continued. "I need a favor, Jacob. And I need it fast."

"Okay, buddy. I'll see what I can do. What is it?"

"The president has appointed a guy named Rutherford Eastwood to his charitable compliance commission. I need some background on him. He runs a corporation called Bio-Gen. I have heard some things about him that aren't very flattering, that he borders on illegal trafficking of antique relics. Can you look into it for me?"

"A little late for that, isn't it, Garrett? I mean if the president has already appointed him. I did see something in the paper about it. You all didn't vet this guy first?" Middleton asked, clearly irritated.

"What the president gives, he can take away. Better we learn the mistake now than down the road. *If* the appointment was a mistake. I don't know that it was, but the few feelers I put out weren't promising."

Sawyers heard a prolonged sigh on the other end. Middleton's tone was clipped, short. "BioGen, you say? All right Garrett, but this squares us, okay? I'll call you in a day or two with whatever I come up with. Have a nice day."

Sawyers hung up the phone and gazed out his window. *Christ, these Bureau guys, what prima donnas.*

ⱷⱷⱷ

Doyle settled back into the plush seat of the Hawker 800 and dialed Eastwood's private number on his cell phone. The two pilots were buckled into the cockpit, having done their walk-around, and the hanger tractor was pulling the sleek jet onto the tarmac of Teterboro Airport. The trip promised to be long and grueling, for the Hawker's cruising range was only about three thousand miles which meant there would be numerous refueling stops along the way—San Francisco, Anchorage, Tokyo—until finally arriving in Beijing. Roughly fourteen hours flying time, plus time for refueling. Fortunately, the Hawker was a plane built for comfort and for the comfort of the wealthy. The three men he had chosen to go with him were adjusting their seats and all were experienced combat-hardened ex-military types.

Eastwood picked up the phone on the first ring.

"You about ready?" His husky voice boomed in Doyle's ear.

"They're pulling us out of the hanger as we speak, sir. Should be airborne shortly."

"The necessary luggage aboard?"

Doyle knew the question referred to the firepower his team had assembled and stowed in the luggage compartment.

"Yes, sir. Safely aboard. The men are anxious to get started, sir. They do love these adventures."

"Adventure or not, Ben, you're there to do a job. Remember that. Now keep me informed along the way. And good hunting."

With that, Eastwood hung up, and Doyle gazed out his window at the inky clear sky above. No wind. Should be a smooth flight to San Francisco. The sun had just set leaving a thin orange glow on the horizon, and only the brightest stars could be seen. He heard the aircraft's twin jet turbines begin their whine and watched the pilots go through their final checklist. Settling deeper into the soft leather seat, he buckled his seatbelt and motioned to his men to do the same. Besides each man's personal 9 millimeter automatic pistol, the team had brought Persuader twelve-gauge shotguns, M-16 rifles with silencers, and two Browning Automatic Rifles that fired 30-06 ammunition from a twenty-round magazine, at a rate of five hundred rounds per minute. More than enough firepower for whatever they should encounter. The weapons were hidden in a false bottom of a crate of computer parts and should pass uneventfully through customs once they landed in China.

It didn't take long for the Hawker to reach its cruising altitude of 35,000 feet and speed of 450 miles per hour. Doyle calculated landing in San Francisco in six hours. Taking his iPod and headphones from his flight bag, he switched on a Metallica album, retrieved his copy of the *Times,* poured three fingers of bourbon into an old-fashioned glass, and started work on the daily crossword puzzle. An hour later, and halfway through the puzzle, he set the paper aside and tried to nap. His glass was empty and it was growing dark outside the plane.

ᲔᲘᲔᲘ

Kesler stood beside the thermal cycler and waited impatiently as the machine did its work in silence. The thermal cycler, a device which held the block of tubes containing DNA material, was raising and lowering the temperature of the block in pre-programmed steps. Doing so separated the DNA into smaller strands then amplified them, creating many copies of the strand. Even small or degraded samples could be analyzed using this method. However, then the DNA still needed to be sequenced. Sequencing read the exact order of letters—A, C, T and G—corresponding to the nucleotides along a segment of DNA. Large-scale sequencing involved two stages. The first was to set up the sequencing reaction and the second was to read the results. The process used by the thermal cycler was called polymerase chain reaction, or PCR for short. The material was then placed in a DNA sequencer and the instrument determined the precise order of the four bases—adenine, guanine, cytosine, and thymine—composing pieces of the sample. In sequencing, a single-stranded DNA fragment was copied with the use of an enzyme, making the fragment double stranded. Starting at one end of the DNA fragment, the enzyme sequentially added a single nucleotide that was the match of the nucleotide on the single strand. Nucleotides were paired one-by-one as the enzyme moved down the single stranded fragment to extend the double-helix ladder structure.

Kesler's friend and colleague, Dr. Chloe Rawlings, was chief of the forensic DNA lab at California Pacific University. She was running a DNA sequence on the small piece of bone the professor brought her. Dr. Rawlings wore a crisp white lab coat and peered at the machine through wire-rimmed glasses. Kesler noticed she smelled of a perfume, that was familiar, but whose name escaped him. She was tall and her blonde hair hung loosely on her shoulders. Every now and then, she nodded, as though willing the machine to its completion.

The lab was a large affair, filled with strange machines of all kinds, most of which Kesler hadn't the slightest idea what they were used for. The whole process of DNA analysis was mysterious and foreign to him. He understood the basics but when it came to working on a sample, he let Dr. Rawlings do all the work.

"Professor, once the thermal cycler is through, we'll stick the sample in the sequencer, and go to lunch while it runs. Is that agreeable?"

"I would love to buy you lunch, Chloe. I rarely use the faculty dining room anymore."

"I have missed seeing you there of late, Julius, why is that?"

"Well, over the years the university has hired so many new

faculty, most of whom I do not know. So I would rather bring a lunch and eat in my office."

"I didn't know you were so shy, Julius. You would rather hide away and not socialize with an old friend?" Dr. Rawlings chided, smiling.

Kesler felt himself blush at the comment, *old friend*, and shook his head.

"We used to have such interesting conversation over lunch," Rawlings continued as the thermal cycler hummed behind her.

"I remember," Kesler said. "You shared the latest findings of your work and I complained about my grad students."

"You wished you could find a smart one with a good work ethic if I recall. That changed when...now let me see...what was his name? Your protege?"

"Olson. Harry Olson," Kesler said. "Got his doctorate a few years ago and stayed on here at the university."

"I remember you thought very highly of him," Rawlings said after taking the sample from the cycler and placing the plate in the sequencer. After verifying that the machine had begun its cycle, she took Kesler by an arm and the pair strolled toward the faculty dining room.

"Yes, Chloe, he's special. He's become the son I never had. I love the man."

"Well, here we are," Rawlings said. "Let's get some lunch, and I'll fill you in on your sample. It'll be like old times."

Over salad, dinner rolls, and pie, Kesler tried to assimilate Dr. Rawlings's simplified version of what was happening to his sample. Genetics was never his strong suit and he struggled to follow along.

"Years ago, a man musing about work while driving down a California highway revolutionized molecular biology when he envisioned a technique to make large numbers of copies of a piece of DNA rapidly and accurately. Known as the polymerase chain reaction, or PCR, Kary Mullis's technique involves separating the double strands of a DNA fragment into single-strand templates by heating it, attaching primers that initiate the copying process, using DNA polymerase to make a copy of each strand from free nucleotides floating around in the reaction mixture, detaching the primers, then repeating the cycle using the new and old strands as templates. Since its discovery, PCR has made possible a number of procedures we now take for granted, such as DNA fingerprinting of crime scenes, paternity testing, and DNA-based diagnosis of hereditary and infectious diseases."

"So far I'm following you," Kesler said.

"DNA is first extracted from its biological source material and then measured to evaluate the quantity of DNA recovered. After isolating the DNA from its cells, specific regions are copied with PCR. This produces millions of copies for each DNA segment of interest and thus permits very minute amounts of DNA to be examined. The resulting PCR products are then separated, detected, and sequenced. What we have then is a DNA profile called a genome for that individual or specimen."

"You will be able to compare that genome with known Neanderthal genomes and see if they are similar?"

"Yes. Computer software makes the comparison process faster and simpler."

"You seem to be married to these machines, Chloe. Do you ever leave the lab?" He patted her hand across the table. "I mean socially."

Rawlings laughed and tossed her head back, her blonde hair dancing on her shoulders, eyes sparkling. "Sure seems like marriage, sometimes, Julius. I do get out some, however."

"Any special fella?"

Rawlings shook her head and laughed again. "Not at the present. But there have been a few over the years. I'm just extremely busy right now."

"The biggest mistake of my life," Kesler said, "was that, as I got older, I was always too busy for love. Don't make the same mistake, honey." Kesler finished his coffee and dabbed his mouth with a cloth napkin. "Let's go see if the sequencer is finished running."

ℰ∽ℰ∽

Doyle stepped off the plane into a biting north wind in Anchorage, Alaska. Since leaving San Francisco, a large, bright moon had risen, bathing the tarmac in a silvery light. It was four a.m., and he needed to get some fresh air while the Hawker was being refueled for the long flight to Tokyo. He pulled the collar of his shirt around his ears to ward off the chill, while the ground maintenance crew worked in silence. The pilot had gone into the operations dispatch center for a briefing on the weather, leaving the copilot to inspect the plane's exterior. Ted Stevens International Airport was located on a shelf of land that jutted into Cook Inlet. The resulting water-cooled breeze pierced Doyle's thin shirt like tiny needles and, for a moment, he thought of retreating into the plane. There wasn't much to see, anyway. The airport was all but shut down. Only a few lights were burning in the terminal building.

The flight into Japan was expected to take eight hours and Doyle had yet to get any real sleep. He was hoping he would be able to over the Pacific. By the time they landed in Beijing, he would have spent over fourteen hours sitting in the Hawker. Eastwood had thought of everything—a fully stocked bar and enough food to feed an army.

The plush captain's chairs in the plane's cabin reclined and were comfortable to a fault. Doyle just had too much on his mind to relax and sleep.

Once in China, the plan called for taking the train into Mongolia and finding someone to guide them to the research site. Not having a contact and not speaking the language was the main thing that worried Doyle. And they had a crate of weapons to lug around, which caused an additional headache. Eastwood wasn't going to be very patient or tolerant if the search for a guide took a few days. But a couple of days in Beijing would give the men a chance to get over jet lag and rest up for what was going to prove a difficult journey.

The wind felt good on his face, like tiny icy needles massaging his skin. He sauntered over to the operations center and peered in a window. Only one sleepy-eyed employee chatting with the pilot. Ted Stevens Airport was dead at this hour.

The pilot boarded and Doyle followed, inquiring about the

weather. Clear sailing at present, only one thunderstorm down near Hawaii that shouldn't affect them.

The Hawker shot down runway 7L and, when airborne, banked left on a broad turn, out over the Pacific. At cruising altitude, Doyle resumed his crossword puzzle. His men were sound asleep.

෫ඁ෫ඁ

Harry woke with a start. Someone was shaking his arm. Struggling to come alert, he noticed Li standing over him.

"Boss, it's the professor. He's on the video conferencing network. Needs to talk right away. Come now."

Harry rubbed his eyes and pulled on his boots. "At this hour, Li? What time is it?"

"Three, boss. Professor said it could not wait. He sounded excited. I am going to wake Dixie now. You awake?"

"I'm fine, Li. I'll meet you both in the command tent."

Li disappeared out the tent door, leaving Harry to don his field jacket. He noticed Li had already lit the lantern in the command tent and its light cast eerie shadows on the canvas walls. Late summer on the steppe made for cool, if not brisk, nights. With a clear sky, the temperature had dropped farther than usual.

Harry sat at the table in front of the laptop and saw Kesler on the screen, frowning. Dixie rushed into the tent and took a seat next to Harry with the trailing Li choosing to stand behind them.

"All right, Professor. You've got us all out of our beds and interrupted our peaceful slumber, so what's the emergency?" Harry yawned and rubbed his eyes. He was still not fully awake.

"Harry, you know that bone fragment you sent me by Fed-Ex?"

"Sure do. It took three days to get it to Ulaanbaatar so we could ship it to you. What about it? Something interesting?"

"Not just interesting, guys, earth-shattering. I took the spec-imen to Dr. Chloe Rawlings. Her lab does the genetic and

DNA testing and research here at Cal Pacific. That specimen was dated at a hundred thousand years ago, but it is not Neanderthal. And here is the real shocker—it's not *Homo sapien* either. The genome of the specimen you found did not match Neanderthal or human DNA sequences. It's neither."

There was a long, silent pause while the weight of the professor's words sank in. Harry, Dixie, and Li looked at each other, as if not comprehending.

Dixie spoke next. "So what are you saying? If the bones and teeth we found don't belong to a Neanderthal or modern human, to whom do they belong? Have you figured that out?"

"Unfortunately, no. We have the genomes of most hominids and *Homo* species, including *Habilis* and *Erectus* and this specimen isn't any of them. It's definitely hominid because certain of the nucleotide base pairs are the same, but I don't know what it is at this moment."

"A lower primate, perhaps," Dixie asked.

"No," Kesler said. "We have the genomes of the major hominids that have been excavated and the DNA doesn't match any of them."

Li leaned closer to the monitor. "An entirely new species, possibly?" Li said, his voice betraying his sudden excitement.

Harry was awake now, his sleepiness jolted away by this unforeseen turn of events. His attention was focused on Kesler's every word, his stomach gripping him in a tight knot.

"Can't rightly say but anything is possible at this juncture." Kesler's demeanor betrayed his calm speech as he smiled and fidgeted during the call. "However, I think you all need to continue digging. More specimens are always better. A skull would be perfect. The more skeletal remains and genetic material you can dig up will help shed more light on this mystery. But please be careful. Because of my stupidity, someone may be on their way there right now. The men who kidnapped me didn't seem like nice folks at all."

"We've added a few more nighttime sentries for extra security, Professor," Harry said. "But it's quiet here for the present. Those bones and teeth were on a crashed Russian airplane so they could have been coming from or going to anywhere. The plane was apparently heading west when it went down so, the flight's origin could be in Mongolia. Or China, possibly."

"I've thought of that," Kesler replied. "You might search the wreckage more thoroughly and see if you can come up with more information about where it came from or where it was going. In the meantime I want you to keep digging."

"We can do that, Professor. We can."

"Harry," Kesler said, his voice had a pleading tone, "please be careful. Keep digging but watch your backs. This discovery may turn out to be extremely important, but not as important as everyone's safety."

"I promise," Harry replied.

After they had signed off with Kesler, the trio looked at each other and started laughing.

Li summed up their thoughts. "I think we may be on the trail of something big."

# Chapter 9

Sleep would not come to Harry. Returning to his cot after Kesler's bombshell, he tossed and turned, but his mind was on the expedition and its security. The professor's last words haunted him. Who would care about their research enough to kidnap and rough up an elderly university scholar? Unable to drift off, he decided to call his brother and check on his mother. He pulled himself to his feet and stumbled over to the command tent. Dixie had turned the lantern down, but its low light made it easy to dial the satellite phone.

This time Max sounded eager to talk. "Harry, I tried several times to call yesterday but could not get through. The satellite must have been malfunctioning or something."

"Yeah, Max. How's Mom?"

His brother never took responsibility for anything. When things went poorly it was always someone else's fault or due to circumstances beyond his control.

"She's back in the hospital, little brother. Went the night before last. She started having breathing difficulties again, so the doctor put her in. A cardiologist saw her and I think they are going to put in a pacemaker tomorrow."

"You *think*, Max?" Harry was getting agitated.

"Well, it's pretty much decided. The doctor wanted to look at a new heart tracing in the morning but I think it's her only hope of getting better. It's that damned heart failure."

"How's her spirit, Max? She was always a fighter, you know?"

"She thinks Dad needs her so she wants to go home as soon as possible. She seems happy every time I call and talk to her."

Harry's head began to throb at the mention of his father. "And Dad, has he been to see her at the hospital?"

"No, he says that hospitals make him nervous so he will wait for Mom to come home. He's going to fix her a special dinner."

"Won't visit. That's about right," Harry said. The throbbing was now making his eyes hurt.

"I'll try and call if there are any new developments, Harry, or when Mom makes it home. Keep yourself safe over there."

After signing off, Harry sat in the command tent, staring at the lantern. He felt horrible about being so far away when his mother was ill. Should he leave the expedition and go see her? He knew she would reciprocate if the situation was reversed. It would require a week of travel and take a big chunk out of the expense fund to do so, but the professor would agree to it. But Harry wasn't sure Dixie and Li could direct the digging in his absence. An argument against going was that Max was near and was keeping him informed as to Mom's condition. If things got worse, he could always leave. Hopefully, the pacemaker would fix her up. But Dad gave Harry ulcers. The sonofabitch hadn't changed in all the years since Harry had left home. Everything was still always about dear old Dad.

Harry turned off the lantern and headed back to his tent to grab some sleep before breakfast. Early morning twilight was starting to form, off to the East, and the stars were fading from view. In the west, the mountains looked like dark pyramids bearing down on their little compound. The steppe could be eerie this time of night with its vastness and the dark forbidding mountains. A cool gentle breeze rattled his tent flaps as he fell onto his cot, not bothering to remove his boots. Lying there, he listened to the rustling of the tent and slowly eased into a hazy fog.

&2&2

Harry was slurping his oatmeal when Li approached him

with a young woman Harry had never seen on the expedition site. They hired a few women to work in the kitchen but this woman was new to him. She was short and had dark, straight hair that flowed from underneath her woolen knit cap. She wore the traditional brown Mongolian robe, a deel, which covered western-style denim jeans. The deel was held closed by way of a bright, green sash. Her thick leather boots seemed too big for her as she followed Li to Harry's table.

"Harry," Li said in a quiet tone, "this is Jing Wu. She lives in the mountains two days ride from here. We went to school together. She was on her way to Kastum to buy her mother a birthday gift when she saw our worksite. It was pure coincidence that we met here after so many years. I explained what we are doing and what we have found. I took her to see the plane wreckage. She is very impressed. And she knows English almost as well as me."

Harry smiled and shook Jing's tiny hand. It was a firm grip, the skin tough like leather. Jing flashed green eyes when Harry dropped her hand then Li motioned for her to sit opposite Harry.

"Would you care for some coffee or water, Jing?" When Jing shook her head, Harry continued as he filled his mug with coffee from a carafe in the center of the table. "So you and Li went to school together?"

"Yes, at Kosh-Ut. Li went on to college in the United States and I attended the National University of Mongolia in Ulaanbaatar."

"What do you do now?" Harry said.

"I teach grade school in a small village way up in the mountains. I wanted to be an engineer but, back then, the university's faculty were Russian men and they frowned on women engineers. So I became a teacher instead."

"It's an admirable profession, Jing. Helping kids and all."

Li interrupted the conversation. "Jing here has some things to say to you, Harry. You should listen. They may pertain to our research."

The morning sun had warmed the kitchen tent and workers were strolling to their work assignments, chatting and laughing among themselves. Harry suggested they move to the command tent for privacy.

When they had all gathered around the table, Jing began. "Li tells me you are looking for skeletal remains of humans. That is right? Very old skeletons?"

"We are, Jing. We are researching early human or proto-human development here in Mongolia. Actual bones are greatly needed for scientific study."

"And you have found something you think is important, some bones and teeth?"

"Well, Li knows better than to speak to outsiders of what our work has uncovered. I'm afraid he spoke out of turn."

"But it's true, right? You have uncovered some bones?"

Harry was beginning to get irritated by the woman's persistent questions. "Well—" he said.

Jing smiled and interrupted. "I don't mean to intrude but I know of the existence of a skull. It is supposedly very old. And it is considered sacred among the elderly mountain people. But it is not human."

Harry stared at the young woman. His pulse rose. "Not human? Animal?"

"It is like a human skull, but it does not belong to an animal. At least no one seems to think so."

The workers' voices were now in the distance. Li spoke up. "Please, Jing. Tell Harry everything. Please."

Jing loosened her deel and Harry offered her a bottle of water, which she gratefully accepted. "Well, it is only by accident that I stumbled across your work here and I assure you it was not my intention to be so inquisitive. But if I can help an old friend, Li, here, I want to do it. Dr. Harry there are many, many things we of the younger generation have put aside here in Mongolia. One of these are the strange tales of wild men living high in the mountains. Some of the old folks call them Almas while others call them Yeti."

"Yes," Harry said. "I have heard of them and some of the stories. Interesting."

"Yeti appear in the legends of local people, who tell stories of sightings and human-Yeti interactions, dating back several hundred years. Around 1941, shortly after the German invasion of the Soviet Union, a wild man was captured somewhere in the Altai by a detachment of the Red Army. He appeared human, but was covered in fine, dark hair. When they tried to interrogate him, the creature was unable or unwilling to speak, so the unfortunate thing was said to have been shot as a German spy. It is the skull of that creature that I am aware of."

"But we know there is no such thing. In America, that creature is called Big Foot. Some places have their Sasquatch. In the Himalayas, it's the Abominable Snowman. Most people laugh at such tales. These creatures just don't exist."

Harry shot a glance at Li who nodded in agreement.

"I don't understand what any of this has to do with our research here," Harry added.

"Dr. Harry, like I said, most Mongolians my age have entered the twenty-first century and regard these tales as just that—tales perpetuated by fertile imaginations. However, I have seen this skull I mentioned and I can assure you it exists. Li says you are looking for skeletons. Exactly what it is, I cannot say. Maybe you can, Doctor. If you would like to see it I can take you there." Jing Wu finished her water in a long gulp.

"Where is it located?" Harry asked.

"High in the Altai. Three days ride from here there is a small Buddhist monastery near a village named Tenduk. It is very remote. The monks there hold the skull sacred and keep it locked in a special room. Only a few people have seen the skull and no outsiders that I know of."

Harry was interested now and he smiled at Jing. "How did you come to see it?"

"My father took me there years ago. He was a childhood friend of one of the monks. While there, the monk showed the skull to my father and me. My father said it was of an Alma, a Yeti."

"Yes, Jing, I would love to see the skull. You will take me there?'

"Wait a minute," Li exclaimed. "I'm going as well. And you know you won't be able to keep Dixie here once she hears of the skull. Wild horses couldn't keep her from going."

Harry sighed in resignation. "I suppose you are right, Li. How do we get there, Jing?"

"Like nomad travel centuries old—horses and camels.

"Three days journey you said?"

"More like two and a half days. Up an ancient yak herder's trail."

"When could we leave? Weren't you on an errand?"

"I'll be back the day after tomorrow, so we can leave then. You can spend the time packing provisions until I get back."

Harry did some quick mental calculations then nodded. "We'd be gone seven or eight days, you think, Jing?"

"Yes, a day or two at the monastery should be enough, I would think."

"Fine. Li, leave Cheng in charge when we go. Tell him we should be back in about a week and to keep the nighttime sentries posted. After that, start getting our gear and provisions packed and ready to load as soon as Jing returns." Li nodded. "And find Dixie and send her here," Harry added. "I'll bring her up to date."

Li bolted from the kitchen tent. Jing rose and tightened her deel around her tiny waist. "Don't expect too much in Tenduk, Doctor. It is a small village and monastery. For most of the inhabitants there, time has passed them by. They only got electricity ten years ago."

"How do the villagers eke out a living?"

"They are farmers, mostly, growing large gardens of vegetables. They raise goats and sheep as well. The mayor there used to have the village's only TV."

After seeing Jing on her horse and off to Kastum, Harry relayed Jing's news to Dixie and told her of their plans for the trek to the monastery. Delighted, she ran to her tent to find clothes that needed washing.

❧❧❧

Garrett Sawyers picked up the ringing phone in his Georgetown apartment.

It was Middleton at the FBI and he sounded bored. Sawyers

threw himself into an oversized chair and listened.

"You were right, Garrett. Your man, Eastwood, isn't squeaky clean. His company, BioGen, as you suspected, has been involved in some mighty shady dealings over the recent years. Mostly, Eastwood is a relic hunter, or should I say, he's a stealer. The proof is shaky at best but here is the scenario. BioGen locates or steals priceless relics, from art to fossils, then sells them to private collectors or museums for exorbitant fees. How they find these things remains unknown. There are rumors of extortion and outright theft involved in some of these transactions. But they have been extremely adept at keeping the details of their dealings shrouded in mystery. How BioGen managed to get its hands on the complete fossil skeleton it just sold the Saudis is anyone's guess. Eastwood has a security force of former military commandos, or something. One man was court-martialed for insubordination. Eastwood's board of directors must be in the dark about the company's methods, because there are a few big wheels serving on it."

Sawyers mixed himself a martini. "Anything that could be prosecuted, Jacob?"

"Nothing that would stand up in court. Lots of complaints from competitors but no one wants to go on record or file a formal complaint."

"Why is that, do you think?"

"Probably fear of exposure or recrimination would be my guess."

"Who is on BioGen's payroll?"

"That's the strange thing, Garrett. Like I said, besides Eastwood, most of the employees are ex-military or quasi-hoodlums. Pretty strange for a company with a scientific name. And no scientists, none. A company that does business in scientific specimens ought to have at least one scientist, wouldn't you think? My guess is BioGen is a well-organized, efficiently run extortion racket but I can't prove it. Anything else?"

"Well, I don't know how the president will take this news or what he will do with it. Do you mind sticking with it a while longer, ole man? Something more concrete might turn up."

"You mean the president would still keep this guy as head

of his prized commission, knowing what I just told you?"

"I dunno. He is loyal to a fault, just as with his other nominees. But I can't predict what the man will do."

"All right, Garrett, I'll stay on it a little longer. Give you a call next week."

"Damn," Sawyers said aloud after hanging up the phone.

He opened the small cabinet that served as his bar, mixed another vodka martini, sauntered back to his chair, and sipped his drink. This was news the president was not going to like, as the commission's team, along with the assistants, had already been chosen. Fortunately, news of the team's participants had not been leaked to the press yet, so the fallout might not be so bad. Sawyers hoped the fallout wouldn't find its way to his office. How this man Eastwood had made it onto the president's list, he didn't know, but whomever had floated his name might well now be in jeopardy. The commander-in-chief was not a man to be out on a limb all by himself. Sawyers knew there would be someone else out on that damned limb with him.

However, he put it out of his mind for the present as he had a date. He was taking his girl to the Kennedy Center.

# Chapter 10

Eastwood sat ensconced behind his carved mahogany desk, pondering where Doyle was. The sun sat low over the East River, bestowing a shimmering quality, like pearls, over the water, while a late afternoon haze settled over New York's skyline. The Brooklyn Navy Yard was barely visible. His security chief's last communication informed him that they had safely landed in Beijing, cleared customs without incident, boarded the Trans-Mongolian Railway, and were headed to Kastum. There they would pick up their guide and begin the trek to the expedition site. The Chinese Customs officials didn't even give the crate with the hidden weaponry a second look, just glanced at the bill of lading and stamped it before handing it back to Doyle. So they were almost in country. Traveling northeast out of Beijing, it was a eight hundred mile train ride to Kastum so the team should be on site in another two or three days.

He had a map spread out on his desk so he could keep track of the team's progress. The town of Erlian was on the Mongolia-China border and was, potentially, the next hurdle in getting the weapons into the country. Fortunately, Doyle was experienced in handling covert activities so the possibility of trouble was remote. Once in country, there were the towns of Airag and Bayat before arriving in Kastum. He would spend an anxious several days waiting for word and holding his breath until he learned they had safely crossed the border.

Eastwood's pulse quickened as he imagined Doyle and his

men nearing their destination. Whatever it was this Dr. Olson uncovered in the Altai Mountains, Eastwood would soon have his hands on it. Or maybe it would be best to let the research team go about their business until a real discovery was made, then Doyle could move in and seize whatever it was. Eastwood had a few days to decide.

The intercom buzzed and his secretary announced that Garrett Sawyers was on the phone.

"Hello, Mr. Sawyers," Eastwood said with a lighthearted tone.

"Mr. Eastwood, I'm afraid the president may have been a trifle premature in asking you to head his charitable donations commission."

"Oh?" was Eastwood's serious reply.

"Yes, and I don't know how to put this exactly, but—"

"Just spell it out, Mr. Sawyers. Be blunt."

"Well, uh, during your vetting process, and that of BioGen, a few things have turned up that are rather puzzling—er—concerning information and—"

"Exactly what information, Mr. Sawyers?" Eastwood's tone took on a more somber note. "What are you trying to say?"

"I'm not at liberty to divulge anything at present but the president feels it prudent to hold off on a formal White House announcement and photo op for another week or so. I'm sorry but it's his decision."

"I don't understand, Mr. Sawyers. Can't you be more explicit? What's really going on here?"

"I wish I could be more forthcoming, sir, but I am just relaying the president's decision. I am terribly sorry."

"You started to say something about something having turned up. What, exactly?"

"Again, sir, if you could just be patient for another week or so, I think everything will work itself out. The president is certainly hoping so."

"Well, if it can't be helped, it can't be helped."

"I'm sorry to be the bearer of bad tidings, Mr. Eastwood, but if you can be patient, like I said, maybe everything will work out. If it does, then we can make a formal announcement in the Rose Garden with you by the president's side. It would be a nice photo-op for the both of you."

"Well, Mr. Sawyers, if that is what the president wants, than that's what we'll do."

"Thank you, Mr. Eastwood. I'll keep in touch."

Eastwood poured a generous amount of bourbon into a tumbler and fought the hot bile building in his gut. While sipping the amber liquid, he hoped that Doyle would use caution and good judgement in his tactical approach to the Altai site. What was Sawyers referring to when he mentioned *puzzling information*? The latest Saudi deal had involved arm-twisting, bribery, and even outright theft, but he doubted that any of the aggrieved parties would go public with their complaints. The Saudi prince who helped them obtain the skeleton was a high-roller who jetted all over the world, partying and wooing starlets and wealthy matrons. The man, known as Fariq, was introduced to Eastwood at a party while the royal entourage was housed in the St. Regis Hotel. Eastwood had been invited to a gala affair and the two men began a casual friendship that culminated with Fariq offering his services when he learned that Eastwood was searching for a buyer for a dinosaur he had recently acquired. The prince acted as the middle-man negotiator with the Saudi museum, arranged the transfer of funds, and assisted in the clandestine movement of the skeleton to its final testing place.

Eastwood never questioned the prince's motives, actions, or the men with which he did business. They were as dirty as BioGen when it came to procuring these ancient relics and fossils. Thievery and money were part of the game. His father had taught him that.

ോ

Dixie watched as Li supervised several workers loading wicker baskets with the food and cooking utensils for their journey. Metal mugs, bowls, utensils, and a stainless blackened pot were loaded as well as their food and water. The baskets would then be lashed onto the camels for the trek into the high mountains to the monastery.

She was eager to get started and had packed her bag as soon as Harry told her of their plans. During the past year, the pair's working relationship had evolved into a close one. Dixie prided herself on knowing what her professor wanted, or needed, and she was there, lending a hand. Back at Cal Pacific, he was more formal in his demeanor toward his graduate students, even distant most of the time. But here at the research site, he had warmed considerably, as if the pressures of academic life had been left behind and he was now doing what he truly loved to do. At times, she thought they were actually becoming friends, but then he would holler for Li and the two would jaunt down to the diggings together. It wasn't that she was looking for romance—it would be hard to juggle that out here on the steppe—but if it happened...well, and here she smiled. Harry seemed like a nice guy. She had to admit that it was becoming more difficult to remain focused on work when they were together so she said a silent vow to keep her dissertation and their research upmost in her mind.

The discovery of the Russian plane and its mysterious cargo stimulated her scientific curiosity but unnerved her as well. She had a vague feeling, one she couldn't really put a finger on, that the reason for their being on the steppe was devolving into something other than the reason they came to Mongolia. Not knowing where the bones and teeth originated made their discovery meaningless, in her opinion. But, nonetheless, they made for fascinating speculation. She was eager to view the skull Jing mentioned and to see more of the mountains that loomed to the west.

Li finished with one basket and started on another. His hands worked deftly with the cords and canvas covers as the workers filled the basket. He hummed an unfamiliar tune until the work was finished then sat at the mess table, surveying the baskets.

"Li, where is the Tenduk Monastery?" she said, sitting beside him.

"Like Jing said, three days journey. Very high altitude."

"What's the monastery like? Have you been there?"

"I was there years ago when I was a teen. It is a Buddhist monastery, as are ninety percent of all monasteries in Mongolia, and it dates back to the fourteenth century."

"I know a little about Buddhism," Dixie said. "It is a beautiful religion."

"Buddhism in Mongolia is a form of Tibetan Buddhism and shares the common Buddhist goal of individual release from suffering and the cycles of rebirth. Ours holds that salvation, in the sense of release from the cycle of rebirth, can be achieved through the intercession of compassionate Buddhas, the enlightened ones, who have delayed their own entry to the state of selfless bliss to save others."

"Yes, I've read about nirvana," Dixie said. "I took a world religions course in college."

Li smiled and continued. "Buddhism was introduced into Mongolia during the periods of the pre-Mongol states and came here from Nepal. Therefore, many of the Buddhist terms are of Sanskrit origin, which are still used in Mongolia, were adopted via the Nepalese language.

"By the beginning of the twentieth century, Outer Mongolia had over five hundred monasteries and temple complexes and controlled an estimated twenty percent of the country's wealth. Almost all Mongolian cities have grown up on the sites of monasteries. Over time, the monasteries acquired riches and secular dependents, gradually increasing their wealth and power. Some nobles donated a portion of their dependent families—people, rather than land, were the foundation of wealth and power in old Mongolia—to the monasteries. Many herders dedicated themselves and their families to serve the monasteries. All of that means that, today, Buddhism is deeply rooted in Mongolian culture, and the people willingly support the monasteries. Christian outsiders usually have a negative opinion of Mongolian monks, condemning them as lazy, ignorant, corrupt, and debauched, but they simply do not know the truth." He stood and shrugged. "Well, Dixie, enough of the history lesson. I need to pack a bag if I'm going to be ready when Jing returns."

⌒⌒⌒

A blazing sun was high overhead with only a few cumulus clouds floating near the horizon. The party trekking through the steppe was made up of four Americans with a Mongolian guide. The men were on horseback, leading a line of three smaller horses. The yellow-, green-, and straw-colored grasses stretched out before the small group like an ocean with only small rolling hills interrupting the flatness of the land. The narrow path that stretched out before them led them past small glades, over gnarled roots, and sometimes beside a small river.

It was quiet on the steppe. Nothing stirred, not even a small animal. Not a pheasant or marmot had they seen, or the gray wolf.

They stopped for a short rest at a green glade alongside a shallow river and drank the cold, clear water before continuing on their journey. The sun warmed their backs and they cheered the little gusts of wind that sprang up, bringing refreshing relief to the heat.

Doyle adjusted himself in the Mongolian saddle, attempting in vain to ease the aching in his legs and back. The saddle was a strange affair, wooden in construction, with the pommel and cantle raised high, which was supposed to stabilize the rider and protect him from forward and backward falls. Anyway, that was according to their guide, Gang Shun. Doyle's assistant, Riley Gillum, had never been on a horse in his life, so mounting the animal had been a comedy of errors. Gillum had been unable to swing his leg over the tall cantle, forcing Gang to have to push the man's leg over it. The smallness of the saddle and the short stirrups made riding awkward and unpleasant.

The five men wormed their way over the grassy plain, taking a short break now and then to dismount and stretch their legs. As the sunlight began to fade and the cool evening breeze picked up, they made camp for the night next to the small, fast-moving stream. Doyle and Gillum lay their saddles next to each other while the other men of the team, Kurt and Marley did likewise near where Gang was building a small fire in an antique metallic stove with a chimney. While Gang boiled water in a copper pot, in preparation for dinner, the team gathered near the stove and warmed themselves.

"Can you believe this place?" Gillum said. "It's like being on another planet."

"Like Mars," Marley said, standing close to the small stove.

"This region of Mongolia has its own beauty," Doyle said. "These nomads, however, are a bit backward." He shot a glance toward Gang, hoping he was out of earshot.

Kurt laughed and pulled a jacket over his shoulders. "Gang said the nomads have been living like this for centuries. But they have yurts to sleep in. Going to get downright cold under the stars tonight."

"Hope he packed warm sleeping bags," Marley added, who lit a cigarette and watched the smoke drift skyward.

"Another night and we should be nearing the expedition site," Doyle said, turning to Gang. "Hey, Gang, when will we see the mountains?"

Gang brought each of the men a large mug of steaming, thick, salted tea with milk and sat beside them on the heavy blanket spread over the ground.

"Tomorrow. You will see the Altai tomorrow afternoon."

Kurt frowned at his mug. "What is this stuff?"

"Traditional Mongolian salty tea. We call it *suutei tsai*, which means milk tea. It is one of the most common drinks in Mongolia. Do you like it, Mr. Kurt?"

"Make mine without salt next time, Gang," Kurt said, casting an angry look at their guide.

Gang returned to his stove and stirred the copper pot.

"What's for supper?" Kurt asked. "At least that's starting to smell good."

"A nomad specialty, Mr. Kurt. Boiled dried mutton with vegetables and noodles. You will like." Gang went back to stirring his pot.

Marley, the quiet team member, stood and walked over to where Gang was working. He watched silently while Gang added some spices to the bubbling concoction.

"Once we are at the research site, boss, what then?" Kurt asked.

"Eastwood wants us to surveil them from a distance. See if we can determine if they have found anything of significance. Once we have determined that, I'll give him a call and learn what our next moves are. Ultimately, we are going to find this Dr. Olson and grab whatever it is he has discovered. Eastwood tells me it is momentous."

"Kill him?" Kurt said. "The doctor, I mean."

"Kill everyone. Leave no witnesses, Kurt."

Marley had returned to the group and had been listening. "Including Gang?" he asked, pointing a thumb at their guide.

"We won't need him to get back," Doyle said, smiling. "So yes, him too."

"Listen, Ben, I came on this little excursion for one reason, fun and excitement. If we don't blast these bastards to kingdom come, I'm going to be really pissed." Kurt's tone had turned sour.

"All in due time, my friend, all in due time," Doyle said, patting his eager team member on the shoulder.

Gang handed each man a wooden bowl filled with a thick, pungent broth in which chunks of meat were immersed. As the men ate, the conversation turned to the nomadic way of life in Mongolia. Doyle listened half-heartedly, his mind on their mission, as Gang talked.

"I have heard," Gillum said, "that Mongolian pastoral herders make up one of the world's last remaining nomadic cultures."

Gang smiled. "Yes, for many, many years they have lived on the steppes, grazing their livestock on the lush grasslands. But, today, their traditional way of life is at risk."

Doyle spooned chunks of meat into his mouth and swallowed. "How so?"

"Everything is changing in Mongolia," Gang said. "Our economy, our climate, even our deserts are disappearing. And they threaten our nomadic way of life. The herds and grazing lands die. The harsh winters and poor pastures have caused herders to seek employment in mining towns and urban areas."

"Sounds dire."

"Most herders, who stay on the steppe, want their children to have an education and get jobs in the cities, believing that our way of life is no longer an option."

"I can't believe anyone would choose to live out here," Kurt said, slurping his noodles.

"The Mongolian pastoral nomads rely on their animals for survival and move their habitat several times a year in search of water and grass for their herds. Their lifestyle is precarious, as their constant migrations prevent them from transporting reserves of food or other necessities. Rarely having the luxury of surpluses to tide them through difficult times, they are extremely vulnerable to the elements. Heavy snows, ice, and droughts jeopardize their flocks and herds and heighten their sense of fragility."

Overhead the Milky Way extended from horizon to horizon. There was no moon so the millions of stars formed a broad ribbon in the sky.

"So why do they continue in this outmoded way of life?" Kurt asked, shaking his head at Gang's description.

"It is all they know, Mr. Kurt," Gang said through mouthfuls of the stew. "It has been a way of life for their families for many generations. But these days, many children of nomadic families attend school in the cities and live with their parents during the summer months. The nomad numbers here in the Altai Basin are dwindling."

"I can see why," said Kurt. "There's nothing to do way out here."

"Ah, but Mr. Kurt, that is the beauty of it."

Gang finished his stew, stood, and patted Kurt's shoulder on the way to his stove.

"Kurt, my friend," Doyle said as he gave a hearty laugh. "I guess you will never make a nomad. No matter how hard Gang tries."

# Chapter 11

Li had the camels loaded, and Harry, Dixie, and Jing were ready to climb aboard the horses for the trek to the Tenduk monastery. Harry gave last-minute instructions concerning security to Cheng, who was being left in charge of the site. Dixie and Jing chatted idly until Harry was finished, then the group mounted and headed west with the snow-peaked Altai shimmering in the distance.

Sure-footed horses were a necessity in the mountains and Harry hoped that his horse, named Mouse, would deliver him safely, as he had originally delivered him to the research site. Growing up in a large city never afforded Harry the opportunity to become comfortable with animals of any kind, especially horses. He always viewed them as unpredictable creatures, not one of the smarter barnyard animals, one that could inflict injury at any moment. After climbing aboard Mouse, the first hour had been spent worrying when the animal was going to take off across the barren steppe with him holding on for dear life. But as the day progressed and Mouse plodded along without incident, Harry settled into the saddle, relaxed, and marveled at the vistas surrounding them.

Jing led them along a narrow path, first through the level grassy lowlands, then gradually climbing the narrow ridges that formed the Altai foothills. In this arid region, drought-resistant feather grasses and sheep fescue dominated the landscape and provided much-needed fodder for the yaks and other animals raised by the nomadic families that moved throughout the steppe. The Altai represented the northern most region affected by the tectonic collision of India into Asia. Massive fault systems ran through the area, including the Kurai fault zone and the recently identified Tashanta fault zone. Although seismic activity was generally a rare occurrence, a massive earthquake had occurred in the Chuya Basin area to the south of the Altai region in 2003. This earthquake and its aftershocks had devastated much of the region and wiped out an entire village.

Leaving the banks of the river behind as they continued upward, Harry realized the Altai were some of the highest and remotest mountains in the world. The mountain valleys were forested with spruce, fir, and pine, interspersed with grassy meadows. As they ascended, the pine and fir trees gave way to aspen, birch, and finally larch and dwarf conifers. Stands of those trees were part of a mosaic landscape that also included meadows with an alpine component. Jing had told them that many varieties of deer populated the valleys and mountain goats, sheep, and yaks grazed the open areas.

The mountains, divided by several river valleys, formed a great variety of landscapes. There were hollows with semi-desert landscapes, alpine peaks, narrow river canyons, broad valleys, highland tundra, deep limestone gorges, open steppes, permanent snow and glaciers, and tracts of forest, as well as lakes, wild rivers, and waterfalls. Nearing the break for lunch, the group passed through a burned forest and traversed a transparent turquoise river that flowed from a towering waterfall. As they followed its snaking shoreline, the roar of the falls grew dimmer until, when they arrived at a small grassy meadow surrounded by high rock walls, its sound was only a soft murmur. Here, Jing called a halt for a quick rest and food.

"Up there," she said, pointing at a rock knoll to the northwest, "we will cross the first pass. The going gets more difficult after that."

Harry, glad to be off his horse and on firm soil, walked about, easing the ache in his knees. The camels immediately folded their legs and plopped to the ground, groaning.

"How many passes to the monastery, Jing?" he said.

"Three. And each one gets narrower as we ascend. There may still be a little snow on the ground at Tenduk. You'll be glad you have the deels I provided."

After a quick meal of beef jerky and bottled water, the small band continued on their journey. The trail became a serpentine line ahead of them, winding along a precipitous ridge overlooking a deep green gorge. Massive granite boulders with jagged outcroppings glistened with quartz and jasper. The Mongolian steppe was a treeless land, harboring, at most, squat bushes and low-growing junipers. But in the higher elevations, Harry noticed, sparse vegetation had given way to tundra grasses sprouting in sporadic locations among the rocks. Dominant tundra groundcover in the Altai were mosses and fungi, as well as small numbers of vascular plants well-adapted to this extreme environment. How the fragile ecosystem flourished up here was a mystery to him. Now and then, he shot a furtive glance down the deep gorge and prayed Mouse would keep steady footing.

Later that evening, the group gathered around the portable stove and sipped the tea Jing had brewed. The sky had turned overcast with low dark storm clouds swirling overhead. A cold wind surged down from the icy peaks, dull gray in the distance. Harry pulled his deel tighter around his neck.

"So what about these mountain wild men, Jing. Any hopes of catching a glimpse of one?"

Jing laughed. "I doubt it, Dr. Olson." She shot a glance at Li and shook her head.

"What about them?" Dixie asked, as if cued by Jing. "I have heard a few stories by the camp workers."

"Wild men, Almas, Yetis—they are all the same creature. Different people call them by different names. My uncle claims to have seen one and he retold the story many times. One evening at dusk, he was walking in the mountains when he heard a strange noise. The source of the commotion ahead of him was a humanoid figure, wandering about in an upright fashion, pausing to tug on dwarf rhododendron bushes as it passed. The creature's dark figure was in stark contrast to the white snow and it was easily distinguishable. It wore no clothes. The beast moved into some thick shrub and disappeared before my uncle could get a closer look at it. He followed its tracks for a while, until they became illegible in the snow, then he returned home. We children heard this story so many times, we could repeat it from memory.

"But across the Altai, the Yeti has been seen as real, known for generations in a half-dozen countries from Tibet to Mongolia. It is a region flush with wildlife, where tigers, bears and wild dogs roam thick mountain forests and remote river valleys. Here, if nowhere else, the Yeti was always simply one more creature."

"You have never seen one?" Dixie asked.

"No. I have never seen the tracks of one, either."

"What do they supposedly look like?" Dixie said, obviously intrigued by Jing's tale.

"The Almas are reputed to be six-foot tall, upright creatures, covered in reddish brown fur, with human-like facial features, including pronounced brow ridges, flat noses, no chin. And, unlike the Himalayan Yeti, their behavior is considered far more human than ape-like. They reportedly inhabit the mountains of central Asia and the Altai Mountains of southern Mongolia. Modern accounts documenting footprints, as well as native traditions dating back hundreds of years, attest to the existence of the Almas, including the exchange of trade goods between remote Mongolian villages and Almas."

"It's hard to believe that people actually traded with the creatures," Harry said, a smirk now appearing on his face.

Jing continued without addressing Harry's comment. "In 1953, Sir Edmund Hillary and his Sherpa reported seeing large footprints while scaling Mount Everest. Hillary would later discount Yeti reports as unreliable. In his first autobiography, the Sherpa said that he believed the Yeti was a large ape and, although he had never seen it himself, his father had seen one twice. But in his second autobiography he said he had become much more skeptical about its existence.

"At one time, your American government thought the existence of the Yeti likely. One theory is that the Alma is a remnant human species such as the Neanderthal. To date no conclusive evidence for the existence of the creature has been found."

"But you have never seen one?" asked Harry.

"Again, no. I don't believe they exist. But when we get to Tenduk, you will meet people who have seen the Yeti and know they exist. Maybe you can speak with some of them."

ℰℐℰℐ

The next morning, the group continued onward and upward. As they climbed higher, Harry began to feel the effects of the thin air. Riding side-by-side, Jing and Li appeared not to be suffering in the slightest, as they laughed and chatted with each other. All during the morning, the sky remained overcast and the wind that stung their faces blew sleet a few times. Harry worried that the clouds threatened frank snow but, by afternoon, the sky cleared and a warm sun greeted them.

Dixie's cry pierced the mountain quiet. "Help!"

Harry jerked in his saddle, his eyes searching in the direction of Dixie's plea. She was nowhere to be seen and her horse galloped, saddle empty, ahead of the group. He yanked hard on the reins and spurred Mouse to where he had last seen Dixie. Jing and Li followed at a gallop.

Harry reined to a stop at the edge of a sheer precipice and gazed over the drop-off. There, clinging to a rock outcropping, hung Dixie, her eyes wide. He jumped to the ground.

"Help, Harry. My horse spooked and threw me. Hurry! I only have one foot on a small ledge."

"Hold on, Dixie," Harry said. Far below her, he could see a river pounding along. "Stay calm!"

Jing and Li vaulted from their saddles and rushed to the edge of the cliff. Then Li ran to a nearby camel. "I've got a rope," he cried. "We'll get her up."

He returned with a coil of rope. Harry took one end and fashioned a bowline around his waist. "Tie the other end to a saddle," he said to Li in a voice that betrayed fear. "I'll go down and get her. You can have the horse pull us up. Understand?"

Li nodded and did as Harry commanded. As soon as the rope was attached to the saddle, Harry took a deep breath and started over the edge.

"Be careful," Jing said. "These rocks are jagged and sharp."

Harry's heart pounded as he began the descent to Dixie. He noticed her hair was a tussled mess, there were scrapes on her face and neck, and the leg that was perched on a small ledge was trembling. Her eyes darted between him and Li who was peering at them from above. Harry could hear her whimpering as he picked his way slowly down over the rocks.

"Hold on, Dixie. I'm coming," he said, trying to calm the fear in his voice.

If Dixie fell before he could reach her, it would mean her certain death. His temples pounded and sweat burned his eyes but he fought to keep himself under control and continued to maneuver his way to where she clung to the cliff. The rocks were jagged and sharp and several times an edge nicked his hands as he wormed his way down the gorge. His boots were a bit large for the cracks he used for support, causing the muscles in his calves to start burning. He searched for handholds and inched downward, all the while praying Dixie could hold out until he reached her.

Midway the rope got caught in a crack that was in a rock twenty feet above him. His descent stopped. He tried flipping the rope out of the crack but it was stuck. He looked up and yelled at Li. "Li, the rope is caught in a crack! See if you can flip it out!"

Li struggled to free the rope but it was in vain. "No dice, Harry!" he called down.

Dixie screamed again. "Harry, I can't hold on much longer! Do something, please!"

Harry looked for a handhold, and finding one, pulled himself up enough to release tension on the rope so Li could flip it out of the crack. His mouth tasted of metal, his head pounded, but he continued picking his way toward Dixie.

When he reached her, she was shaking and tears stained her cheeks. Harry found a narrow rock outcropping where he could stand and held out an arm. "Grab hold of me, Dixie.

Grab hold and don't let go until we're back up." He noticed she wasn't looking at him.

"Did you hear me, Dixie? Grab hold of my waist and the horse will pull us up."

"I ca—can't," she said, still not looking at Harry.

"Dixie, look at me. No, look here at me now. Dammit, Dixie, you're going to die here if you don't look at me and do as I say." Harry was screaming at her. His legs were beginning to tire.

Dixie turned her head and stared vacantly at Harry. She did not utter a word.

"Focus, honey. Focus on me. Good. Now put your arm out and grab my waist. I won't let you fall, I promise. You've got to do it, honey."

Slowly, Dixie extended her right arm and placed it around Harry's waist. She grabbed tight and let go of the boulder with her left hand.

Harry folded his arm around her and looked up at Li. "Okay, Li. We're ready. Start pulling us up."

The rope tightened then the two began moving upward over the rocky mountain face. Harry kept a tight grip on Dixie with one hand and kept them on course with the other. Dixie was breathing hard and continued to sob softly as they ascended, her face buried in Harry's shoulder.

Twenty feet from the top, they hit another snag and quit moving upward.

Li hollered. "Harry, the rope is caught again somewhere. Just a minute, I'll look."

Harry watched Li survey the problem from the edge of the cliff above them. He had no place to prop his legs so he was just hanging with Dixie at the end of the rope. She still had not uttered a word.

"I see the problem," Li called down. "But the rope is too taut to free it. Can you step up a foot or so to relax the rope like you did earlier? I can scramble down and free it."

"I'll try," Harry said.

As he tried to gain a foothold on the nearest outcropping, he felt Dixie's grasp on him tighten more. He used his free hand to push himself over the rock but try as he might he could not find even one small bulge to stand on. His legs were starting to feel like rubber and Dixie's clinging was making it difficult to breath. A vision of his mother flashed through his brain while the sweat continued to sting his eyes.

His hand felt along a crack and his body swung sideways on the rope. He felt the rock with his feet and there it was—a small ledge, just wide enough for the tips of his boots. He found solid footing then looked up at Li. "This is it, Li. There's nothing else down here. Can you free the rope now?"

Li scampered over the edge and picked his way to where the rope was tangled. It was wedged tight in a crack but, after several attempts, he pulled it free. Harry watched him climb back to the horses and they resumed their ascent to the top.

Lying on the soft grass, Dixie and Harry took a moment to regain their wits. At last, as Harry stood, Dixie looked at him and smiled.

"Thanks," she said. "You called me *honey.*"

"What?" Harry said.

"Down there. A few moments ago. You called me *honey.*"

℘↻℘↻

Dr. Julius Kesler was in his office at California Pacific University. With him was Brinley Foreman whom Kesler had called and asked for a meeting. The two men watched the boats in San Francisco Bay for several minutes then Kesler spoke.

"It is a beautiful view. I am extremely fortunate. Please, Mr. Foreman, take this seat here." Kesler ushered the man to a chair beside his cluttered desk. "I appreciate you being able to meet with me here. I know you have a busy schedule."

"Dr. Kesler, the privilege is mine. After all, cryptozoologists usually aren't consulted by academics. You mentioned some strange bones on the phone?"

"If I speak candidly, Mr. Foreman, can I rely on your utmost discretion in this matter?"

"Of course, Doctor. Our conversation will be held in the strictest of confidence."

"Fine, fine, and thank you. Now let me begin and get right to the point. I have never had the need to ask for help from someone of your...how should I say?...unusual qualifications. You come highly recommended."

"I understand. Cryptozoology is the study of hidden or unknown animals. It is not a traditional mode of scientific investigation. In fact, the scientific community does not recognize it as a valid science. There are no degrees in it, and therefore, there is no such thing as a cryptozoologist. Nonetheless, we search for animals whose existence has not been proven. This includes looking for living examples of animals that are considered extinct, such as dinosaurs—animals whose existence lacks physical evidence but which appear in myths or legends. Cryptozoologists contend that because species once considered superstition, hoaxes, delusions, or misidentifications were later accepted as legitimate by the scientific community, the descriptions and reports of folkloric creatures should be taken seriously."

"And so to continue," Kesler said, "let me describe what my associate, Dr. Olson has unearthed in Mongolia."

⌘⌘⌘

The next mountain passes were more difficult as the trail became nonexistent and the path was rocky. Mouse plodded slowly, wheezing in the rarefied air. A thin crust of snow blanketed the rocks and trail while the wind blew in swirling gusts. Up ahead, Harry could see Dixie's head bowed on her chest, her face out of the biting wind.

Dixie had weathered her fall without serious injury. Bruised and slightly battered, she never complained during their night camp but listened to the group's idle chatter without entering much into the conversation. Jing had made her a brew of tea with some added herbs and she slept soundly through the cold night.

The ambiguous trail they were on rose sharply after breakfast, forcing a slowdown in their progress. Harry had not felt like eating much, a fact that he attributed to the altitude but Jing forced him to drink the hot tea she had made. Dehydration was a killer, she said. He knew many people succumbed to the altitude and weather, so he gulped down the liquid and felt somewhat better. He watched her with fascination, as the altitude did not seem to adversely affect her at all. She scampered around, making camp, fixing their dinner and breakfast like she was on a holiday. She smiled and hummed. He, on the other hand, was dragging.

At the summit of the final pass, Jing stopped and slid off her horse. Harry followed suit, as did Dixie and Li. A milky soup of clouds and mist hung low over the mountains, threatening rain or snow. Visibility was reduced and the mountaintops were obscured from view, while the thick air made breathing difficult.

"Look down there," Jing said, pointing off in the distance. "You can make out the monastery from here."

"I see a pagoda on a hill," Harry said, trying to catch his breath.

"That's it," Jing said.

"Doesn't look like much from here," Dixie said.

"I told you it wasn't much of a village, but there's more to it once we get there."

"How long, Jing, till we're there?" Li said.

"Three or four hours more. Not long. The worst is over." Jong turned her attention to Harry who was still breathing hard. "You okay, Dr. Olson?"

"Yeah, Jing. I'll be fine once we descend a little. I'm not used to this altitude."

They mounted their horses and began the descent to the monastery of Tenduk.

# Chapter 12

Nestled high in the Altai Mountains, between the peaks of Mount Belukha and Mount Kuitan, the small monastery of Tenduk overlooked a vast plain. Situated on a large knoll at the base of rugged cliffs, the ancient monastery and its affiliated buildings stood sentinel over the rocky steppe below. The village of Tenduk, sprawled out around the base of the promontory, consisted of several dirt roads, along which stood rows of low-standing stucco houses, all constructed of the same ubiquitous brown mud so common in the steppe. As the small group made their approach into the village, a few people stared but most of the residents ignored them. Bicycles lined the roads and herds of sheep and cattle grazed together nearby. Originally built in the 1300s, Tenduk monastery was a large multi-storied affair with many smaller living quarters terraced around the main temple building. The buildings were interconnected through steps and stairways made of rocks and a few rickety wooden bridges, which enabled the monks to pass easily over gaps between the various levels. The main stone-and-mortar structure was in the form of a stepped-pyramid of three rectangular stories, three circular terraces, and a central pagoda forming the summit. The whole structure was in the form of a lotus, the sacred flower of Buddha. There were ponds surrounded by bright multi-colored columbines, poppies, and anemones.

Buddhism came to Mongolia with the Khan Dynasty. The Mongolian Khan's choice of this religion seems to have been based on cultural similarities between the Mongols and the Tibetans. Both Mongolia and Tibet formed the high plateaus of Inner Asia, and their open steppes along with a cold, arid climate made them well-suited to nomadism. It was, thus, easier for the Mongols to mingle with semi-nomadic Tibetans than with purely agricultural Chinese, who were far different in their social and cultural institutions. The dedication of Genghis and Kublai Khan to Tibetan Buddhism insured the religion's foothold in Mongolia.

During the repression of the 1930s, which was an off-shoot of the Stalinist purges in the Soviet Union, more than 20,000 monks were killed and over 800 temples and monasteries destroyed in Mongolia. In 1990, all barriers to religion were removed. Since then 160 monasteries and nunneries had been reopened.

Abbot Bo Zhing stepped out of his quarters into a brisk dawn morning, relishing the gray mist that covered the valley beyond the monastery. The morning's dullness matched his mood. The electrical power to the kitchen was out and there was the ordination of a novice to consider later in the day. He had already organized the other monks in redistributing the food stores and was now on his way to the temple for early morning chants and prayers. The twenty other monks gathered again at nine a.m. for additional chanting before beginning their daily chores.

Zhing crossed a wooden bridge over a small clear creek and sauntered up the stone steps leading to the temple. He wore a brown robe of Tibetan origin, called the Kashaya—a large rectangle, about six by nine feet, wrapped to cover his left shoulder, leaving his right shoulder and arm bare. He breathed deep lungfuls of the crisp air and realized the altitude taxed his sixty-year-old body. As he reached the massive wooden doors to the temple he was approached by Pu Yang, the monastery's senior monk. Each man pressed his hand together over his heart and bowed slightly.

"Namasta, Lama Yang," Zhing said, smiling.

The elderly monk smiled in return. "Namasta," he said.

"We lost power to the kitchen during the night," Zhing

said. "Several of our brothers will miss early chant. They are busy trying to save the food."

"It is understandable," the older monk said as he entered the temple.

Zhing followed him inside.

Buddhist temples were designed to represent the five major elements of Buddhism. The pinnacle at the top represented wisdom of the Buddha and the Buddha's teachings. The base of the temple, or the plinth, represented earth. Earth was important to the Buddhist religion because earth signified solidity and durability. Water, which in a Buddhist temple was represented by the dome, signified liquid, fluid, and moisture. The crescent of a Buddhist temple represented air, which in Buddhism symbolized movement and openness. Last of the elements, fire, was represented by the spire representing energy and warmth.

The temple's large room had a floor of tile with alternating green and tan squares, contrasting with the small alter at one end, which was draped with red tapestries. It was otherwise bare, except for an enormous statue of Buddha perched against the far wall. The other walls were adorned with frescoes depicting scenes from Buddhist legends. Monks filed into the temple in silence and formed two groups on each side of the statue of Buddha, each man standing next to a thin mat that lay on the floor. When everyone was in their place, Pu Yang stepped in front of Buddha and faced the monks.

"Let us begin," he said.

᠎᠎᠎᠎᠎᠎᠎᠎᠎᠎᠎᠎᠎᠎᠎᠎᠎᠎᠎᠎᠎᠎᠎᠎᠎᠎᠎᠎᠎᠎᠎᠎᠎᠎᠎᠎᠎᠎᠎᠎᠎᠎᠎᠎᠎᠎᠎᠎᠎᠎᠎᠎᠎᠎᠎᠎᠎᠎᠎᠎᠎᠎᠎᠎᠎᠎᠎᠎᠎᠎᠎᠎᠎᠎᠎᠎᠎᠎᠎᠎᠎᠎᠎᠎᠎᠎᠎᠎᠎

Brinley Foreman took the cup of coffee offered him by Dr. Kesler. He had listened with much interest to the professor's description of Harry's Mongolian discovery and of his analysis of the specimens. After sipping the dark liquid, he sat back in his chair and shook his head. "Quite a story, Professor Kesler," he said, returning his cup to Kesler's desktop. "And very interesting."

"What do you make of it?" Kesler said. "I would be interested in your thoughts."

"Well, remember the old saying, 'you get what you pay for.' I'm not sure my thoughts are worth much." Foreman laughed and continued. "What I hear you suggesting is that there is a Neanderthal-like hominid in the Altai region of Mongolia. One that is different from the Neanderthals we know. What it could be is uncertain at present. However, I am at a loss as to why you would call me at this early juncture in your investigation. As a scientist, I would think you would be overjoyed at the possibility of discovering a new species in the evolution of the human race. But you don't seem all that excited. Why?"

Kesler rose from his desk, adjusted his spectacles, and paced his office. "The problem is, Mr. Foreman, that I have an uneasy feeling that there is more to this than the obvious. Scientifically, the most logical explanation is a new species of some sort. But what? That's the rub. It doesn't fit with what we currently know. To date, there are no known human cousins to *Homo Sapien* other than *Homo Neanderthalensis*. These specimens recently uncovered in Mongolia do not fit a pattern that would allow them to belong with the *Homo* genus nor any known hominoid pattern. So, what primate these specimens belong to remains a puzzle beyond any reasonable speculation. Unfortunately, we have only a few specimens with which to work and form a hypothesis."

"I see," Foreman said. "That's where I come in, right? Sort of think outside the box. Well, let me suggest this. What if what you currently know isn't all there is to know? What if there's more to the puzzle of human origins than scientists can possibly imagine? In addition, another big part of your problem seems to be that you don't actually know where these specimens were originally located."

"That's right. We don't."

"But isn't that what makes your field so interesting, Doctor Kesler? The discovery of something heretofore unknown?"

Kesler returned to his chair and folded his arms across his chest. "Another possibility are the Denisovans."

"The what?" Foreman said. "Never heard of them."

"A relatively new addition to the hominid tree," replied Kesler, who had picked up a pencil and was toying with it. "Harry—er—Doctor Olson believes they may be a subspecies of humans. A couple of years ago, a finger bone fragment was discovered not far from his research site. It was of a juvenile female who lived around 41,000 years ago. Analysis of its mitochondrial DNA showed it to be distinct from Neanderthals as well as modern humans. However, study of its nuclear genome suggests that it shares a common ancestor with Neanderthals, and that they ranged from Siberia to Southeast Asia."

"Interesting," Foreman said. He was taking notes on a small pad.

"In another bone the scientists were able to achieve near-complete genomic sequencing, dating it around 400,000 years ago. It is the oldest hominid DNA sequenced. They were able to demonstrate that some living humans can trace a portion of their ancestry to the Denisovan genome. It is all very interesting, of course. It goes to your point, Brinley, that new discoveries cause us to revamp our theories constantly. But I am interested as to what thoughts you might come up with. There might be more here than I can envision. I was hoping you could expand the possibilities."

"This part of the world is notorious for its legends of wild men."

Kesler leaned forward on his elbows. "Wild men?"

"Beasts of the Himalayan and Mongolian regions. The Abominable Snowman. The Yeti."

"I have heard of them, of course," Kesler said, "but I never thought anyone actually believed they existed."

"In the Tibetan language, Yeti means *man-bear*. The term Abominable Snowman was coined in 1921, by Lieutenant-Colonel Charles Howard-Bury of an Everest climbing expedition. In his book Howard-Bury included an account of finding footprints that he believed were probably caused by a large gray wolf, which in the soft snow formed double tracks rather like a those of a bare-footed man. He added that his Sherpa guides at once volunteered that the tracks must be that of The

Wild Man of the Snows, to which they gave the name *metoh-kangmi*. *Metoh* translates as man-bear and *Kang-mi* translates as snowman.

"In 1925, a photographer and member of the Royal Geographical Society wrote that he saw a creature at an altitude of about 15,000 feet, near a Tibetan glacier. He later wrote that he observed the creature from about 200 to 300 yards, for about a minute. Its outline was exactly like a human being's, walking upright and stopping occasionally to pull at some bushes. It was easily distinguishable against the snow and wore no clothes. About two hours later, the photographer and his companions descended the mountain and saw the creature's prints, described as human, but only six to seven inches long by four inches wide. The prints were undoubtedly those of a biped.

"To catalog all the reported cases of this mystifying beast would be next to impossible, due to numerous sightings and encounters that attribute to this beast's existence. One cannot hope to compile all this data, but one can come close, and shorten it down in the process. In the final analysis, all these sightings start bearing a striking resemblance to one another. This adds to the credibility factor, but also makes for less interest. No one enjoys reading the same story repetitively. But as one reads on, it becomes impossible not to observe this data in one way or another and not to notice the sheer amount of it, physical and not."

Foreman drained what was left of his coffee. He had loosened his tie during his discourse and, finishing his coffee, retrieved a file folder from his briefcase. He pushed the folder across the desk toward Kesler. "Here is something interesting," he continued. He waited for Kesler to open the folder and examine its contents. "It's a recent report from Dr. William Smythe, a professor of Human Genetics at the Oxford Institute of Molecular Medicine. It just so happens that I have recently read this article and have been carrying it around with me. A British expedition set out in search of this elusive creature when mysterious hairs were found in the hollow of a cedar tree in the eastern Tibet area. Naturally, the hairs were carefully removed in a forensic manner and flown back to Britain. The report speaks for itself. DNA found in the hairs were not human or animal. In fact, Dr. Smythe could not identify the source of the DNA. It did not match anything known. What these hairs are and to whom they belonged, are unknown at present. The cryptozoologist in me wants to think they belong to the Yeti, but until there is more evidence I am putting those thoughts aside."

Kesler closed the file folder, set it aside, then removed his glasses. With a handkerchief, he methodically and quietly wiped the lenses. "I was unaware of any of this," he said as he replaced the glasses on his ruddy face.

"And so it remains to this day," Foreman said. "Shrouded in a riddle and surrounded by a mystery, as we like to say. And with insufficient material. Putting the issue of the hairs aside and, in spite of all this supporting evidence and mounting physical evidence, it seems that we have not progressed much farther from the time that the Western world first heard of this enchanting tale. If there is indeed a bulky, hairy bipedal hominid roaming the remote valleys and woods of Nepal, Tibet, and Mongolia, it is possible that it will elude science for many years to come. Or perhaps, its discovery is right around the corner. Who knows? Then again, the entire Yeti phenomenon may be nothing more than our imaginations running wild. Odd things can happen at high altitudes where air is icy and thin. Less oxygen to the brain, as it were. But you scientists could help a lot by uncovering some hard physical evidence, like skeletal remains, a good photograph.

"You know Dr. Kesler, we humans have always wanted to believe in other-worldly creatures. Look at the Nephilim— offspring of the sons of God who copulated with women on Earth. They were the giants found in the Old Testament book of Numbers. The whole story is related in the book of Enoch. Did they really exist? I, for one, don't believe so. But I digress. These Mongolian creatures, I predict, will simply be added to the tree of life then forgotten like the mountain gorillas unless some tangible evidence of their existence is found."

დოდ

Doyle and the others followed Gang Shun up a narrow trail. The green vegetation of the lower altitudes had given way to brown grasses as they rode higher. The sun, more intense in the thinner air, burned their skin and parched their lips. The mountains to the west began with craggy cliffs interspersed with long plateaus. The trail continued along a wide river that filtered out of the snow banks much higher up. Along its banks grew a collection of ferns, dwarf evergreen shrubs, and lichens of various colors.

During a quick break for lunch, Gang rode ahead to the summit of a high ridge to scout the afternoon route. Beyond the ridge, the mountains began in earnest with the trail becoming more treacherous. Leaving the river behind, their progress was slowed as they picked their way over sharp rocks and around boulders. Late in the day, the trail descended and leveled out before them, and they found themselves alongside the river once again.

That evening, under a clear sky, the group huddled around Gang's stove, sipping his strong tea.

"How much further to the digging?" Kurt asked Doyle.

Doyle retrieved a map from his pack and unfolded it on his lap. The pair studied it in the fading light of dusk.

"We follow the river for another ten miles, cross this plateau here," he said, pointing at the map, "and it should be in this valley here. We'll be able to surveil them from the plateau, using our night vision binoculars."

"When do we move in?" asked Marley, who had joined the pair with his cup of tea.

"I will contact Eastwood and let him know we have them in our sights. It will be up to him at that point."

"I think we should go in and force them to hand over whatever is so damned important or we kill them," Kurt said, pouring the dregs of his tea onto the ground.

"Hopefully, it won't come to that. Eastwood wants to avoid a massacre, if at all possible. Apparently, he's taking some heat for the Saudi deal. Needs to keep a low profile for a while."

Marley spat and slapped Kurt on the shoulder. "We didn't

use excessive force over there. We just got them to see things our way, that's all."

"We need to be careful," Doyle said. "Orders from the boss. If we can get them to provoke something—well, that's different.

Marley frowned into his tea then shook his head. "This stuff he brews could use some good whiskey to sweeten the taste and help ward off the chill."

Kurt nodded his agreement. "Well, maybe soon things will pick up." He ambled over to the stove and poured himself another cup of the tea.

Gang waved and said the meal was ready. Everyone gathered around the small stove and watched their guide dip large spoonfuls of stew out of the copper pot.

# Chapter 13

Li and Jing Wu labored over the portable stove while Harry and Dixie walked about camp, stretching their legs. Dusk was beginning to settle over the vast steppe that engulfed them, and a few stars glittered overhead. The blazing sun had settled behind the peaks of Belukha and Kuitan, leaving the four travelers donning their jackets and sweaters. Satisfied that the kinks had been worked out of their joints, Harry and Dixie reclined on woolen blankets Jing had spread out near the warming stove.

Dixie spoke first. "Jing says we should be at Tenduk tomorrow afternoon. I'm excited about seeing it, aren't you?"

Harry didn't answer but stared at the peaks fading in the dwindling magenta twilight. Dixie noticed him looking at the mountains.

"What's the matter, Harry? You look worried."

"I was just thinking of mother. Her health is declining and I'm not there. And I can't seem to really talk to my brother about her. That's all."

"Is she very ill, Harry?"

"Heart is failing. Max—that's my brother—Max says she probably is going to need a pacemaker in the near future."

"When did you talk to him last?"

"A few days before we left the diggings. She may have already had the pacemaker by now."

"Your father, is he there with her?"

"I dunno, possibly. Not that he cares all that much."

"You care to tell me about your parents? What are they like?"

Harry shifted his weight and leaned back on the blanket. He looked into Dixie's large, brown eyes for a while before he spoke. "My father is an alcoholic, foul-mouthed asshole whom my mother should have kicked out of the house years ago. He rarely works and, when he does, he drinks up his paycheck. Mother is a sweet, kind, once-beautiful woman who raised Max and me with little help from her husband. She worked two jobs to keep us in food and clothes. Many a time, she was too tired to take us anywhere, like to the movies, if she had a little extra money. When he was drunk, my father verbally abused my mother and me. I remember her crying a lot. Not much else to say. I've always considered him a mere sperm donor, not my father. Fathers care about their children, think of them first. No, I never considered the man my father."

"You love her very much, your mother. I can tell," Dixie said. "But she has stayed with him all these years?"

"I don't know why. Security, I guess."

"Maybe she really loved him, Harry. Ever think of that?"

"What kind of love would it be? More like pity."

"People do strange things when they're in love. It sounds like she was a good mother."

"The best. Once, while I was in graduate school, I went through a tough period. Didn't think I would make it and thought seriously of giving up and quitting. When I told her, she really let me have it. Told me I was carrying her dream. She always wanted to go to college but never could afford it, and it was her dream that her two boys would, even if she didn't. She told me if I quit, it would be her failure as a mother. So I sucked it up and kept plugging away until I had my doctorate. She cried at my graduation."

"She sounds like a remarkable woman."

"She is. What about you, Dixie? Any brothers or sisters?"

"Just a brother. I'm the classic rich kid. My parents sent me to all the proper schools, trying to teach me all the proper ways of a proper society. Except they failed."

"Failed? How?" Harry said.

Now it was Dixie who stared at the dark peaks silhouetted against the western sky. "Oh, nothing really. I was just thinking of something."

"You said your parents failed. You seem to be doing just fine to me. You're a bright, curious student. One of my best."

"You don't know, Harry. I'm not at all what I seem."

"How so?"

"Well, for starters I have made some mistakes—"

Harry chuckled. "Welcome to the club," he said.

"No, I made a big one once. I—I feel I need to be honest with you, Harry, but I'm afraid. No one at the university knows—but you should know, you're my professor. But I'm afraid you might not understand."

"Understand what?"

"Harry, I—"

"It will be all right, I promise. Go ahead. Let it out."

"Well, when I was sixteen I thought I was in love with this boy in my algebra class. He seemed so nice. Well—well, he introduced me to cocaine. There, I said it. We started doing cocaine after school at his house. His parents were gone. It seemed like fun at first and it felt so good. Soon we were having sex and doing cocaine almost every day. Then one day, I overdosed. Got some strong stuff and almost died. I wound up in the hospital and, after that, my folks stuck me in rehab. While I was in rehab, I got an abortion. At the time, I thought there was no way I could raise a kid by myself. My parents were going nuts. It's haunted me ever since. I feel so ashamed. But, Harry, that's not all. I relapsed when I was in college and had to go back to rehab. When my brother was killed in a car accident, I was devastated. I thought my life was over. He meant so much to me. We used talk about everything. After that, however, I never went back to the stuff. At my brother's funeral, I dedicated the rest of my life to his memory and vowed I would make something of myself. I got my life turned around and went back to college. I've been clean and sober ever since."

"I never thought—"

"You're upset with me now, aren't you?"

"No, never."

"You don't mind if your student was a druggy and had an abortion?"

"Dixie, Dixie." Harry placed a hand on her soft cheek and felt its warmth. "Everyone has a past and done things they wished they hadn't. Myself included. I could tell you something shocking about your professor. The important thing is that we learn from our mistakes and move on. Become a better person. You certainly have done that."

"It's just that I keep feeling that something is going to happen. Something bad. My life is so perfect right now."

"Dixie, you are the best graduate student I have ever had. You are bright, energetic, and you work hard. Nothing has been given to you at Cal Pacific. You've earned everything by hard work and dedication. My other students could learn a lot from your example."

She smiled. Tears welled in her eyes. "You won't mention this to anyone will you? Especially to the professor."

"I promise your secret is safe with me. And, Dixie, I am fortunate to have you on this expedition. Now it looks like supper is ready, so let's see what Li and Jing have cooked up."

❧❦❧

Eastwood let himself into his Upper West Side penthouse and mixed himself a drink. His phone call with Garrett Sawyers earlier that afternoon had left him in a sour mood. He tugged at his tie and slouched in his favorite chair, facing a large window overlooking FDR Drive and the East River. Mill Rock stood like a sentinel in the hazy distance.

Sawyers had telephoned from the White House to talk about his appointment to the nonprofit commission the president was forming. To Eastwood's dismay, the presidential aide informed him that no decision was forthcoming and might not be for many weeks. Eastwood wondered if the Saudi deal had anything to do with the president's decision. He had broken a few laws, sure, but what American corporation hadn't? As far as he knew, there were no trails leading back to him. To make matters worse, he had not heard from Doyle in several days, which increased the tension in his chest and neck. The unknown status of the Mongolian mission cut through him, and not being able to control operations on the ground made him antsy. His star had risen profoundly since dropping out of school at age eighteen. After joining the army, he became a platoon sergeant and went to Vietnam. Those days were long past but the urge to lead men was still a driving force within him. He had used those skills learned in the military to build BioGen to a company whose tentacles reached throughout the world. These days, there were no bullets to dodge, just laws to skirt around and avoid getting caught.

Eastwood got up and fixed himself another drink. Standing in front of the large window, he allowed the whiskey to calm his frazzled nerves, while his mind wandered back to a time in the jungle, a time when decisions seemed simpler—kill or be killed. He was alone in a bunker at Kham Duc, situated in the northern section of Quảng Tín Province, South Vietnam. It sat beside National Highway 14, which paralleled the international border with Laos, and was surrounded by high mountains on all sides. Located in the northwest of South Vietnam, just ten miles from Laos, for years the camp at Kham Duc had served as a base for intelligence gathering operations along the Ho Chi Minh Trail. And in the spring of 1968, the communists decided the time had come to take it out for good. By early May, intelligence sources realized that a large number of North Vietnamese were gathering in the mountains around the camp. After it was reinforced, an outlying camp was attacked, which soon fell to the enemy, and the marines were evacuated by helicopter to Kham Duc. That evening, General Westmoreland determined that Kham Duc was indefensible and, wishing to avoid the headlines of American troops being overrun, decided to evacuate it, beginning at dawn the next morning. The special forces camp was named after the main village, which was located about 800 meters to the northeast. It was night. The camp was surrounded by the enemy and they were outnumbered. Help was supposed to be on the way, but no one knew for sure. The air force had pounded the surrounding hills for days, but North Vietnamese mortars kept raining down on them. Several helicopters and a plane were shot down and burned on a small runway next to the outpost.

It was the longest night Eastwood could remember. Enemy fire pounded them all night. He sat in his hooch, waiting for death. He wrote his parents a letter and told them he missed them. The small candlelit dugout closed in on him and his few buddies, who were huddled with him. The night wore on, as did the incoming artillery. He prayed in earnest. He was never a religious young man but, that night, buried in that hooch, he was as religious as they came. Finally, after dawn, Chinook helicopters arrived and began the evacuation. He had survived, but it was a terrible retreat.

Finished with his drink, he decided to go to bed. Maybe he would hear something from Doyle in the morning.

*       *       *

Doyle sat perched behind a rock outcropping, squinting through the night-vision binoculars. The expedition site lay spread out on the steppe, a half a mile below, and all appeared quiet. No one was moving among the numerous tents and no lights burned. Doyle counted a dozen tents—four large ones, the rest being of the smaller variety. He noticed two sentries dozing at the far side of the compound. He stumbled from his overlook and retrieved the satellite phone from his duffle. After punching in a series of numbers, he waited while the clicking commenced then breathed a sigh of relief when the ringing began.

Eastwood answered. "Hello?"

"Sir, we're here. Got them under surveillance now. Everyone is asleep. Only two guards and they appear to be sleeping."

Eastwood's voice crackled over the phone connection. "Good. Now here is what I want you to do..."

Doyle listened for a long while to Eastwood. Finished, he replaced the phone in the duffle.

"Gather around, men, and listen up."

Gang, Gillum, Kurt, and Marley sat in a semicircle around Doyle, who shook his head. "Not you, Gang. This is company business."

Gang nodded and sauntered off to where the horses were hobbled.

"Kurt," Doyle said, "this is where you start earning your pay. Go take care of Gang. And do it quietly."

Kurt smiled and left to join Gang who was adjusting the saddles. Doyle watched as Kurt put an arm around Gang, led him behind a section of rocks, and disappeared from view. There were muffled sounds of a brief struggle then stillness, after which Kurt rejoined the group.

"Never uttered a sound," he said. "Just smiled at me and the knife."

"We'll cover him with rocks in the morning," Doyle said. "Right now, we've got a job to do down there." He pointed in the direction of the expedition site.

"No need to cover him," Kurt said, sporting a broad grin. "I threw him down a deep ravine. No one will find him, trust me."

"What's the plan, Ben?" Gillum said.

Doyle looked at his second-in-command, studying the deep lines etched in the man's face. Riley Gillum was a study in contrasts—tough but smart, outwardly quiet but possessing an analytical mind that worked incessantly, calculating options, weighing percentages. He had a muscular build, as all of Doyle's men did, dark curly hair, and deep-set eyes. He had been a navy SEAL and, as a member of Operation Urgent Fury, participated in the invasion of the island of Granada. A chance for the United States to flex its military muscles after Vietnam, Gillum had said. After his wife divorced him for her boyfriend, he began drinking heavily and was separated from the navy. He tried his hand at law enforcement but found that chasing petty criminals wasn't his cup of tea, eventually meeting up with Doyle at a gun range in Pennsylvania. The two men hit it off and, when Doyle took Eastwood's job offer, his first recruit was Gillum. The man had no social life that Doyle knew of, no women or steady girlfriend, just played video games alone in his apartment until the wee hours of morning. But Gillum was rock steady. Doyle trusted the man with his life.

"Time to break out the weapons. We'll go in and find this Dr. Olson. Once we have him, we force him to give us what we came for. I will interrogate the doctor. The rest of you will keep the compound secured. Believe me, he'll hand over whatever it is they have found. Remember, we don't shoot first. Let's get moving. It'll be daylight soon."

Doyle grabbed a Persuader shotgun while Gillum and Kurt each slung an M-16 over a shoulder. Marley brought up the rear with the BAR. The group slogged single-file over rocky terrain then entered the steppe grassland, leaving them exposed. Doyle hoped the sentries were still asleep at their posts. From his vantage point, the expedition site was quiet, the early kitchen crew not having awakened for the day. Crouching low and maneuvering at a trot, they made their way to the compound's edge and halted behind one of the larger tents. With no moon overhead, they created no shadows to betray their arrival. Darkness lay over the compound like a black velvet blanket, while only the occasional chirps of a few crickets pierced the night.

Doyle peered around the tent. Two men sat at a small table at the far side of the row of tents. Security, most likely. He signaled Kurt and Gillum to capture and disarm the two men. They disappeared from view as they rounded the corner of a tent filled with tables and chairs.

Doyle waited with Marley, pulse pounding in his neck. He fought to bring his breathing under control. Waiting in a semi-crouched position caused Doyle's back to ache. His brain pleaded to get moving and relieve the pain now shooting into his legs. After what seemed an interminable length of time, the two men returned and shot Doyle a thumbs up.

Following Doyle's hand signals, the group spread out through the compound and began to search each tent. Ten minutes later, Doyle heard Gillum's whistle and ran to the central clearing, where he found the man pointing his M-16 at a young Asian. Kurt and Marley joined them in short order.

"Man's name is Cheng." Gillum said, pushing the man to his knees with the barrel of his rifle. "Says he's the foreman on the digging. Says the doctor is not here."

Doyle walked up to the man as a small crowd of workers began milling about, all talking, some crying.

"You speak English?"

The man shrugged.

"So, where's your leader?" Doyle said.

The man stared at the ground in silence.

"I'll ask just once more, young man. Where is Doctor Olson?"

"Gone," came Cheng's hesitant reply.

"For the last time, gone where?" Doyle pumped the Persuader shotgun he was carrying, pushing a shell into its chamber with a loud *clack*. The sound made Cheng jump.

"He and the woman went to Tenduk monastery. Two days ago."

"What have you all been digging for up here?"

Again quiet.

"And what have you found?"

"An airplane and a few bones, that is all."

"An airplane?" Doyle's voice rose in pitch.

"Over there," Cheng said and pointed in the direction of the foothills.

"An airplane? Really? What kind of an airplane?"

The man remained silent.

Doyle smiled and pointed at Gillum. "Riley, you and Kurt go check out what he's talking about."

After the men left, Doyle returned his attention to Cheng. More of a crowd had gathered and Marley paraded back and forth around them, brandishing the BAR.

Doyle couldn't believe the expedition workers' unwillingness to cooperate. They appeared to be waiting for a chance to overpower his men. One false move and Doyle knew there would be a blood bath, initiated by Kurt—something that neither he nor Eastwood wanted.

His men were battle-hardened veterans with mostly level heads but if Kurt killed one of the workers, Doyle feared a slaughter would result. He concentrated on a calm voice and slow movements.

"Now, Mr. Cheng, why did the doctor go to this monastery?"

Cheng shook his head. "I do not know for sure. It had something to do with the bones we dug up, I think. Please, mister, do not kill us. We are but simple workers here. We know nothing."

"I believe you, Cheng. We aren't going to kill you. We are not monsters, after all." Turning to Marley, Doyle continued. "I'm going to see what this plane business is about. I want you to go back and bring up the horses. After we eat, we're going to find this monastery.

# Chapter 14

A disturbed Professor Kesler sat alone in his office and looked out over the calm waters of the San Francisco Bay. It was a bright day and there were many boats on the water, but the idyllic scene did not match his mood. He had tried numerous times unsuccessfully to reach Harry on the satellite phone and over the satellite video conference caller. Each time there was no answer. The time difference made things difficult, as the research site was fifteen hours ahead of Pacific Time. He had risen earlier than usual and gone to bed much later in the last two days, in an effort to reach his colleague, but was unable to do so.

Earlier in the day, he had attempted to work, trying in vain to concentrate on a talk he was scheduled to give on human evolution the following month. He was upset. Not being able to reach Harry, after the threat on his life, caused bile to spill out of his stomach and into his throat. His hands trembled as he thumbed through the papers before him, his mind unable to focus. So he had put the speech in a drawer, reviewed Dr. Rawlings's DNA data from her sequencer, and compared them once again to his notes. As his brain calmed, he was able to process the data but, once again, the result was the same. Unmistakable. The DNA sequence of the bones did not match the human genome nor what they knew of the Neanderthal genome. He checked and rechecked, but the answer always came up the same. The bones did not match any known DNA sequence. This meant it had the potential to be a very big discovery, but he could not savor the moment. Not while he couldn't locate Harry.

He was worried—no, in fact, he was afraid. It was unlike Harry to be out of touch for so long a time. Usually, they communicated every two days, if nothing more than a hello and an update from each other. But now it had been three days and Harry did not answer his calls. To make matters worse, Kesler had not heard from the police and he feared something might have happened to Harry. The men who kidnapped him had been deathly serious and, for all Kesler knew, Harry could be dead. Whomever was behind it seemed to think the scientists had stumbled onto something worth killing for. But, Christ, it was only the beginning of the scientific work. The inadvertent religious slur didn't make him smile. It might take many months before they developed a workable hypothesis explaining the significance of the uncovered bones. And there might still be more discoveries to come. Who could tell? It all might amount to nothing. He thought of calling Dr. Rawlings, thinking that to hear her cheerful voice would take his mind off his worries, but as he picked up the phone, he thought better of it. She was busy and she had done him an enormous favor by running the DNA analysis on the Mongolian specimens. He might call her later in the evening.

Kesler stood, clasped his hands together, looked out at the waters again, and quietly recited the first lines of the prayer that was the centerpiece of Jewish daily life, the Shema. As a boy, he'd learned that, according to the Talmud, the reading of the Shema morning and evening fulfilled the commandment, *You shall meditate, therein, day and night.* He had said the prayer each night before sleeping:

> *Sh'ma Yis'ra'eil Adonai Eloheinu Adonai echad.*
> *Barukh sheim k'vod malkhuto l'olam va'ed.*

> Hear, Israel, the Lord is our God,
> the Lord is One!
> Blessed be the Name of His
> glorious kingdom for ever and ever.

Sitting once more at his desk, he picked up the telephone and dialed the number for the satellite phone.

*ɕͻɕͻ*

The afternoon sunlight was fading as Harry, Dixie, Li, and Jing trekked into the village of Tenduk and kicked their horses up the small knoll to the monastery. The mountains of Belukha and Kuitan framed the rounded hill upon which the monastery had been built centuries earlier. Jing led them up the knoll to the temple, where they dismounted then climbed a short series of steps to a pair of heavy, oaken doors. The crisp, thin air formed a thin layer of haze that obscured the lower elevations of the mountain peaks.

While Harry and Dixie waited on their horses, Li followed Jing to the temple doors but, before either of them could knock, they opened.

A short, roundish man in a brown robe emerged and greeted the pair with an impish gleam. He bowed slightly at the waist and spread his arms in a warm welcome. "*Namasta*, travelers. You look weary. Please come in, all of you."

"You speak English, great," Harry said from atop Mouse.

"But, of course," said the man in the brown robe. "We have studied the language here for many years. And we are no longer removed from the rest of the world."

*So you say*, thought Harry, as he and Dixie dismounted and followed the man into the temple behind Jing and Li.

Inside, the roundish man turned and smiled. "My name is Bo Zhing, the abbot of Tenduk monastery. I welcome you in the name of Buddha. May I offer you some tea?"

"That would be very nice, Mr. Zhing, thank you," Jing said.

"Then please follow me," Zhing said.

He turned and strolled through a side door to the large temple room. The group followed the monk through the temple and into a smaller room, which was located at the end of a narrow hall.

In a corner stood a small antique stove with a large copper kettle. A small wooden table with several wicker-style chairs sat in the room's center. The room was very warm.

"Please, sit here," Zhing said, offering the chairs. He made his way to the stove, poured tea into mugs, and brought them to the table. "What brings you to Tenduk? Are you trekking tourists?"

Harry shot a glance at Jing and, when she did not answer, he spoke. "Hardly, sir. We are part of a scientific expedition from down on the steppe. We are searching for early human skeletal remains. I am Dr. Harry Olson from California. This is Dixie Zinn also from California. Li Chao there is our guide and foreman, and Jing Wu brought us here."

"Scientists," Zhing said as more of a statement than a question. "How wonderful. You are anthropologists studying human evolution?"

"Yes," Harry said. "We hope to advance scientific understanding of how humans got to North America from Africa."

Zhing smiled broadly. "But, Doctor, through Mongolia, of course. I thought that was all settled."

Harry returned the abbot's smile and gestured with a hand. "Yes, but it is the details that we seek. And specimens. Any specimens can only serve to augment our understanding."

Zhing nodded but remained silent, as if contemplating Harry's answer.

"Jing," Harry continued, "told us about a certain skull you have here, one from a wild man, a Yeti. We would like your permission to examine it, if possible."

Zhing appeared taken aback by the request, visibly startled. He sipped his tea for a while then stood. "You must be tired from your journey. Of course, you will stay the night as guests of the monastery. We find the quiet very refreshing and spiritual. And you will eat with us later, meet the other monks. And after the meal, if there is time, we shall discuss your request. But, for now, let's get you to your rooms where you can rest before dinner."

Zhing stood and clapped his hands. A small boy in western dress appeared. The abbot stooped and whispered into the child's ear. He grinned and started out the door.

"Please," Zhing said. "Cam will see you to your rooms and

will call for you in about an hour for dinner. There is water in the rooms so you can clean up. We will attend to your animals, so please don't worry. I will see you later."

With that, Zhing turned and disappeared from the room. The group hurried to catch up with Cam.

Later, after dinner, Zhing was nowhere to be seen. Pu Yang, the senior lama, took Harry aside and addressed Zhing's absence. "He does not think it wise to allow you access to the Yeti skull. Its existence is not well known outside our monastery," he said in a mild-mannered voice. He tugged at his robe as he spoke. "He wishes that it remain so. The abbot believes that the Yeti is a figment of one's imagination. According to him, it does not exist. Our educated young people scoff at the possibility, but our elders know better. Many have seen the creature. Many have seen its footprints."

"It's not a matter of believing or not believing, Senior Lama," Harry said. Most everyone had left the dining hall except for Dixie, Li, and Jing. Only a few novice monks were left to clean the tables. "We are scientists. We wish to examine the skull, that is all. I doubt we can confirm its authenticity up here."

"I don't even know why we still have it," Yang said. "The outside world is largely unaware of its existence. If you think it could be helpful—"

"If you choose to not let us examine it, that is your choice. It will be fine. We will not trouble you further. However, we have trekked for several days with the hope of examining it, so if it can be arranged, I promise you, we will not make a political event of it. It would be extremely useful to take measurements of it and make a drawing of it."

Yang took Harry's arm and guided him down the hallway. Halfway to the end of it he stopped. "I will do what I can to change the abbot's mind. I am senior to him, you know, so my wishes carry a lot of weight around here." He laughed and his gray eyes twinkled. "I will let you know tomorrow after morning vespers. Now, I bid you a restful night in Buddha's name."

えつべの

Dixie was alone in her room. A small kerosene lamp filled the space with a soft light. The room, at the end of a short hallway in the monastery dormitory, was spartan with only a bed, small wooden desk, and straight-back chair in the way of furnishings. Upon returning to the room after dinner, she noticed someone had replenished the pitcher with fresh water. The bed was firm, almost hard, and, as Dixie tried to rest, she could not get comfortable. She closed her eyes and tried to relax but sleep would not come, for her mind was on the events of the past two days. And on Harry.

He had called her *honey*. They had exchanged secrets. She had revealed dark mistakes that no one at the university knew, and he had accepted it. Just accepted that her past sins were just that—past.

Her pulse quickened.

Why did she feel this way? She thought it crazy but he made her knees weak. She trembled around him. Oh, not so much that it was noticeable, but enough that she felt unsure of herself in his presence. She felt awkward. It had not been so back at the university or initially in Mongolia—only since he had called her *honey*. So her view of her world had changed in the last few days, changed in a more complicated way. Could she continue to work with him and keep that professional distance necessary in a professor-student relationship? He was vital to her obtaining her doctorate and, if she mishandled the situation, it might spell disaster for her. He seemed not to realize his effect on her, continuing his professional demeanor around her. She hoped she could remain as professional as Harry.

She took a deep breath.

Harry had touched her face. She could still feel his warm fingers on her cheek. Turning over in the bed, she tried again to get comfortable but failed.

There was a soft knock on her door.

She opened the door and Harry stood in the doorway.

His eyes sparkled and he smiled warmly. "Were you sleeping?"

"No," she said. "Come in."

Dixie closed the door behind Harry, who crossed the room and eased his tall frame into the chair at the desk. "I—I couldn't sleep either. I hope you don't mind me coming here. I just wanted to see you."

She put a hand on his shoulder and felt the firmness under his shirt. "It's funny. I was just thinking about you. Then you knocked."

"When I spoke of my parents, I'm afraid I presumed too much. I'm sorry if I burdened you unnecessarily. At the time you...I don't know...you seemed like you cared."

Dixie sat on the bed, her heart racing. The room was getting stuffy. "I do care, Harry, very much. More than I can say, actually. I had a friend in college who had parents much like yours. A father who drank too much and a mother who supported the family. She couldn't decide if she loved or hated the man. It caused her much stress and grief. So I feel I know a little of what you must feel. And I hurt for you."

Harry rose from the desk and sat on the bed next to Dixie. She looked deep into his steel-blue eyes, seeing strength and compassion. She fought an urge to put her arms around him, draw him close, and touch his cheek as he had hers. He seemed vulnerable, something she had not experienced before. He was showing a human side to his methodical, professional demeanor and it touched her heart.

"You don't know the half of it, Dixie. I'm not at all what I seem. You should know—"

"You shouldn't feel it necessary to confide in me, Harry. Your business is your business but I do care for you."

"I did something about a year ago. It was stupid and foolish and, in doing so, I hurt the man I admire the most."

"The professor?" Dixie said.

Harry nodded. "It was because I wanted to make a name for myself. It was so stupid." He seemed to struggle to find the right words. Dixie's heart pounded as he continued. "I forged some data on a paper I wrote for a journal. I changed it so it would fit a theory I proposed in the article. The professor caught it and confronted me. I didn't know what to say. There was nothing to do but admit what I had done. It was the darkest day of my life, for the look on his face has all but destroyed our relationship. Not a day goes by that I don't regret my actions but I can't undo it. Fortunately, the professor corrected my mistake in a letter to the journal and took responsibility. Christ, he's my father. I love the man. But I have let him down immensely—more than that, I hurt him, Dixie. It's hard to look at myself in the mirror anymore."

"Forgive me if I don't know what to say to be of comfort. Just know I care about you," she said. "I think it's natural to feel guilt over it."

Dixie's mind was in a whirl with this revelation from her professor. She hadn't expected it, not forging data in a journal article.

"I've tried to understand why I did what I did. I guess I just wanted a shortcut to fame and fortune. It was so stupid."

"Harry," Dixie said, her voice faltering. "I—"

"Now, you'll be thinking differently of your professor. Probably want to work under someone else. I wouldn't blame you."

"No one but those involved in the academic life, Harry, understands the tremendous pressure to make discoveries and publish them. I'm sure Dr. Kesler understands the motivation behind what you did. He seems caring enough."

"The fact remains I all but have destroyed his confidence in me, I am sure of it. He's the only father I ever had. I—"

Without thinking, she placed her hand on his. She startled herself in doing so. Then she did the unthinkable—she took him into her arms and they gazed at each other for a long, silent moment. He brought his lips to hers and kissed her. Dixie felt her spirit melt into his and, for a brief few seconds, they were kindred souls suspended in space and time.

When they parted, Harry shook his head. "I'm sorry," he said.

"I'm not."

"But I'm your professor. And now you know *my* secret. I'm sorry."

Dixie laughed. "Harry, we're not in high school and I'm a full-grown woman. I loved the way you kissed me."

"Well," he said, letting go of her, a weak smile on his face. "We'll just have to do it again sometime."

# Chapter 15

Breakfast at the monastery was a simple affair of oatmeal with honey, unleavened biscuits, and strong tea. The small dining hall was quiet, as the twenty monks with somber faces ate in relative silence. Sunlight streamed in two large windows, filling the room with a brilliant golden warmth. Morning prayers and chanting were over and they were readying themselves for the day's work that lay ahead. Harry, Dixie, Li, and Jing sat by themselves at a table and endured the stares of the monks.

Harry smiled at Dixie and thought of the previous evening. After leaving his assistant and returning to his room, he had lain on his cot, savoring the taste of her lips. At first, he found it hard to believe that he had kissed his graduate assistant, an act that normally would spell the end of the student working under him. It had never happened before. What *was* happening? What *was* he feeling? His emotions were a jumbled mess—a high he had never experienced, along with a low, and a realization that their relationship was different now. She had smiled at him, an indication that the kiss meant something important to her. In spite of the possible complications it might pose, Harry couldn't get Dixie out of his thoughts. Even this morning at breakfast, he smelled a faint fragrance from her hair. He had confided to her his monumental mistake that, under any other departmental chairman, would have spelled the end of his academic career. He considered resigning but felt indebted to Kesler and was working to restore the man's confidence in him. Sleep had been difficult in coming but, finally, as a gray dawn filtered through his window, he drifted off for an hour before being awakened by the morning bell. As they finished their breakfast, abbot Bo Zhing approached their table.

"*Namasta*," he said, clasping his hands and bowing slightly.

"*Namasta*," said Harry. "Good morning, abbot Zhing."

"I wish to apologize, Doctor, for my rudeness last evening. After speaking with Lama Yang, I realize your curiosity in our skull is purely scientific. Please forgive me for thinking of our monastery's reputation. It was just that I did not wish to politicize our custody of the Yeti skull and have to deal with a deluge of unwelcome inquiries."

"I quite understand," Harry said, finishing his mug of tea.

"Thank you so much, Doctor. Lama Yang has led our small conclave here at Tenduk for forty years and his opinions are highly regarded by us all. It is his feeling that you and your colleagues can be trusted."

Dixie, Li, and Jing nodded their agreement.

"Of course you can," Dixie added.

"Well then, if you all will follow me, we shall go to the catacombs where the skull is kept."

With that, Zhing ambled out of the dining hall and led the group to another smaller room whose walls were decorated with faded murals of the Buddha in various poses. The abbot lit a kerosene lamp that sat on a carved mahogany table next to a locked door that was much shorter than the one through which they entered. Zhing fumbled under his robe and retrieved a large key ring containing numerous keys. Finding one, he unlocked the door and opened it into a dark passageway.

"I will lead," Zhing said, "and light the way. Please be careful and watch the steps. They are narrow and can be slippery."

Zhing disappeared and began a descent down a series of stone steps that curved in a counter-clockwise spiral. Harry followed with Dixie and Jing behind him. Li brought up the rear. The only light was from Zhing's lamp and it cast flickering shadows against the stone and timber walls of the staircase. The air was cool and damp and smelled of loam and moist earth.

Down they descended. The walls glistened and, in several places, water dripped from the stones overhead. In the pale yellow light, Harry noticed that some of the stones had a dull green moss covering them while others were covered with an orange lichen. He estimated fifty steps before Zhing stepped into a wide passageway that angled sharply to their left. There, Zhing hung the lamp on a peg in the wall and lit another kerosene lamp. Its light illuminated the tunnel enough for Harry to make out that they had stopped in front of another heavy oaken door. Once he unlocked and opened the door, the abbot led the group along a dark hallway, his swaying lantern shooting shafts of light over its rock walls. The air was dank and heavy.

*Where are we going?* Harry wondered as the group stumbled down the passageway in single file. His lungs burned from the heavy, languid air. *We must be a hundred feet underground.*

Zhing stopped in front of a metal door secured with a padlock. The abbot unlocked the door and carried his lamp over its threshold. The door creaked as he pulled it open. The group was greeted by the odor of old parchment, leather, and dust.

"This is our antiquities room," he said, "where we store certain items we wish to keep from public view. The constant temperature and low humidity seems to help keep the items in good condition."

"What sort of items?" Li said.

"Artifacts of our history—illuminated manuscripts from the Khan Dynasty and statues from the Mergids when they were defeated by Genghis Khan. And, of course, the Yeti skull. We don't use this room much anymore, as you can tell."

The room was musty. A pungent odor of dust and mildew singed Harry's nostrils upon entering. Sturdy wooden cabinets, whose shelves contained books and various items, lined the room's walls. Zhing led them to a dark corner and stood in front of a waist-high metal box. Using a key from a separate key ring, he unlocked the box, opened the top, reached in, and pulled out a frayed canvas bag.

"Here it is, Doctor. Here is what you wanted to see. Please handle it with care."

He handed the bag to Harry, who took it in both hands and retrieved the skull.

☙☙☙

Kesler sat across the desk from police sergeant Stu Walcott and toyed with his handkerchief while the detective questioned him. Walcott was a large man with a bulbous nose from his years of weekend beer drinking. The smoke from his cigarette irritated Kesler's nostrils and eyes and he thought he noticed a mustard stain on the man's wrinkled white shirt.

Located west of Mission Bay on Bryant Street, the San Francisco Hall of Justice housed the San Francisco Police Department. Kesler had made the trip from his office at Cal Pacific University after calling Sergeant Walcott. From the sergeant's window, he could barely make out the clock tower of the Ferry Building on the Embarcadero.

"So, Dr. Kesler, let me get this straight. Two men abducted you, threatened you, and forced you to tell them the whereabouts of your colleague in Mongolia who is doing archeological research there. Is that it?" Walcott blew smoke into the air above Kesler's head.

The professor shifted in his chair and wiped his chin with the handkerchief. The question sounded more like a rebuff than a request for information. "That's correct, Sergeant."

"And this happened over a week ago?"

"Yes."

Walcott's eyes narrowed as a frown formed on his face. "Why are just now getting around to reporting it?"

"I don't know exactly. I am worried about my colleagues doing research in Mongolia."

"What did these men look like?"

The sergeant retrieved a pad from a desk drawer and began taking notes as Kesler spoke.

"I don't know. It was dark and they blindfolded me." Kesler squirmed in his chair and continued to stroke his handkerchief.

"Come now, Doctor. That doesn't give me much to go on. Surely you can do better."

"One of the men had a scarred face. Like a burn or…"

"A bad case of acne, perhaps?"

"Yes," Kesler said. "That could be it. He was a big man."

"So a big man with scars on his face kidnapped you. That's not much to go on, either. Nothing, really."

Kesler explained who Harry was and why he was in Mongolia. He suggested a reason why they would want Harry and what he had found. He explained about the teeth and bones and the DNA analysis. The sergeant frowned, all during his explanation, as if he didn't follow most of it. He wrote on the pad through the entire discourse.

When he was finished, Kesler threw up his hands. "I'm sorry. It all sounds so silly now that I talk about it. I don't know what I was thinking. I hoped you could help. And I'm sorry for not coning to you sooner."

"Not much we can do, really, at this point. It would have helped if you had reported this right after it happened. Now, however—"

"Sergeant, I understand. At the time I was just too shook up to think straight."

"Well, what's done is done. Any inkling where they took you?"

"No. But possibly south of the city. I thought I heard planes taking off."

"Big planes? Like airliners?"

"Yes," Kesler said. "I was in an empty room, like in an abandoned warehouse, but I have no idea where."

The detective snubbed out his cigarette. "Doctor, I can do this. I know Mongolia has recently joined INTERPOL. Let me contact the INTERPOL office in Paris and see if they can forward this information to the Mongolian authorities. We can at least do that and then see what happens or what turns up. Beyond that, at this point, there's not much more I can do."

"Thank you very much, Sergeant Walcott."

"You're welcome, Dr. Kesler."

On the drive back to Cal Pacific, Kesler wondered if anything would come of the visit with Walcott. Embarrassed by the detective's questions, he now realized how stupid it was for not going to the police right away, but he felt he couldn't risk it. Could INTERPOL do anything? He would have to wait and see. All he knew about the agency was that they helped countries with international crimes. But it wasn't a known fact that the kidnappers were even in Mongolia. The threat to Harry and the team might be nonexistent. Kesler could be worrying needlessly. Trust in Walcott was his only option for the present. The man seemed to know what he was doing. Kesler was still aching from all the rough handling the men had given him. Hopefully, his delay would not cost Harry or Dixie their lives.

*eↄeↄ*

Doyle and his men climbed onto their horses and headed into the Altai Mountains. He did not know what was so special about the bones the research team had excavated but, from his association with Eastwood, he knew that those sort of relics could be worth big money. He also knew leaving the expedition workers behind unharmed was a risk, as they might contact Dr. Olson or the authorities, but Eastwood wanted this operation done without collateral bloodshed. The murder of their guide could be explained as a necessary casualty. So he was begrudgingly doing as he was told. Eastwood's decision could prove their undoing with the one killing already on their hands but he wasn't the boss.

Without their guide, Gang, they would have to make their way to Tenduk alone in strange territory but he and Gillum studied the map and thought they could find their way. He ordered Kurt and Marley to check on Gang's body, and the two men returned assuring him Gang would never be found.

Doyle didn't know how far behind the research team members they were—could be a day or possibly as much as three. If Dr. Olson was staying at the monastery then perhaps they had a chance of overtaking them. The doctor must have the bones with him for no one gave them up at the digging site and they didn't find them during their search of the compound.

Kurt and Marley had pressured Doyle to do away with the entire research team, an unthinkable act in Doyle's mind. He wasn't opposed to violence, as disposing of Gang testified, but needless mass murder was abhorrent to him. It was against all rules of civilized warfare and those rules were in place for a reason. If someone deserved killing…well, that was one thing, but to blast away indiscriminately at innocents, was another—and out of bounds. Doyle hoped those two could keep a lid on their emotions and not let things get out of hand. They were professionals but if they decided to act on their own, against Eastwood's orders, the entire mission would fall apart.

The sun burned the mist off the mountains, foretelling a warm, cloudless day. As the Altai came into sharp relief against the brilliant azure sky, the group assembled their gear and filled their water bottles. Once mounted, the four men guided their horses over a rocky trail and along a deep crevasse with a fast-moving stream at its bottom. Ahead, the mountains loomed large and foreboding causing Doyle to momentarily doubt the sanity of their *raison d'être*. When they returned to the States, he was going to demand a pay raise from Eastwood.

೧൞൞

The skull which Harry held in his hand was a brown, weathered object, larger than a modern human skull. It was a low, flat, elongated skull that featured a prominent brow ridge and a projecting mid-face. Fascinated, he turned it over in his hands a few times while he examined it, eyes narrowed in concentration. It seemed overall larger than a typical Neanderthal skull.

He handed it to Dixie, who took it with eager hands and let out a low whistle. After studying it for a few moments, she passed the skull to Li.

"What do you make of it, Harry?" she asked.

"It has features of a Neanderthal but seems too large. Let's measure it."

"It has a protruding chin which is definitely *not* Neanderthal," Dixie said as Harry took the skull from Li. She removed a tape measure from her pocket and handed it to Harry.

"Also, notice there are no ridges in the occipital bone, either," he said. He wrapped the tape measure around the skull both lengthwise as well as crosswise. Doing the math in his head, he calculated the cranial volume.

"Twenty-one hundred cubic centimeters," Harry announced, "far too large for a Neanderthal. Or human for that matter."

Zhing moved in closer and looked over Li's shoulder. The lantern's flickering light caused their shadows to undulate on the floor and walls of the tiny room.

"Where was this found?" Dixie asked Zhing, returning the tape measure to her pocket.

"Not far from here, higher up the mountain. The story is that many, many years ago a man was riding on a yak near mountain Almasyn Ulan which is three days' ride from the monastery. There, in a ravine, he saw something in the fog laying between two trees. Moving ahead and nearer to it, the man came to a corpse of a human-like animal, very big and covered by hair. In spite of being terrified, the man approached and examined it closely. The animal lay on one side. One hand, a leg and head were raised. The corpse was extremely similar to human, but it wasn't Mongolian, Russian, or Chinese. The old man understood that the creature in front of him was not human.

"The animal obviously had been dead for a long time. Its head was large, the neck thick, hands and legs were long. The hair on its head was long, while other parts of its body were covered by shorter hair. Its armpits and undersurface had minimal hair. The creature's groin, armpits, and other similar places had a dried up leathery look. Sections of its hair were separated from the body and had been scattered by the wind. There were no implements found nearby that people use, like tools or utensils.

"When the old man saw the corpse was neither human nor animal, but nonetheless terrible, he thought about devils and malicious ghosts. He became so frightened that he did not tell either his wife or children. Due to his shock and fear, the time and other details of the corpse became firmly fixed in his memory.

"Years later, the old man, along with his close friend and some villagers, returned to the place, but found no remnants of the dead creature. The landscape had changed and everything looked different.

"Eventually, the old man, once again with help of his friend, was able to locate the site. They searched for days but never found its body but they did find the skull near the location of the man's original sighting. The corpse got carried away, or eaten, by predators. So they found only the skull. The old man brought it here."

"I see," Harry said. "That is a different story that the one Jing told us. Why the discrepancy, I wonder?"

"I have heard many tales of this skull," Zhing said, "all of them wild and untrue."

"The eye sockets are smaller than Neanderthals as well, Harry," Dixie said.

"Well, the skull is definitely not a Neanderthal, that's for sure. It is equally not modern human, either."

"What about early hominoid, like an ape or other primate?" Li said.

"No, the cranial capacity is too large. Nothing we have seen has a cranial capacity as large as this skull."

Zhing tugged on Harry's sleeve. "Doctor," he said, "people believe it is from a Yeti. I can understand that you don't believe it is, but the people who live up here *know* it is a Yeti. They have seen them or at least glimpses of them."

"But there has never been an actual corpse or skeleton uncovered, no bones. Isn't that right, abbot Zhing?"

"What you hold in your hand is the evidence you seek, Doctor. I, myself, have not made up my mind, one way or the other."

"If what you say is true, abbot Zhing, then you owe it to the scientific community to allow scholars a chance to examine it and run tests. It is the only way to verify whether this tale is true or not. It could provide a giant leap forward in our understanding of human evolution."

"But, Doctor, there are a lot of people who do not believe in evolution, who do not wish for these tests to be done." The abbot frowned as he spoke.

"It is not a question of belief, sir," Harry said. "Evolution is the scientific community's best explanation as to how modern humans got to be on this planet. Whether you believe or not does not change the scientific facts. You can choose to believe the Earth is flat, if you so desire, but that does not change the fact that it is actually round. This is potentially a great discovery, abbot Zhing. You owe it to the world and the scientific community to allow more complete studies of it."

"I am sorry, Doctor, but you said you only wished to examine the skull. I have accommodated your request. Anything more is out of the question."

Zhing took the skull from Harry, replaced it in the canvas bag, then returned it to the small metal cabinet. He led the group back through the dark stairwell to the temple room where they gathered around the abbot.

"We thank you for your hospitality, abbot Zhing," Harry said. "I did not mean to offend you by my little speech back there. We will be returning to our research site as soon as we can gather our belongings. Thank you for allowing us to view the skull."

Back in the dormitory, as Harry, Dixie, Li, and Jing began to put their bags together, they talked in Harry's room.

"Well, the thing is definitely not human, not Neanderthal," Dixie said.

"What is it, Dr. Olson?" Jing asked. "Is it possible it is a Yeti?"

"I don't have the slightest idea," Harry said. "I have never seen anything like it. The evolution of the genus *Homo* is an important transition in hominid development. Early hominids, including the *Australopiths*, have traits that distinguish them clearly from other apes and make them much more like us.

These traits are not only anatomical but behavioral and ecological as well. Walking on two legs, bigger brains, use of complex tools, use of fire, all make these hominids different."

"And now today we see a hominid skull markedly larger than any uncovered to date. Right?" Dixie's eyes were wide and she gestured with a hand for emphasis. "These monks don't realize it, but they are sitting on something that could revolutionize our thinking about human evolution."

"Right," Harry said. "Neanderthals had larger brains than modern humans—our brains actually shrank about twenty percent. But this skull is way larger than Neanderthal. So what is it? I just don't know. It is too bad I could not convince the abbot to allow scientists to examine it more completely. "

"The monks have an answer to your question," Jing said. "It is from a Yeti."

# Chapter 16

Sitting in his office at the National Police Agency of
Mongolia, Colonel Yuli Bronislav looked out his window over the street below the Parliament Building.
Drivers in Ulaanbaatar never paid any attention to the simple
traffic rules in Mongolia's capital. Ulaanbaatar had a long cultural history, but only now was undergoing an industrial revolution. He thought it was one of the most drab looking cities on
the face of the planet—a travesty, really, considering it was the
capital of one the most beautiful and hospitable countries on
Earth. Still, as a traditionalist, he loved his capital. He understood it was not an Asian beauty, but was aware of the city's
history, culture and numerous struggles. The city was a caul-
dron of concrete and dirt. New buildings, thrown up on any
available patch of ground, crowded boulevards where
Humvees battled Land Cruisers and yellow taxis for right of
way. On the high street, tourists and new-moneyed Mongols
hunted for bargains in European-fashioned shops and Mongolian cashmere boutiques.

Between these chaotic scenes were islands of serenity—
quiet monastery courtyards, public squares, and the odd beer
patio. The river, the Tuul Gol, offered a cool respite to the
south, while the four holy mountains surrounding the city provided its backdrop. Ever-expanding yurt suburbs still surrounded the city, offering a glimpse back to before Soviet urban planning.

Bronislav lit a cigarette and studied the alert just received from INTERPOL over the I-24/7 global police communication system. Also, he held the teletype from the General Customs Office and wondered if they were related. Four Americans recently passed through customs and were possibly involved in a kidnapping and assault on a college professor in the United States. The report coincided with a notice fresh on his desk of Americans possibly involved in unknown crimes in Mongolia at an anthropological research site near the Altai Mountains. A local Mongolian had called in a report of four men brandishing weapons, threatening the workers, and asking about the expedition leader, a Dr. Olson. The local thought they were Americans. Bronislav snubbed out the cigarette and pushed the intercom.

"Tell Captain Stepan to come in," he said to a female voice.

A knock on the door, ten minutes later, announced Captain Semyon Stepan who took the chair offered by Bronislav.

The captain was a short, wiry man with a pencil-thin mustache. He had deep-set eyes and a receding hairline, which gave him a certain distinction for his age of thirty-two years.

"Read this, Semyon," the colonel said, handing the papers to his captain.

Stepan took the alerts and studied them for a few minutes. "This Benjamin Doyle, is he the only name we have?"

"Apparently, Semyon. This American professor, who someone abducted, claims that the research team here in our country has uncovered some skeletal remains of possible scientific significance. This Doyle character was involved in negotiations of an American company with the Saudis for a prehistoric skeleton. Doyle might be connected to confronting the team doing research here."

"This professor thinks this Doyle might be here in Mongolia?"

"The professor did not know the man's name. In fact, he could not identify his captors. A police sergeant in San Francisco did the legwork to get this information on Doyle. His company, BioGen, has had some pretty shady dealings in the past."

"Nothing more to go on, sir?"

"Not really. The research site is southwest of Kastum. It's a large affair so it shouldn't be hard to find. Doyle and three other men passed through customs four days ago."

"Nothing unusual with their passports, I take it?"

"No."

"You have orders, Colonel?"

Bronislav lit a cigarette and blew smoke toward the window behind him. "Well, this may not amount to much, Semyon, but then again, one never knows. I want you to take a small cadre to this research site and find out what is going on. I'm choosing you because you speak English extremely well and are proficient in these exercises. If everything is on the up and up, then report back to me and return, but if anything is suspicious, then I want you to check it out. If you should stumble upon these men, bring them to me and we will sort it all out after you get back. The American government can't squawk too loudly since INTERPOL got us involved."

"What if they resist, sir?"

"I want you to be prepared for that eventuality, Captain," Bronislav said.

"Will do, Colonel."

"And, Semyon, be careful. Take enough men and weapons with you."

∽∾∽

Zhing had petitioned Harry to take one of the novice monks with him on his return trek, as the young man no longer wished to be a part of the monastery. At dawn, the group began their descent down the mountain back to the expedition site. From there, the former monk would make his own way to Kastum to catch the train. A dull gray sky, billowing ominous dark clouds, greeted them and a brisk wind stung Harry's face as he struggled to keep a comfortable seat in his saddle. The horses were skittish from two days of rest and forged ahead against their reins. Harry brought up the rear of the column which was led by Jing.

By noon, the weather turned worse with sleet pelting their

eyes and ears. Soon after a hurried lunch of jerky and tea, a light snowfall began, forcing them to break out their parkas to shield themselves from the large flakes. By the middle of the afternoon, the snow was coming down so heavily that Jing called a halt to the day's trekking. Harry and Li built a make-shift lean-to using a canvas tarp while Dixie and the monk got a fire going in Jing's portable stove.

Huddling with the others in the lean-to in front of the stove with a mug of steaming hot tea improved Harry's spirit. Jing mentioned that, at the high elevations, early freak snowstorms were possible, and the group watched the snowfall continue into the evening. Reclining around the stove however, they remained warm and dry. As daylight faded, Jing put some dried vegetables into the pot of boiling water and in fifteen minutes, they were eating soup. After a mug of tea and one of soup, Harry was satisfied and stretched out, his boots facing the fire. The wind quieted but the snowfall continued, building tall drifts along the rock ridge that lined the trail. Tired, but warm, he found himself drifting in a dark abyss.

Once again, he was with Dixie in her room at the monastery. He kissed her. She lay back on the small cot and took him in her arms. He put his head on her chest, while she stroked his temple. She smelled of roses and lavender. His brother did not matter. Work no longer mattered. Only the touch of Dixie's soft caress mattered. She held him there all night and the next morning they were in San Francisco at her parent's home. Her father was dressed in a suit and smiled at him. He shook his hand and welcomed him into the family. He told them he loved them both. But Harry could not remember marrying Dixie. It was all mixed up.

They drove into Napa Valley to a small farm where Harry grew grapes. He was building a winery. Professor Kesler, who was now head of his vineyards, welcomed them and showed them into a large stucco house filled with servants. His father labored in the field while his mother presided over the household.

Harry and Dixie strolled the vineyard each evening at sunset, basking in each other's company and the beautiful rolling hills covered with grapes. Dixie stooped, picked up a handful of soil, and brought it to his nose where he breathed in its rich and fragrant aroma. It was going to be a good year for the grapes.

When Harry awoke, the snow had stopped and the sun was peaking over the eastern horizon. Everyone was still asleep so he rolled out of the lean-to and stirred the ashes in the stove. A small flame flickered. He placed another camel patty in it and went to check on the animals. Snow blanketed the ground and his boots made a soft crunching sound as he walked.

The horses were grazing on some grass they had found so he returned to the lean-to. He counted three sleeping bodies, the novice monk not there.

*Must be using the bathroom.*

Harry started to make tea when Jing awoke and took over the job.

"I'll go find our monk friend, Jing, if you'll wake the others," Harry said.

Jing nodded and Harry left to scout the camp's perimeter. Six inches of snow covered the ground, which clung to his boots as he walked to the rear of the lean-to. Footprints led away from the shelter then continued into some low-lying brush. After about fifty feet, the footprints stopped and the snow was trampled down in a large circle. Then, leading away from the trampled area, another set of footprints headed off into the distance.

Harry kneeled to get a closer look at the prints. Strange, he thought. The footprints leading away from the trampled area were not the same as those going into the brush. These were much larger and were barefooted.

Much larger. Barefooted.

What he saw didn't make sense. The footprints from the lean-to to the brush had to belong to the monk, but these—what were these? To whom did they belong?

Harry followed the larger prints for a short distance but then stopped and returned to camp. Dixie and Li were up and sipping tea.

"Our monk friend has disappeared," Harry said.

"What?" a startled Dixie and Li said in unison.

Jing looked up from her stove, eyes wide.

"He's gone. Tracks leading back that way," Harry said, pointing in the general direction. "But there's more. I think there was some sort of scuffle or fight because something messed up the snow in a spot back there. Then another set of footprints lead away, going in the same direction. But those prints are different. Very different."

"How so?" Li asked.

"Come and see for yourselves."

Harry led the group to the rear of the shelter and the footprints. When they arrived at the spot that was all trampled down Harry pointed out the new footprints.

"Wow," Dixie said. "Look at those, Li."

Li and Jing moved for a closer look. Jing's face had a look of surprise and horror. "I have seen footprints like these before. In pictures," she said.

Harry, Dixie, and Li all looked at Jing.

"It is - the Yeti," she said.

"Are you sure?" said Dixie, shaking her head as if not believing what she had heard.

"Yes, Dixie, I am sure. Footprints such as these are famous in this part of Asia. Photographs of them have appeared in magazines and newspapers for decades."

Harry bent over the footprints and measured them using his own foot as a measuring tool. When finished he rejoined the group. "Bigger than any known primate or hominid. Probably stands nine or ten feet tall."

"Are you serious?" said Li. "Where would it have come from?"

Jing frowned. "I have heard my grandfather say that they live in the high mountains and come down to the lower elevations in search of food."

"They? You said *they*? Jing, that is all just talk, speculation," Harry said.

"Maybe just talk, maybe not."

"Come on, Jing. I, for one, don't believe that a Mongolian wild man appeared out of nowhere and dragged our monk to

God-knows-where. If you choose to believe these wild tales, please keep them to yourself. We need to search this area thoroughly for our monk. He might be lying dead or injured around here. If for some reason he's not around here, I think we should follow these footprints and see where they lead. Maybe find him. We can't just leave him out here. If you all can start looking, I'm going to try and raise the professor on the satellite phone."

They nodded and fanned out over the area surrounding the footprints, leaving Harry to return to the lean-to. Soon the group was back at the shelter and Harry was sitting, phone in hand.

"Able to reach him?" Dixie said as she poured herself another mug of tea.

"Yes, he was at dinner with some cryptozoologist he had located in the Bay area. I brought him up to date with what's happening here."

"Tell him about the events of this morning, the missing monk?" Dixie said.

"No. He would have worried himself sick. You all find anything?"

"Just this," she said, producing a blue parka. "I believe it belonged to the monk."

"Yes, it did," Harry said. "Jing, I'm sorry for my outburst earlier. I'm just a little stressed, I guess."

"No problem, Dr. Harry," Jing said without meeting his gaze. "I understand."

"So, what's next, boss?" Li asked. "You still think we should follow these footprints? No telling where they will lead."

"I do think we should follow them. Like I said, we can't just leave the guy out here without attempting to find him. Besides, I would love to get a look at this thing, if, indeed, it is some sort of primate or Yeti as Jing insists. What do you think, Jing, are you up to it? I know it's more than you counted on."

"It's a grand adventure, to be sure," Jing said. "I don't have any pressing plans at the moment so, yes, I will tag along. But I warn you, I am not familiar with that part of the mountain."

She pointed in the direction of the footprints. "Maybe you can use your satellite phone to call the police in Ulaanbaatar and report that this monk is missing."

"I think we should wait on that, Jing. After all, we may find him wandering around out there. He could have gotten lost during the night and snowstorm."

Jing and Dixie nodded in agreement.

"Okay then. Let's gather our gear and get moving while the weather lasts. No telling when it might start to snow again."

"Up here at this altitude," Jing said, "and at this time of year, the weather can change in a matter of a few hours."

After packing and loading their gear, they followed the strange footprints. Their horses, plodding through the snow-pack, blew short breaths of steam from their nostrils. The tracks led in a serpentine fashion higher into the mountains, where, at times, the snow had drifted into three-foot piles, while in other places, tufts of grass poked through only a thin layer of white carpet. When the ground was visible, Harry noticed they were on a narrow trail that continued into a rocky portion of the mountain. The footprints were spaced around four feet apart making the creature, whatever it was, very tall. And heavy, for the prints were sunk deep into the snow.

They crossed a trickle of water that splattered over rocks above them and spewed over the trail. Small tufts of green grass covered the path where the running water melted the snow. Rounding a bend to the north, they began to climb a series of wide step-like tiers that slowed their progress. The horses panted hard and, upon reaching a plateau, they decided to let them rest awhile. The snow was deeper now and the footprints more visible, still leading upward. Jing dismounted and checked everyone's saddle cinches before the group continued on.

Above the plateau, the going was more difficult, the route steeper. They crept along with Jing leading them past a series of switchbacks and, as they snaked their way higher, Harry wondered where their trek was going to end.

The mountain peaks were closer and loomed menacingly over them like birds of prey, waiting for them to make a mistake. Just one slip. One fall. But they continued upward.

At last, they reached a small clearing and decided to make camp for the night. Daylight was fading and the sky shown in brilliant shades of orange and indigo. They had settled into a routine with Li and Dixie starting a fire, Jing manning the stove, and Harry constructing the lean-to.

That night as the fire crackled, the stars shimmered with the brilliance of large blue-white diamonds. Later, as a yellow moon rose over the basin to the east, the wind died to a light breeze, making for a beautiful night. Dixie sat beside Harry while the group talked of their plans for the future.

"I very much would like to get a master's degree," Jing said. "I want to teach at the university. I enjoy teaching children but my dream is to teach at the university I attended. What about you, Li?"

Li laughed. "I have no plans for the future. I like working with the research team because I believe it is important work. And I am well paid. My parents want me to do something useful, like banking or the law. Beyond that, it is, as we Buddhists say, in simply being that I find happiness."

"A noble calling, to be sure, Li," Dixie said. "As for me, my plans are to finish my damned dissertation and get my doctorate."

Jing and Li laughed at Dixie's wording. Harry didn't add anything to the conversation. He just stared at the moon and thought of Dixie.

# Chapter 17

Arriving in Tenduk, Doyle and his men rode straight to the monastery. They had ridden all night through a snowstorm and he was cold and hungry, his patience for their mission wearing thin. Doyle pounded on the large doors until a small boy opened them. Grabbing the boy by the collar, he demanded to see whomever was in charge of the place.

"Get the boss man here now, boy. And be quick about it."

He shoved the boy away and watched him dart inside the temple and disappear. He pulled his 9 millimeter pistol from its holster and signaled for Gillum to do the same. The group waited inside the temple doors while Doyle paced about, grumbling.

"What if they're not here?" asked Marley who, still at the bottom of the steps, held the reins to Doyle's and Gillum's horse.

"Then we find out which direction they went and take out after them," Doyle said, a notable irritation in his voice.

He continued to pace and curse.

A man in a brown robe appeared in the doorway. He bowed. "*Namasta*, travelers," he said.

"Stop with that crap," Doyle said and shoved his pistol in the monk's face.

The man in the robe recoiled, stumbling, at the sight of the gun.

"Are the Americans here, old man?"

The monk hesitated, shooting furtive glances at Doyle then the men with him. Doyle waved his pistol in front of the man.

"Don't make me ask again," he said.

The monk shook his head. "They are not here," he said. The monk turned to go back inside the temple but Gillum blocked his way.

"Which way did they go?" Doyle asked, continuing the inquisition.

Again the monk shook his head.

Doyle crashed the butt of his pistol into the monk's forehead causing blood to spurt down the man's face. He hissed. "Dammit, man. I asked you, which did they go when they left here?"

The monk said nothing. His eyes blinked wildly as they filled with blood.

Doyle noticed the small boy looking beyond the knoll on which the monastery sat to a ridgeline behind the village. The boy pointed in that direction. "They went up that way," he said.

"Thanks for nothing, old man." Doyle placed his pistol to the man's temple and pulled the trigger.

લ્જીજ્જી

The Russian Mi-24 Hind helicopter touched down in the Altai Basin next to the research compound. Captain Stepan bolted onto the steppe under the still-whirling rotors then waited while the rest of his six-man team exited the aircraft. People from the site began gathering around the helicopter, creating a buzz that Stepan could not make out clearly. As the aircraft noise lessened, he noticed a young Mongolian man wave as he approached them.

"My name is Cheng," he said. "I am the foreman of this research site. What is going on?"

"Good morning," Stepan said. "I am Captain Stepan of the National Police. Is there somewhere we can talk?"

Cheng led Stepan and his men to the command tent and, when everyone was seated around the table, the captain continued. "We are looking for a group of Americans. They may be coming here to disrupt your research. We really don't know. They may want something you have dug up. Have any strangers showed up here recently?"

"Actually, yes," said Cheng. "Four men were here several days ago looking for Dr. Olson, our expedition leader. I told them they had gone to Tenduk and they left. They had guns. We were very frightened. Is Dr. Olson okay?"

"That is not known at present. Why was this Dr. Olson going to Tenduk?"

The captain's men fanned out from the command tent and began searching the compound.

"This is an anthropological research project. We are searching for human ancestors here. Dr. Olson and his assistants went to the monastery in Tenduk to view something related to our research, possibly a skull of some sort. They never confided in me, Captain. I just overheard two of them talking. Earlier in the week, we unearthed a plane and some bones were in it."

"An airplane? What kind?"

"A Soviet transport plane. I can take you to it if you like. It's not far from the compound."

"Have you reported this to the defense ministry?"

"I believe Dr. Olson was going to do that, yes. I do not know if he has done so, however. May I offer you and your men some tea, Captain?"

"That would be nice, thank you. We will be going soon. I wish to be at this monastery before dark but I want to see this crash site before I leave."

After tea, Cheng led Stepan to the hole containing the Soviet airplane. The captain scrambled through the battered wreckage before returning empty-handed. "What a grisly scene in the cockpit," he said. "To think they have been sitting there, strapped in their seats, all these years. I wonder when it crashed."

"Before the Soviet Union dissolved. We found a Soviet pilot's cap as well."

"You say there were bones in this wreckage? Did I hear that right?"

"Yes, Captain. Some sort of bones. What they were or are I cannot say. But Dr. Olson and Dixie were very excited about them."

"Dixie?"

"Yes. Dr. Olson's assistant. They called their boss back in America after we found the bones. That is about all I know, Captain."

Stepan started back to the command tent with Cheng at his side. The two men were the same height but the captain struck an imposing figure in his uniform.

Men and women workers were still milling about staring at the police officers and their military helicopter. Inside the tent, one of his men studied an aeronautical chart and conferred with Stepan upon his return.

"We are about to have lunch, Captain," Cheng said. "You are more than welcome to join us."

"No thanks, we'll be off now. Thanks for the tea and answering my questions."

"What will become of these men you are after?" Cheng said.

"If, and when, we catch up with them, they will be arrested and taken back to Ulaanbaatar for further questioning. Did they harm any of your workers, Cheng?"

"No, just threatened us and scared us. I hope you catch them. Foreigners should not be allowed to break the law in our country."

"I agree, Cheng, I agree. Now listen to me. In the off chance that these men should return, do not try and be heroes. Give them whatever they demand then call for help after they leave. Keep your sentries posted at night."

Stepan scurried to the waiting chopper and, at his approach, its twin turbines started winding up. His men followed behind. After they boarded the aircraft, it lifted several feet into the air, hovered for a few seconds, then rose and sped northwest.

Cheng watched it until it had disappeared over the farthest ridge.

ඏඏඏ

Harry was up before everyone and sat alone in front of the fire he had stoked into life. The sun was not yet up and the fire felt good. Before retiring the night before, he had tried without success to reach Max on the satellite phone. The morning found him thinking about his mother and what might be happening back home. He filled Jing's copper teapot with water from a canteen and set it on the portable stove. Leaning against his Mongolian saddle, he let his thoughts drift back to his mother and her condition. Not knowing her present state had left him fretful, and not being able to talk to Max, as hard as that was, made matters even more difficult. He decided to put the thoughts away and concentrate on present matters.

Like what had happened to the young monk? He certainly did not just walk off on his own. Harry was certain of that. There were obvious signs of a struggle and, in addition, there were the large footprints. But as the day wore on the tracks became less discernible because the wind began to erase all traces of them. Now they were in the midst of the great Altai Mountains, and a long way from their expedition site, with Harry having no idea where they actually were. He doubted Jing did either. What he wouldn't give for a map and compass. Or better still, a GPS. They left the one used for plotting the latitude and longitude of discovered artifacts back at the compound. What he wouldn't give for it now.

Should they give up searching for the monk and head back? Or should they continue on, in the face of mounting evidence that he had been abducted by a large creature? What were the possibilities that something other than an abduction had happened? If a large animal had killed the monk, wouldn't there be some of his remains still laying about? There surely would have been blood. And yet, there was none. What other explanation could there be? Harry's mind drew a blank.

Could it be a Yeti as Jing believed? His scientific mind told him it was impossible. Yet here was proof that something *did* live up here. Not all the tales could be false. *Something* unusual, inhuman, stalked these mountains. He might not know what it was but the Mongolian elders did.

Dixie sat beside him and Harry filled mugs of tea then

passed one to her. She looked beautiful, fresh and alive, hair askew, but radiant.

She noticed him looking at her and blushed. "I know, I must look a mess," she said, smoothing her hair. "When we get back to the States, I am going to soak in the tub for a week."

"Not in the least," Harry said. "I'm glad you came along."

Dixie smiled and took a sip of her tea. "I am too. What do you think happened to our monk friend?"

"He disappeared is all I know. I don't think it was his own doing, however. There were definite signs of a struggle back there. But no blood. And that's odd."

The rising sun was a large orange ball on the eastern horizon and the sky was clear. The air was warming. Li and Jing joined them around the stove.

They exchanged greetings and Jing fixed a breakfast of oatmeal while Harry and Li saddled and loaded the horses.

As they ate, Jing continued her earlier dialogue about Yeti. "I have always been skeptical, Dr. Olson. Most every one of my generation is. But seeing those footprints yesterday brought back the stories of my grandfather and my uncles. Suppose all the sightings and photographs of tracks are real, what then? Those footprints are certainly real, right? You tell me, Doctor, what do you make of them?"

Harry tossed his mug in the utensils bag and stood by Jing. "I don't know, yet. Those tracks are real, yes. But they could have been made by a bear or some other animal. The poor man could have had a fatal encounter with a wild animal."

"If it was a wild animal, where is the blood? Those weren't animal tracks and you know it, Doctor." The way she said *doctor* indicated that she didn't think he was being honest with them. "We all know it."

"You're saying you think the tracks belong to a Yeti?" Dixie asked.

Jing's eyes narrowed and a frown appeared on her face. "I'm saying that the evidence says they do, yes."

Li, who had been silent during these exchanges, shrugged his shoulders and looked at Harry. "So, boss, what is our next move now?"

"I think we need to try and find the damn thing, whatever it is. We might stumble across the monk in the process. He is still missing, you know."

"Count me out," Jing interjected. "That's a stupid thing to do," The force of her words stunned Harry. "I'm heading back."

"Let's suppose you're right, Jing. Think of the opportunity this is. If we could run across the thing, think what it would mean to science, to mankind."

"Thinking about making history, Harry? Is that it? You would put our lives at risk for that? For fame?"

Her words cut deep into Harry's soul. He had no response.

"Besides," she continued, "we have no weapons to defend ourselves. We might wind up like the monk. It's an insane idea to go after the thing. We need to return to the research site and notify the police."

"I think Jing is right," Li said. "I vote we turn around and go back."

Harry looked at Dixie who looked away and finished her tea.

"How about you, Dixie? What do you say?"

"Don't make me the deciding vote. You're my boss, Harry. I go with you. But don't make me choose."

Harry thought for a while, with the group loading their gear in silence. Finally after ten minutes, he stood. "Okay," he said. "We go back. Let's mount up and get moving."

On the way down the mountain, Harry argued with himself. In his heart, he knew going back was the right decision but he could not help thinking they were passing up a once-in-a-lifetime opportunity. Whatever the thing was, it walked upright and had human-looking feet. His scientific mind ached—no, longed—to find out what it was. Never mind personal risk, it could turn out to be a great discovery. And if the monk was still alive, they were leaving him behind.

Before mounting his horse, he had tried to reach Max but could not link up with the satellite. He tried getting through to Ulaanbaatar but could not do that, either. His mind was a jumble of emotions, making it difficult to think straight. Not having any news about Mother worried him. Had she died? Max hadn't answered the phone in two days.

Why?

Something was up, he was sure.

# Chapter 18

Kesler sat in his favorite chair in the study of his San Mateo home. From his study window, he could see the San Mateo Bridge that crossed the bay into Hayward. He had just talked to Sergeant Walcott, who informed him that he had notified INTERPOL who had then passed the information on to the Mongolian authorities. It was about all he could do for now, he said, without more to go on from Kesler himself.

The cars passing over the bridge looked like tiny insects from Kesler's vantage point. A delicate haze hung over the bay, muting the water's color to a dull gray. He glanced at the pictures of his parents in an antique pewter frame beside his chair. It was a photograph of them garbed in the old world clothing of their native Lithuania, his father with a somber countenance, and his mother smiling. He could not remember leaving the country during the Nazi invasion but his adopted mother retold the story often enough that he could recite it from memory. His father had been an optician, a maker of glasses, a trade that had provided a comfortable living. His mother was a seamstress and made fashionable dresses for up-scale debutantes. When the Nazis invaded, they dissolved the country's government and used the Lithuanian army to execute Lithuanian Jews. When large numbers of their fellow countrymen were sent to Germany, his father attempted to find smugglers to get them to Russia, hoping to sell their jewelry to finance a Trans-Siberian Railway trip across Russia and a sea voyage from Vladivostok to Vancouver, Canada. But, unfortunately, this father's contact turned him in to the Gestapo and they arrested his parents and deported them to a concentration camp. Upon his father's arrest, his mother took little Julius to a friendly couple who took the boy into their home as their own. Kesler remembered the German soldiers pounding on their door and dragging his father away. He also remembered his mother's terrified look. He never saw his mother after going to live with the family's neighbor. After the Russians annexed the country, driving the Nazis out at the close of the war, they began deporting masses of Lithuanians to Siberia. Kesler and his new parents managed to make their way to the US-controlled sector of Germany and from there to America.

The phone rang. It was Harry.

"Where have you been, my boy? I've been trying to reach you for days," Kesler's demanded in a loud voice.

"Professor, we are on a trek into the mountains. Examined an old skull of some sort of primate or hominoid, don't know which. I'm sitting on a ridge right now. We are heading back to the research compound."

"Harry, when I couldn't reach you, I went to the police and they have contacted INTERPOL and the Mongolian authorities about the men who kidnapped me. Are you all safe and sound?"

"Calm down, Professor, we are all fine. A little tired perhaps but fine. I'll fill you it when we get back to the site."

"As long as you assure me everyone is safe, Harry. It's hell being halfway around the world. Hopefully, the local authorities there are taking action."

"Like I said, Professor, we are all fine."

"Well, I had to hear your voice. Is Dixie with you?"

"Yes, she is, and she is fine as well. Relax. When we get back to the compound, I'll give you all the details. We've had an interesting few days."

"Those bastards that roughed me up may be in Mongolia so, Harry, I worry a lot. Just be careful, please."

"We will, Doctor Kesler, I promise."

After hanging up, Kesler sat and watched the haze over the

bay get thicker, until the far shore disappeared from view. Harry's predicament saddened him. The young man had made a dreadful mistake and it had stunned Kesler. He couldn't believe that Harry had falsified data in an academic journal and over a theory that mattered very little. Feeling betrayed by his star pupil and assistant, Kesler had isolated his feelings and had emotionally distanced himself. But during the past year, he'd observed what the mistake had cost Harry. His pride and self-respect were gone. The man still possessed a brilliant mind. He appeared to have learned from the mistake. Only he, Julius Kesler, knew the complete story and he was resolved to see that Harry was made whole again.

Satisfied with the phone call, he ambled into the kitchen to fix his dinner.

⌒⌒⌒

Doyle and his men were traveling along a winding trail leading higher into the Altai Mountains in the general direction they had seen the boy point. Whether it was the correct direction, Doyle didn't know and the uncertainty unnerved and angered him. What angered him more was the complete breakdown of his self-control when he shot the monk. What the hell had he been thinking? He knew what the men were thinking—how their leader couldn't control himself in the heat of their mission. Now his preaching concerning bloodshed would fall on deaf ears, especially Kurt's. *When Eastwood learns of the two murders, he is going to be madder than hell.*

They wormed their way, single file, with Doyle in the lead, their horses plodding nose to tail. The path followed a small brook that cascaded in brisk, dark ripples to the basin below. At a broad ledge overlooking the peaks of Belukha and Kuitan, Doyle called a halt to their progress and dismounted. Gillum, Kurt, and Marley followed suit. The sun was out, the mist burning off the mountains.

"Where the hell are we?" growled Marley, pacing along the edge of the ridge.

"I have no idea," Doyle said. He retrieved his map from a

saddlebag and, kneeling, unfolded it on the ground. Gillum squatted beside him. "Here is Tenduk," Doyle continued, pointing a finger on the map. "We have been traveling in this direction here, along this small stream, so we should be somewhere near this point right here. Agree, Gillum?"

Doyle's assistant squinted at the point on the map and nodded. "Sounds about right," he said.

"Look here," Marley said from a short distance away.

Doyle and Gillum joined Marley who was pointing at the ground. "Look at all these tracks in the mud here. Must have been made in the snow and it melted, making mud."

Doyle studied the tracks for a while. "Something happened here," he said. "A scuffle, or a struggle, something like that. Horse tracks lead up that way."

"What's this kind of track?" Marley asked. He was pointing to a different-looking track, a footprint.

"Looks like a track of a large person. A large, barefooted human." Kurt broke his silence. "But why would they be barefooted up here?"

Doyle walked back to their horses. "Beats me but those tracks must belong to the research team. I can feel it. Let's go."

ლ৩ლ

Captain Stepan viewed the corpse at the Tenduk monastery, studied the single bullet wound to the man's head. According to the account told by abbot Zhing, the old monk had been murdered execution style on the temple steps. His brothers had brought the dead man to his room until the monastery could notify the authorities. It was fortuitous luck that the captain's helicopter landed just as abbot Zhing was making the call.

"He was such a kind man," Zhing said. "He meant so much to the monastery and to all of us. He was my Dharma teacher many years ago when I was a novitiate. We will all miss him."

Stepan shook his head at the senseless violence. "What were the circumstances surrounding his murder?"

A small lantern lit the room and the monks who crowded in it made it stuffy.

"Four Americans arrived, asking questions about the research team that had been here a day earlier. I was in the maintenance office when it happened. The other monks were going about their usual afternoon duties. When Lama Pu Yang did not answer, the big one shot him. The others had guns as well. They had an evil look about them, sir. I heard the shot, ran to the front, and saw them mounting their horses. Lama Yang was lying there and blood was all over his face. He didn't move. I knew he was dead."

Stepan examined the rest of the monk's body, satisfying himself there were no other signs of injury. He covered the man with his brown robe.

"Can you describe them?"

"The big one, the one who shot lama Yang, had scars on his face. All of them wore black. They looked mean."

"Scars," Stepan said, thinking on what the monk had said. "All right, clear this room and lock the door." The captain began moving everyone out of the lama's room. "Where can we talk further, abbot?" When settled into a chair in the main monastery office, Stepan continued to question Zhing. "Why was the research team up here? Their site is down on the steppe."

Zhing sat behind a small primitive desk, surrounded by statues of the Buddha and paintings of Khan history. He poured two small cups of tea and offered one to Stepan. Then he took a sip of the liquid and eyed the captain. "They were here to examine a certain relic in our possession," he said. "After doing so, they left. The doctor said they were going to return to their compound."

"Relic? What kind of relic? A skull perhaps?"

Zhing shifted in his chair and toyed with his teacup. "I'd rather not say, unless it is absolutely necessary."

"Abbot Zhing, a murder has been committed here and this is not the eighteenth century. Yes, it is quite necessary." Stepan's voice was hard and cold as steel.

"Of course. Yes, it was a skull they came to see," Zhing

said and, with that, the captain raised his eyebrows. "But it is not a human skull."

"A skull of some animal? A Buddhist holy artifact?"

"Not quite, Captain. People who live up here in the mountains claim it is of a Yeti. This Dr. Olson and other members of his team came to examine it."

Stepan blinked then stared. "You serious?"

"Yes. A Yeti. People say it is the skull of a wild man, an Alma, a Yeti."

"People up here in the mountains still believe in those tall tales?"

"Old habits die hard, sir. Some of our fellow monks here believe the creatures exist."

"So, after examining this skull, this doctor just left?" The captain's expression did not change.

"His woman assistant was with him and two other people on the research team."

"So they left. Where were they going?"

"Like I said, I believe they were returning to their research site. Have you been there?"

"Yes. They were not there. Probably on the trail somewhere. So the murdering Americans are, in all likelihood, pursuing them. How far behind the doctor are they?"

"A day. They arrived here the day after the doctor and his group left."

Stepan and the monk returned to the front doors of the monastery. Stepan turned to a sergeant standing near the two men and gave a circling motion with his index finger. "Wind up the chopper, Sergeant. Inform the pilot we are airborne in a few minutes."

The man saluted and ran off in the direction of the helicopter.

Stepan resumed his discussion with the abbot. "You may bury your friend now. And we will go and search the mountainside for these murderers."

"He will be cremated, Captain, and his ashes we will store in our relic room. It is our highest honor."

"I understand. If need be, we will return and borrow horses at the village. So long."

He turned to leave but the abbot grabbed him by his elbow. "Our people are always willing to help the police. If I can be of help in the future, you can find me here or have Tenduk's mayor call me. Good luck."

Stepan returned to his waiting helicopter and climbed aboard. As the aircraft lifted off the grassy knoll, he watched the small monastery get smaller and smaller.

ℰↃℰↃ

Harry and Li finished setting up the lean-to while the women got a fire started and put the copper pot on the stove for tea. Harry unloaded the horses and laid their saddles by the fire. The campsite was in a grassy gorge, off the trail that cut through the shallow neck of a knoll. A rock-covered ridge on the one side, which blocked the gentle breeze that had sprung up late that afternoon, sheltered it. When the tea was ready, all but Harry gathered around the campfire.

"I still cannot believe our monk has disappeared," Jing said, taking a long drink of the steaming liquid.

"Neither can I," said Li.

Harry, carrying a bundle of firewood and hearing that the talk was about the monk, interrupted.

"Listen, all. He's gone. Where, we don't know. Carried off by that…thing…most likely. We don't know if he is alive or dead, but we need to get a good night's sleep then make it back to the compound as quick as we can. We have to report this."

"That thing was a Yeti, Dr. Olson," Jing said. "It doesn't matter if you believe or agree or not. I know what it was." Jing's voice shook with emotion as she spoke.

"We don't know any such thing, Jing. I was upset earlier but now, listen. Just who the creature was or is remains pure speculation and all this talk fuels needless worry. Why you insist that it must be a Yeti is beyond my comprehension. A few days ago, you were telling me how these stories were just tales, birthed from fertile imaginations, and that they couldn't possibly be true. Now you seem to have changed your mind, all because of a few tracks in the snow. I would appreciate it if you would refrain from such mindless gossip."

Harry stared at Jing until she looked away and started their supper. He was in a foul mood and wasn't interested in prolonged conversation about the missing monk. Hoping for a quick meal, he planned to crawl into his sleeping bag and stay there until morning. The evening sky was turning from a light purple to a dull gray, and golden eagles were soaring through the thin air.

Dixie came and sat beside him. "You don't need to bite her head off, Harry," she said. "Jing comes from a culture that believes Yetis do exist. Her uncles and grandfather saw something they claimed was the creature. And she led us to a skull that supposedly belonged to a Yeti. You can't blame her for that."

"I know, I know. The missing monk has put my nerves on edge. The sooner we get back to the compound, the better. At first I wanted to see where those tracks led, but now I think we need to call the National Police."

"Then that's what we'll do. Just try to be patient with the people we ask to help us is all I'm asking. Understand?"

"I do," Harry said. He accepted a bowl of dried vegetable soup from Jing and smiled at her, touching her arm with his free hand. "Jing, forgive my impertinence. I shouldn't have lost my temper. Please forgive me."

"Yes, Dr. Olson. I will try to not mention the Yeti again."

That night, after the group retired to their sleeping bags, Harry lay awake, sleep not forthcoming. He tossed and turned, long after the others were breathing regularly. His mind was a jumble of thoughts of his mother, the monk, Yetis, and Dixie. And Jing. He had hurt her feelings, he knew. For the rest of the evening, she sat silent, sipping her tea, looking at the stars. The fact that his research had been interrupted by this Yeti business unnerved Harry. It was a distraction to the main purpose of the expedition and his career. He wanted dearly to leave this place with enough artifacts to eventually provide material for an earth-shattering scientific paper, one that would redeem his reputation in the professor's eyes. Was that such a horrible, selfish goal? He was tiring of fieldwork and hoped the Mongolian dig would be the last he would be required to endure. Someday, Professor Kesler would retire and Harry hoped to fill his shoes. A monumental discovery would cement his place as *heir apparent*. And maybe repair their damaged relationship. But now, what else would slow his progress, and threaten to derail the research? Harry had a distressing premonition that something dreadful was about to happen.

And when the sun rose in the morning, it had.

Dixie was missing.

# Chapter 19

Eastwood was in a foul mood. He had just received a call from Garrett Sawyers, informing him the president would be choosing someone else to head his commission on charitable organizations. Eastwood sat behind his desk and toyed with a cigar before finally lighting it. He'd wanted this appointment like he had wanted nothing else in a long time. It would have meant a great deal of welcome publicity for BioGen, whose detractors had been increasing, amid spurious rumors, after the Saudi deal.

It was unfortunate that his parents were no longer alive to appreciate what he had accomplished with BioGen and the wealth he had accumulated. His father, a tough, grizzled veteran of the depression and Second World War, would be proud, no doubt. But with his mother, he wasn't so sure. She had wanted him to be a musician, to play the violin like Isaac Stern. He remembered listening to those records of the master violinist while he fell asleep each night. No, he wasn't so sure that his mother would be proud of him.

He took a deep puff on the cigar and endeavored to calm the growing apprehension that mounted inside him. He had not heard from Doyle in several days and had no idea what was happening with his team. Not knowing was worse than having to deal with a problem. He prided himself at his ability to make quick decisions but, at present, there were no decisions to make. He was left to wallow in his chair, waiting for the next shoe to fall. Reacting. Since Vietnam, he had schooled himself in being proactive, creating, not reacting to whatever life handed him. Waiting for Doyle to call was a formidable task.

He didn't know what had been discovered in Mongolia but whatever it was, the professor in California said it had the possibility of being something monumental. Eastwood's knowledge of archeology or paleontology was limited but, most often, he could determine the value of things and evaluate a market for potential buyers. In a way, he was glad that this was happening in Mongolia. If killing became necessary, it would be good to have it happen in a third-rate, backward country, where it would be difficult for the authorities to trace it back to him. The thought, however, did not make the waiting any easier.

He studied the map of Mongolia on his desk and tried to pinpoint Doyle's last known position. It was imprecise, for his security chief had never given him exact coordinates. He took a deep puff on the cigar and exhaled slowly blowing smoke over the map. *Give me a call, Doyle. Give me a call and let me know where you are.*

؏؟؏؟؏

The Russian helicopter circled a small group on horseback riding along a ridgeline next to a rocky gorge. They were in single file and Stepan noticed that each person shot a glance skyward as the chopper buzzed overhead. He directed the pilot to land on a small knoll next to the ridge and as, they descended, the group halted and dismounted.

On the ground, Stepan commanded his troops to exit the aircraft with their weapons at the ready. He could not tell if these people were the scientific team or the American murderers. He drew his pistol and jumped to the ground, while his men fanned out around him.

A man approached him with a woman following close behind. Stepan took a deep breath and relaxed as he realized this was the group of scientists.

"At ease men," he said. "Stow your weapons." Captain

Stepan faced the man leading his group. "I am Captain Stepan of the National Police. You are Dr..."

"Dr. Olson. I am the scientific leader of a research team excavating at the base of these mountains. Am I glad to see you. Glad you speak English."

"Glad to see us?" Stepan replied, ignoring the *English* comment.

"Two of our team are missing. My assistant, Dixie Zinn and—"

"When did this happen?" Stepan said. The whine of the chopper's turbines were winding down, making conversation easier. "You mentioned two people are missing?"

"A monk from a nearby monastery was traveling with us."

"When did this happen?" Stepan repeated.

"My assistant disappeared sometime last night. When we woke up this morning, she was gone. We searched all around our campsite but there was no sign of her. The monk disappeared several days ago. There were signs of a struggle at that camp. We were on our way back to our compound to notify the authorities."

"Where was your last night's campsite?"

"Only about a mile back up the trail."

"I would like to look around. Can you show us? I can walk beside your horses."

"Absolutely, Captain. Follow us and we will take you there. Why are you in these mountains, sir?"

"Actually, Doctor, it is for your and your group's safety that we have flown all this way. I will explain on the way."

こうこう

Harry could not believe their good fortune at having the police land right in front of them. He led Stepan to the previous night's campsite and showed the captain where the lean-to was located. The small frame structure looked eerie, abandoned and alone. Stepan strolled the area, looking for clues of her disappearance. The ground was barren of any sign that might shed light on what had happened to his assistant. Harry caught up with him some distance from the campsite, where he was squatting, peering off in the distance.

"She just up and disappeared as best as I can figure," Harry said. "She and the monk both, but something happened to the monk 'cause there were signs of a struggle with him. And strange footprints led away from the site of the struggle. Jing here thinks it was a Yeti."

"A Yeti?" Stepan said, eyes wide, alert. "Really? Have you all seen anything up here?"

"No, nothing. Just the large footprints where the monk disappeared. What are you doing way up here, Captain?"

Harry and Stepan walked back to the horses. The sun was up and the air was warming.

"We had a report of a group of Americans in this region looking for you and your team."

Harry stopped short.

"Really? Why?"

"Had something to do with your excavation. Have you uncovered something important?"

"Not really. Just some old bones and a few teeth that we don't know what they are. Might turn out to be important, might not. It's too early to say right now. How do you know all this?"

"We have just come from there, Doctor. I talked to an abbot...Zhing, I believe. Apparently, these men are after whatever you have found and they will stop at nothing to get their hands on it. They must believe it is worth a lot of money. They have been to your compound and terrorized your team and foreman. After learning that you were headed to the Tenduk monastery, they followed and murdered a monk there."

Foul-tasting bile formed in Harry's mouth, along with a sudden knot in his stomach. "Are you kidding? Surely not. Which one?"

Li fell to his knees and Jing began sobbing.

"The older senior monk. Yang, I believe, was his name. When I first began this mission, Doctor, I didn't know what to think. A lot of our INTERPOL alerts turn out to be false leads or outright mistakes. But after I spoke with your foreman and, from what I saw at the monastery, I do believe these men are out to do your team harm, possibly murder every one of you. I believe you and your team are in grave danger."

Stunned, Harry was at a loss for words. Lama Yang had convinced Zhing to allow them access to the skull. He was a kind and gentle man. But, as Harry was about to ask Stepan what they should do, one of the captain's men came running up and saluted.

"Sir, I found something back there," the man said, pointing off in the direction of the ridge.

"Okay, Corporal, lead the way and show me."

Harry followed the two men with Li and Jing close behind. When they reached a clearing in a field of low-lying brush Harry found several of the captain's SWAT team members standing over a series of footprints in the sandy soil. Stepan studied them for a minute then turned to Harry. "Look at these, Doctor. Look familiar? You mentioned seeing footprints when the monk disappeared."

Harry bent down in order to get a closer look. There were a series of human-looking footprints similar to what he had seen before. Large, humanoid prints. "Yes," he said. "Exactly like the other day."

"Any ideas, Doctor?"

"Originally, I thought an animal of some sort, maybe a bear or something like that. But they're too large."

"I think they look like they belong to a large human. You don't?" Stepan said.

Before Harry could answer Jing stepped forward, her eyes flashing. "It's like I said. It belongs to the Yeti. They live higher up but come to lower elevations in search of food. You may not believe, as I did not believe, but this is proof. They live."

Captain Stepan stared at Jing for a moment then paced around the footprints, hands on his hips, thinking. "The bottom line is that we have two people missing. I need to report to my colonel and then we will see what is next. In all likelihood, he will want me to investigate these disappearances. Excuse me while I get to the radio and check in."

Without waiting for Harry's reply, Stepan walked over to the helicopter and climbed aboard. Harry marched about the tracks, casting periodic glances in their direction.

Li joined him. "Doctor, this is nasty business. Dixie was my friend. I can't believe something has happened to her."

"Neither can I, Li. But it has. I just hope and pray she is all right."

"She used to laugh at my attempts at American slang. If I used a word in the wrong way, it made her laugh. Not at me personally, just the way I said it. Her laugh made me happy."

"I know, Li. She makes me happy, too. And on top of that, the captain says there is a group out here wanting to do us harm, steal our relics. It's getting to be too much."

"But we don't know if what we've uncovered so far is worth anything at all, Harry."

"That's it, though, isn't it? You said it—*so far*. Who knows? Later, after we have finished with all the scientific study, they might be worth a lot."

When the captain returned he smiled. "We will fly back to Tenduk, obtain some horses, and get on the trail. Dr. Olson, can you all wait here until we catch back up with you? We can then proceed together. I want to follow these tracks."

Harry turned to Jing, who nodded. "Yes, we can do that," he said.

"How long will it take us to get back here, do you think?"

"Three to four hours, probably. Depends on how long it takes you to find horses."

"We'll try to rent them, of course. Hopefully, that won't take too long."

Harry watched Stepan and his SWAT team board the helicopter and take to the sky. In a few seconds, the chopper was gone, leaving him, Li, and Jing in silence. Li pulled the saddles off their horses and hobbled them so they wouldn't wander off while grazing.

Jing wanted tea so she set to making a fire.

Harry strolled down to where the tracks were located, trying hard to reconcile their meaning. Unable to fathom their origins, he returned to the campfire and retrieved his satellite phone. He knew the professor would be in bed but he needed to talk to him.

"Sorry to wake you, Professor," Harry said when he had Kesler on the line. "Something terrible has happened and you need to know."

Harry could hear Kesler fumbling with the phone then, in a sleepy voice, he answered. "Yes, Harry. What is it?"

Harry thought his voice sounded far off, even frail. "It's Dixie, she's disappeared." The words came with difficulty for him.

"Wh—what? She's what?"

"Disappeared. When we woke this morning, she was gone. No trace of her leaving. It's horrible. I can't believe it."

Kesler sounded more alert now, his voice stronger. "The police. Have you notified the police?"

"Well, actually, they have been here."

Harry brought Kesler up to date with Stepan's arrival and his reason for being there. He told him about the monk disappearing and the murder at the monastery. He told him about the Americans on their tail and their terrorizing the expedition compound. After a long discussion about the events of the previous days, Harry waited for Kesler to say something else but there was silence on the professor's end.

Finally the man spoke. "I guess I need to inform Dixie's parents. It's going to be a shock. No one ever expects anything like this to happen on a scientific expedition. I will have to inform the university, as well. Do the police have any ideas as to what might have happened?"

Harry didn't know how to answer Kesler's question. He had his suspicions and Jing certainly thought she knew what had happened to Dixie and the monk. Should he relay those thoughts and fears to his boss? Dixie could have just wandered off and gotten lost. He decided to tell all he knew. "At both places where the monk and Dixie went missing, we found large, human-like footprints. Looked exactly like a human, but much bigger. Where the monk disappeared there were signs of a struggle. That's about all any of us know for sure right now."

"My God," Kesler said. His voice sounded far off again.

"You know, Harry, what they say lurks in those mountains and in the Himalayas, don't you? I have been talking with a cryptozoologist and he thinks they could be real. Just because science hasn't proven otherwise is no reason—"

"I know what they say," Harry interjected, cutting Kesler short.

"Harry, listen to me. It would fit with the bones and teeth you found, don't you see? Those bones were of a larger than human primate or hominid. You have seen footprints of a large hominid. What other possibilities could there be?"

"Professor." Harry tried to sound calm, even though his pulse was going through the roof. "There are three possibilities, as I see it. One, we have uncovered a new species of hominid, one larger than humans or Neanderthals. Two, we have found a different branch of the Neanderthal line, one that survives to this day, and one that evolved much larger than its predecessors. And, finally, there's the remote possibility that a creature like the Yeti exists and it has abducted Dixie and the monk. Personally, I favor the first possibility and discount the Yeti theory. However, the police are here and together we are going to follow the tracks we have found. I won't leave this country without finding Dixie."

When Harry finished there was a pause until Kesler spoke. "Harry, for God's sake, be careful."

"Don't worry, Professor. You can count on it."

❧❧❧

Jing was sitting on the ground, leaning against her saddle, thinking of the events of the past few days. She was tormented by recent events. After completing her studies at the university, Jing considered herself an educated person, a person not given to believing folk tales and mountain legends. But, as a child of Mongolia, she had heard the tales of the Yeti most of her life and, although in adulthood she never gave them much credence, they lurked in the hidden recesses of her mind. In her subconscious. She realized that being a Westerner made Dr. Olson much more skeptical when it came to these stories.

And him being a scientist added to his unwillingness to accept what she now considered fact. There were beasts in these mountains, wild men.

Harry, as everyone called him, seemed to Jing to be a nice guy but totally involved in his work. In the few days of knowing him, she admired the way he worked with his subordinates, a leader but treating everyone as equals with an easy sense of humor. She had noticed the way Dixie acted around him and looked at him. Women noticed these things and understood. The pair worked well together. Dixie seemed more inclined to believe in the existence of the Yeti than the doctor, Li, or the police captain, and Jing wondered why. Maybe she was not as ensconced in her profession as Harry. Or maybe it was a woman thing. Jing was amazed at the turnabout in her own thinking regarding the creature's existence. It had happened overnight but, seeing the tracks coupled with the disappearance of Dixie and the monk, had convinced her. The beasts were no longer legends to her, no longer just tales heard by a frightened child. And the longer they stayed in these mountains, the more Dr. Olson would come to embrace the truth as she had. Eventually he would become the believer she was.

# Chapter 20

On a windy ridge, overlooking a vast series of rolling hills interspersed with rocky ledges, Doyle stood with raised binoculars. Beside him were Gillum, Kurt, and Marley. The sun had passed its zenith, and it was on its downward arc, filling the valley below with elongated shadows. Their horses grazed methodically on the few parcels of grass sprouting on the ridge.

He pointed and passed the binoculars to Gillum. "There they are," he said. "See them? They are perched right next to that rocky gorge off to your right."

Gillum turned and began looking in the direction Doyle commanded. "There's only three of them," Gillum said. "I thought there were four."

"Let me see," Doyle said, jerking the binoculars away from his assistant.

After several minutes of looking, Gillum spoke. "Do you see a fourth person?"

"No, I don't. There were four of them. The doctor, his female assistant, and two others. But there are only three of them there."

As Doyle returned to the horses, he heard voices and a horse whinny right below them. He signaled for Gillum to be quiet and to move the horses into the brush nearby. Doyle crawled behind a rock then strained to locate the source of the voices. Peering around the boulder, he looked over the edge of the ridge and saw them—men on horseback. He scanned back to the first group who seemed to be waiting for someone or something. One man appeared to be talking on a phone. Back below him, Doyle watched the other group of men on horseback. They stopped, jumped off their mounts, and fanned out over the edge of the rocky gorge. Doyle watched the scene unfold at a distance below him where two men were talking.

Gillum and Marley crouched beside Doyle while Kurt remained with the horses.

"Who are they?" Gillum said softly.

"I have no idea," Doyle said. "They are wearing black fatigues, see that?"

"Yeah. We could pick them off real easy from here boss," Marley said. "Want me to get the rifles?"

"Don't be a fool," Doyle commanded in a sharp tone. He continued to study what was happening below. "We wait, for now."

The men on the ridge below Doyle now mounted their animals and began plodding across the mountainside. They were heading toward the group ahead of them. Doyle put the binoculars down then, in a rush, bolted to where their horses were waiting.

"Mount up," he said. "We're following."

ℰᴑℰᴑ

Li took a mug of strong tea from Jing and sat beside her while Harry talked to the professor. He looked at her oval face and her dark eyes smiled back at him.

"So, Jing, you really think this creature is a Yeti?" he said.

"Like I said earlier, Li, at one time I thought it was all just rumor, wild tales. But, now, I have changed my mind, yes."

"What changed it?"

"I think those footprints did it. Actually seeing the footprints made a huge difference for me. And of course, Dixie and the monk disappearing where the footprints were did a lot, as well."

"What more can you tell me about these creatures, Jing?"

Harry was still on the satellite phone, pacing back and forth.

"Li, I grew up hearing about these beasts. For many years, the legend of the Yeti remained confined to a remote area, where they worshiped it, inscribed it in scrolls, and represented it in an annual festival. The Yeti is vaguely mentioned in ancient writings, perhaps first by Alexander the Great. He would have liked to have one, but the native people told him that the creature was unable to breathe properly at lower altitudes. They told him they had human-like bodies and, because of their swiftness, could only be caught when they were ill or old.

"You know in the Altai foothills there are lush, overgrown valleys. My grandfather used to tell me that strange-looking animals roamed these valleys. They were covered with shaggy hair and had a long horse's tail. When left to themselves they stayed in the forest and ate tree sprouts. But when they heard the noise of approaching hunters and the barking of dogs, they ran with incredible speed to hide in the mountain caves. They were masters at mountain climbing."

"I, too, have heard such tales," Li said. "But I never gave them much thought."

"Yellow skin below matted hair, extremely robust body, cone-shaped head, and an oddly human stance—this is the common description of the Yeti. As with most strange beings, people have attempted to link it with a presumed extinct prehistoric animal and have succeeded in doing so. The similarities between the Yeti and what is known as the giant ape is almost uncanny. This ape, with proportions that coincide with those of the Yeti, was discovered in the unlikeliest of places—a jar full of teeth in a Chinese medicine shop. Later, a jawbone of this beast was found in a Mongolian cave. When compared with the jaw of a gorilla, the proportions of this monstrous creature were almost identical. Or so my grandfather said. I was a young child when I heard these tales, so they made quite an impression on me."

"Wow," said Li. "I had no idea. And I'm Mongolian like you." He finished his tea and stood.

"The Yeti have been part of the Altai culture for centuries,

Li. It is a fact that I don't think Dr. Olson truly comprehends or appreciates. Or wants to."

Li smiled at her. "Is there a man in your life, Jing?"

"No. I haven't had the time or the inclination, Li, teaching school in the mountains. Most all the young people have left for the cities, the good looking ones, anyway." They both laughed and Jing's eyes sparkled. "How about you?" she said.

"I have a girlfriend in Ulaanbaatar," Li said. "She works in a tourist office. I hope we can get married after I am finished with the expedition."

"I hope nothing else happens," Jing said.

☙❧

After hanging up with Kesler, Harry joined Li and Jing and took the mug of tea she handed him. It was nearing the middle of the afternoon, so Stepan and his SWAT team should be returning at any moment. As soon as they arrived, Harry wanted to be on their way, so he paced about, waiting. Together, the three of them chatted about Dixie.

"She was a good team member," Li said. "Never shirked a task."

"I liked her a lot," Jing added. "She was always happy, always smiling."

"Yeah, as if she knew something that the rest of us didn't," Harry said. "I could always count on her."

Li fumbled with his parka zipper and looked at Harry. "Do you think she could have gotten up to use the bathroom and wandered off?" Li said.

"We searched all around here and found nothing."

"But we didn't find those footprints until the SWAT team arrived," Jing said.

"I don't think it's merely a coincidence," Harry said, "that she goes missing at the place we find those strange footprints. But I can't explain it."

"You guys refuse to believe, don't you?" Jing said. "Soon, everyone will know what I know." She looked down at her boots and didn't say anything further.

There was a rustling in the brush to the west of them and Stepan and his men appeared, riding horses. Harry jumped up and greeted the SWAT leader. Li offered the new arrivals each a mug of tea. After downing their drinks, the team remounted and Harry took a place alongside Stepan at the head of the column. Li and Jing followed, with the rest of the captain's men bringing up the rear.

The group followed the tracks left in the soft ground along the ridgeline, which then turned abruptly into the brush and disappeared. The captain had his men fan out into a wide arc until one of the men located a series of broken limbs on the low-growing vegetation. Beyond the mangled brush, the tracks reappeared. Harry swallowed hard and continued following them.

The trek was not easy, for the tracks did not follow a straight line but went in a seemingly random path, circling first in one direction then another. Harry rode alongside Stepan, rarely exchanging words as the two men kept a close eye on the tracks.

Harry was puzzled. Puzzled and uneasy. Dixie's disappearance had turned his world upside down, casting his new-found relationship into uncertainty. He was beside himself with worry. Thoughts of never finding her, or finding her dead, now crowded most other thoughts from his mind and he found it difficult to concentrate on the task at hand. In addition, where were these tracks leading? Every now and then, they would come across signs of a struggle—many tracks with the ground torn up. If Dixie had been abducted, could these areas be where she decided to fight? Why were the tracks meandering all over the place? He thought back to their time in the monastery when he kissed her and wondered if his disclosure had destroyed any chance of them being together. She had become more than a graduate assistant, for his feelings went far beyond that of a boss for a valued worker, one for whom he cared. He had crossed the Rubicon, crossed that imaginary line no professor should cross with a student, and the realization of the fact both thrilled and unnerved him.

The tracks ended at a shallow stream that surged down the

mountain from high above them. Low-growing junipers and other shrubs were interspersed along the water's edge with bare areas of sand and boulders.

Stepan eased his horse across the creek, scouted the far side, then returned. He shook his head. "Nothing," he said, dismounting.

Harry slid out of his saddle and paced the edge of the stream, searching for footprints.

"Sergeant," Stepan said, "you and another man ride up and downstream and see if the tracks leave the water. We'll wait here while you do so. Holler if you find something."

Two men rode in opposite directions in the stream's middle, leaving the rest of the group at water's edge.

"What do you make of all this wandering around, Captain?" Harry said.

"I have no idea," Stepan said. "Where these tracks are leading is a mystery at the moment."

"There were signs of a scuffle at certain points. Even you commented on them."

"Could have been a scuffle," the captain said. "Could have been something else."

"Like what?"

"Can't say right now."

"Captain!"

The shout came from upstream so Harry and Stepan remounted their horses and rode to where a SWAT team member was pointing. Deep footprints in the mud led away from the stream. Harry spurred his horse up the shallow bank and onto a narrow trail that continued into the mountains. The sandy trail wove around a cobbled rocky outcrop, reaching ever higher into the Altai. The afternoon light was fading into a magenta gloom, causing the temperature to drop by several degrees. The trail was cut on a gentle slope at right angles to the stream.

Hours later, they reached a broad grassy embankment as the sun dipped behind the peaks, casting the landscape in purple shadows.

Harry was thankful Stepan stopped the trek for the night and ordered his men to make a simple bivouac. Jing set up her stove while Harry and Li once again created their lean-to.

After a quick and simple meal, Harry and Li chatted, while Jing reclined in her sleeping bag.

"We have to find her," Li said. "I really care for her."

"We will," Harry said. "I believe we will. I hope it's just a matter of time."

"How did she come to work with you, Harry?"

"She showed up at Cal Pacific one day, saying she wished to begin graduate work in paleoanthropology. She had good grades from college so I became her major professor, meaning I directed her studies and suggested her dissertation research project."

"Is she a good student?"

"The best," Harry said. "No one has worked harder than Dixie. Plus, she has a good mind for understanding difficult concepts."

"She has always been helpful to me," Li said. "Always has a smile. That's what I remember. Her smile."

"I know," Harry said and crawled into his sleeping bag. Lying in the dark, he thought of Dixie's kiss, the way her soft lips felt against his. *We have to find her. We just have to find her.*

⸙⸙⸙

Kurt was pissed and he told Marley so. Having to make do with a cold camp and cold rations made him irritable and short-tempered. The ground was cold, the breeze was colder, and there was no whiskey or women. Sitting in the dark, waiting for his boss to decide something, rattled his brain, made him jumpy.

"I don't mind telling you, Marley," he said, "this jerking around in the middle of nowhere is getting on my nerves. We're just spinning our wheels. It's time for action, don't you think?"

Marley glanced around, making sure Doyle wasn't close by, before answering. "Can't do much about it right now, Kurt," he said. "Doyle is in charge and we take our orders from him. That's how we get paid."

"That can change, you know."

"I'm not going to change it, are you?"

Kurt gnawed at a piece of jerky then took a drink of water.

Marley continued. "You going to walk up to Doyle and tell him you know better how to run this operation? Go ahead. He's sitting right over there. Or don't you have the balls?"

"The doctor is only about a mile away. We could get over there tonight and kill them all before Doyle knew what had happened. Then we take the relics and return home. It's simple."

"Except that ain't what Doyle or the boss wants," Marley said. "Killing our guide then the monk has changed some of the strategy, to be sure, but I'm in no mood for a confrontation with Doyle. I, for one, value my head."

"You gotta admit him shooting that monk was a surprise. I never would have believed it if I hadn't seen it. Our leader losing his cool."

"Knock it off, will ya?" Marley snarled. "Just knock it off."

"This rotten country is giving me the creeps and the sooner I get out of here the better," Kurt said. "This wait-and-see game we're playing is making me jumpy as hell."

"Kurt, this may come as a surprise to you, but I'm here to do the boss's bidding—for however long it takes. Understand? I suggest you calm down and do the same."

Kurt returned to his saddle, which lay on the ground, and reclined against it. *All right, maybe I'll wait a few more days and see what develops.*

# Chapter 21

Doyle and company were camped on a ledge next to a formidable rock outcropping. From their hidden perch, they could barely make out the light of a campfire far up the mountainside. They had been following at a safe distance, to prevent their discovery by the police and research team. Momentarily losing them at a small stream, Kurt had picked up their tracks farther up the trail, and Doyle had ordered his group to hang back until the research group was out of sight.

Now that neither party was on the move, Doyle could relax and place a call to Eastwood.

The man demanded frequent updates on their progress, an order that Doyle considered especially unprofessional. Updates in the military were unheard of. One was briefed on a mission, one left on the mission, and one was either killed or returned for debriefing. There was none of this *Call me at the next stop* sort of thing.

Eastwood sounded like he had been asleep. "It's three o'clock in the damned morning," he growled. "Where the hell did you think I'd be?"

"Sorry sir," Doyle said, trying to sound contrite. "But you wanted me to call."

"So, anything new?"

"We now have them under surveillance. The National Police have joined them. Looks like a SWAT team, from what I can see."

The satellite phone crackled. "Makes your job a little harder," Eastwood said.

"Look, boss, this has become real tricky. Are you sure you still want to go through with your original plan? We're going to have to kill police. It will make getting out of the country nearly impossible. I suggest we reevaluate the situation. After killing our guide, I had to shoot a monk, so everything has changed."

"You killed a monk?" Eastwood's tone was incredulous.

"This has become more complicated than at the beginning. And they are not returning to their research compound. It appears they are following some strange tracks going higher up the mountain."

"What kind of tracks?"

"I dunno. Looks like a giant human of some sort. At any rate, now they have the police with them for some reason."

"I want you to keep following them," Eastwood said. "Just don't let them know you're there. Maybe the circumstances on the ground there will change and allow you to move in."

"Move in and do what? They outnumber us. It will mean a firefight."

"They might split up. Who knows what might happen?" Eastwood now sounded irritated.

"All right, boss. Will do."

After hanging up, Doyle finished his dinner of water and jerky. He disagreed with Eastwood's long distance assessment of their situation. Nothing good could come from having the National Police SWAT team in the vicinity. Not just in the vicinity but now as members of the scientific team they were following. He would much rather pull his men back to the research compound and simply wait for Dr. Olson's return. Their stock of food and water was not infinite and eventually they would have to turn back to replenish their supplies. It made good sense to Doyle to return through Tenduck where they could restock, then simply wait at the digging site until a more advantageous time for a confrontation presented itself. Presently, numbers were not on their side. If it came to a show of force, they were outnumbered and most likely outgunned.

Gillum sat beside him. "What did Eastwood have to say?"

"Keep following at a safe distance. Keep surveilling. That's it."

"In a battle, we'll lose."

"I know."

"Did you tell him that?"

"Yes."

"And?"

"He doesn't understand the situation here. The man is obsessed."

Gillum frowned and shook his head. "We have food for only three more days."

"I know," Doyle said. "And, at that time, we'll turn back. Not before."

The pair sat in silence for a while, eating, then Gillum spoke again. "I overheard Kurt complaining to Marley. He's getting antsy with an itchy trigger finger. I hope he's able to keep his cool."

"So do I," Doyle said.

"If he decides to go off on his own, what will you do?"

Doyle sighed out a long breath. "I hope it doesn't come to that, my friend. But I need you to watch my back."

Gillum smiled. "That's what you pay me for, isn't it?"

ev∋ev∋

The early morning sunlight cast soft shadows over the campsite as Harry readied the horses for the continuing search for Dixie. Not hungry, he had gulped a mug of Jing's strong tea and set to work. The SWAT team was busy with their own chores. Captain Stepan sat on a narrow ledge studying a map. A somber mood hung over the entire group, for it was going to be another long day in the saddle. Harry was conflicted. He longed to be back at the digging site, but he was fascinated by the possibilities offered by the footprints. But with Dixie missing, a sour feeling settled in the pit of his stomach, while a premonition that this search would not turn out good hung like a somber pall over the entire team. The thought of not finding her, or worse, finding her dead body, was driving him to near panic and he struggled to drive those thoughts from his mind. His career would be over, for he doubted he could carry on without her. But erasing the dark thoughts was impossible. He watched Stepan fold his map and approach him.

"Another day, Doctor," he said, smiling. His uniform was wrinkled and dirty from days in the saddle and he looked drawn and haggard. "I'm getting too old for such excursions."

"My thoughts, exactly, Captain," Harry said. "Maybe today we will find her."

"Here's hoping. If we don't, I will call for more help and get a larger search party out here. This has gone from a murder investigation to a missing person search as well. The fact that Miss Zinn is an American puts additional pressure on our department."

Harry swung into the high-backed Mongolian saddle and kicked his horse into a walk. Stepan moved alongside him and the pair hastened up the narrow trail. The crisp air was noticeably thinner at this altitude and the temperatures cooler, in spite of a brilliant sun overhead that illuminated the Altai peaks in an orange alpine glow. Harry focused his gaze on the footprints ahead. With each turn of a switchback, his guilt over Dixie's disappearance increased. He was the expedition leader and, as such, was her supervisor, making him and him alone responsible for the safety of the team. When he returned to the university, he was sure there would be a reckoning—even if she were unharmed.

It was when they were at the edge of a deep gorge, that Harry spotted the cave. A massive rock promontory located a good distance from the gorge contained a black cavity at its base. Harry signaled to Stepan and the group headed toward it, horses at a trot. As they neared the cave, Harry noticed its opening was large enough to accommodate a large truck, wide at the base, narrower at its top, and a good ten feet tall. At the cave's entrance, the group slid off their horses and stretched their legs.

"Sergeant, search the ground around here for more footprints. Sing out if you find any." the man barked at the SWAT team, who began scouring the area around the cave. After a five-minute search, the sergeant shook his head.

"What do you think, Captain," Harry asked as Stepan walked to his side and peered into the black emptiness of the cave.

The captain looked into the dark cave, as if trying to fathom its depths. "We'll get our lights and go in. Your assistant and the monk could be in there." Stepan turned and yelled another order to his sergeant, who began organizing the men and unloading the animals.

Li and Jing stood beside Harry and watched while the SWAT team members moved their equipment to the mouth of the cave. Stepan adjusted the headlight he had donned then checked his Russian OT-33 Pernach machine pistol. Its magazine held twenty-seven rounds and could fire them at a rate of nine hundred per minute. The rest of the team was armed with Bizon submachine guns and AK-12 assault rifles. Harry let out a low whistle.

"Not going to back away from anything," Li said to Harry as they watched the men beside them.

"I just hope they don't panic and shoot Dixie, if she's in there," Harry said.

The two scientists continued to watch as Stepan and his men strapped on their weapons. Harry's pulse quickened to a pounding beat and his mouth felt as dry as cotton. What they were about to do was a far cry from digging for hominids. He felt strange, almost as if separated from his body. He was somewhere else looking down on the scene, disbelieving what was about to happen. If there was something in the cave, whatever it was might have Dixie and the monk and, most likely, would not give them up without a fight.

"I think we're ready," Stepan said, approaching Harry, his shadow dancing over the rocky ground.

"What's your plan?" Harry said.

"You three follow us and take these flashlights," Stepan said, handing several small lights to Harry. "Stay a ways back and let us lead. If we encounter anything, we'll let out a shout."

"Not much of a plan, Captain. Please don't shoot my girl by mistake."

"This is a typical SWAT extrication drill. We play things by ear but we have practiced these scenarios many times. There will be two men left out here for security and as a back-up if needed. Now let's go."

Stepan waved his arm and headed for the cave's entrance. Harry fell in behind the SWAT team. He turned on his flash-light, as did Li and Jing. Harry grabbed Jing by the arm.

"I think you should wait out here," he said.

"Not on your life," Jing replied. "I got you into this mess. I'm going."

With that, she pulled out of his grasp and continued into the cave beside Li, leaving Harry to bring up the rear.

The first thing Harry noticed was the sharp drop in temperature once inside the mountain. The hollowed out entrance was high enough so members of the group were able to walk up-right. Once inside, the cave opened into a large room, the ceiling of which, Harry surmised, was at least twenty feet high. Beams from headlights danced on the walls and floor as they moved toward the rear of the cave.

About fifty feet from the entrance, the room narrowed to a wide tunnel, which veered to the right then began a gentle de-scent. Green and orange moss covered the damp rock walls, creating a pungent, stifling odor. As they continued along, the air temperature steadily decreased and the tunnel grew darker as the filtered light from outside dissipated. Harry was glad he remembered to wear his parka and he noticed that Li and Jing had theirs on as well. No one was talking. It was eerily quiet. Only the plodding sounds of their footsteps echoed off the rocky walls.

Deeper into the cave, the green moss gave way to a purple lichen and the air became damp as well as cold. The cave had just enough light to see, but not enough to reveal all its secrets. Harry could hear dripping water inside and smell its ancient age. The stalagmites and stalactites looked like huge teeth, even the stains on them looked like dried blood. The feeble rays of sun waned, throwing the room into a velvet gloom. The howling sound from the wind coursing through it didn't improve his bravery, but his curiosity was heightened, so he plunged deeper into the darkness.

To Harry, they had entered an alien world, hostile and unforgiving to trespassers. He looked to the head of their column and saw Stepan stooped over a rock outcropping. He picked his way to the captain's side.

"Look here," Stepan said to Harry.

Harry bent to take a closer look and saw a jagged piece of cloth stuck to the rock. "That looks like something the monk was wearing," he said. "But I can't be sure."

Stepan called Li and Jing to the rock and asked them if they could identify the piece of cloth but neither could do so.

Continuing on, the tunnel took another sharp turn to the left while the walls closed in on the trespassers, forcing Harry and the group to walk single file. The low rock ceiling loomed barely above their heads. Water seeped from the rock and dripped down the sides of the tunnel.

With another sharp turn, a rush of cold air greeted them. Harry shivered and tried to get his bearings when Stepan called out. "Up here, Harry!"

Harry rushed to the front of the column and gazed into a remarkable abyss. The tunnel transformed into a huge cavern, several stories tall. Stepan shined his headlight around and the sight took Harry's breath away. The cavern was enormous. Its glistening gray limestone walls contained fissures several feet deep.

The team's lights glittered off the crystal and quartz embedded in the rock. At the far end of the cavern, and barely visible through dense mist, a waterfall emptied into an emerald stream. The water gushed over lichen-covered boulders then crashed into an emerald pool below, sending showers of mist high into the cavern.

"Shit," Harry said. "What is this place? It's breathtaking." He marveled at the numerous stalactites that hung from the roof high above. Water dripped from their tips.

"Mongolia has hundreds of caves," Li said. "When the ground water combines with atmospheric carbon dioxide a weak acid is formed. That acid eats away at the rock until a cave is formed."

"Must take millions of years to create something like this," Harry said. He noticed a few stalagmites pushed up from the floor of the cavern.

"Well guys," Stepan said, "we need to cross that stream which will require the use of ropes which we left at the entrance. I suggest we return to the surface, make camp for tonight, and get an early start back here in the morning."

"I'm totally blown away by this place," Harry said. "I wonder if anyone has ever been in here before us. Maybe we're the first."

"I'm afraid of bats," Jing said. "I hope we don't see any. One could bite me. Plus, there must be all sorts of creepy crawly things that live in here."

Li laughed. "Jing, you don't strike me as the sort of girl who would be afraid of a few bats and spiders."

"They can suck your blood," she said.

"But wear a bat bone around your neck and it will bring you good luck," Li said.

She glared at Li. "I don't have a good feeling about this."

The group reversed its route and soon were back at the mouth of the cave system. The afternoon sun was heading toward the horizon. In quick succession, lean-to's were built, fires started, and sentries posted.

Harry hoped for a peaceful evening.

ℰ∾ℭ∾

Stepan called his sergeant to a meeting and the two men sat a short distance apart from the rest of the group, who were lounging by the campfires. The sergeant was a burly man in his fifties. He bore a scar across his forehead and had large, stubby hands. Stepan liked the man and had been through a few tough skirmishes with him. They talked in their native Mongolian language.

"Zaya, this is likely to be some dirty business." The sergeant nodded but said nothing. "I don't have good feelings about this American woman, the doctor's assistant. In all likelihood, if we find her, she's going to be dead, and a gun battle with bloodshed will erupt. So I want the men to be ready, whenever it comes. Will you see to preparing them?"

Zaya shifted his large frame and smiled at his captain. "Of course," he said, hoarsely.

"We have trained extensively on these kinds of missions and now it's time to put that training to work. I don't want to have to break bad news to parents or wives. Something tells me this cave is the only place the girl and monk can be, dead or alive. Even though we haven't found them yet, this cave is the logical place—it's secluded and out of the weather. Whatever we run into, it is going to result in a shootout and I want the men on their toes."

Zaya nodded again. "The men will meet the challenge, sir. I know them well. They are good men and they will fight hard. Whatever the eventuality, the men will follow you without question."

"I know them, too, Sergeant. And you and I have been through some tough times ourselves, right?

Zaya nodded once more and smiled again. "Yes, Captain, we have fought many wars together. You have been like a brother to me."

"Fine, Zaya. Get some rest and tell the men to relax tonight. Tomorrow we begin in earnest."

# Chapter 22

Doyle watched the National Police SWAT team place sentries around the camp. He had climbed to the top of a ridge to get a better look at the group who had come to a halt outside a large cave. The team was well armed and it would be a toss-up as to who would have the advantage if a firefight broke out. Their gear was in piles around several campfires and, up to now, they were seemingly unaware of Doyle's presence. He scrambled down the small ridge to where his men were assembled.

"No fire again tonight, men," he said. "They are less than a mile away in front of a large cave. They may have already scouted inside it."

Gillum sat on a flat rock and put a plug of tobacco in his mouth. "If they go back in tomorrow, we'll have them trapped. We can move in right behind them."

Doyle zipped his parka as the evening temperature dropped. "That is the plan. Now listen up, everyone. If they decide to enter the cave tomorrow morning, we will give them an hour or so before we go in ourselves. Let's hope we can surprise them without much gunplay."

"Fat chance of that," Marley said. "What if they shoot first?"

"We defend ourselves, of course. Remember, we're after information and relics not a body count."

"And once we have them cornered, they won't be able to do anything but give us what we want," Gillum added.

"I vote we kill every last one of the bastards," Kurt said, sneering at Doyle.

"We do this Eastwood's way," Doyle said, "or not at all. I'm the hard case here and, until Eastwood says otherwise, I decide what we do." He looked at Kurt for a long, silent moment. "Understand, Kurt?"

Kurt looked away but when he returned Doyle's gaze, the sneer was gone. "Understood."

"Gillum, make sure that all the weapons are ready to go for tomorrow and everyone turn in. I'll take the first watch."

The men sat in the dark and checked their weapons. Finally, they stretched out on the ground and fell asleep.

Except Doyle, who was worried. They had come to Mongolia ill-prepared for an extended expedition requiring specialized caving equipment. He and Eastwood planned for a quick strike at the research compound, seizure of the artifacts, and then a quick escape and flight back to the States. Doyle had not counted on a pursuit through the Mongolian mountains, a pursuit that now included the country's law enforcement. Nor the killing of two Mongolians. They had weapons, sure, but beyond that, he was not convinced they could manage alone in a maze of underground caves. He had heard that some of Mongolia's caves were quite extensive and dangerous. Caving was not on the list of things he had been trained to do. It wasn't that he was worried about the dark—more like he was somewhat claustrophobic. This venture was turning into an extended game of chess and he had a peculiar feeling that his team wasn't far from checkmate. However, maybe he was worrying too much. The cave up ahead might turn out to be nothing much at all. If that turned out to be the case, they could have this showdown over within a matter of hours and be on their way back home in a few days. His limbs ached for a nice soft bed with clean sheets.

∽∾∽

Harry had Kesler on the satellite phone and the professor sounded agitated. Harry didn't want to worry the professor needlessly but felt the situation required total honesty. After all, one of their team member's life was at stake.

"You still haven't found her?" Kesler said, obvious distress sounding in his voice.

"Unfortunately, no. We are camped at the entrance of an immense cave system and, in the morning, we'll go in and see if she is in there. I hope to God she is and that she's okay."

"If she is in the cave," Kesler said, his voice still sounding apprehensive, "she just didn't wander in there by herself. She had to have been taken there. Against her will."

"No, Professor, it's possible she could have sought shelter to get out of the elements. Or she might have been injured in some way and could have been wandering around, dazed. But you're right. Dixie is not the kind of woman to go exploring on her own without telling someone. I must admit my worst fears are being realized."

"Harry, remember what I said about the possibility of the Yeti. It's sounding more and more like—"

"Professor, you're jumping to conclusions. She could just as easily been abducted by bandits who are holding an American scientist for ransom. We don't know at this point."

"Really, Harry? Then how do you explain the footprints you found and have been following? That doesn't sound like bandits to me."

Kesler's anguish was producing a foul taste in Harry's mouth. A lump formed in his throat as he thought of Dixie and what might have befallen her.

"We'll keep looking, Professor, that's all I know to do. The SWAT team is with us, so we're ready for whatever happens."

"I talked with Dixie's parents," Kesler said, his voice now sounding more controlled.

"I don't envy you," Harry said.

"They took it pretty well, I thought, considering. They realized she is in a foreign country and complete safety is not always possible. They seemed relieved when I said the Mongolian Police are involved as well as INTERPOL. They were going to call the State Department and their senator to enlist their aid."

"Well, Professor, that's about all here. I'll try and call soon for another update."

"Harry, don't take what I'm about to say the wrong way. God knows I pray for Dixie's safe return..."

"Yes?"

"If it isn't bandits you're dealing with but something more...er...more sinister, then try and bring back some tangible evidence. Understand?

"Completely. First priority is to get Dixie. Then obtain some proof as to whatever this thing is, if it's not human. I'll do my best, Professor."

"I know you will, Harry."

☾☽

Eastwood settled himself into the canvas seat of the helicopter that sat on the tarmac of Chinggis Khaan International Airport outside Ulaanbataar, Mongolia. He was anxious to get airborne. The Mi-8T twin turbo engines were revving up and the two pilots were finishing their checklists. Eastwood had arrived from Beijing earlier and rented the sixteen-seat helicopter to transport him to Doyle's location, if he could find him.

Sitting alone in his Manhattan office had been nerve-wracking and impossible. His attempts at controlling the mission from behind a desk proved too much for his anxiety-wracked nerves. He needed to be near the action, where he could call the shots, direct the strategy as the situation demanded. He was not good at supervising from a distance and, now that this enterprise was becoming difficult and unpredictable, he needed to be on the scene. Doyle was not going to appreciate his arrival but both men understood their relationship, one of boss and employee. He paid the man more than he could make elsewhere and Eastwood wasn't worried. So he had quickly packed a bag and charted a jet to get him to Mongolia.

He thought about retrieving his satellite phone from his overnight bag on the seat next to him but decided to wait until they were in the air heading to the research site. Doyle could give him his coordinates in route and the pilots could adjust their flight plan accordingly.

One of the pilots opened the cockpit door and gave him a thumbs up. Eastwood settled into his seat and tried to relax as the large aircraft shuddered briefly then rose off the tarmac. With a jerk, they were speeding down the runway, gaining altitude, followed by a banking turn to the west. The flat plains below grew smaller and in the hazy distance he could just make out the mountain range.

*Relax*, he told himself. *You'll be there soon.*

☙☙☙

Morning found Harry, Li, Jing, and the SWAT team gearing up in preparation to re-enter the cave. Weapons were checked, headlights and flashlights switched on, canteens filled. Although the thought of returning to the dark didn't seem quite as eerie to Harry as it had the previous day, he wasn't looking forward to it. The SWAT team extinguished their campfires while Stepan paced about, checking on his men. As a brilliant sun peaked over the steppe, the captain assembled everyone for last minute instructions.

"Stay close, people. Keep the person ahead of you in sight at all times. If you need to stop for any reason, sing out and we will all stop. Try not to touch any vegetation or moss, as some of them can be poisonous. If we meet with trouble, let my SWAT team handle it." Stepan paused for a moment as his words settled upon Harry like a heavy mantle. "Ready?" Everyone nodded. "Then, let's move out."

Tramping through the dark tunnel, they soon found themselves in the large cavern and grouped themselves next to the stream. The roar of the waterfall sounded like a locomotive, while the stream, looking cold and deep, rushed past in swirling eddies. Their headlights flashed bright beams about as they huddled.

Stepan sent two men up and downstream to check for a safe place at which to ford. One returned and reported a narrow portion of the stream close by. It looked waist deep. They joined the other man where he waited.

"Tie onto this rope," the captain said after one of his men pulled it out of a pack and uncoiled it.

One by one they did as instructed with some SWAT team members tying on just ahead of Harry and Jing.

The water swirled around Harry's ankles as he waded into the stream. It was freezing cold. He felt his feet go numb as he lumbered deeper. Bringing up the rear of the column, he watched the group slowly make its way through the dark, churning water. Harry pressed forward through the swift and foreboding water, using a shuffling gait. He refused to think what might be lurking in its depths.

Ahead of him, Jing was saying something he could not hear over the roar of the waterfall. He could tell she was struggling against the current, for she had almost fallen several times. Once he caught an earful and realized she was cursing.

In the middle of the stream, the going got more difficult, the current much swifter. Harry watched Jing fight to maintain her balance in the churning water. She was tugging against the rope, frantic to remain on her feet, in spite of being forced downstream. Even with the headlights and flashlights, it was difficult to determine how far to the opposite shore. Harry's feet were numb and his legs seemed ineffective in moving his body. His foot struck a rock and the impact sent shock waves of pain up his spine.

Jing was having more trouble maintaining her balance. She floundered, arms askew, and grabbed hold of the rope to steady herself. Ahead of them, Harry saw that the SWAT team was pushing forward, their black uniforms drenched. He reached out and managed to grab Jing's arm, pulled her erect, but sensed it was a losing battle.

As Stepan stepped onto the opposite shore, Jing fell into the frigid water and disappeared below the torrent. Harry made a frantic grab for her but missed. The rope pulled taut against him as Jing was pulled downstream. Fighting to keep his footing, Harry jerked hard on the rope and Jing's head popped to the surface. She gasped and rolled under a second time. Harry pulled again on the rope but nothing happened, Jing's head didn't roll to the surface. He definitely had her by the rope—he felt her weight pulling against his grip. He gave the rope another yank and she breached the surface like a whale, taking great gulps of air. The swift current pulled the rope in Harry's hands, stinging his fingers, turning two of them raw.

She disappeared again.

Stepan noticed what was happening and hollered for the team to get onto dry land. As they steadied the rope, Harry reached into the water, prayed for a miracle, found an arm, and pulled Jing to the surface again. When the dim light from his flashlight illuminated her, a look of terror greeted him.

"I've got her!" he called to Stepan.

The rest of the group stumbled onto shore.

Harry supported Jing by an arm as they made their way through the stream until they fell, gasping, on rocks at water's edge.

"Are you okay?" Harry asked her.

Jing coughed several times and nodded. She lay on the sandy ground, taking deep breath after deep breath.

Stepan kneeled at her side. "Feeling better?"

"I'm okay," she said. "But I'm freezing." She began shivering so Harry removed his parka and placed it over her shoulders. Jing looked past him with a vacant stare. Her lips and cheeks were blue.

Harry started rubbing her arms and hands in an effort to stimulate warmth. "Jing," he said, turning her face toward his. "Are you okay?"

She nodded. "Thanks."

"Listen up," Stepan said, standing. "We need to get warm before we move on so let's look around and see if there's anything we can use to build a fire. There might be some wood around here somewhere."

Harry stayed with Jing while the rest of the group began searching for anything that would burn. The darkness engulfed them like a velvet hood. Soon several of the SWAT team members arrived carrying small branches and they soon had a warming fire going. Jing huddled near the growing flames to dry her clothes, as did the rest of the team. Once her shivering stopped, Harry thought she looked better. After the short delay, they were on their feet again.

At the far end of the large cavern, the stalactites grew larger, longer, and more numerous. Some hung almost to the cavern's floor making it necessary to walk a meandering path as they approached the far wall. There the room grew smaller and Harry noticed what looked like a series of steps leading down into another tunnel. The stones of the steps were rectangular and encrusted with moss and dirt.

"These steps look as if they were made and placed here," he said as the group descended.

A short distance down the tunnel, it leveled off; the air was heavy and languid, the roar of the waterfall less deafening. The group continued making their way, with Stepan in the lead. Here the narrow tunnel was devoid of debris and the ground was smooth, which made walking easier. Harry stopped to inspect the walls. His flashlight danced over the rock illuminating strange markings.

"Look here," he said, and Stepan and Li gathered next to him. "What do you make of this?"

Stepan took a closer look and shook his head. "Hieroglyphics of some sort, it looks to me."

The wall was marked with black designs that Harry could not decipher.

"I can see a figure like a man and an eye but that is all I can make out. I certainly don't know what they mean, however."

"No telling how old they are," Stepan said. "Maybe thousands of years."

"Some form of intelligent life drew them, no doubt," Li said. "Maybe an ancient human."

"It's obvious that something intelligent lived down here," Harry said. "Pre-historic man, probably."

"Maybe a Yeti," Jing said, joining them. "There are legends that they are as smart as humans."

"But can they communicate like that? I doubt it," Li said.

"Just wild talk," Stepan insisted. "Let's keep moving."

Farther into the tunnel, they came to a small alcove off to one side of the tunnel. A startled Stepan bolted from the anteroom's entrance with a frightened look on his face. "Christ, Harry," he said. "Look in here."

Harry pushed through the SWAT team and peered into the small room. His flashlight cast an unearthly light onto the floor and he followed its beam until it came to rest on a ghastly sight. Strung on the wall, like a puppet, hung the mangled body of the monk. His head was half-gone, as if chewed by a wild animal. His eyes were missing as well as one of his arms, blood congealed on the mutilated stump. The rest of his naked body bore numerous rips and wounds, betraying a vicious attack.

Harry swallowed hard, choking down a desire to vomit. Li and Jing came to his side. Jing began crying and retching.

"H—how did he get here?" Li stammered. "We're a long way from our campsite."

"He was brought here, for sure," Stepan said, stepping into the small alcove to examine the body more closely. "He didn't come of his own accord. This is what I feared."

The sweet, putrid smell of decaying flesh filled the room and overwhelmed their senses. Back in the tunnel, Jing was doubled over, vomiting what was left of her breakfast. Li went to her side, placed a hand on her back, and tried to comfort her.

Harry fought to keep his head. His world was out of control, crashing down around him. How could he have wound up in this godforsaken mountain on the edge of the world looking for a missing team member? Where was Dixie? What was happening? The answers were not forthcoming, only the questions remained. He felt so alone.

Now he was scared, really scared.

# Chapter 23

Doyle's satellite phone rang as he and his men approached the cave. It was Eastwood and Doyle wondered why he was calling as he punched the *TALK* button. "Yes sir," he said to his boss.

"Ben, where are you? I'm on the way. In fact, I'm in a chopper and heading to the digging site. Is that where you are?"

"You're here? In country? But how? Why?"

"Couldn't stay away, Ben. Now, are you at the research compound?"

"No longer, sir. We've moved to a location in the Altai Mountains. We have the doctor and the police cornered in a cave and are about to enter."

"How did that happen?" Eastwood yelled.

"Quite by accident. They were apparently returning to their compound, than changed their course. We stumbled upon them yesterday."

"Give me your coordinates, Ben, and wait for me to arrive. I want to go in with you. Just wait until I can get there. Understand?"

Doyle's stomach took a sudden lurch and he held up a hand in a halting gesture. He couldn't believe what he was hearing. "Understood. We will await your arrival, boss." After giving Eastwood the coordinates from his GPS, he continued. "What's your ETA?"

"Just a minute, Ben, the pilot is plugging the numbers into

the chopper's autopilot. Oh, he's got it. Right at an hour—fifty-five minutes to be exact. See you then."

"I copy," Doyle said and switched off the phone.

His temples pounded, his mouth felt like cotton. Not only had he been ready to move into the cave and now had to stand down, he would have to put up with Eastwood trying to run the show. He didn't need the aggravation or the delay. He'd watched as Dr. Olson and the SWAT team entered the cave earlier in the morning. In the gray dawn, they had rolled out of their sleeping bags, eaten a quick breakfast, donned gear and weapons, then disappeared into the mountainside. He was surprised to see that no sentries were stationed outside the cave's entrance, the place was quiet. Hurriedly, Doyle and his men drank water, ate jerky, and checked their weapons once more before moving out.

At the cave's entrance, Doyle peered into the darkness beyond. No sound or light emanated from its depths. He told Gillum, Kurt, and Marley to relax until Eastwood arrived and watched their eager smiles turn to frowns.

"What's the point?" Kurt sneered.

"Point of what?" Doyle said.

"The point of them being here with what looks like a SWAT team? I don't get it. What are they doing in a cave?"

"And why aren't they going back to their digging site?" Marley added.

Gillum studied the darkness beyond the cave's entrance then sat on the ground.

"You boys think I've got the answer to all those questions?" Doyle demanded. "Well, I don't. We followed them here. It's that simple. I don't care what they're doing in there. Eastwood wants whatever they have so that ends it, as far as all of us are concerned."

"Then each minute of delay puts them that much deeper in the cave, that much harder to locate," Kurt snarled. "What's the old man going to do when he gets here, anyway? Take over? Why can't the bastard leave well enough alone and just let us do our job without his interference?"

"Maybe he wants to safeguard his precious discovery," Gillum said. "I admit having him here doesn't make me very happy either, Ben."

So Doyle paced.

കൗകൗ

Two members of the SWAT team cut down the monk's stiff body and covered him with a blanket. The man was mutilated. His empty eye sockets were covered with white vitreous fluid. His right arm looked as if it had been ripped from his body by tremendous force. The white bone protruded from dried brown muscle. Part of the monk's brain was missing, the surrounding skull showing gash marks from what could have been teeth. The man presented a grisly scene. Jing sobbed nearby.

Stepan scouted the far end of the tunnel. When he returned, Harry and the rest of the group, including the SWAT team, gathered around him. The light from his headlight danced from person to person as he spoke. "Empty down that way," he said, indicating the dark tunnel beyond them. "What do you think, Dr. Olson?"

"A violent death for sure," Harry said, glancing at the lump underneath the blanket. "Can't tell if he was killed here or not but it doesn't matter. I pray Dixie hasn't met a similar fate."

"The fact that she's not here," Li said, "gives us hope she's still alive."

"We shouldn't waste time here," Stepan said. "Need to keep moving."

The others nodded and he led the group down the musty-smelling passageway past the monk's corpse. Bright green moss covered certain portions of the rock wall on either side of them, while the damp air felt heavy and pressed on Harry. It made his breathing strenuous.

As they continued to make their way forward, the walls of the tunnel converged upon them. The passageway narrowed dramatically, forcing them to once again walk in single file. Harry still brought up the rear of the column. *How deep are we going to go?*

He became disoriented in the dark with light beams flickering wildly and the tunnel meandering through the earth. The narrowness closed in on Harry, sending convulsive waves through his body and brain. Being claustrophobic, he felt a slow panic build within, a desperate need to get out of the tunnel.

He fought to keep his nerves under control. Maybe it was a mistake to venture into this strange, foreign place.

Their progress slowed to a snail's pace. Harry noticed the SWAT team ahead stooping to scramble under a limestone arch from which dripped brackish, sulfur-smelling water. The arch was only about four feet high, requiring him to stoop to maneuver his tall frame underneath and, in the process, got drenched.

Beyond the arch, the tunnel opened up enough to allow the group to walk several abreast. Jing walked alongside Harry.

"Feeling better?" he asked her.

Jing nodded. "Much. Thanks for helping me."

"Wondering what we're doing in here, Jing? I'm asking that myself about now."

"I'm hoping we can find Dixie and that she's okay. I hate to think otherwise. But our monk friend—what do you think? "

"I dunno. It's peculiar, for sure."

"More than peculiar," Jing said. "It's downright gruesome. I pray we find Dixie unharmed."

"Me too," Harry said.

The group continued along in silence. The lights dancing on the tunnel walls reminded Harry of Plato's *Allegory of the Cave*.

A scream pierced the darkness.

A woman's scream.

It came from up ahead.

Not far.

Harry shuddered and stopped, head pounding, ears alert. The whole group stopped. Everyone heard the scream. Stepan moved back to Harry's side and shook his head.

Then another scream.

Stepan pointed his headlight into the dark tunnel ahead but

there was nothing. "Let's go," he said and moved to the front of the column.

"Dixie!" Harry called, his heart pounding in his chest.

The team groped their way down the passageway until it widened into another large room. A room that was decidedly different. Scattered on the ground were a variety of bones and there were remnants of clothing strewn about the room in disarray. The SWAT team scrambled throughout the cavern, weapons at the ready. Harry and Li continued to look about while Jing fell to the ground and waited. Around the room's periphery were smaller chambers sculpted into the rock. Each chamber contained more bones cluttered on the floor. On the walls were more of the undecipherable hieroglyphs they had noticed earlier.

Harry and Li searched each of the chambers but found them empty. Rejoining Stepan, Harry let out a long, low whistle. "I've never seen anything like this before," he said. "It's like someone's residence down here. Someone or something is using this cavern as an apartment, living quarters."

"More than one something, by the looks of things," Li said.

"You're right, Li." Harry noticed Jing was up, approaching them. "What do you think, Jing?"

"It's creepy, that's what it is. Any sign of Dixie?"

Harry shook his head.

"Not yet," Stepan said, holding a scrap of blue cloth. "These bits of clothing don't match with hers. But I've got an uneasy feeling that she's down here, somewhere. It's just a matter of time before we find her."

"I hope not like we found the monk," Jing said.

"Let's not think about that," said Harry.

"But those screams," Jing said.

"I know, I know," Harry said. "But there's no woman here. Stepan, what now?"

The captain glanced at his watch. "It's getting late and we need rest and food. We've had a rough few days. I suggest we eat something, and then rest for a few hours before continuing. What do you think?"

"Good idea. Jing is about all in and the rest of us could do with a few hours' sleep. Let's bed down here."

The SWAT team dropped their packs to the ground and Harry found a comfortable place for Jing to rest. They chewed jerky and sipped water. Harry volunteered to remain awake and take the first watch so Stepan gave him his Russian OT-33 Pernach machine pistol. One by one, the headlights and flashlights clicked off until darkness and quiet engulfed them. Harry propped himself against the rock wall and tried to relax. Only the sounds of muffled breathing broke the menacing silence.

Harry's pulse and breathing slowed as he worked to calm his frayed nerves. He shifted his position to get more comfortable, laid his head back on the rock, and closed his eyes. It was strange how much closer to Dixie he felt since her disappearance. The fleeting moment they shared in her room at the monastery had altered his earlier resolve not to get involved with graduate assistants. He was no longer the aloof professor where she was concerned, but an impassioned friend who longed for her company. He felt drawn to her in a way that was different from other women in his life, which had not been very many. He almost married Lisa but her father's money got in the way.

She had wanted to purchase him, almost as one would a car or a house, and let him know that Daddy's money would help see him through graduate school. She wanted the marriage but he knew in the end it would never work. She needed her father's wealth and he needed freedom for his scientific research. So when he told her how he felt, she left with only a short note of explanation. And that was it—she was no longer in their small garage apartment one afternoon when he arrived home from class.

Dixie was different. Originally, their relationship consisted of nothing more than working together or discussing her dissertation. He had viewed her as a colleague only. That was until the kiss at the monastery. One kiss and his life had been turned upside down.

လ၁ယ၁

From the Mi-8T helicopter, Eastwood could see the orange smoke wafting from the spot that marked the location Doyle had chosen for their landing. The chopper banked sharply then circled the smoke, losing altitude as it did so. From his seat, he saw Doyle standing by a large gaping hole in the mountainside. His security chief shielded his eyes as the chopper descended. As it settled on the ground, Doyle ran to its side and opened the door while the pilot powered down the aircraft's engines. Once the rotors stopped moving, Eastwood climbed out and greeted the man.

"Good to see you, Ben," he said, pumping his hand. "What's the situation?"

"The research and SWAT teams went in yesterday and have not returned. They are still in there. It must be a large cave system."

"Are we all ready?"

"Ready. Locked and loaded, sir."

"How many of them are there, Ben? Your best guess."

"I'd say probably a dozen. But they are well armed. Some of them look like they are a SWAT team, so they may be willing to shoot it out."

"Maybe not. If we get them cornered, it's possible they will listen to us. If it comes to that, of course, we fight Ben. We fight."

"The guys know that, sir, and are ready," Doyle said.

"Well, let's get after them. Why are they in there, anyway?"

"I don't know," Doyle said. "But it must be important whatever it is."

"But the police, Ben. Why the need for the police?"

"Don't know that, either.

Eastwood shrugged. "Okay, Ben. Lead on."

ᄅᄀᄅ

Harry jumped. *Had he been dozing?* He didn't know. His senses were on full alert. He peered into the darkness and listened, straining to hear.

Something was moving about in the dark.

Everyone was asleep, no other sounds could be heard, except their regular, soft breathing.

There it was again.

Something was definitely moving about at the far end of the cavern.

Soft, muffled sounds, like someone walking, crunching the dirt beneath their feet. He thought someone might be up using the bathroom in a dark corner but no one returned.

He grasped the Pernach machine pistol and felt its cold metal in his hand. He strained to see past their little group but it was no use. He could make nothing out. Sitting dead still, he waited. The sound had stopped.

The silence pounded in his ears.

Then...

There it was again.

Muffled steps.

Moving to his left.

Harry's mouth was dry and tasted like metal. Something was different in the darkness. His conscious mind couldn't register it, but something had triggered the primitive part of his brain. Adrenaline surged through his body, putting his nerves on edge, heart rate doubled, ready for fight or flight. Out of the corner of his eye, he thought he caught a glimpse of a dark shape. Bigger than a person. He quickly counted the dark outlines of the team members and all were sleeping.

He lost the shape in the darkness. The footsteps stopped. He thought about switching on his flashlight but a curious fear gripped him. He couldn't bring himself to illuminate whatever was in the cavern with them. He thought he should wake the others but they needed rest. So he remained frozen, gripped the pistol, and waited.

Again the muffled steps.

This time closer.

With ears attuned to the slightest sound, Harry scanned the cavern.

Two red dots, like eyes.

In the darkness.

Staring at him.

He jerked the pistol up and fired two shots in rapid succession. The noise crashed through the cavern and the team jumped up, screaming.

"What's that?"

"What's going on?"

"Harry, what is it?"

Stepan switched on his headlight at the same time Harry clicked his flashlight and pointed the beam in the direction of the red eyes.

Nothing.

Everyone was now awake and up milling around. Jing was sobbing.

"What happened," Stepan asked Harry. He walked around, surveying the cavern while the SWAT team searched its periphery.

"Something was in here," Harry said. "Moving about. I couldn't see what it was in the dark."

Jing sobbed. "It's the Yeti, like I told you. They must live here, in these caves. They must come down to the lower elevations in search of food."

"Jing, stop that," Harry said in a stern tone. "You are freaking everyone out."

But Jing continued to sit and sob softly.

One of the SWAT team yelled at Stepan and he and Harry went to look at what he had discovered. At the far end of the cavern was a cluster of large human-like footprints that led to where the group had been sleeping.

There were large drops of blood on the ground.

"These weren't here earlier," Stepan said. "We looked, remember?"

Harry nodded. He was still shaking from the shooting. He had to get himself under control, but doing so was difficult.

He walked over to Jing, stooped, and put an arm around her. She turned, looked at him with her large brown eyes, then put her head on his chest, and cried again. He felt helpless, not knowing what to say or how to comfort her.

When she finished crying, he stood and walked over to

where Stepan was talking to his men. The captain was giving instructions to his sergeant, pointing first in one direction then another.

The sergeant nodded then ambled off toward the other SWAT team members.

Stepan turned to face Harry, a somber look on his face. "I don't mind telling you, Doctor, we need to find this assistant of yours, and soon, or it may be too late."

"I'm afraid you're right, Captain. And I'm beginning to think Jing has been right all along. There's something evil lurking in these caves."

# Chapter 24

Doyle, Eastwood, and their men stood beside an underground stream, which ran through a large, high-domed cavern. They had just traveled through a long, narrow tunnel, emerging into a great room filled with stalactites dripping water. A cold draft blew through the groups' clothing, causing Eastwood to pull a fleece sweater out of his pack.

"Wow," he said, scanning the immense underground room. "I've never seen anything like this. There's a waterfall at the far end. See it?"

"Yes, I do," Doyle said. "Pretty impressive. It's going to be tough crossing this stream. Looks fairly deep and swift right here."

"There's bound to be a better crossing around here somewhere," Eastwood said. "The research team made it over, obviously."

Doyle shuddered at Eastwood's use of the term, *obviously*, but sent Kurt and Marley to look for a spot at which to cross. Waiting alone with Gillum and his boss, Doyle thought how much more complicated things were going to be now that Eastwood was along for the duration. Although the two men always enjoyed an amicable working relationship, there was an undercurrent of mistrust that came through Eastwood's dealings with his subordinates. Doyle was usually able to put his feelings for his boss aside and concentrate on the job or mission at hand, a fact that was made easier because the two men rarely worked side by side. But now that Eastwood was on site, he would want to take charge and Doyle realized that, sooner or later, conflicts would arise. He hoped that they would not be serious ones and jeopardize himself or his men.

Kurt waved and the pair ambled to where he stood alongside a narrower portion of the stream. Small rocks lay scattered over the sandy shore, which sloped gently to the water that appeared deep and swift. It glowed an emerald green hue as their lights danced over its surface.

"There's footprints here," Kurt said. "The scientists must have crossed here as well."

When Marley joined them, he pushed into the frigid water and then let out a yell.

"It's damn cold," he said above the sound of the rushing water that was around his chest.

Gillum followed, then Kurt, and Eastwood, leaving Doyle to bring up the rear. Despite the freezing temperature of the water, crossing posed no problem and soon all were on the far side, safe but chilled. As they neared the waterfall, it became harder to hear while the mist soaked their clothes. The water plunged over mammoth boulders, filling the air with a storm of spray turning the river below into a churning soup. Damp and exhausted they found an indent in the rock a short distance from the waterfall and huddled there as Doyle contemplated their next move.

"Start a fire and let's dry out," commanded Eastwood. He pointed to Kurt and Marley.

"We need to push on," Doyle countered. "They are up ahead somewhere."

"I doubt there's a way out of this cave at the far end," Eastwood said, his voice shaking. "So they will be coming back this way on the way out, and we will be blocking their exit. Now get a fire going."

Doyle nodded his assent to Kurt and Marley, who stumbled off in search of anything that would burn. They managed to find a few limbs from dead shrubs and soon had a small fire blazing. Eastwood took off his sweater and laid it on the ground near the flames. Doyle opted to keep his clothes on and sat as close as he dared to the growing fire. Marley sat at the entrance to the small rock recess, with his Persuader shotgun in his lap. Kurt and Gillum rested on the ground near Eastwood.

"Got anything to eat?" Eastwood asked Doyle.

"Sure," he said and tossed a pack to his boss.

Finding a small bag of jerky, Eastwood chewed and surveyed the large cavern. "I never would have believed anything like this was possible," he said. "It's astonishing, simply astonishing."

"Unbelievable, for sure," Marley said from his seat at the recess's opening.

Doyle tried to keep a lid on his temper, as he was prone to let it get the better of him. Eastwood's sudden appearance and taking command sent Doyle's emotions into a tailspin, on the verge of being out of control. He now had two problems with which to contend—his boss showing up and Kurt's mental state. Kurt had a surly disposition, prone to second-guess every decision he, Doyle, made. The man could go off at any moment. As for the other problem, he was going to have to have patience. In any given operation, he knew there could not be two commanders, two leaders. He realized he would have to take a back seat to Eastwood, swallow his pride, and make it work. What had allowed their association to work in the past was that they operated separately and Doyle was his own boss and the leader of his team in Eastwood's absence. It was a system that worked well. But now? He wasn't sure.

Eastwood got up and headed beyond the rock recess that formed the niche in which they rested. "I need to take a leak," he said, and disappeared past Marley.

Kurt moved to sit beside Doyle. He had a dark frown on his face. "What the hell is he doing here?" he said. "Did you know he was coming?"

"Not until he was in the chopper and almost here. And no, I didn't know he was planning on being here."

"He's so condescending," Kurt said. "Why do you work for him?"

"Most of the time we're not together on a mission such as this. We just converse over the phone."

"Is he really all that rich?"

"Apparently. Never seems to worry about money matters that I know of."

"If I had all that money, I'd be fishing in the South Pacific, not grubbing my way around a damn cave in a forgotten country."

"He's excited by all this. Thinks he's still a bigshot in 'Nam or something," Doyle said.

"I just want us to end this mission soon. I'm getting sick and tired of wandering around, doing nothing with our thumbs up our butts. If we move in, kill every last one of the bastards, I doubt any of them would ever be discovered in this place." His voice snarled and hissed venom as he spoke.

"Kurt, you can always turn back. Leave any time. You ought to be able to find your way back to Ulaanbaatar alone."

Kurt snarled again and lowered his eyes. "I don't want to go back alone, Ben, I want to get this damned thing over and done with. All this jacking around makes me jumpy."

"Look," Doyle said, putting a hand on Kurt's shoulder, "this will all be over soon. Then we will be enjoying cold beer on a nice vacation. Eastwood has promised."

Eastwood returned and Kurt moved back to a spot farther from the dwindling fire. The BioGen CEO reclined against the rock wall and soon was sleeping.

Doyle nearly blew a fuse.

*Now we have to wait while the boss naps.*

�

Dr. Kesler sat in Stu Walcott's office in the San Francisco Police Department, waiting for the sergeant to return. He had not heard from Harry in days and was worried that some misfortune had befallen the team. He fidgeted and looked out the sergeant's window overlooking downtown and listened to the faint moan of cars on the Bayshore Freeway.

Walcott entered, closed the door, slouched in his chair, and lit a cigarette. His white shirt was wrinkled and sported a mustard stain on the front. He looked at Kesler with stone gray eyes and smiled. "And how are you, Doctor? How is Cal Pacific these days?"

"I'm not doing very well, Sergeant, but the university keeps plugging along as usual."

"Any news from your scientist colleague, Dr..."

"Olson," Kesler interjected. "Dr. Olson. No, I haven't heard a word from him and that is why I'm here. I'm terribly worried. I hoped maybe you had heard something from Mongolia or INTERPOL."

Walcott blew a large smoke ring toward the window and took a sip of coffee from a Styrofoam cup. He made a face and set the cup on his desk. "Police coffee, Doctor. Don't ever try the stuff. Like battery acid. Actually, we have not heard anything back from the Mongolian police. The language barrier makes things like that difficult. Which is why INTERPOL is usually the liaison between countries in situations such as this. They have sent an initial message to them outlining what happened to you. I don't suppose you can add anything to the descriptions of the men who abducted you?"

"Unfortunately, no, Sergeant. I have the worst feeling about all of this. Harry—er—Dr. Olson is a dear friend as well as colleague. I'm just sick at the thought that something may have happened to him. Not knowing makes the worry all the more fearful."

Walcott smiled, snubbed out his cigarette, and got up from his chair. "Tell you what, Doctor," he said, taking Kesler by the arm and leading him toward the door. "I'll contact INTERPOL again and see if I can't prod them along on this. Maybe some gentle nudging from my office can produce some results. That sound all right with you?"

Kesler nodded. "It's fine. And thank you."

"I'll keep in touch."

Leaving the Hall of Justice, Kesler prayed again for the team's safety. The potential scientific implications of the latest DNA revelations from the bones and teeth Harry had sent no longer mattered. At least for now. The possibility of discovering a new hominid paled in comparison to Harry's, Dixie's, and the team's safety. He couldn't fathom what his life or his career, let alone his professional reputation, would be like if they did not return. Talking to Dixie's parents had been the hardest thing he had ever done and he doubted he would be able to give them ultimate bad news if it came to that. The fact that he had allowed Harry's mistake to remodel their relationship grieved him to the point of sadness. One didn't hold a son's blunder against him, not if they were loved like he loved Harry. And Harry seemed truly repentant. The reasons behind Harry's actions were understandable in the current world of academic promotions, a world of publish or perish, of discoveries earning pay raises or a notable book. He vowed things would be different if Harry and the team made it back.

Outside, the warm sunshine brightened his spirits somewhat. It was a beautiful day on the San Francisco peninsula. He found his car then headed back to his San Mateo home.

ᘓᘓᘓ

Eastwood woke and looked around. Everyone was sleeping and, in the large cavern, it was quiet as a church on Monday night. He stretched and sat up. It was difficult to believe that he was here in the middle of the earth, scurrying after a bunch of scientists in the dim hope of making a few million dollars. He wondered if he wasn't beginning to lose a grasp on his sanity, what with the trouble in obtaining the president's appointment and now this idiotic stalking. He was no longer sure he knew what he would do when they found them. They might not have anything he wanted or be willing to kill for. And it was that point that concerned him. If the scientists had nothing to show for their efforts, then a confrontation was pointless. Worse yet, if there were needless deaths, then Eastwood would have to bear that responsibility. He was not opposed to killing, just senseless killing. He realized the killers whom Doyle hired were eager for a confrontation, possibly Doyle himself. Many years had passed since Eastwood had soiled his hands with that sort of action and the prospect of doing so in the near future troubled him. Now that he was bottled up in this damned mountain, he was losing his appetite for the pursuit. He had often thought of selling out, finding a nice young woman he could bed, and simply relaxing. But the lure of the next deal, of adding more riches to his name, forestalled that action. He worried that he was addicted to wealth.

Others stirred and soon Doyle was up. Eastwood listened to the idle chatter of the men as they prepared for another trek deeper into the cave. He donned his backpack and strapped his 9 mm pistol to his hip.

Shouting from the front of the small indent caught his attention. Doyle hurried to address him.

"Sir, Marley's gone," he said, looking frantic.

"What?" Eastwood said, suddenly alert.

"Marley was on watch and now he's gone. Disappeared. Gillum and Kurt searched close by and there are no signs of him."

Doyle picked at his ear as if waiting for Eastwood to issue orders.

"He couldn't have just up and disappeared," Eastwood said after a few moments of silence. "He has to be somewhere close, there's no place for him to go. Go look for him."

"I've searched near where he was sitting and the ground is churned up but nothing definitive there. There are occasional footprints scattered about that are Marley's size so he may have decided to explore down the tunnel. But the guys ran down there quite a ways and found nothing."

Kurt came running up, his flashlight casting beams of light back and forth. He was panting hard as he spoke.

"Boss, we found something farther down in the tunnel," he said, gasping. He held out a black boot for Eastwood and Doyle's inspection. "It belongs to Marley. Found it nearly fifty yards down the tunnel."

Gillum walked over and stood by the three men. "Yup, that's Marley's boot all right," he said. "Only he wore a shoe that large."

Doyle grabbed his backpack and nodded at Eastwood. He removed his pistol from its holster, then racked the slide. "Let's go," Doyle said. "Gather up the equipment and let's go find Marley."

Doyle led the way into the tunnel down a series of steps, followed by Eastwood, then Kurt, with Gillum last in line. A short way into the tunnel, they passed strange markings carved into the rock wall.

"Hieroglyphics," Eastwood said. "I've seen them before."

Stopping only briefly to look at the markings, they continued farther. Eastwood halted after a short distance and sniffed the air. "What's that smell?" he asked. "Smells awful."

"Like rotting flesh," Gillum said, as a pungent, sweet odor greeted them. He bumped into Doyle who had stopped.

"Shit," Doyle said.

There on the floor of a small recess carved into the tunnel wall was a mound covered with a blanket. Doyle bent down and pulled back the blanket. Eastwood retched.

They stared at the grisly face of a dead man whose head was half missing. There was nothing left of his eyes but empty sockets. One arm was missing. Dried blood was spattered everywhere.

"Who is he?" Gillum asked, crowding in for a closer look.

"Hell if I know," Kurt said. "Who covered him with a blanket?"

"Look at the robe he has on," Doyle said, raising a portion of it into the light from his headlight. "He's from the monastery. They wore robes like this one."

"How did he get in here?" Eastwood said. "He's a long way from the monastery."

"Who knows?" Doyle said, standing. "The monk at the monastery never mentioned any of their members being missing. Let's keep moving. The research team can't be that far ahead."

As they filed past the corpse, Eastwood couldn't help thinking, *Just how* did *he get in here?*

The tunnel narrowed then widened into a room filled with bones.

# Chapter 25

Harry and his team had moved beyond the bone room, but just how far he wasn't sure. The narrow tunnel twisted and turned and, as they progressed deeper underground, he became completely disoriented. Once, he thought he saw a patch of sunlight but it was just a beam from a headlight reflecting off a rock ahead of them. There were fewer stalactites, a fact Harry thought was due to there being less water at the greater depths. But, so far, their search had only turned up a dead monk, murdered by creature or forces unknown. To wander aimlessly deeper into the mountain no longer seemed an appropriate idea to him, one that might bring disaster to the entire team. Other than the violent death of the monk, there were no clues that pointed to anything substantial. Not a hint as to Dixie's whereabouts. *Hell, she might not even be in this infernal cave.* But he knew different. The screams he heard had to be her. The glowing red eyes had unnerved him and shooting at them had made him jumpy, scared. They were in the creature's world now, one as alien to Harry as the moon, and the creatures were able to attack at will. The team's food and water were limited so, at some point, Stepan was going to call a halt to their search, return to the surface, and take his SWAT team back to Ulaanbaatar. If that happened, Dixie would be left behind.

The tunnel widened and they encountered a deep chasm that was meters in diameter. Stepan came close to stumbling into it and, after regaining his balance, stood at its edge, calculating its depths. Harry pointed his flashlight into the dark abyss.

"Deep, huh?" Stepan said. He picked up a rock and tossed it into the dark hole. No sound indicated that it ever hit bottom.

"I wonder how deep it is," Harry said.

"Step in there by mistake and you're dead," said Li as he came to stand at Harry's side.

The chasm filled most of the space offered by the tunnel leaving only a narrow ledge on one side for a path. One slip and it would be over for the unlucky person. The hole was forty or fifty feet across, as best as Harry could estimate, and what lay beyond no one could fathom.

"I'll scout up ahead," Stepan said as he peeled off his pack. "The rest of you stay put."

Harry watched Stepan creep along the shoulder of the chasm while clinging to the rock wall next to it. It was slow going with just enough room to put one foot in front of the other. The ledge was covered with small stones and gravel, making his footing more precarious. Step after step, he inched along, glancing first at his feet then ahead toward the opposite side of the hole. Along the wall, bordering the hole, numerous rock projections forced Stepan to come dangerously close to disaster. Midway, he stopped, kicked a rock out of his way and into the chasm. The light from his headlamp cast its yellow beam into the dark, flickering, as the captain peered into the hole. When he stepped forward to continue, his foot slipped and he fell into the chasm with a loud *crash*. Harry rushed to the edge of the hole and saw Stepan hugging a large rock twenty feet below. Blood streaked his face and he winced in the light of Harry's flashlight.

"Stepan," he called.

"Shit," the captain called back. "I lost my footing."

"Are you okay?"

"I bruised my ribs and hit my head. But I'm all right if you can help me back up. I was lucky to grab ahold of this rock. It kept me from falling farther."

A SWAT team member arrived with a coil of rope, tied a large loop in it, and then tossed it over the edge to Stepan. The captain, after some struggling, managed, with one hand, to get the rope loop over his head and around his waist.

"Okay," he yelled up to Harry, and soon they began hauling the captain upward.

With each pull of the rope, Stepan helped their effort by finding a rock with his foot and pushing himself toward the chasm opening. After several final tugs, he was out and lay on the ground while two SWAT members checked him over.

"Maybe we ought to turn around," said Jing. "One of us is going to get killed."

Stepan sat up. "We can make it around the hole," he said, softly. "We just need to be careful."

"You sure you're okay, Captain?" When Stepan nodded, Harry continued. "We'll proceed a little farther at least," he said, putting an arm around Jing. "If we don't find Dixie pretty soon, we'll turn around." He looked into his guide's dark eyes in the dim light. "I promise."

Difficult as the going was, one by one they clambered their way around the chasm. Once safely around it, Harry saw that the tunnel widened into still another, larger room. As they dropped to the ground for a rest, four dark forms appeared out of nowhere at the room's far end. The forms were large, covered in long, dark hair, and moved toward them.

"Stepan! Up ahead!" Harry yelled.

Stepan looked into the darkness in time to see the dark shadows moving rapidly toward them. The stench of putrefaction filled the room.

"Weapons ready!" he ordered.

The SWAT team responded and the room was filled with the sounds of AK-12s and Bizon sub-machine guns being locked and loaded.

"Jing and Li, get behind us," Harry said, pushing the pair back toward the chasm.

The dark forms appeared out of nothingness and, as they neared, Harry saw they were large, bear-like creatures, with long dark hair instead of short fur. They walked upright. A long snout sat between two eyes that pierced the darkness with a red glow. The putrid odor that accompanied them stung Harry's nose. It smelled of death and decay and Harry fought to keep his stomach calm.

Stepan's headlight flashed a bright beam at one of the creatures. It stopped, growled, and ambled toward them.

"Got something I can shoot?" Harry shouted at Stepan.

The SWAT team took positions in front of the two men, their weapons ready. The captain handed Harry a 9 mm pistol from his backpack. "Rack the slide and you're ready to shoot," he said.

They waited.

The four creatures moved closer, grunting with each step.

Harry gripped the pistol, his mouth tasting like bitter alum.

The creatures stopped, as if surveying what was ahead of them.

Harry looked at the one in the lead. It was slightly larger than the others, a good eight or nine feet tall. With a flat black snout and upper limbs that functioned like hands and arms, it was more like a giant gorilla or chimpanzee. But its eyes were what caught Harry's attention. Blazing red eyes like fiery, molten steel, leered at him.

With a grunt from the large creature, the group moved again, coming closer.

"Now!" Stepan commanded.

A hail of bullets plowed into the dark forms. A loud roar emerged from the large creature and two of them fell in the barrage of gunfire. The large one and another scampered off into the darkness, grunting and howling. Just before disappearing, the large creature stopped and shot a glance over its shoulder at Harry.

For a moment, their eyes locked on each other.

Then the creatures were gone.

 espeso

Captain Stepan stooped over the corpse of a dead Yeti, felled in the SWAT team's gunfire. His headlight danced over the hulk, its light coming to rest on the creature's large head. Its eyes were open, still gazing with a certain intensity into the darkness beyond. The Yeti's mouth, partially open, revealed long fangs stained dark and Stepan shuddered at the thought of them sinking into his flesh. The feet were enormous and he realized they matched the footprints seen earlier on the steppe. The beast's putrid odor smelled of death and decay, and churned Stepan's stomach.

Harry ambled to his side and squatted beside him. "My God," he exclaimed. "What a beast. I can't believe it. I'm looking at the thing but I can't believe what I'm seeing."

"The damned thing must be ten feet tall. Those feet match the footprints we saw earlier."

"Sixteen inches at least."

"The room with all the bones must be where they live. We stumbled into it and disturbed them. They were protecting their territory."

"What kind of creatures are these?" Harry asked. "Where do they come from?"

"From hell, most likely."

Harry reached out and ran a hand over the Yeti's side. Li and Jing joined him and the captain. Hearing Jing's muffled sobs, Stepan rose and Harry followed suit.

"See, Doctor?" Jing said, wiping her nose on her sleeve. "I was right all along. The Yeti live."

"I never dreamed," Harry said. "I never in my wildest imagination thought something like this could exist in today's world. It just seemed impossible."

"Neither did I," Stepan said. "It's unbelievable. And there's more of them. Two got away and no telling how many more lurk in this mountain."

"We need to find Dixie and get the hell out of here," Harry said. "I fear it may be too late."

"You're right, Harry," Stepan said. "Let's get organized."

"I've heard stories of these beasts since I was a child. I never—" Li began.

"My grandfather knew," Jing said. "And now we all know."

*ଏଓଓ*

Doyle and Eastwood finished sifting through a pile of bones they found scattered about in the large cavern. Most of them looked like small animal bones that neither could identify. Each had gouges on them that resembled teeth marks, indicating that they had been the victims of vicious attacks. Kurt and Gillum had gathered them and stacked them in a large pile for Doyle and their boss to inspect.

"Something big has been gnawing on these bones," Doyle said to Eastwood. "Look how deep these gashes are."

"I still can't get that poor monk out of my mind," Eastwood said. "The poor bastard was torn apart."

"Don't think about that, boss. Look at these bones. What could possibly have made these marks? I have heard talk that evil beasts lurk in these mountains."

Eastwood had stooped to pick up a bone when sounds of gunfire echoed through the large cavern.

"What was that?" said Gillum.

"Sounded like gunshots up ahead," Doyle said. "Rapid fire. Machineguns, most likely."

"The SWAT team?" Eastwood said.

"That would be my guess," Doyle said. "But what could they be shooting at? Have they encountered something?"

"Let's find out, Ben. Take the lead again."

The four men moved out of the cavern into a tunnel, their headlights shining brightly ahead of them. Doyle stumbled over small rocks that were scattered over the narrow pathway. Moving quickly, the group hurried toward the sound of the gunshots while Doyle uttered a silent prayer, his pistol at the ready. The temperature in the tunnel cooled with their further descent into the mountainside and the air became denser, weighing on them like a heavy, invisible cloud.

They were a hundred feet into the tunnel when the pungent odor of cordite hit them. Doyle stopped short and flashed his light into the far reaches of the darkness ahead of them. Nothing.

They continued to move, now more cautiously, their talking abandoned. When the trail turned to the left, Doyle stopped. A faint glow flickered in the distance.

"There's light up ahead," he said. "Stay alert."

Slowly he led the group toward the shimmering lights and, as they approached, he thought he could hear voices.

Yes. Definitely, voices.

"Douse the lights," Doyle commanded. "They're not far away."

Doyle had to make his way in total darkness, which slowed their progress. Unable to see the ground ahead, they crept along with Doyle feeling his way, one hand on the tunnel wall. He heard Eastwood's labored breathing behind him and hoped he was not having a heart attack.

His foot came to the edge of a precipice. He dropped to his knees, probed the ground, and discovered a large chasm, its hole filling most of the tunnel area. It was like moving forward in a blind world and, for a moment, he felt empathy for the visually challenged. Standing against the wall Doyle took several deep breaths. He had been inches from disaster. He wanted to turn on his headlight to get his bearings but feared giving away their presence.

Then ahead were more lights and more voices. They were all talking at once, making it impossible for Doyle to understand what they were saying. In the dim glow, he could make out vague figures huddled together, their headlights and flashlights piercing the darkness. The men carried rifles and approached the opposite side of the chasm with caution.

Doyle switched on his headlight.

"Attention!" he called across the chasm. "At ease! Don't shoot!"

The cacophony of voices ceased and a series of lights were trained on Doyle and Eastwood.

"Who's there? Who are you?" came a call from across the giant hole.

"What are you doing here?" yelled another voice.

"Was that you shooting?" Doyle said, not answering their questions.

"It was," answered a voice. Doyle put his light on the voice and noticed it was a tall, American-looking man. Men in fatigues surrounded him, with their weapons pointed Doyle's way. "I'm coming your way. I see you have guns. Don't shoot."

"Come ahead," Doyle said and he watched the American-looking man inch his way around the chasm until he was facing Doyle and Eastwood.

"You must be Dr. Olson," Doyle said.

"How do you know my name?" the man said.

"We know all about you," interjected Eastwood. "You and your research team."

"But how? Who are you people? Why are you armed?"

"We're here to relieve you of your discovery," Doyle said. "The relics you have uncovered."

"We haven't found anything of scientific significance," Harry said. His thoughts flashed to Kesler's and Stepan's earlier warnings. "We're here looking for a colleague abducted a few days ago. We've been warned about four men wanting to steal our discoveries. You are them?" He glanced at Stephan who had a scowl on his face and a pistol pointing at Doyle.

"We missed you at your research site, Dr. Olson," Doyle said. "You're a long way from your compound."

"We're looking for my assistant," Harry informed them.

Eastwood moved to stand in front of Harry and stared at him with cold eyes. "What was all that shooting about?" he said.

"Yeti."

"Yeti? You've got to be kidding, Doctor."

"I'm serious. I didn't believe they existed either until we were attacked a while ago. Four of the creatures jumped us back there," Dr. Olson said, pointing back across the chasm. "We killed two of them but the other two got away. We still haven't found my assistant."

"We lost one of our men," Doyle said. "He was on guard duty and simply vanished."

"Dixie, my assistant, disappeared, or rather was abducted from our campsite while we were returning to our research compound. Signs of a struggle there led us to these caves. The police arrived and have been with us since."

"How did the police get involved?"

"I don't know. They just showed up."

"You think these creatures will attack again?" Eastwood asked. He was now joined by Gillum and Kurt.

"I don't know," Dr. Olson repeated. "Seeing all these bones and the many rooms around the other cavern leads me to believe a family of the beasts live down here, so anything is possible. Our guide, Jing, has told us that mountain legend says these things live in the high altitudes and venture lower down in search of food. They could drag their prey in here."

"We stumbled across a dead man in what looks like a monk's robe behind us. He was ripped to shreds."

"Yea, we cut him down. He had been hanging in that little room. He was traveling with us as well."

"You think our man and your assistant are in these caves?" Eastwood asked. He paced along the rock wall after asking the question.

"Anything is possible at this point," Dr. Olson said. "I'm sure the police are going to want to return to Ulaanbaatar pretty soon. If we don't find Dixie soon, we'll be on our own."

"Dr. Olson, I suggest you get your team over here where we can discuss this further. If there are more of these Yeti monsters lurking about, we need to have an organized, combined plan to deal with them."

Dr. Olson signaled Stepan, and the SWAT team began filing past the dark hole. Once everyone was together, Stephan approached Eastwood. "Now exactly what were you saying about relics?"

Eastwood took a deep breath, exhaled it slowly before speaking. "Don't lie to me, Doctor, I know different. Whatever it is that you unearthed back at your diggings, I am now confiscating. And the sooner we get out of this creepy cave, the better I'm going to like it. We need to be heading back now."

"My assistant is in here somewhere!" Dr. Olson shouted. "I won't leave until we find her."

Eastwood smiled. "Doctor, be reasonable."

Kurt stood alongside Eastwood and sneered at the scientist. "Please, boss, let me have a go at him."

"Go sit down, Kurt," Eastwood said in a stern voice. "I'm sure the doctor can see he can't win in this."

Stepan, who had been listening, stepped forward. "But, I believe we have the superior firepower. If it's a fight you want, I doubt you'd fare very well."

"That remains to be seen, doesn't it," Eastwood said, his tone more conciliatory.

Doyle started to speak when a woman's scream pierced the quiet.

"Help! Someone help!"

# Chapter 26

Garrett Sawyers's small office, located on the West Wing's second floor, was an isolated affair, crowded with steel files and piled with books and reports. It was stuck inconspicuously in a corner by the elevator. He liked the quiet but cramped space, for it offered a retreat from the hectic grind below him. Across his desk in a leather chair sat Hugh Grant, one of the chief of staff's many administrative assistants. Grant did odd jobs for the COS and, as a result was not well known among West Wing insiders, but the two men had become friends during the president's campaign. Sawyers had called him for this meeting because he needed someone with a foot into the Oval Office.

"Coffee?" Sawyers said.

"Sure."

Sawyers rose and poured two Styrofoam cups of the liquid and handed one to Grant as he returned to his desk. "How are things downstairs?" he said.

"The usual chaos," Grant said, taking a sip of the coffee. "Getting close to re-election time, you know. People are starting to freak out."

"I can imagine. Listen, could you to deliver a message to the COS?"

"Be happy to, Garrett, unless it's about leaks or something." He chuckled at the word *leaks* and took another sip of his coffee.

"Nothing so onerous, Hugh. POTUS was all set to name a

man named Rutherford Eastwood to head his charitable donations commission. Now it turns out the man isn't what he seemed."

"Oh?" Grant said with raised eyebrows.

"According to an FBI investigation, it appears his company, BioGen, using an unknown negotiator, tried to extort a rare prehistoric skeleton from the American Museum of Natural History in New York. Apparently happened last year. A museum curator has recently come forward with the accusation and Justice is investigating. In addition, there have been grumblings concerning a business deal with the Saudis—that Bio-Gen extorted the money out of the Saudis by threatening to go public about one of their royal princes. So Eastwood is not as clean as we thought. Can you deliver the message?"

"Sure, no problem."

"Thanks, I owe you one."

Grant was busy writing as Sawyers spoke. "Any evidence other than the curator's accusation?"

"Like I said, something about the Saudis getting a rare relic furnished by BioGen that might not be on the up and up. But the details don't matter. He's out, as far as the commission is concerned. The president will want to know what the investigation turned up."

"Anything about the man himself?"

"Vietnam vet, built his company from nothing, has a large security detail. Rumor has it he has been stockpiling a large cache of weapons. The Bureau has turned the results of their investigation over to the attorney general's office."

"I'd hate to be in his shoes with Justice on my tail."

"Agreed," said Sawyers.

❧❧

Kurt was incensed. Being told off by Eastwood left him confused and angry. It was time to settle this affair once and for all, and he couldn't understand why the boss didn't see it that way. The solution was simple—kill the bastards, find the relics, and return home. He didn't care about the damned beasts. Let them rot in here. Once the scientists and SWAT team were all dead, it would be an easy matter to find their way back to Ulaanbaatar and board the train to Beijing where the Hawker was waiting. A surprise attack on the SWAT team would neutralize any resistance, and the rest would be like shooting ducks in a barrel. And no one would find them in this infernal cave. It was the perfect burial place.

He had spent most of his younger years either in reform school or behind bars. Being a member of the *Hombres del diablo* gang in Los Angeles had given him a toughness and indifference that made him Doyle's most skillful assassin. In his youth, he had carried out execution orders from his gang leader and had many kills of the *Crips* and *Bloods* to his credit. No one dared venture into their territory, on pain of death.

At age nineteen, he served five years for second-degree manslaughter for a shooting that should have been for first-degree murder, except that the DA had no evidence directly linking Kurt to the crime. So he copped a plea and did his time in a minimum-security facility in Sacramento. Once out, he put the gang life behind him, headed east, and landed in Philadelphia where he found a job in a meat processing plant. He married a girl who worked in the plant's distribution center and thought he had things going his way, when her brother approached him with a plan for making some easy money. The plan was to rob the plant's safe and, when the attempt went haywire, Kurt found himself on the run. He ditched his wife and her brother and took the train to New York.

He was working as a stevedore for the Port of New York at its container terminal on Staten Island when Doyle found him, took him to his walkup apartment, and offered him a job. Liked the way Kurt handled himself, he said. Doyle encouraged him to get his GED and introduced him to Eastwood. Soon he was a member of the inner sanctum, along with Gillum and Marley.

Sitting alone, he fingered the clip in the M-16. One spray of the gun while their backs were turned, and it would be all over. He needed to talk to Marley. If Doyle wouldn't go along with them, maybe they would have to do it themselves.

❧❧❧

"That's Dixie's voice," Harry exclaimed. He jumped to his feet and stared in the direction of the scream.

"Everybody up," Stepan said. "We're going to find her."

The SWAT team rose, shouldered their weapons, and followed their captain and Harry as they hurried toward the sound. Eastwood, with his men, followed suit, with Jing and Li at the rear of the column.

The panicked call for help came only once, a fact that disturbed Harry as they scurried back toward the waterfall. The group hurried in silence, their headlights and flashlights illuminating the path ahead. The tunnel got wider and the roar of cascading water became louder. As they turned a corner, six Yeti blocked their way.

The grotesque creatures screeched and flashed long teeth, their red eyes blazing in the dim light. They blocked further progress, the course hair on the nape of their necks erect.

"Shoot!" cried Stepan.

The Yeti advanced in a rush.

Gunfire erupted that sent the Yeti into a screaming frenzy. Blood splattered the ground and walls as two Yeti fell.

The remaining four animals stopped in their tracks, as if stunned and contemplating their next move, and then they advanced again. Two scurried to their left, one ambled to their right, and one lunged straight at them. Blood dripped from their dark hair, their red eyes glancing side to side. Snarling and showing their fangs, they blocked the tunnel, making escape impossible.

Another volley of gunfire sent the animals howling in obvious pain, but one lurched forward, grabbed Kurt, and snapped his neck in one fluid motion. When the creature released him, Kurt slumped motionless on the ground.

Stepan and the SWAT team fell back, but the Yeti kept coming. More shots were fired but none of the animals fell. They had fired over a hundred rounds but only two Yeti were dead. Harry's pistol was empty.

When the center Yeti lunged forward again, the SWAT

team fired another long volley at them, the gunfire echoing throughout the cavern.

The Yeti scurried back through the tunnel and out of sight.

Doyle rushed to kneel at Kurt's body. Finding no pulse, he stood and faced Eastwood. "Those bastards," he hissed. "Kurt was a good man. Always ready to watch our backs."

Stepan and Harry stumbled around the dead Yeti. At the far edge of the cavern they entered a small alcove obscured by stalactites.

Dixie, strapped by her arms to pegs in the walls, hung unconscious.

"Get some help," Harry cried to Stepan while he worked to free Dixie's bindings. Stepan left while Harry lifted his assistant off the wall and gently laid her on the ground. She took short shallow gasps of air. Her face, contorted in pain, was covered with blood and sported large purple splotches. She didn't move, but lay limp as a rag doll. Harry placed an arm behind her head and spoke to her.

"Dixie," he said in a faltering voice. "Dixie, can you hear me? It's Harry."

Stepan returned with Doyle and Eastwood. They rushed into the alcove and peered at Dixie's body. She was not moving, not responding to Harry's pleadings. A few SWAT team members stood nearby, anger and confusion etched on their faces.

Dixie moved an arm and opened her eyes. She coughed and Harry touched her face with his free hand. He looked at Stepan, then Dixie.

"Ha—Harry?" Dixie stuttered, rubbing her head, wincing as she did. "I—is that you, Harry?"

"It is. Feel like sitting up?"

Dixie nodded and Harry helped her into a sitting position. She blinked at the bright light from several headlights that were focused on her. While Harry stroked her hand, she licked her lips, and tried to swallow.

"Here's water," Harry said, offering his water bottle.

The woman gulped several deep swallows then looked around with wide, dazed eyes. Doyle and Eastwood crowded next to her while Stepan gathered his men into a tight circle.

"How did you get here?" she asked. "Who are all these people?"

"We have been desperate to find you, Dixie. Your friends are here."

"Oh." Dixie took more gulps of the water.

"Feel like telling me what happened?" Harry brushed a wisp of hair away from her eyes.

"I—I had to—to use the bathroom. The monster—"

Dixie's head fell back, eyes rolling upward.

"Dixie?" Harry said.

She focused her gaze upon Harry again. "The monster—grabbed me."

"It's a Yeti," Doyle said, kneeling next to Harry. "What happened then?"

"I don't remember. Some—somehow I got here. The thing tied me up. It hurt me, Harry."

With that, Dixie burst into tears and sobbed on Harry's shoulder. It was awkward but he placed an arm around her and let her cry for a long while. Finished, she looked at him with tear-stained eyes and smiled faintly. "I'm sorry," she said.

Jing came to Dixie's aid and pushed the men aside.

"Doctor, I'll help her, please. Leave me with her for a few moments. You men leave us alone."

Harry nodded and watched as Dixie got slowly to her feet and was escorted by Jing to a darkened corner of the cavern.

After they were gone, Eastwood spoke. "All right, we've found the girl—let's get out of here."

"What about Marley?" Doyle said.

"He knew the risks. I can't worry about him now," Eastwood said.

"We can't just leave him here," Gillum said. "And Kurt."

Eastwood confronted Gillum, his face inches from the man's nose. "Shut the hell up. Who is the boss here, anyway?"

"Gillum's right, Mr. Eastwood," Doyle said, using the formal *mister*. "We can't leave one of our team behind. Didn't do it in Nam and we can't do it here."

Harry watched the argument from a distance while Stepan

stood with his men. Eastwood pointed his pistol at Gillum.

"As I said, Gillum. I'm the hard case here and I call the shots. You'll do as I say or else."

Gillum flinched at the pistol. "All the same, Mr. East-wood—"

Before he could get another word out, Eastwood pumped two rounds into Gillum's chest. Blood engulfed the front of the man's shirt and he fell backward without uttering a sound. Bloody froth issued from his mouth in a final gasp.

"My God!" Doyle screamed. "Why?"

Eastwood holstered his pistol, stepped over Gillum's body, and pointed a finger at Doyle. "Like I said. We're getting out of here. Now!"

The SWAT team surrounded Eastwood, AK-12s pointed at him. Eastwood looked surprised and started for his pistol.

"No, no, Mr. Eastwood. That's your name, right?" Stepan ambled up to the man and removed his pistol from its holster. "You sir, are under arrest. You can't murder someone in front of the Mongolian Police and not expect to be arrested. Ser-geant, bind this man's hands."

Two SWAT team members shoved Eastwood into the cav-ern wall and tied his hands in front of him. Li and Jing stood by Harry, eyes wide with shock.

Doyle shook his head and looked at Stepan. "Captain, are you sure you want to do this? He might be of help later."

"Actually, Mr. Doyle, why don't you hand over your weapon as well? At least for now. We would all feel better, I'm sure."

Doyle grumbled but did as requested then sauntered to Eastwood's side.

ೲೱೲ

Eastwood sat in darkness, hands bound, fuming while Doyle stood next to him, not returning his stare. He was in a state of disbelief. Two of his men were dead and one was missing but he didn't care about them in the least. They were expendable, like pawns in a chess game, given up as a sacrifice in pursuit of a larger objective. Now his security chief seemed to be waffling in his loyalty, leaving him alone to figure a way out of their current predicament.

He struggled against his bindings but found they were tight. A SWAT member had shoved him to the ground and he sat at an odd angle, his legs aching and his feet numb.

In the hail of gunfire, the creatures had looked as if they had been loosed from hell. He had never seen anything like them before. In spite of their hideous appearance and menacing manner, they were awesome creatures and a further thought began to slowly materialize in his haggard mind. To have a Yeti in his possession, alive or dead, would make him fabulously wealthy. It would command millions, or more, if he decided to put it on tour. If, somehow, he could pull it off.

But Doyle was a problem that was not going away. Eastwood knew him well. If they managed to return to New York, the man would have to go. Eastwood would not tolerate disloyalty.

におに

"Now, everyone, listen up," Stepan said. "We are going to get out of this infernal place, one way or the other. If those creatures attack again, we'll fight."

"Li, Jing, gather your belongings along with mine," Harry said. "I'll help Dixie."

Stepan led the SWAT team into the tunnel, followed by Eastwood and Doyle, then Li and Jing, with Dixie and Harry last in line. A weakened Dixie stumbled along, Harry supporting her with an arm around her waist. The group formed a serpentine line with their lights dancing off the tunnel walls.

Stepan and his men forged ahead while Harry's group staggered a few meters behind. Doyle and Eastwood dawdled in the middle causing Harry to wonder if they were planning something.

They paused at the stream to reconnoiter a way across. Harry walked downstream a few paces to where he had crossed before and signaled Stepan.

"Give me a rope," he said to the captain. "I'll wade across. The rest of you can tie into the rope and follow."

Jing began to cry.

"Please, Harry. Don't make me do it. I almost drowned before."

Li came to her side and hugged her. "Don't worry," he said. "I will hold on to you. Nothing will happen, I promise."

Harry tied one end of the rope around his waist and waded into the water. The freezing cold encircled his ankles and his legs but he forged ahead, progressing deeper. He waited while Jing tied herself onto the rope and entered the water, then one of the SWAT team put an arm around her waist. Li followed and came to support her other side. Harry noticed that there was a faint smile on her lips. Halfway across, at the point where Jing had previously gone under, the current picked up, the dark water pushing against his legs. But she continued without a word, leaving Harry to utter a silent prayer of thanks.

One by one, the group's members tied themselves onto the rope and followed Harry, Jing, and Li into the water. Dixie followed, then a few of the SWAT team members brought up the end of the line.

It was when they were all in the water that the Yeti reappeared.

# Chapter 27

Kesler was on the phone with Sergeant Walcott. He was in his office at Cal Pacific University when the police detective called. Kesler listened with a racing pulse as Walcott spoke.

"The situation is this, Doctor, at least as best as I can uncover. A Mongolian SWAT team has been sent to the research site to find Dr. Olson and warn him that he and his people may be in some danger. This was done about a week ago. There has been only sporadic news from the SWAT team since leaving Ulaanbaatar. They traveled by helicopter so they should have been there days ago. That's all I can tell you for now."

"No word on Dr. Olson or the rest of the team, then?"

"Sorry, no. I do have a number for the National Police but when I tried it, all I got was someone who didn't speak English. No way to get through to anyone who did. If anyone *does* speak our language there. INTERPOL is supposed to help with these language barriers and they usually do, so I'll keep after them to provide us with an update."

"Sergeant, not knowing anything is taking its toll on this older man. Dr. Olson and his assistant, Miss Zinn, are very close to my heart. I couldn't go on if something happened to them."

"Now, Doctor, it hasn't come to that and I doubt that it will. I will keep trying to find someone there who speaks English and, in the meantime, you keep the faith."

Kesler hung up the phone and stared out at the Pacific

Ocean. Dark thunderclouds were building far out over the blue water, promising much needed rain. At least there was the beginning of some action. *Keep the faith.* Wasn't that the way Walcott put it? The man didn't know how many prayers and *Shemas* he had said already. He needed to be there, to help in some way.

He took the phone book from a desk drawer and looked up the number to Air China, thinking he would fly to Ulaanbaatar and see if he could move things along or offer help. Realistically, however, what could he do? No much, really. But just being there might provide the motivation the police needed to continue their investigation.

He placed the phone book back in the drawer and drank from the bottled water on his desk. It was premature to leave the States now. Harry could be out in the field as he was supposed to be and this could all be a stupid mistake and wild goose chase by the SWAT team. Kesler trusted Harry's judgement, so he would wait a little while longer before getting on that plane. Harry would be upset if he showed up and there was no reason to do so. In the meantime he would do as Walcott instructed—keep praying.

※

This time there were three hairy creatures. They ambled to near the water's edge and stood snarling, their red eyes blazing, blocking the tunnel behind them.

Jing screamed.

Stepan loosed himself from the rope, aimed his Russian pistol, and fired at the beasts. The Yeti howled and moved back a few meters allowing the SWAT team to take up a position along the shoreline. They fired at the Yeti, who again retreated into the dark tunnel.

Harry pulled Eastwood onto dry land where he stood with Doyle, Li, and Dixie. Harry could hear the snarling and growling ahead but could not make out the Yeti in the darkness.

The Yeti had them trapped. Behind them was the stream and the seemingly endless cave system that was a confusing morass of rooms and tunnels. The only known way out to the surface was through the tunnel now blocked by the Yeti who were proving difficult to kill.

More beasts kept coming, taking the place of their fallen comrades.

Harry dropped to the ground and crawled next to Stepan. "Any ideas?"

The captain shook his head. "Not at present, Doctor. As long as those beasts are in the tunnel, we are stuck right here. There seems to be an endless supply of them."

"When we run out of ammunition we'll be done for," Harry said.

"Let's hope that doesn't happen."

"What if we could get them out of the tunnel?"

"What do you mean?"

Harry glanced around, noticing that the SWAT team still had their weapons ready.

"If we could lure the Yeti in here somehow," he said, "maybe we could manage to get into the tunnel. The route would take us to the surface."

"Force them into this cavern here?"

"Exactly. Force or give them some sort of bait to lure them in."

Doyle had joined the pair and was listening to the conversation. "Captain," he said, "get a few of your men at the far end of the cavern and see if the Yeti will go after them. If they do, we can scramble into the tunnel. Use them as bait."

"Once in the tunnel, the beasts will just follow after us," Stepan said.

"Not if we can block it behind us," Harry said.

"Not much around to do that," Doyle said. "I don't think we can outrun them, either."

"We have some C-4 plastic explosive with a few blasting caps," Stepan said. "We could blow the tunnel and trap the bastards in this cavern."

Eastwood stepped next to Doyle. "Are you nuts?" he said. "You'll kill us all."

"It seems to be our only chance, Eastwood," Harry said. "I

say we try it, Captain. If we don't do something, we're gonna die, anyway."

"You think it will work?" Doyle said to no one in particular.

Eastwood threw up his bound hands in anger and frustration. "Wait a minute. What you're thinking of doing is suicide. A blast like that will surely kill every last one of us."

"We don't have many options," Stepan said. "We could try to kill them all, right here but they have proven difficult enough to kill."

"No other viable options," Harry said. "Let's get to it."

Li and Jing nodded.

"Do it," Li agreed.

"We all are going to die in here," Eastwood complained, whining now.

"Sir," Doyle said, "we don't have any other options. We have to try it."

Stepan called to three of his men and explained the plan. They ran to the far side of the cavern and began throwing small stones into the tunnel. More snarling and growling emanated from its depths. Stepan moved everyone next to the cavern wall where the darkness obscured them.

They waited.

More rocks were thrown into the tunnel.

A Yeti appeared, barely visible, in the tunnel entrance.

When Stepan flashed his light illuminating the creature, it ducked back into the darkness. He turned his light off.

More rocks thrown.

This time, three Yeti trudged into the cavern and lumbered in the direction of the SWAT team. When they were a good distance from the tunnel, Stepan signaled *now* and scrambled toward its entrance. Harry pushed Jing and Dixie ahead of him. Once in the tunnel, Harry took Dixie by the waist and held her close.

"You okay?"

"I'm fine, Harry. Just weak and shaken up. Get us out of here, please."

Harry frowned. "I plan on doing just that."

He helped her as she collapsed onto the ground beside Jing. The three SWAT team members rushed into the tunnel behind Doyle and Eastwood and their other comrades.

"Put the C-4 around the entrance," Stepan told one of his men who dug into a pack and produced the plastic explosive and blasting caps.

Two men worked quickly, stuffing the explosive into cracks around the tunnel entrance. In the cavern the Yeti were heard shuffling about, growling, and snorting. Finished with the explosives, the men connected the caps to a small electronic detonator and set the timer. They gathered their equipment and started for the world outside. It was still dark inside the cave system but Harry felt a surge of hope that they might get out alive.

A tremendous explosion rocked the mountain when the C-4 blew. The ground shook and the tunnel walls rattled, sending smoke smelling of burnt oil billowing down the tunnel and to engulf the group. Harry's nose and lungs burned. Dixie gagged and wheezed.

Harry grabbed his assistant's arm and pushed her ahead of him down the tunnel. The dense smoke made seeing impossible even with his flashlight. He groped along, not knowing where Stepan was ahead of him. Panic shot through him and caused his head to throb. He stopped and peered into the dark ahead.

Nothing but smoke and dust.

Then he saw a headlight flickering in the smoky haze.

Another rumble in the darkness.

A boulder crashed into the tunnel from above.

More deep rumbles.

The ground shook as if in an earthquake.

All at once, the tunnel walls gave way and collapsed on them, rocks and boulders landing everywhere. Harry pushed Dixie to the ground and lay over her, hoping to protect her from the falling rock and debris. In the confusion, he heard Jing scream but could not locate her. Beams from several headlights pierced the dark and danced wildly amongst the rubble.

Then, quiet.

Total darkness.

One by one, members of the group started to move. Harry stumbled to his knees then stood, trembling. He groped about, found Dixie, and helped her to her feet while he searched for Stepan. Finding his flashlight half-buried in the rocks, he switched it on and noticed a crushed, blood-stained body protruding from beneath a large boulder. It was a SWAT team member. Jing also noticed it and began crying.

Stepan knelt beside the man and shook his head. "He was a good soldier. Always followed orders. I loved the man."

Eastwood sat in the dim light, silent. Dense dust hung in the small space, filling lungs with unbreathable air. What had been a tunnel had been reduced to barely a crawl space.

"We're all dying, one by one," Jing sobbed. "We're not going to make it."

Stepan ignored her and attempted to rally the group. "We need to find a way through all this rubble, the sooner the better. We don't have much water left, but if we work as a team, I believe we'll make it."

Two of the SWAT team pulled the soldier's corpse behind a pile of rocks while Stepan began searching for a way out of the impasse in which they found themselves.

જીૐજી

Eastwood sat on a rock ledge with his back against what was left of the tunnel wall watching the flurry of activity around him. His body ached and his stomach rumbled as he stared at his hands bound at his waist. But he humored himself by scrutinizing the work being done by the others. He was covered with a fine layer of dust and was in desperate need of a hot shower, a martini, and a good cigar. Those items, however, seemed far off at the moment.

He leaned back and took in a deep breath. He had learned one thing. The trip had not been in vain, for he had discovered something of greater value than anything he could have hoped for back in New York. It would take some doing to pull it off but maybe he and Doyle could do it. And he didn't believe the captain could keep him and Doyle secured all the way back to Ulaanbaatar.

As he contemplated the possibilities, Doyle, as if beckoned by his thoughts, came to sit next to him. "Doing okay, sir?" he asked in a low voice.

"Yeah, just great, Ben. You couldn't loosen these bindings could you? My hands are growing numb."

"Sorry, boss. They watch me all the time. You need some water?"

"No, I'm not thirsty. But listen, I have idea once we get out of here."

Doyle's scowl faded.

"You realize we have discovered something immensely more valuable in these caves than anything thought of before."

Doyle's eyes widened, his face brightened. "Yeah? Like what?"

"These creatures, stupid. The Yeti. Just think what a specimen would mean if we could produce one. What do you think something like that would be worth?"

"I dunno. Lots, I guess."

"It's incalculable, that's what it is. Probably millions."

"Yes, I'm sure you're right."

"And, Ben, they are right here under our noses, just waiting for us to drag one out and show the world. The Chinese would pay anything for an actual Yeti specimen."

"Better still, boss, why not tranquilize one and take it back as living proof of their existence."

Eastwood could hardly contain himself. "Ben, you're a genius. Like King Kong or Mighty Joe Young, eh? God, I can see it now. We would not only be rich but famous to boot. I love the idea."

Doyle frowned and placed a hand on Eastwood's arm.

"It would be difficult to pull off," Eastwood continued. "These bastards aren't going to just let us up and walk out of here, are they?"

"Maybe we can make that happen, boss. At some point, while they are busy figuring a way out of here, they're going to take their eyes off us. If only for a moment or two."

"If we can escape, we can always come back later and get ourselves a specimen, huh Ben?"

"But everyone here knows where these beasts live just as we do. What if one of them comes up with the same idea?"

"Yes, Ben. You're right. But it's a problem that's not without a solution, I am sure. We just need to begin thinking in the right direction, that's all."

# Chapter 28

Eastwood had new life. A brilliant idea was taking shape in his mind, an idea that would make him the envy of every scientist and propel him to the forefront of the world's richest men. First, he needed to get free of his bindings. That done, he and Doyle would overpower the SWAT team and take their weapons. Killing no longer held a moral impediment when wealth beyond belief was within reach. Too bad, for Dr. Olson seemed a likable fellow. *Maybe he could be persuaded to join BioGen.* But the rest would have to go, that much was clear.

A Yeti specimen, dead or alive, would seal Eastwood's reputation. A living Yeti, touring the world, would assure his place for posterity, his name forever written in history books. The *how* of capturing a Yeti alive would have to wait, however. His immediate problem was freeing himself and overpowering the captain and his SWAT team. Eastwood would have to bide his time until Doyle could free him.

❧❧❧

Harry struggled to pull rocks and boulders aside while Stepan directed the SWAT team in assisting. Being underground without the sun's daily ritual of rising and setting had completely upset Harry's bodily rhythms, making it difficult to focus on the task at hand.

The explosion had not only blocked the creatures from getting at them but also caused a general cave-in from which he feared there might not be an escape. Enormous rocks, boulders, and rubble blocked the tunnel leading to the mountain surface, and it dawned on Harry that his plan might have sealed their fate underground. While he worked, he thought back on Eastwood's words. *I want the relics you have uncovered.* What did he mean by that remark? Did he know of the bones and teeth discovered in the Russian plane? They had since been involved in fighting off the Yeti attacks, leaving the statement's meaning shrouded in mystery.

Eastwood was obviously a big-shot back home as the man called Doyle addressed him with some deference. But what or who he was had not been forthcoming. When Stepan confiscated their weapons, Harry was surprised at the firepower belonging to them.

He paused, wiped the sweat and dust from his eyes, then continued laboring over a large rock sitting on an even larger pile of debris. The dust, combined with his sweat, made a thick mud pack that caked his face, forcing him to stop and peel it off.

They worked at a fever's pace but did not make much headway. The tunnel, blocked off from any circulating air, became a miserable sauna, reeking of week-old sweat, body odor, and grime. They were confined to an area no larger than a small room and the atmosphere was stifling. So far, not much progress had been made in clearing a hole through the rubble and Harry was losing his resolve.

A shout rang out.

Harry scrambled on his hands and knees over to Stepan. The man peered into a narrow shaft that opened up when a boulder was rolled away. The captain aimed his flashlight into the dark recess that led into a passageway different from the tunnel. It was more like a low crawlspace, just big enough for a person to negotiate on their belly.

"It's not the main tunnel," Stepan said, removing his head from the hole. "Can't tell where it leads. Maybe nowhere."

Harry watched the captain's light flash beams of illumination down the small crawlspace, dust heavy in the dank air.

"Should we try it?" Harry asked. "Looks big enough to crawl through."

"We have no idea where it leads," Stepan said, shaking his head. "I don't know. Could be a false passage."

"Well, our retreat is blocked. We don't have much of a choice."

"Yeah, that seems to be the size of it. Okay, I'll lead, then we'll push Eastwood and his man through, followed by the women, then you and your man. My SWAT guys can bring up the rear."

"If the way gets blocked, we'll just have to back up and re-think."

"It won't matter. We're running out of water. We either get out of this miserable place today or we die here." Stepan wiped his perspiring face on a sleeve. "All right, let's move."

Stepan freed Eastwood's hands then crawled on his abdomen into the shaft and disappeared. Harry grabbed first Eastwood then Doyle by an arm and shoved them toward the crawlspace opening.

Eastwood protested. "You expect to get us out of here through that hole?"

"Look," Harry said, "I don't really care if you die in here or not. But if want to try and save yourself, you'll get to crawling. Understand?"

Eastwood shook his head in disgust and squirmed his way into the passageway. Doyle followed him. Jing, Dixie, and Li followed them. After they had inched their way down the shaft, Harry followed. The light from his flashlight cast a beam on the rocks as they slinked forward on their hands and knees. The SWAT team brought up the rear.

The cramped space was thick with dust and it quickly became inhospitable. Ahead, Harry heard Dixie cough and realized his lungs were feeling heavy, making it difficult to breath. The walls of the crawlspace pushed in on Harry from all sides, oppressive, overwhelming. Using one hand to steady himself, he reached out with the other and found a bandana in his shirt pocket. With difficulty, he tied it around his nose and mouth and continued to worm his way along. Soon everyone was coughing. Harry's lips were parched and his mouth felt like bitter sandpaper. What he wouldn't give for a nice cold beer.

Forward, his vision was blocked by Li's small frame but he could make out the dancing lights of Stepan's headlight. *Still making progress.*

As a child, Harry was claustrophobic and had been terrified when his brother had locked him in a closet. In a panic, he screamed for someone to find him and when, finally, his father heard his cries and let him out, he spent the remaining afternoon in his room shivering and whimpering. The terror of that time never left and now, as an adult, he detested tight spaces. He fought to keep his mind focused and his emotions under control. Any moment, he feared he would break down into a screaming, whimpering mass like on that dreadful afternoon. The sooner they got out of this mess, the better.

Crawling on his belly and using his legs to propel himself forward, he inched along. His lungs burned. With each cough, pain seared his breathing passages. His face was caked in a thin layer of mud. Every now and then, the group's progress was halted by something unseen and Harry took the time to wipe his face and nose with the bandana. Then he would begin creeping along, once again, hoping—no, praying—for survival.

A deep rumble passed over them. The shaft quaked. Behind Harry, the wall of the tunnel gave way and collapsed with a roar, spewing a cloud of dust over everyone.

Another rumble.

Then another.

Then quiet.

Harry peered through the thick dust behind, sensing a catastrophe.

The SWAT team was gone.

Where they had been was a mass of rocks and boulders. The air was thick with dust making visibility in the low light next to impossible. He aimed his light behind him but saw nothing but rock. The shaft had collapsed on the SWAT team.

He heard shouts up ahead but could not make out the words.

Li twisted in the narrow confines and shot a terrified glance at Harry. "Oh my God!" he said.

"What's the shouting ahead?" Harry said.

"The Captain wants to know what happened. What should I say?"

Harry forced down an urge to vomit. "Tell him there has been a cave-in. The SWAT team is lost. There is no way to get them out."

Harry heard Dixie and Jing begin to cry. Li shouted Harry's message ahead and the group began to move forward once again.

℮↷℮↷

Eastwood could hardly contain himself. *What a stroke of good luck!* The SWAT team had perished. In spite of his current situation, that single fact made his predicament less worrisome and his future a little brighter. The odds were decidedly improving in his favor, making his and Doyle's escape more probable. Although the dust and cramped conditions made breathing difficult, he relaxed a little, knowing that things were looking up. If they could find a way out of this miserable mountain, he and Doyle now stood a much better chance of escaping—only the doctor and the police captain stood in their way. Once out of the cave, it would be an easy matter to overpower them, seize their weapons, and head for home. Boarding the train might present a problem without clean clothes, but he would cross that bridge when he came to it. His Hawker was waiting in Beijing. He managed a small smile. The grit in his mouth wasn't as disagreeable as he pushed forward on his hands and knees in the dark.

Things were definitely looking up.

℮↷℮↷

Dixie was near panic and sobbing. Her tears mixed with the dust caked on her face, turning the mess into a dried mud facial. It was difficult to move her mouth with the dried mud and the dust choked her and made it hard to breathe. It was surreal being in this place. Almost like a dream. No, a nightmare. She knew she was going to die.

When the Yeti grabbed her and carried her off, she had put up a fight, but the creature's strength easily overpowered her. Its hot, fetid breath, smelling like rotten garbage, overwhelmed her senses. Its eyes, piercing, red, glowed were like embers in a dying campfire. Most of all, she remembered its fangs, long and pointed, stained yellow and brown.

At first, she waited in fear for it to sink those long canines into her neck and was surprised when the Yeti carried her to a cave and deposited her in a small room. It then tied her to the wall, using crudely fashioned straps made of dried vines. The monster knew what it was doing, acted almost human. There she had hung until rescued by Harry.

During her three-day imprisonment, Dixie was in a state of exhaustion, as she silently watched the Yeti come and go. Was it a hallucination that they seemed to be an extended family? One male creature seemed dominant over the others and appeared to be their leader, while a smaller female was never far from the leader's side. In her tortured mind, Dixie thought the other Yeti completed the family, although what the exact nature of the unit was she couldn't say. Had it even been real? She was beginning to doubt her memory of that time. But they did seem to be some sort of primate unit, for they knew each other and worked together. They grunted some sort of language that only they understood and, surprisingly, seemed to have affection for each other. At one time, Dixie thought she saw the male caress his mate.

The Yeti came and went, never paying her much attention. They seemed content to have her confined and helpless, giving her no food or water. As the hours dragged on, she became weaker and it was as if she was in a dream, looking down on her body. But then, one of the hairy beasts would amble into the little room, shove its ugly face into hers, and snarl, its hot breath smelling of rancid meat. But not once did one of them harm her. It was as if they were studying her, like in the movie *Planet of the Apes.*

Or, maybe, she was just a piece of Yeti art, stuck on the wall for them to enjoy.

Nearing collapse, she lost her fear of being eaten alive and accepted her predicament. Dixie remembered the moment she realized she was not going to survive because Harry had no idea where she was. Never very religious but spiritual in her own way, she felt that there was some sort of soul's existence after death, although exactly what it was, she couldn't say. But she knew it would be a good existence—of that she had no doubt. So she wasn't afraid of dying, exactly, but dying without knowing Harry saddened her. She so much wanted what had begun to form between them to have a chance to grow and blossom. There was no one like Harry and she longed for him, as she grew weaker and weaker. She needed his comforting look and soft, reassuring words. As she passed from consciousness into a dream state, she saw the two of them together, happy.

By the second day of her imprisonment, the Yeti hardly noticed her as they came and went. Sometimes the large male would saunter up to her, stare for a moment or two, then turn and leave. Rarely did he snarl anymore. None of the Yeti touched her, except one of the young females did feel her breasts as if they were something she had not seen.

By the third day, Dixie was having frank hallucinations. Dehydrated and weak, she was near total collapse, and she had only short lucid periods interspersed with unconsciousness. At one point there were bug-eyed snakes spewing from the cracks between the rocks and their tongues flicked at her, as they hissed. When a tongue touched her, it burned and left a mark. It was the one hallucination she could recall.

She did not remember Harry cutting her down from the wall. Trudging along in this dank, dark, miserable underground shaft full of inhospitable dust, she refused to believe that he rescued her only for her to die now of suffocation and thirst. It wouldn't be fair if her life was to end this way. She had so much to live for. So much to give someone.

CSCS

Harry continued to inch his way forward, close behind Li. The walls of the shaft felt as if they were closing around him, squeezing the breath out of his lungs, crushing him into a small mass of skin and bones. The crawlspace continued snaking its way through the dark bowels of the mountain like the river that flowed through the Mongolian steppe. Periodically, Stepan had to clear rubble or large rocks that hindered their progress. The work required tremendous effort and during those periods of rest, Harry was able to catch his breath. His lungs felt as if he had inhaled a gallon of dust. When he coughed, his airways burned. On top of everything, his stomach ached and churned, causing waves of pain to ripple through his weakened body. The cave-in had shocked him into weighing his own mortality and the scorecard did not look promising. Everyone was coughing but, to his relief, Dixie's and Jing's crying had subsided.

As he wormed his way through the dark crack in the mountain, Harry realized his death was imminent. There was no way they were going to be able to get out of this horror alive, and that thought sent a shiver through his pain-racked brain. He'd never counted on anything like this, never thought he would end up swallowed by a mountain cave-in. A coughing spasm overcame him and he spat out a bolus of dust-filled mucus.

*Damn.*

Then—

A shout from up ahead.

A sudden rush of cool air.

"What's that?" Harry called out.

More shouting.

"There's light," Li said over his shoulder.

Shuffling behind Li, Harry could make out a small shaft of light coming from beyond the group ahead of him. Inching forward, he saw what the shouting was about—a hole, a glorious hole. And beyond it Harry could see blue sky.

They had made it.

One by one, they scrambled out of the small rock shaft and into bright, cool sunlight. Slowly, each stood, stretched, and filled their lungs with the fresh air.

Stepan patted Harry on the shoulder. "You all right?" he asked.

"Yeah, fine," Harry said.

"Is it too late for them? My men, I mean. Are they dead?"

"Crushed, I'm positive. I'm sorry."

"They were good men, all of them. They cared about the law and Mongolia."

Stepan went to check on the others and Harry found Dixie. When their eyes met, she ran and threw herself into his arms.

"Oh, Harry. I thought I would never see you again."

"I can't believe how good you look, Dixie," he said.

"Are you kidding? I look horrible."

"You don't understand," Harry said, smiling. "You look fantastic."

# Chapter 29

Harry fell to the ground exhausted. Sucking in deep gulps of the sweet smell of loamy earth, he lay on his back and marveled at their miraculous escape from a prison of darkness, rock, and dust. Dixie lay beside him, crying softly, but now her tears seemed to be of joy at being alive. Doyle and Eastwood were sprawled next to each other while Captain Stepan sat with his head in his hands.

Harry was wasted, mentally and physically. His bones ached, his head pounded, and his mouth cried for water. Visions of the Yeti danced in his mind, their menacing advance, the gunfire that killed several of them, the knowledge that more of them were still alive somewhere in the cave. Struggling to focus his thoughts, he realized that the encounter, horrible as it had been, was of great scientific significance. Who were these creatures and how did they fit into the pattern of primate and hominid development? They were obviously more developed than present day primates, as they appeared to have advanced language and cognitive abilities. But they were larger, had more body hair, and had different facial construction than what scientists believed *Neanderthals* were like.

Anthropologists did not think in terms of an evolutionary tree, *per se*, but more along the lines of a bush with many branches, springing from a common ancestor. And the clear implication of this bushy family tree was that there is no single central tendency in hominid evolution. Rather, new variations on the hominid potential were continually thrown out to compete in the ecological arena, until one species finally emerged that somehow contrived to eliminate the competition—an unprecedented event in all hominid history.

Current thinking placed the earliest possible fossil hominids in Africa between about seven and four million years old. They formed a peculiar group, united mainly by the fact that they moved upright when on the ground. Bipedalism was definitively established over four million years ago among the *Australopiths* who had ape-sized brains, projecting faces, and small bodies that retained excellent climbing capabilities.

So, Harry wondered, could these Yeti be a heretofore undiscovered branch of that evolutionary bush? Living in isolation for centuries in the high Himalayan and Altai Mountains could account for their peculiar development similar to the way species of wildlife developed on the Galapagos Islands. Isolation such as that did strange things to species' development over time.

When one population of a species became isolated from the rest of the species, that population formed its own distinct gene pool. Over time, by means of natural selection, the gene pool of this isolated population produced mutations and acquired new traits that other groups of the same species did not develop. Eventually, over a very long period of time, so many mutations built up that the two populations of this species became so different and incompatible with each other that they were unable to interbreed. At this point, the two groups had become two distinct species.

Tired as he was, the scientist in Harry attempted to put these thoughts into clearer perspective. In reality, evolutionary biology did not imply linear progression. Modern species did not morph into other modern species, and evolution was not the outcome of some mystical force. Modern evolutionary theory had three basic concepts. One, modern species existing today had descended from pre-existing ancestral species. Two, during this process, single evolutionary lineage had repeatedly split into multiple lineages. And three, the primary force driving evolutionary change was a mechanism that Darwin labeled *natural selection*.

As a consequence, any pair of existing species, such as humans and chimps, shared a common ancestor that existed sometime in the past. Modern day evolutionary theory did not claim that we evolved from chimps, rather that we shared a common ancestor with chimps. The process of evolution led to a branching pattern of relationships among organisms, not a linear progression. A bush, not a ladder.

Great as these principles were, they did not help explain the exact *why* of these Yeti. Why now? Why here?

Maybe the more appropriate scientific question was *how*. How did these creatures come to be here? How did they fit into the evolutionary bush? Maybe the *why* questions were best left to the philosophers and theologians.

ᘓᗷᘓᗷ

Stepan's hand on Harry's shoulder woke him. It was late afternoon and shadows were forming over the small meadow next to where the group had exited the cave.

"They're gone, Harry," the captain said with scowl on his face.

"Who is gone?" Harry asked, stumbling to his feet and brushing the dust off his clothes.

"Eastwood and his man."

"Doyle? When?"

"Must have disappeared when we were napping. An hour ago, maybe longer."

"The horses?"

"They took two, of course."

"Where could they have gone?" Harry was now awake. He reached down and shook Dixie's arm.

"Away from here. Off this mountain, I am sure of that. They need to get out of the country so they'll be heading back to Ulaanbaatar. They are wanted by INTERPOL. I figure they arrived in Mongolia by private jet or the railroad."

When Harry and the group had stumbled out of the cave, a short distance from the original entrance opening they found their horses grazing peacefully at a stream nearby. Filling their canteens with the sweet, cold water and drinking their fill revived them only to be lulled into sleep by their exhaustion. To find Eastwood and Doyle gone distressed Harry. The men were killers.

"They could be heading to our research site," Harry said as Dixie joined the pair.

Jing and Li were sitting on the ground looking at them.

"What for?" said Stepan.

"Oh, God," Dixie interjected. "We left all our computers, notes, and findings back there."

"But there's really nothing of any great value," Harry said.

"What about the bones and teeth? Now that we have seen the Yeti wouldn't that make them a highly valuable prize?"

"I am sure they now know about the skull at the monastery," Jing said, now standing next to Dixie, who nodded her agreement.

"A couple of our weapons are missing," Stepan said.

"They will kill anyone who stands in their way, innocent site workers or not."

Awake and alert, Dixie wrung her hands. "We need to get back there as soon as we can."

"Hold on," said Harry. "How would we stop them if we found them? Most of our weapons were lost in the cave-in."

Stepan pulled his pistol from its holster. "I have my trusty Russian OT-33 Pernach machine pistol. Not much, but it's something."

"I doubt it's more than what they're packing," Li said, smiling at his use of American slang.

"Captain, what about radioing Ulaanbaatar for help?" Harry asked. "You had your radio when we entered the cave."

"No luck, Harry. It got lost in the scramble and cave-ins. Sorry. So it seems we are on our own for the present."

"Maybe I could make it back to the monastery while you all go on ahead," Jing suggested. "If I get there, I can call the police and get some help out here."

Harry smiled at Jing, her sharp facial features softened by the waning sunlight. "Unless, Eastwood and Doyle decided to head for the monastery, then it could be dangerous."

"No," Li interjected. "If they are smart, they are going to get out of the country, pronto."

"What do you think, Captain? Send Jing to the monastery? If Li is right about the two, it would get her out of the line of fire. Dixie could go with her."

"Not on your life, Harry," Dixie said forcefully. "I'm going with you, period."

Stepan laughed. "I'm glad that's settled, Harry. Okay, Jing will take a horse and make her way to the monastery. When you get there, call the National Police and talk to Colonel Bronislav. I will give you the phone number. The rest of us will head to the research site. Maybe we can overtake them before they get there, if that's where they are heading. What happens when we find them, we can talk about along the way."

ფფფ

Doyle bent over the shallow stream refilling his and East-wood's canteens while his boss sat on a rock and surveyed the valley below them. They had pushed themselves hard for a few hours after mounting two horses and leaving the sleeping party behind. Now, in the fading evening light, Doyle handed East-wood his canteen and the men climbed back in the saddle. Making their way along a narrow trail into the basin below, they rode in silence with Doyle listening to the plodding hoofs and the horses' raspy breathing. The valley was devoid of any lights and, as the twilight deepened into purple hues, he switched on his headlight and searched the brush alongside them.

Eastwood rode behind him and Doyle heard the man slurp water periodically. He was worried about his boss's health. Never an athletic man, Eastwood suffered from the usual medical illnesses of middle age—high blood pressure and being overweight. His face was bright red and he limped around like an old man.

As they followed the small stream down the mountain, the grade became easier. Arriving at a level area, Eastwood pulled his horse to a stop and dismounted.

"Let's rest a moment, Ben. My knees are killing me."

"Fine, boss." Doyle dismounted and sauntered over to Eastwood. "Feeling okay? You look bushed."

"I'm fine, Ben. Just tired. That cave-in about did me in, however."

"Do you still want to go to the research site?

"Yeah. They've found something there, and I've got to know what it is. More than that, I want it. If it relates to these Yeti, it could prove helpful."

Not having a science background, Doyle never understood why these relics commanded so much interest and money. Eastwood wasn't a scientist either but he had an innate sense of what things were worth and didn't mind breaking a few laws to obtain them. The man had built a billion-dollar company finding anthropological and paleontological artifacts and selling them to the highest bidder. Doyle's own fortunes rose as his boss made millions. Italian suits, a fancy sports car, and a large bank account kept him content for the present.

"How will you know if you find it?" Doyle said.

Eastwood paced and stretched his legs. "I will know, Ben, I will know."

"Let's push on a while longer," Doyle said. "We can sleep in a few hours. I want to put as much distance between us and that police captain as possible before bedding down."

They continued their descent to the Altai steppes. A large yellow moon rose behind them and the sky was filled with bright stars, as if someone had thrown a handful of diamonds across the heavens. The day's warmth turned chilly as a slight breeze pawed their faces. The indistinct solitary trail was in soft relief, even in the bright moonlight, but their horses kept trudging along without a stumble.

Doyle was tired of Mongolia and longed for a hot shower and a large steak dinner. He hated horses and had a basic fear of the unpredictability of the animals. What had begun as a simple mission to Mongolia had turned into a nightmare, his men killed and him on the run. But the thoughts that haunted him the most were the faces of the creatures in the cave. Yeti, Dr. Olson had called them. Where had they come from? They looked like pictures he had seen back in the States of Sasquatch or the Abominable Snowman.

They had confronted an evil he had never seen nor understood. Thankful that they had survived the encounter, he only wished to get home as soon as possible. He sympathized with Eastwood, but to stop at the research site was a waste of time and effort that would not produce anything of real value. He and his boss needed to get out of the country before there was a national search underway for them.

But Doyle could read the handwriting on the wall. Eastwood had other plans. The man was obsessed now with the Yeti, wanting to obtain one of the creatures to make his fortune. Alive or dead, it didn't matter.

And the man expected him to help. Which was fine, except they needed to get out of the country, return home, regroup, and plan for an eventual return. Specimens were one thing but one needn't die for them.

As the vast Altai steppes spread out before him, Doyle called a halt to their trek and made a cold camp on a tiny escarpment next to a dark bluff. Eastwood collapsed on the ground, pulled his jacket around his ears, and huddled against the bluff out of the wind. Doyle unsaddled the horses and gave a saddle to his boss who propped himself against it and closed his eyes.

"I'm getting too old for this sort of thing, Ben. Think we can find our way back to the site?" he asked, trying to ward off the evening chill.

"Follow this stream until the buttes then go northeast. I think we can get there," Doyle said, putting an optimistic tone in his voice. "Out here on the steppe you can see for miles."

"I wish I had a cigar," Eastwood said. "Nothing like a good smoke for relaxation."

"I always used three fingers of scotch," Doyle said, forcing a smile.

"That wouldn't be bad, either, Ben."

The two men sat in silence, gazing at the stars. After a few moments Doyle spoke. "Remember the military, boss?"

"Sure, Ben. Viet Nam. Overall, it was a miserable experience and I almost didn't make it out. I've never really spoken about it. Making money became my interest."

"When that IED exploded in my face I thought I was done for. I actually enjoyed my tour in Iraq until then. It blew me up pretty good—you can tell by the scars on my face."

"You've never talked about it either, Ben. What was it like?"

Doyle could sense the compassion in Eastwood's voice and shook his head. "Bad. Just very bad. I had six operations in a month's time in Germany then came home for retraining. I didn't want to get out. But the scars are still painful, even to-day."

"I would have opted out after that."

"But, you see, I had nowhere else to go. My parents were both dead. I needed a family and the army was it. At least for a while. Then I got into trouble and after that I wanted out."

"It was my luck, Ben. I'm glad you're here."

# Chapter 30

Dixie's horse stumbled and bolted her awake. She was still in the saddle, riding behind Captain Stepan with Li and Harry behind her. A brisk biting wind jabbed her face, sending a shiver through her aching body. The silver moon gave enough light that she could see the trail ahead, outlined in the dark. Stepan and Harry had agreed that they would ride throughout the night but she wondered if her battered frame could stand it. She was stiff and sore and it was only a little past midnight. But Harry thought by riding all night and most of the next day they would arrive at the research site by evening. She lowered her head against the wind and said a silent prayer that she could hold out until then.

The Yeti no longer consumed her thoughts, which drifted to Harry—what he was beginning to mean to her and the possible future. Thinking of him eased the pain in her shoulders and legs. At first, she thought it was just a schoolgirl infatuation with her teacher. After all, Harry—Dr. Olson back then—was a nationally recognized scientist in his field. He had taken her under his wing and into his confidence, and she blossomed academically. Under his patient tutelage, she had grown in her scientific knowledge and had come to admire the man. By his example, she learned what it meant to be a professional and a scientist and earned his praise when she performed to his high standards.

Her doctoral thesis was all that was left and, with Harry's help, it would be completed within the coming year. After that, her plans were vague, and a lot depended on her relationship with Harry. She was in love, of course. But was he? She didn't know. He acted as if he cared for her but was he willing to make a commitment? Once back in the States things might change.

Harry reined his horse to a halt and jumped to the ground. He came to stand beside Dixie and looked up.

"Let's rest a spell, Dixie. I know you must be tired."

Dixie fell into Harry's arms and he helped her to a small copse of trees where she settled against the largest one. Li followed and sat on the ground next to her. Stepan paced around, stretching.

"Thanks," she said. "I was getting pretty bushed. Where do you think that Doyle fellow and his boss are headed?"

"Ulaanbaatar and out of the country if they're smart. I can't believe they would hang around in Mongolia at the risk of being caught. If Jing managed to call the police, they will be searching all over the steppe for them. It will hard to hide or escape."

"But what if they return to our site?" Li demanded. "They'll kill more people, most likely."

"I do remember something Eastwood said," Harry mused. "He wants whatever relics we have uncovered. Your worry is well-founded. He just may be heading to our site. What do you think, Captain?"

"Entirely possible. We'll know soon enough."

"Tomorrow evening," Li said, nodding his head. "What happens if we all get there at the same time?"

"A confrontation, most likely," Stepan said. "They can't have much more in the way of weapons than we have."

"One nine millimeter pistol?" Harry said. "Can't do much with that."

Stepan smiled, patting the pistol on his hip. "Don't forget my trusty machine pistol."

"There's three of us and two of them," Li said. He pulled his jacket tighter around his shoulders. The wind had lessened but the night's chill lingered.

Harry frowned, deeply concerned. "Not much of an advantage there. I hate the thought of a confrontation without any idea of a plan ahead of time. We can't just stumble into our site with no plan, can we?"

"But we can't sit idly by and let them kill innocent people, either," Li argued.

"Maybe Jing will have called in reinforcements," Dixie said, pulling a blanket around her shoulders.

Stepan squatted amidst the group and shot a glance at each person. "If we keep pushing we could catch up with them before they reach the research site. As much as I am hoping for a helicopter full of more SWAT members, I don't think we should count on it happening."

"Then, as exhausted as we all are, I vote we push on right now," Harry said.

Stepan sighed and rose to his feet. "Let's mount up, then."

Dixie shot Harry a resigned look then proceeded to climb into her saddle. The rest followed suit and soon they were back on the trail.

The eastern horizon was beginning to lighten with the faintest streaks of gray. Riding behind Stepan, Dixie could barely make out the vast steppe ahead and, while she feared meeting up with Doyle and Eastwood, the police captain gave her confidence that he could handle whatever came their way. She rode along in a fog, as if she was moving slowly toward a preordained climax over which she had no control. Was it really happening?

She thought back to her days at Smith and her stay in rehab. *That* she knew had been real. Her brother's death had certainly been real, too real. They had been close, probably closer than most brother-and-sister relationships and when he was killed by a drunk driver, the life had gone out of her. She never felt close to either parent. Her father always talking about money and her mother giving incessant parties for their Wall Street friends. It was Dixie's brother, Franklin who kept her sane, in spite of her semester-long drug fling. Once she was out of rehab, he had talked to her as only a brother could and got her to see the folly of her behavior.

With his death came the realization that she would have to

build a life by herself and she had dedicated herself to that task.

Her horse's stumble jarred her back into the present. Streaks of yellow and orange light shot skyward from the horizon. Dixie took a drink from her canteen and rubbed her eyes. Dawn was upon them.

❧❧❧

Doyle was up with the early morning twilight and got the horses saddled while Eastwood slept. Finished, he sat beside his boss, took a drink from his canteen, then shook the sleeping man by the shoulder. Eastwood sat up, looked around, and coughed several times.

"Time to get moving, sir," Doyle said, helping the man to his feet.

Eastwood relieved himself then climbed into his saddle. Doyle led the way and shifted back and forth, as he searched for a comfortable position. The sun was pushing up over the distant hills, flooding the steppe in pale light. The air was brisk but the wind was still calm.

The rocky trail meandered alongside the shallow stream that tumbled from out of the mountain behind them. Mosses and ferns dotted the shoreline, causing a fragrant perfume to titillate their noses. Doyle turned in the saddle toward Eastwood.

"Once we are out of these foothills, the going should be much easier and faster. Hopefully, we can reach the research site by mid-afternoon."

"I could use something more to eat than a few strips of jerky," Eastwood said. "My stomach is rebelling right now."

"Yeah, mine too. Frankly, boss, the sooner we're out of this damn country, the better I'll like it."

Eastwood forced a laugh. "I was thinking the very thing myself, Ben. Neither one of us is suited for living on horseback and sleeping under the stars. I prefer a soft bed and a roof over my head."

Both men chuckled and Doyle's attention returned to the

trail ahead of them. The going was slow, despite the gradual descent, due in part to the altitude and the rocky terrain. The sun was now a piercing, blinding fireball so Doyle kept his attention fixed on the trail ahead. They stopped a few times so Eastwood could stretch his legs and have a drink of water.

When the time came, he would persuade Eastwood to put Mongolia behind them and return another time to fetch a Yeti specimen. He didn't see how two men armed with only one pistol stood much of a chance against the beasts. And if the man was intent on capturing one alive and pirating it out of the country, it was going to take weeks of planning and more men. He hoped he could get Eastwood to see it his way.

❧❧❧

Jing Wu woke with a start.

Something had startled her. Her heart pounded. It was dark. The moon was behind a cloud, which cast a filtered light around its edges. The small campfire she'd built to cook her dinner was a heap of cold ashes. The mountain was quiet.

But something definitely had awakened her. She sat up, rubbed her eyes, and tried to focus through the darkness.

She had ridden long into the night, hoping to make it to the monastery in Tenduk before daylight but fatigue overtook her resolve and she opted to rest for a few hours before continuing. She prayed that the monastery's phone was working so she could notify the National Police of their predicament.

But the noise had startled and scared her.

She tried to calm her frazzled nerves. Years of trekking alone in the mountains had accustomed her to the strange music and sounds heard at night. These sounds she accepted without fear as a part of a nomad's life. But this sound was different. She couldn't put her finger on it, but it *was* different. Her heart pounded in her temples.

She found her flashlight, switched it on, and plied the darkness with its beam, but saw nothing. She worked to stoke the cold embers of the dead campfire until a small flame flickered to life. The fire grew as she piled on more wood. In a short time, a bright blaze was burning. She paced, worried about the sound she heard, scanning the darkness, seeing nothing.

Finally satisfied, she sat and warmed herself beside the fire and contemplated starting toward the monastery. She estimated that it was only four or five hours more. She took a long drink from her canteen and gazed up at the stars. The Big Dipper was high overhead and the Milky Way stretched across the sky like a silvery veil. She thought of Harry and Dixie and wondered how they were faring. How close they were to the research site. She had grown to like them both during their ride to the monastery, with Dixie doing her best to explain what they were digging for. Jing did her best to understand, but the science of it eluded her. Nevertheless, she had formed a bond with the American pair and hoped she could make it to the monastery in time to call the National Police.

There it was, again.

The sound off in the darkness.

It sounded like a twig snapping.

Jing stood and flashed her light all around, its beam piercing the velvet black.

"Who's out there?" she shrieked. Her stomach rumbled and her sticky palms grasped the flashlight all the tighter.

Nothing.

She shuffled beyond the ring of firelight and was startled by the stench of decaying matter—pungent, burning her nostrils. She glanced around but saw nothing. Heard nothing.

Her horse, who earlier grazed methodically, now danced at the end of its tether. Its ears were laid back against its head. The animal sensed something.

She located her saddle and shoved it onto the animal's back. The horse nickered softly and shuffled away from Jing.

"Hold still," she said, irritated and worried. When she tightened the cinch, the horse nickered again and pawed the ground.

"What's the matter with you?" she said, this time in a loud, commanding voice. "If you don't cooperate, we'll never get going."

Satisfied the saddle was secure, Jing turned and suddenly stared into the face of a large hairy Yeti.

The red eyes of the creature blazed like burning coals from her campfire and spittle dripped from its long fangs. Its hot, putrid breath hit Jing in the face and drove her backward. She tried to scream but the sound stuck in her throat.

Glancing to her left, she saw that the Yeti had friends, one on each side of the large one. They approached, snarling, hissing. Jing turned to run but the large Yeti grabbed her in a powerful grasp and pulled her to him. Her head spun, her stomach revolted, she vomited. Warm liquid ran down her legs. Her vision tunneled around the hideous creature.

The hair on the animal was course and long. It smelled of dead, rotten flesh. Jing fought to breathe. Frantic, she struggled against the Yeti's hold on her but it was no use. The animal brought her close to him, clutching her with powerful hands. She fought with every fiber of her being, for her life depended on it. She struggled but its hold crushed the air from her lungs, making it difficult to breath. A kick to the Yeti's knee did nothing except focus her mind on the helplessness of her situation. For a moment, their eyes locked on each other and Jing wondered if it knew she was human, almost like itself in many ways.

Then she felt its jaws close around her head and everything went black.

# Chapter 31

The sun was up and the air was warming, a promise that fall was still a few weeks in the future. Harry shifted in his saddle and was glad that they were now back on the level Altai steppe, for it made travel easier and faster. The steppe was verdant and luxuriant, compared to the stark beauty of the mountains. The clear stream they followed tumbled languidly now, instead of plunging headlong down the steep embankments found in the higher elevations.

Harry was hungry but the jerky was gone. They would have to put their cravings aside until they reached the research site. Up ahead, Stepan swayed rhythmically in his saddle and Harry noticed that he continually scanned the horizon in front of them. Li and Dixie appeared to be asleep as they were not moving; Li's head was on his chest.

The white peaks of Mount Belukha and Kuitan loomed behind them as if propelling them forward toward their destination. Since leaving their diggings for Tenduk, and with their narrow escape from death, Harry had all but forgotten his mother and her health. Did she ever get her pacemaker? Was she even alive? If she had died while he was off chasing hominids, he would never be able to face his brother. No, never be able to live with himself. Maybe Max had been right—he was selfish to the core, thinking only of himself and his idiotic career. Trapped inside the mountain, his death certain, had made him realize his precious career was not nearly as important as he once thought it was. There *were* more important aspects to living and he was only now figuring that out. Dixie, he hoped, was going to play a much larger role in his life going forward. Harry said a quick prayer that his mother was all right. He would call Max as soon as he could.

Stepan had stopped and was peering through binoculars at the distant landscape. Harry rode up beside him and reined his horse to a halt. "What's up, Captain? See anything?" he asked, squinting his eyes at the man.

"I thought I saw a flash up ahead. Like the sun glinting off metal."

"Yeah?"

Dixie and Li rode to a stop beside Harry and the captain. Li cupped a hand over his eyes and stared in the direction Stepan was looking.

"Nothing, I guess," Stepan said. "Maybe I'm just getting spooked."

"No, you can't be too careful, Captain Stepan," Li said, turning his gaze on the man. He shot furtive glances at Harry and Dixie.

"I guess. Let's keep moving."

The small band continued on their way, leaving Harry feeling uneasy about what they would eventually encounter. The fact that they might overtake Eastwood and his assistant, Doyle, was a cause for concern. Harry wasn't looking forward to a gun battle where Dixie might get hurt or killed. With only Stepan's pistol for protection, he doubted that they would be able to overpower the two men. A profound feeling of dread was building in him, his mouth tasted of metal, and his fingers were numb from the cold.

*ରେଉଡ଼*

The stream that flowed through the steppe took a long, leisurely curve to the north then back again, carving an S-shaped ribbon of silver into the lush green vegetation. Rounding the last curve, Doyle stopped, held up a hand, and waited for Eastwood to ride alongside him. He pointed to white objects in the distance, barely visible on the horizon.

"Tents," Doyle said. "The research site. We're here."

"It looks smaller than before," Eastwood said, putting binoculars to his eyes. "How do you think we should play this, Ben?"

Doyle dismounted and squatted with Eastwood's binoculars. He scanned the site in silence for a few minutes before answering. "Ride in, find the foreman again, demand what we want under pain of death, then ride out. I doubt if they have weapons. They're a scientific expedition."

"Won't they spot us coming? On this flat plain there's no way to get there without being seen."

"Who cares? Where can they go? What are they going to do? Nothing, I tell you. Absolutely nothing.

The afternoon sun was beginning to cast long shadows of their mounts and the light was at their backs.

"Besides," Doyle said, "the sun will be in their eyes. They may not see us until the last moment."

To Doyle, this discussion was moot and pointless. They had the enemy within their sights and the only thing left to do was to waltz in and demand the relics. If the foreman did not comply, kill him. After that, the next person they interrogated would be more cooperative. As a former military man, why couldn't Eastwood understand the tactics involved in an operation such as this? Wasn't it why the man had employed someone with Doyle's unique background?

"You getting queasy about the possibility of shooting someone, Mr. Eastwood? It didn't bother you to put two slugs into Gillum's chest back in the caves."

"That bother you, Ben?"

"Gillum was a good man. It was unnecessary."

"He wasn't going to follow an order."

"You don't shoot someone for not following an order, sir. You might fire him but you don't kill him."

"You questioning my authority here, Ben? Now is not the time."

"Nor the place, Mr. Eastwood. But maybe when we get back home."

"All right, Ben. Stow it until then."

"There is a small promontory there to the south of the diggings, about a hundred yards. Do you see it?"

Eastwood nodded.

"Let's make our way to those rocks so we won't be seen. We can move in from there."

"Okay, Ben."

"We'll leave the horses here and go the rest of the way on foot. Maybe they won't spot us until we are upon them."

Doyle and Eastwood scrambled through the short vegetation, crouching low in the hopes of avoiding detection by the expedition workers. Doyle's back screamed at him, the pain intense. He heard Eastwood's wheezing breath behind him as he zigzagged toward the low mound behind the research site.

Halfway to the hill, Doyle fell to the ground and motioned Eastwood to follow suit. He crawled up next to Doyle.

"Workers milling about up ahead," Doyle said. "There, between those tents. See them?"

Eastwood nodded. "Think they saw us?"

"Don't seem to have. But we're certainly exposed lying on the ground here. Let's get to that mound. Stay low."

The two men crawled on their stomachs toward the promontory. The short grass of the steppe grazed Doyle's cheeks as he wormed his way forward. The earth smelled rich and fertile. With the sun lower, Doyle hoped it made spotting them more difficult. If they could make the little mound, they would have a decided advantage in surprising the site workers.

He worried they were making progress only by inches, as the promontory still seemed a long way off. Eastwood's wheezing was more pronounced and once Doyle thought his boss was gasping for air. Doyle stopped crawling momentarily to allow Eastwood a chance to catch his breath, then he continued on.

Twenty minutes later, they reached the mound and scrambled behind a rock escarpment. Eastwood retrieved his binoculars and scanned the research site then handed them to Doyle.

The area appeared calm and quiet, with only a few people milling about. Work had apparently stopped for the day and everyone was relaxing before the evening meal. There was a row of canvas-walled tents at one end of the compound and another row facing them. One of the tents had a short metal chimney extending from its roof and a thin wisp of white smoke emanated from it. At the end of the row opposite the tents stood two large military-style trucks and two World-War-Two-vintage American jeeps.

"We'll use the tents as cover and enter the compound from their end." Doyle looked at Eastwood, nodded, and then smiled as he continued. "Get your pistol out. We grab the first person we come across and demand to see the foreman. The rest will be up to you. We grab what you want then leave in one of those jeeps. Okay?"

"I hope we can make it back to Ulaanbaatar with the gas in one of the jeeps there," Eastwood said.

"It's a chance we take. There are a few small villages along the way, though."

Eastwood took the 9 mm from his belt and racked the slide.

"I'm ready."

Over the mound they vaulted and burst into the research compound. The area around the tents was devoid of workers. Doyle peered around a tent and moved into the clear area with Eastwood behind, pistol at the ready. A young woman emerged from a tent and bumped into Doyle who grabbed her and covered her mouth with his hand. Eastwood thrust the gun barrel in her face.

"Don't make a sound or you're dead," Doyle hissed.

The woman, eyes wide with fear, looked confused. She shot glances between Doyle and Eastwood. Doyle squeezed her arm tighter and she let out a short muffled noise.

"No sound," Doyle commanded. "Take us to your command tent. Is your foreman there now?"

The woman, seemingly not understanding, began crying. Her eyes were still wide and now tears streamed down her cheeks. Under his grip, Doyle felt her swallow hard.

"Boss. Leader. Which way?" Doyle said.

The woman finally seemed to understand what Doyle was asking and pointed. Doyle pushed her in that direction with Eastwood at his side, his gun pointed at her head.

Out of nowhere, a group of workers formed around them, all talking wildly, frantically. They pointed at Doyle and the woman.

"Stand back, all of you," he said. "Stand back or she's dead."

Seeing the gun, the workers melted away but continued their worried talking, words Doyle could not understand. Women were crying. The woman stopped in front of a tent and Doyle pushed her in.

A man seated at a table in front of a computer screen jumped up.

"See here," he said in a loud voice. Noticing Eastwood's pistol he slumped back down in his chair.

Doyle walked up to the man, stared at him for a few moments. "Yes," he said. "Cheng, isn't it? The foreman here, right?"

The man said nothing.

"Come, come, Mr. Cheng. I think we have been through this before, haven't we? You're gonna answer questions or the woman will die. Understand?"

Cheng shuddered. "Yes, I understand. What do you want?"

Eastwood stepped forward, placed his hands on the table, and leaned over it. "Relics, Cheng. Relics. What you have dug up on this expedition. That's what I want."

"We have nothing, just a few bones," Cheng said. He looked at the woman whom Doyle still held by a hand over her mouth and his other hand gripping her arm.

"Ah, bones, Cheng. Now you have hit upon it. The very thing we seek. Please be kind enough to fetch them, won't you?"

"Stealing artifacts is a crime in Mongolia," Cheng said. "You will never get away with it."

Eastwood pointed his pistol at Cheng's head. Doyle noticed that Cheng's eyes twitched.

"Please, Cheng, do not be so obstinate. Just do as you are told. Besides, we plan to be out of your wretched country before anyone knows we have stolen anything. Now, get the goddamn bones before I lose more patience and shoot this poor woman. Doyle, go with him and make sure he does it. I'll stay here with the woman."

Doyle left with Cheng and, a few minutes later, returned with Cheng carrying a small white box with *Cal Pac U* stenciled on top and its sides. Eastwood smiled and handed his pistol to Doyle. Cheng set the box on the table and stepped aside.

Eastwood rubbed his hands together and opened the box.

# Chapter 32

Eastwood's trembling fingers toyed with the box while he savored the moment. The culmination of their mission lay on the table in front of him. He swallowed hard then opened the box. He lifted a tooth from its interior and examined it. Replacing the tooth, he removed a long bone and held it up for closer inspection. *So this was what it was all about.* Yeti bones. He empirically knew that was what they were. Somehow, in the middle of the Mongolian mountains the scientific team had stumbled upon the skeletal remains of a Yeti. He could do his own DNA analysis back in the States then auction the specimens off to the highest bidder. Later, once they had a living creature to show the world, fame and fortune would be his. He salivated at the thought.

*෧෩෧*

Harry and Stepan led Dixie and Li through the broad Mongolian steppe and approached the research site from the southwest. When they could see the light colored tops of the tents Stepan called a halt and scanned the compound with binoculars. The sun was dipping over the peaks of the Altai Mountains to their rear, shooting rays of sunlight over the lush grassland.

"Seems quiet," he said, passing the glasses to Harry.

"It's after dinner," Harry said. "Nothing usually happens until breakfast. People just hang out, listen to their music, read, play chess, that sort of thing. Pretty quiet, mostly."

"Think they have been here?" Dixie asked.

"Hard to say. We'll know soon enough. Let's go find out." Stepan kicked his horse toward the compound and the others followed.

Closer to the site, Harry was struck by the fact that he could see no one milling about. The place was dead quiet.

At the compound's edge they stopped.

"I don't like it," Harry said. "Where is everybody?"

"Dismount," Stepan said. "Stay alert. Where to, Harry?"

"Need to find Cheng, he's the foreman in Li's absence. Let's get to the command tent first."

Stepan removed his Pernach machine pistol from its holster and motioned toward the compound. "Lead on, Harry. I'm right behind you." He turned to Dixie and Li. "You two stay back a ways. If shooting starts, find cover quick."

Harry ambled into the research site and headed straight for the command tent. Usually, at this hour, there would be workers milling around, walking between tents, talking, and laughing. Now it was quiet, no sounds, no music, and no laughter. Something definitely was going on. The place was like a tomb.

The first tent they passed was the large dormitory tent for the workers. Harry stopped at its entrance and surveyed its interior. Empty. *That's unusual.*

"Something's happened here," he whispered to Stepan.

Usually the dorm tent would have workers in it at this hour, lounging, reading, talking together. A queer feeling erupted in Harry's stomach, a feeling of impending doom, of being on the verge of discovering mass murder. Most of the workers came from surrounding villages and towns, seeking work and the higher wages the expedition offered. They underwent a week of training on how to dig properly and how to handle archeological specimens. To a person, they were a congenial, hardworking group. Some brought their wives who did the cooking for the entire team. Over the past month, he had formed lasting friendships with many of the workers and his head spun at the possibility of anything dreadful happening in his absence.

They continued on and stopped a few yards short of the

command tent. Sounds of quarreling drifted from it and Harry heard a man's voice scream, "Is this all there is?"

Eastwood's voice.

Harry nodded to Stepan who turned and placed a finger to his lips.

The two of them stepped into the tent's doorway with Stepan pointing his pistol at the ready.

Eastwood was standing over the table and the white bone box while Cheng sat with a terrified look. Doyle was at the end of the table and held a woman at gunpoint, his big arm wrapped around her thin shoulders. She was sobbing softly.

Doyle glanced up, startled by the pair standing inside the tent.

"What the hell?" he shouted. He pointed his pistol at Stepan who already had his aimed at Doyle's chest.

Eastwood jerked around and nearly fell out of his chair, a look of panic etched on his face.

"My God! Dr. Olson," he said. "How the hell—"

"Shut your face, Eastwood," Harry ordered.

Stepan advanced closer toward Doyle and waved his pistol. "Put the gun down," he commanded, "and let the woman go."

"Not on your life," Doyle said. "She's my ticket out of here."

Eastwood slumped in a chair and stared at Harry. "Men," he said. "Surely we can negotiate something here like gentlemen. Ben and I have no desire to harm anyone. We only wish to take a few relics and leave quietly."

"Neither of you are going anywhere but jail," Stepan said. "You are both under arrest for murder and attempted theft of Mongolian relics."

Doyle laughed and gripped the woman tighter. "Arrest? I don't think so. Not while I have this weapon and this woman. One wrong move and she's dead. Believe me. I'll kill her."

"He will, too," Eastwood said. "Trust me, I know the man. He works for me."

Harry contemplated the situation, trying to size up their odds. It appeared to be a standoff. Both Doyle and Stepan had pistols pointed at each other. He knew the captain would not shoot, for fear of hitting the woman. So the two men snarled at each other, neither one willing to make the first move. Eastwood was the wild card. He could decide to grab the box of bones and make a run for it. Harry decided if that happened, he would tackle the man before he got out of the tent. Now that he knew the score, his blood was boiling. He was no longer an anxious bystander. He was an angry participant.

A wry smile crossed Eastwood's face and he nodded at Harry. "So, Dr. Olson. What is the next move? Will you dare stop us?"

"If I have to, yes," Harry said.

"It won't work, Doctor, this *bravado* you're showing. You see, we have the upper hand here because my assistant, Ben, will shoot anyone who tries to stop us. And I do not think you or your policeman friend there are so reckless."

"Why?" said Dixie. "What's the point?"

Eastwood looked at her with a whimsical grin. "Why, money, my dear. Money. Pretty simple, really."

"You'll never get away with it," Li snarled.

"Another opinion?" Eastwood snorted. "We have a tent full of experts."

Doyle grunted and made a show of his pistol. "All right, all right," he said. "Let's stop with all the philosophical chatter. It's time we get out of here. You, there." He brandished the pistol at Li. "Go fire up one of those jeeps and bring it here. Leave it running."

Li stood, implacable.

"Move," Doyle shouted.

Li looked at Harry who nodded an assent. Li dashed out of the tent. Harry did not like the way things were shaping up, for it looked as if Eastwood was going to get away, after all. His anger boiled to the surface and he glared at Doyle. *Am I going to stand idly by and allow them to steal what it took months of hard work to uncover?* But what to do? It appeared they were going to be able to walk right out with the bones.

Harry heard a jeep start up and begin its journey toward the tent. Once, in the vehicle Eastwood and Doyle would be hard to stop. Stepan would have to notify his superior and hope the

National Police could find them before they escaped the country.

Eastwood closed the bone box and waited as the jeep neared the tent. Doyle muscled the woman toward the tent doorway. The whine of the jeep grew louder and then it appeared at the tent's door. Li tumbled out, leaving the motor running.

Doyle pushed the woman toward it. "Get in there," he said.

In the instant that Doyle turned his back on him, Harry reacted. Throwing himself into the man, he knocked him to the ground, forcing him to release his grip on the frightened woman.

She dashed out of the tent, screaming.

Doyle spun around and aimed his pistol.

A shot pierced the quiet and Doyle spun again, grabbing his arm.

"Don't move!" Stepan shouted, still pointing his pistol at Doyle.

Eastwood lunged from his chair and bolted into Stepan knocking him off balance. It was enough time for Doyle to scramble to his feet and disappear into the compound.

Recovered from Eastwood's blow, Stepan now had his pistol trained on the man who sat helpless on the ground.

Harry moved to the tent's doorway and glanced about, eyes peeled for Doyle. The man was not in sight anywhere.

"He's gonna take another hostage," Dixie said, her eyes fixed on Eastwood. "I say shoot the bastard right here, right now."

"I doubt it," Harry said. "The workers are all down on this end of the compound. Doyle took off in the opposite direction."

"He can't get far on foot," Stepan said. "If I can use your satellite phone, Harry, I'll phone my boss. I wonder if Jing ever made it to the monastery."

Stepan pulled Eastwood to his feet, cuffed him, and then shoved him into a chair. Dixie followed Harry outside. Dusk was settling over the Mongolian steppe and the air temperature was dropping.

"Be careful," Stepan called from inside the tent. "He could still be lurking around somewhere."

Harry held Dixie's hand as they stood next to the still-idling jeep.

"Well, it's over," Harry said.

"All except for one last criminal. I hope they can find him. I'm surprised he didn't take this jeep."

"Wanted to get far away from here, I guess. I wonder what the professor will say when he learns about all of this."

"Probably laugh," Dixie said.

"I need to find out about my mother. She was going to have a pacemaker the last I heard. I hope she's all right."

A man's scream pierced the compound.

Three gunshots.

Dixie jumped, startled. "What in the world?"

Stepan appeared by their side. "What was that?"

Harry glanced in the tent and noticed that Li now had the captain's pistol trained on Eastwood.

"A man's scream, then gunfire," Harry said. "Coming from the west end of the compound. Let's go."

They ran toward the sounds and soon discovered Doyle's crumpled, blood-smeared body motionless on the ground. His skull had been crushed and white brain matter oozed from the gaping wound.

Harry glanced up and pointed. "There!"

In the waning light of dusk a dark, hulking figure was scurrying away. It stopped, turned, and looked at them over its shoulder, its red eyes blazing fire. Then it turned and disappeared into the darkness.

Harry and Dixie looked at each other, nodded.

"Yeti," she said.

They ambled back to where Li still had Eastwood under guard and Stepan retrieved his pistol.

"Well, Mr. Eastwood, I think it's going to be a long time before you see America again. Our courts here in Mongolia take a dim view of foreigners committing crimes. Now, Harry, where is that satellite phone of yours?"

# Chapter 33

Harry was on the phone to Max. It had taken a few hours to locate his brother but he finally found him at his country club. Sitting in the command tent at the table, Harry doodled while Max talked.

"After Mom had the pacemaker put in, she perked up for a while and felt better. Her breathing improved. Then a few days later, it started all over again, with her breathing difficulties and fluid accumulation. The doctor adjusted her medications and she has improved remarkably in the past forty-eight hours."

"Thank God," Harry said, relieved that the worst had been averted.

"She has been asking about you, Harry. I told her that you would call as soon as you could. I didn't criticize you, either. You can thank me later, brother."

"I'll call today, Max. I want to talk to her. I have felt bad for not being available but when I get home, I will tell you all about it. It's been a helluva week, that's for sure.

"When will you be coming home, Harry?"

"After all that's happened here, I think we are finished with our work. Besides, I don't think Dixie could stand working here much longer. I need to touch base with Professor Kesler first and then it will take another week to wrap things up. Allowing a week for travel, I'd say two weeks at the outside, Max. It will be good to see you."

"You'll come to New York?"

"Well, I'm going to try and get to Chicago to see Mom. Maybe you can fly out when I'm there. We can discuss it when I get home. How is Dad?"

"He's doing his usual complaining about all the work taking care of Mom, so situation normal."

After Harry finished the phone call with Max, Stepan walked into the tent and sat opposite him. He looked haggard with a week's growth of beard on his face.

"Colonel Bronislav is sending a chopper to pick up Eastwood and take him back to Ulaanbaatar. He'll be arraigned in the next couple of days so he won't be going home anytime soon. Maybe never."

"What will become of him?"

"He'll be charged with murder and attempted theft of national relics. Then he'll stand trial, probably sometime next year. He will remain in jail until then. The odds are good that he will be convicted."

"What about you, Captain?" Harry said. He had taken a shower, shaved, and felt human. Stepan, on the other hand, was still wearing his grimy uniform. "I can furnish you with some clean clothes if you wish to shower and clean up before returning."

"It would be much appreciated, Harry. I do feel a bit filthy. I can even smell myself. My boss, Colonel Bronislav, is excited about what has happened. He is pleased that we have interrupted a potentially embarrassing crime and is going to promote me to major. It will mean a nice raise in my salary."

The two men laughed together then sat silent. Harry was going to miss the captain. "You have a family, Captain?" he asked.

Stepan nodded. "A wife and two small boys. It will be good to see them again. I have missed them terribly. My wife, she wants to send our boys to private school so having a major's salary will be of great help."

Dixie joined the men, looking scrubbed and sparkling in jeans and a western shirt. She had applied perfume and its scent filled the tent with a pleasant aroma.

"What about you both?" Stepan said.

"Well," Harry said, looking longingly at Dixie. "For starters, now that I have found the woman of my dreams, I don't ever intend to let her out of my sight."

"Bravo," Stepan said. "I give you both my blessing. May you have many children."

Dixie smiled and put a hand in Harry's. "We plan to."

The next morning, they stood with Li and Cheng at the edge of the compound and waved as the Russian Mi-24 Hind helicopter lifted off, ferrying Captain Stepan and Eastwood, along with Doyle's body, back to Ulaanbaatar. The air was crisp and the sunlight glinted off the beating rotors as the airship disappeared in the distance.

Turning to Li and Cheng, Harry smiled. "Well, Li. Professor Kesler wants to end this project and bring Dixie and me home. The sooner the better, so start tearing it all down. I'll pay off everyone when the work is finished. They've earned a bonus.

Li's eyes glistened and he found it difficult to speak. "Okay, boss," was all that he could manage.

ᥱᕲᥱᕲ

Harry and Dixie relaxed in their room at the Kempinski Hotel in Ulaanbaatar, waiting for their flight to Beijing the following day. Located at the heart of the Bayanzurkh district, a hub in Ulaanbaatar, it was within easy reach of shopping malls, popular restaurants, and business districts. The two had marveled at the marbled lobby and the enormous fountain in its center while they registered and found their room. Their spacious two-bedroom suite included a view overlooking downtown, a sofa, plush easy chairs, and a wet bar full of cold drinks. Lights from the city shone brightly through the window, and a large yellow moon sat in a darkening sky above the horizon to the north.

Harry sipped a beer while Dixie lounged on the sofa, thumbing through a magazine. There was a knock on the door.

"Professor!" Harry exclaimed, seeing Kesler standing there, overnight bag in hand.

"Am I disturbing you?" Kesler asked, smiling.

Dixie jumped up, hugged the man, then kissed his cheek. "But how—I mean—Where—"

Kesler laughed as Harry ushered him to a soft easy chair next to a window. "You're wondering where I was when you called?"

"Yes, how—

"You called my cell phone, Harry. And through the magic of modern technology your call was routed to me while I was in Beijing during a layover. I didn't say anything 'cause you were busy explaining what had happened."

"Gosh, it's good to see you, Professor." Dixie gave him another hug and the old man blushed.

"Harry," Kesler said, "can I speak with you in private for a minute?"

"Sure, Professor, we can talk in here." Harry ushered the man into a bedroom. "What gives?" he said, once the two men were alone.

"Harry," Kesler began, "I want to apologize. This has been weighing on my mind for quite some time. I am sorry for the way I have treated you. After your mistake with the journal article, I was hurt because you have become a son to me—the son I never had." Kesler's eyes moistened as he continued. "It was wrong of me and I'm asking you to forgive me. Please."

Harry hadn't expected this turn of events and was unable to speak, for the words got stuck in his throat. The Professor's eyes were pleading.

Finally, Harry composed himself. "You're much too kind, Professor. Your love and respect mean everything to me and I know how much I let you down. Why I did what I did is difficult to explain but I got caught up in a rush to make a name for myself. I wanted a shortcut to an academic reputation and somehow I lost my personal integrity along the way. I am the one who needs your forgiveness. I'm not sure I can ever make it up to you."

Kesler took Harry by the arms and embraced him, a broad smile on his face. "It's done," he said. "Over and behind us. We forgive each other and now we can go forward. No need to speak of it again. Shall we join the others now?" Back in the main room, Kesler plopped into a chair.

"Care for a beer?" Harry said and, when Kesler nodded, he produced one from the wet bar.

He ushered the Professor to a plush easy chair by a window. Kesler looked drawn and haggard, no doubt fatigued from his long trip. There were dark circles under both eyes.

"I don't believe it," Harry said. "I just don't believe you are actually here. We were hoping to see you as soon as we arrived back in San Francisco but this is an absolute surprise."

"I stopped by the office of the National Police and spoke with a Colonel Bronislav," Kesler said. "I had chatted with him briefly before when I was worried about you two. I have some bad news, Harry. The young woman, Jing, who acted as your guide, was found dead near the monastery at Tenduk. Apparently killed by a large animal or something. Her skull had been crushed. I'm sorry."

Harry and Dixie looked at each other.

"From what the colonel told me it was a vicious attack. Harry, I want you to know—you have made me very proud. Just think, Dixie, a former student of mine making a monumental discovery."

Harry's eyes watered, his voice quaked with emotion at Kesler's praise. "Not just any large animal, Professor. A Yeti."

Kesler's eyes brightened and his back straightened. "A what?"

"A Yeti," Dixie said. "We've seen them. They exist."

Kesler blinked then stared, first at Harry then at Dixie then back at Harry. "You can't be serious," he said. "It's only legend. No one has ever seen them."

"We have," Harry insisted. "What is more, we know where to locate them. There is a family of the creatures living in the Altai Mountains. We've been there, seen them."

"Bring back pictures? Evidence?"

"Unfortunately, no."

Harry spent the better part of an hour describing to Kesler their trip to the monastery, viewing the skull, the kidnapping of Dixie, then getting caught in the cave-in and attacked by the

Yeti. Dixie interjected with pertinent information she thought Harry was leaving out of his narrative.

The professor sat, sipped his beer, and listened intently to their tale.

"These creatures, which have become known as Yeti, reportedly look a lot like humans, except that they are covered in reddish brown hair, have pronounced brows, flat noses, and weak chins. Basically, they look an awful lot like what it's believed Neanderthal men did. Reports aside, it's been consistently debated whether the Yeti is a real creature or just another country's version of Bigfoot. The most compelling proof that Yetis are real creatures comes from two factors: they've been showing up in fairly reliable accounts in a matter of fact manner for years, and their description isn't that far-fetched."

"And now you claim to have actually seen them?" Kesler said, downing what was left of his beer in a single gulp.

Harry held up a hand. "Whenever you hear a story about Bigfoot or the Loch Ness Monster, it tends to have an air of the fantastic to it. People tell the stories of these beasts, as if it was a life-changing moment. However, most older accounts of Yetis treat them as if they were common occurrences. They've even been found listed in an old Tibetan medical book alongside other animals, indexed like all the others. Most accounts put them in perspective as just being a lesser tribe of Mongolians, that weren't as advanced as others, but co-existed nonetheless, even occasionally trading meat for trinkets with the more advanced tribes. I know it sounds fantastic but we have seen these creatures, fought them."

Finished, Harry sat back and waited for Kesler to say something.

"You mentioned a skull?" Kesler said.

"Yes, a Yeti skull, apparently. At the Tenduk monastery."

"Fascinating story. An artifact like that—"

Harry laughed. "Hold on, Professor. Don't get so excited."

There was a pause in the discussion while each person weighed Harry's remarks.

"You two getting married?" Kesler said after a long silence.

"As soon as we are back in San Francisco and we can get

her parents out," Harry said, clutching Dixie's shoulder. He gave her a quick peck on her cheek.

"Good, now that that's settled, maybe we can get on to planning the next expedition."

"The next one?" said Dixie, looking surprised.

"Of course. I'm going to send you both back here to bring back a Yeti specimen. Hopefully alive, of course."

Harry and Dixie looked at each other and shook their heads. Kesler's words caused Harry's spirit to soar. He was free of the past.

"But, Professor," Dixie said, "not before we have had a nice, long honeymoon."

With a wave of his hand, Kesler laughed, then sighed. "But of course," he said. "I was young once."

ໜໜໜ

Deep in a recess on a remote outcropping of the Altai Mountains, a large, hairy creature sauntered to the opening of the cave in which it lived. Large snowflakes swirled as an angry blizzard howled and covered the ground in deep drifts. A blue-gray sky, peeking through dense clouds, caused the landscape to appear as if viewed through a blue filter. Except for the wind screeching outside the cave, not another sound echoed in the mountains. The towering hulk stood in the opening and stared out into the muted world beyond. A thick vapor belched from its maw while its eyes glowed deep red, flickering as it looked around.

After a long moment, it stretched out its huge, muscular arms and shrieked a shattering growl. Then it stepped from the cave, ambled through the deep snow, and disappeared into the mist.

## About the Author

Richard Edde was born and raised in Oklahoma. After graduating from Central State College, he attended the University of Oklahoma College of Medicine, where he earned his medical degree in 1971. After spending a few years in family practice in two rural Oklahoma towns, he completed a residency in anesthesiology. Following a long career in academia and private practice, he retired to devote time to writing. His first novel, *The Photograph*, was released in 2014. Dr. Edde resides in eastern Oklahoma with his wife.